REIGN
OF
EVIL

ALSO BY WESTON OCHSE

Seal Team 666
Age of Blood
Border Dogs

REIGN OF EVIL

A SEAL TEAM 666 NOVEL

WESTON OCHSE

THOMAS DUNNE BOOKS ✠ ST. MARTIN'S PRESS, NEW YORK

This is a work of fiction. All of the characters, organizations, and events portrayed in this novel are either products of the author's imagination or are used fictitiously.

THOMAS DUNNE BOOKS.
An imprint of St. Martin's Press.

REIGN OF EVIL. Copyright © 2014 by St. Martin's Press LLC. All rights reserved. Printed in the United States of America. For information, address St. Martin's Press, 175 Fifth Avenue, New York, N.Y. 10010.

www.thomasdunnebooks.com
www.stmartins.com

Designed by Steven Seighman

Library of Congress Cataloging-in-Publication Data

Ochse, Weston.
  Reign of evil / Weston Ochse. — First edition.
      pages cm. — (Seal team 666 ; 3)
  "A Seal team 666 novel."
  ISBN 978-1-250-05600-9 (hardcover)
  ISBN 978-1-4668-5958-6 (e-book)
  1. United States. Navy. SEALs—Fiction. 2. Druids—Fiction. I. Title.
  PS3615.C476R45 2014
  813'.6—dc23

                                                      2014025162

St. Martin's Press books may be purchased for educational, business, or promotional use. For information on bulk purchases, please contact Macmillan Corporate and Premium Sales Department at 1-800-221-7945, extension 5442, or write specialmarkets@macmillan.com.

First Edition: October 2014

10 9 8 7 6 5 4 3 2 1

To Jon D. Carte, who was there at the very beginning

ACKNOWLEDGMENTS

It took a battalion of professionals to create the book you're holding or viewing or listening to and I owe them all a sincere thanks. Thanks again to Brendan Deneen, Peter Joseph, Pete Wolverton, Nicole Sohl, and the whole Thomas Dunne team. Thanks to Cath Trechman and the wonderful folks at Titan Books. Thanks of course to my agent, Robert Fleck, for being on the front lines of publishing so that I can concentrate on writing. Shout-out to the bands QOTSA, the Beastie Boys, Heavy D, and the Metermaids, for keeping me on edge as I combat-rolled through this novel. And thanks most of all to Yvonne, without whose support, wisdom, and love none of this would be possible.

Special shout-out to Jon Carte, for being there at the real beginning of things and to whom this book is dedicated. Jon and I were in training together back in 1984 and have maintained our friendship. Thanks also to Dave Lake, Brian Wallenius, Barb and Dirk Foster, Hal and Gene, Paul and Shannon, and Eunice and Greg Magill. Thanks also to all of the men and women of ISAF, who welcomed me and watched my back last year while I was in Afghanistan. Thanks again to Brian K and Tommy H, for introducing me to Herb and Diane Harmon and the serenity of Cedar Lodge. And of course thanks to Herb and Diane, for being two of the most special people.

And thanks to you—the readers, reviewers, and bookstore workers—for making SEAL Team 666 such a huge success. I've had e-mails from fans from New Zealand, Croatia, Thailand, and Hawaii, where tourists were buying copies to take out to the beach.

Lots of fan letters. Lots of new friends. I thank each and every one of you for taking the time to write, e-mail, Facebook, tweet, or simply high-five me during a book signing. If you want to reach out to me about this book or anything else, I can be found on Facebook and Twitter under my name and you can always find me at www.westonochse.com.

REIGN
OF
EVIL

PROLOGUE

STONEHENGE. NIGHT.

This was about the coldest holiday Jen had been subjected to in a long time. While she appreciated her old college friend Missy Brautigan taking her to visit Stonehenge, they could have done it when the weather was warmer, or at least during the day. Alas, Missy, who'd always been interested in other religions, hence her Religious Studies degree at Bard College, wanted Jen to witness the Winter Solstice ceremony and the killing of the Oak King by the Holly King.

"It's all pageantry and showmanship, I know," Missy had said during the drive up. "But it's really something special, something you should see in person. I'll make it up to you afterward by filling you with hot toddies and some Yule cookies."

And that was why Jen was standing in the middle of Stonehenge with twelve other strangers while the chants of men in scarlet robes filled the night. The night was frigid cold. She wore one of Missy's wool coats and a pair of gloves, but Jen's face and nose felt as if they might fall off at any moment. Her breath came out in heavy clouds. She brought her gloved hands to her face to warm her skin and wished she were back in San Diego with the love of her life, Jack Walker.

Missy elbowed her. The cold had done absolutely nothing to quench her excitement. "I've never seen them put so much effort into it. You really have come on a special night."

The group of lucky invitees stood in a clutch inside Stonehenge's circle. They'd been asked not to touch anything, not that Jen wanted to touch anything as cold as those monolithic stones had to be. Yet, despite the misery of the cold, she couldn't help but be impressed. Generator-powered lights lit up the exterior and interior of the monument like high noon, casting shadows here and there that were as deep as any darkness. She could almost imagine ancient Britons skulking within them, afraid to taste the modern lights. Scarlet-robed men stood in the center and at places around the circle. They were druids or priests of the wood . . . Missy had been speaking so fast and dumping so much information, Jen couldn't exactly remember. All she knew was that the Oak King, who ruled over the warm months, from the Summer Solstice to the Winter Solstice, was about to be slain by the Holly King.

"Previous years, they've had mock battles. Once they even had a duel and you could tell they knew how to hold swords. It was almost realistic. They keep trying new things. I think that's what I appreciate so much—their inventiveness and creativity and willingness to try anything."

"What are they trying to do?" Jen had asked.

"I think they're just trying to get the ceremony right."

"But why? What does it matter?"

Then Missy had given Jen a shocked look. "For historical accuracy. It's important that they get it right, Jen."

Which was the point at which Jen had stopped asking questions and was just determined to get through it all.

Suddenly a man wearing a green cloak could be seen walking across the frost-tipped grass toward them. The cloak flowed behind him. Where he walked, the snow melted.

"That's the Oak King, or Green Man, as some call him."

He was taller than everyone else in their ensemble. He walked with stately strides, his gaze past them to the center of Stonehenge. Heat radiated from him and she felt herself begin to sweat beneath her heavy jacket as he passed. Then she noticed his skin, which was also green, like a British Isles Caliban. He strode past them and into the center of the circle. The lights speared him, accentuating his green color. Then he dropped his robe. He stood in the frigid air, wearing nothing at all. A twig of something covered his parts, but the rest of him was a muscular, god-like green.

Missy covered her mouth with a hand and whispered, "Now this is something very new."

The snow around him continued to melt. Jen couldn't help but appreciate the special effects. Part of her wanted to know how they did it, but another part of her was transfixed by the figure. Though he was about six and a half feet tall and all green, it was his chiseled features that drew her attention. Dating a U.S. Navy SEAL, she was familiar with good bodies, but this man's contoured muscles were beyond anything she'd ever seen. It was like looking at a statue sculpted by a master.

As her eyes drifted past the twig and down his legs, she saw the ground around him change. Once snow, it was now brown grass. But even as she watched it the dead blades began to change and lift and turn green as if they were really coming alive.

The nature and tone of the scarlet-robed druids' chanting changed. The words came faster and the tones became deeper. One of the druids separated himself from the others and strode toward the Green Man. The druid's face was in shadow, but his hand was visible and holding an ancient stone knife. It didn't seem to have an edge and the tip was rounded, but it was still recognizably a knife. He approached the Green Man and held it up.

The chanting stopped.

Everything was silent except for the whip of wind through the standing stones.

Someone laughed nervously.

The moment drew on long enough that Jen was about to say something when the druid pulled back the knife and then thrust it into the Green Man's chest. The stone knife penetrated and stuck. The Green Man fell to his knees as the druid returned to the circle.

The chanting resumed once again, this time with a higher tone and an even faster beat. Whatever they were saying, it seemed in earnest. Jen felt energy in the air, something like electricity. One of the lights blew, causing everyone to jump. Jen and Missy screamed, then covered their mouths, exchanging embarrassed glances.

The ground around the Green Man was no longer green. It was no longer brown. The snow and frost began to creep beneath him until all evidence of the momentary spring was removed. Then he fell forward. Even as they watched, his skin turned from green to gray to black, mottling through the spectrums.

Jen found that her hand was still covering her mouth. What she was watching was extraordinary. She'd been to plays both indoors and out-, but this was something beyond what she'd ever seen before. She glanced at Missy and saw fear in her eyes.

"What is it?" Jen whispered.

"This has never happened."

"You said they change it every time."

"Yes, but not like this." She gestured with her right hand. "This is so far above what I saw in the past. It's gone from quaint to—"

She fell silent as everyone in the gathered ensemble gasped. The once Green Man made his way slowly back to his feet. When he stood, he had the same features and the same chiseled body, but where he'd been green he was now black. Wind swirled around him and began to peel the blackened skin away. Where it was removed, healthy pink human skin was underneath. Soon pieces of skin were swirling like ash until all the black had been removed.

He shook himself like a great beast might after a kill. Then he leveled his gaze on the gathered ensemble. He spoke in a language Jen couldn't understand. She glanced at Missy for a possible translation but saw her friend's fear had now been replaced by abject terror. She shook and trembled.

"Artur."

"Who?"

The chanting had stopped again.

A druid came and gave the man a crown made of simple iron. He placed it on his head, and as he did, fire began to burn in his eyes.

"Arthur? Do you mean like King—"

A hand grasped Jen's throat from behind just as the hands of the other druids grasped the throats of the rest of the gathered ensemble and Missy beside her. Jen felt a cold breeze pass across her throat, then warmth. She'd been watching Missy the entire time and saw the druid's knife slash deep into her throat and the blood begin to well. It was a moment before Jen realized the same thing had just been done to her.

From somewhere far away she heard a dog howl.

The hand held her erect, but she wanted to fall. She grasped at it, but the druid behind her was stronger than she ever was. She brought her hand to her neck and wiped at it. Her hand came away sticky with blood. She stared at the redness, so much like the color of the druid's robes.

She heard a baying from nearby, then the low call of a hunting horn.

The hand finally released her and she dropped to her knees. She fell to her side.

She watched as furious shadow beasts much like giant hounds cavorted around the feet of the Holly King.

Oh, Jack, where are you?

He'd know what to do.

She felt a tug at something deep inside her, then felt a transformation.

She turned to see her body on the snow, dead and staring eyes above a jugular-red smile. Then the essence of what had been her became something else, something furious and savage and mean, and she bayed like the rest of them, glorying in the return of the hunt.

CHAPTER 1

22,000 FEET ABOVE MARANA AIRFIELD. NIGHT.

JUMPING OUT OF AIRPLANES INDICATES A SEVERE LACK OF BOREDOM was scrawled on the inside cabin of the plane in permanent ink. Jack Walker loved night jumps. In fact, it was his favorite part of being a SEAL. Sure, the free travel, the government rations, the shooting, the fun of getting your ass kicked by supernatural creatures you didn't even know existed held their own special places in his heart, but those were nothing like the feeling of leaping out into the blackness of the night sky and becoming one with the universe.

He stared down the hull to the open door. Red and green lights rested above it. Both were off. Outside was total black.

Sam Holmes, his commanding officer, was with him because it was time to recertify Jack for High-Altitude High-Opening jumps. Not that there was any doubt that he could do them—SEAL Team 666 had sure done their share of them lately—but with all free government food and travel came the necessity of paperwork.

Triple Six had experienced a much-needed rest over the last five weeks and Holmes wanted to make certain everyone was current in their certifications, so this week had been filled with glorious physical fitness tests, rifle and pistol range qualifications, medical exams, SCUBA re-quals, and HALO, HAHO, free-fall, and static-line jumps. Where regular military units made sure their equipment was battle ready, whether it be a tank or a ship or a plane, in the SEALs the men *were* the equipment.

Laws, YaYa, and Yank had been certified the previous evening. Jack would have joined them, but he'd had to appear in traffic court in Los Angeles to try to contest a speeding ticket on the 405. Not that he wasn't speeding; he was just hoping that appearing in his shiny dress uniform might earn some leniency from the hopefully patriotic judge. It had been a waste of time. Jack had been ordered to pay the full fee and received points on his license and wasted a day.

So much for patriotism.

Most important for Jack, once he recertified in HAHO he could go on some much-anticipated leave. Jen had gone to England a week early to spend time with an old college roommate from Bard. She planned on spending time with her friend now so that she and Jack could see the country together once he arrived. They still hadn't set a date for the wedding, but they were thinking about spending their honeymoon in England. This trip would serve as a reconnaissance to see if there was any place with which they might fall particularly in love. As Jen said, only a SEAL would recon his own honeymoon.

But that had to wait. Jack was already a senior parachutist and had almost enough jumps for master parachutist wings. Still, the U.S. Navy in all her wisdom wanted a checkmark on a list in a file. There was no other thing to do but comply.

Normally he'd conduct the jump with the other SEALs of Triple Six. HAHO in and of itself wasn't difficult once you learned and practiced, except for the sheer bulk of equipment, oxygen tank and mask. What was difficult was for all the SEALs to stay together so that they could hit the target simultaneously. With nearly forty thousand feet of room to drift apart, the chances of screwing it up were astronomical. But this was just a certification jump. He and the others would practice another time.

Jack and Holmes were the only two passengers in the rear of

the DCH-6 de Havilland Twin Otter. The seats had been removed and replaced by a single bench along the port side. Jack sat with his equipment hanging to the floor. He carried a one-hundred-pound pack in front. His HK416 was attached to the front. The oxygen tank rested on top. A hose ran from the tank to the mask he wore. He'd been pre-breathing 100 percent oxygen to purge the nitrogen from his blood for ten minutes so he wouldn't experience hypoxia or the bends. A helmet and goggles rested on his head. He stared at the altimeter gauge on his left wrist and watched it creep past 24,000 feet. His MC-6 parachute served as a seat cushion, which he leaned back against.

Holmes sat beside him. He wore a chute, helmet, and mask but wasn't carrying a simulated combat load.

"I know you're aching to get this over with, SEAL," Holmes said through their intra-mask com system, "but slow is smooth and smooth is fast. We're not going to rush anything."

"I'm okay. Last thing I wanted was to spend a week with two chatty Cathies. Talk about feeling like a third wheel."

"Just so. Slow is smooth and—"

"And smooth is fast, I know."

Holmes held up a hand. "Hold. Getting a call from Laws."

Walker watched Holmes. Through his mask, he could only make out the SEAL team leader's eyes. But several times they flicked in his direction. Walker felt worry creep into his system. He'd had a finely honed sense of trouble ever since he was orphaned and left on the streets of the Philippines as a child.

Holmes spoke for perhaps two minutes, then turned to face Walker.

"What's the news?" Walker asked.

Holmes shook his head. "It's bad. We're going to cancel training."

Butterflies with switchblades kamikazied in his stomach. "How bad?"

"Worst."

Walker went through the list of all the worst things that could happen. He was stunned at how few there really were. He glanced at Holmes and then he knew. The emptiness was so complete it was as if his insides had been torn out, leaving the vacuum of space.

He couldn't keep his voice from cracking as he said, "Jen?"

Holmes closed his eyes and nodded.

Walker gulped for air. He felt like he was falling. How ironic he wore a suit made for it and it wasn't helping. "How?"

"They don't know. She and her friend and a group of others were all murdered visiting Stonehenge."

Suddenly he had something to grab on to. "Did you say 'murdered'?"

"I did."

"Do they have the—"

"They have no idea."

"By 'they' you mean MI5?"

Holmes nodded.

"What about our intel? Do we have any?"

"If we did I know it's well above our pay grades."

"To hell with pay grades. She was my fiancée . . . and I want to know. I need to know."

"We may never know."

"That's bullshit."

"Regardless, this exercise is over. Team leader to pilot."

"No!" Walker felt a sense of panic. He had to have something normal. He needed something planned. He had to jump. He glanced at the open door, then back at Holmes. "Let me do this."

The voice came from the cockpit and through their com systems. "Team lead, this is pilot. What's your command?"

Holmes gave him a steady gaze.

"What? You think I'm going to kill myself?" Walker felt his lip curl. "You think I'm going to swan-dive so I can be with Jen in a better place? As romantic as that sounds in movies, it's bullshit. Someone has to be alive to pick up the pieces. Someone has to be the one to get revenge." He paused and couldn't keep from one last desperate whisper. "Is she really dead?"

"Yes, son. She's really dead."

"Let me jump. Just let me fucking jump."

"Team lead, this is pilot; I say again, what's your command?"

"Pilot, this is team lead; continue mission."

"WILCO."

When they reached altitude, the light above the door blinked red.

Walker made to stand and move, but Holmes gripped his arm. They both wore masks, but Jack could feel the intensity in his commander's eyes.

"We'll get through this, Jack. We're your family. We'll help you any way we can." Holmes held on for a moment, then let Walker go.

They both stood and crouch-walked to the door. When the light turned green, Walker stepped out and let the wash carry him back and down. He knew Holmes was right behind him, but there was no way to see him. Not through the darkness. Not through Walker's tears.

Fifteen seconds later he deployed his chute and felt it jerk him free of his fatal fall. He stared at his altimeter and watched as it indicated his descent. Sobs overtook him at 25,000 feet. At 21,000 feet he thought about pulling the release on the chute. Maybe there was a heaven. Maybe there was an afterlife. God knows he'd discovered that there was so much more to this world since he'd joined Triple Six. If there were demons and shape changers why couldn't there be a heaven?

Holmes's voice brought him back. "Walker, you're off course."

Walker checked the GPS compass on his other wrist. He was way off course.

Holmes's voice was filled with urgency. "Walker, what are you doing? We talked about this."

He guided his MC-6 in the proper direction. "Course corrected," he said, then nothing more.

If there was a heaven then he had time to get there. Time probably moved a lot differently in such a place. It might only be a moment for Jen. Then a voice reminded him that it could also be an eternity, but he ignored it. What had initially seemed a comparison of love and revenge and a question of which was stronger had been reconciled. Love was revenge's fuel and by god he'd loved Jen like no one else. He pictured her waiting for him by the famous San Diego statue of a sailor kissing a nurse. The way Jen's red hair had lain against the white nurse's uniform she'd rented from a costume store. The way she and Jack had kissed, mimicking the statue. That had been a hell of a day.

By the time he hit 10,000 feet he knew what had to be done. By hook or by crook he was going to find out who killed his fiancée and when he did he'd do the same to them and everyone else involved.

He'd do it or die trying.

CHAPTER 2

BROMLEY, ENGLAND. MORNING.

Member of Parliament Gordon Miller felt like his head had been stoved in and his brains replaced with porridge. He and that sweet little waitress from Lions Head had drunk enough G&Ts to fill a water tank last night. Now, waking up to the frigid morning and an even more frigid realization that he'd failed to respond to not one but twenty-seven texts from his dear wife, especially the last one, which said: *You might as well go fuck yourself because you're never going to fuck me again,* made his morning complete.

Sigh.

She'd said the same thing twice before and it had proven expensive to get back in her good graces. Real fucking expensive. He'd have to test his mettle and see if her golden triangle was worth it this time.

The bathroom door opened and Veronica stepped out naked, her raven hair still dripping. She held a towel to it as she regarded him, already in his suit, chewing breath mints and guzzling water.

"You gonna run out on me, governor?"

He shook his head. She had the dark skin of a Gypsy and the night moves of an alley cat. He wanted nothing more than to have another go at it, except for the fact he was fresh out of little blue pills. What's a fifty-five-year-old overweight MP to do? Plus, he needed to get home and not with the smell of strange on him.

"Sorry, luv. Mother called and wants me home."

She gave him a smile much like the one she'd offered him in the pub. It promised absolutely everything. "We going to do this again soon?"

Gordon couldn't help but smile. "I hope so. Just need to figure it out."

"Don't leave me hanging, governor. A girl loves to be treated like a woman by a rich man. Especially a rich man who's on television as much as you."

So she knew. So much for his pretense of being a simple businessman. And the damn girl was smiling again. "I'll take care of you."

"I'm sure you will."

She turned and went back into the bathroom. He couldn't help but watch. Even if his body wouldn't cooperate, his mind was creative enough to fill in the blanks.

His cell phone buzzed. He checked it. *Wifey.*

Your shit is on the back porch.

His fingers hovered over the phone as he prepared to answer her. But then it buzzed again. His secretary had sent the schedule for the morning, including an updated time for his conference with the Muslim League about increased funding for their defense account. What another pain in the ass. Not that he didn't mind their considerable support to his campaigns, but they insisted on taking an incredible amount of his time. Still, if he wanted to remain in office this was something that had his full support, which also meant he couldn't afford to miss the appointment.

He texted his secretary to confirm. He also asked that she text his wife and tell her that he'd worked late and stayed at the office. Roxy was a good secretary and would do it with no questions asked. Of course, she'd expect a significant holiday bonus.

Damn but this was proving to be one of his more expensive

days. It was barely dawn and he already owed three women. He couldn't help but chuckle. Of course he could have it the other way. No job. No women. No sex.

He took one more gulp of water, then stood. He straightened his tie in the mirror by the door, then grabbed the keys from his overcoat pocket. He left the room and entered the cold Bromley morning. The wind whipped the fog in the parking lot, making it move as if great objects were passing through. A ship's horn broke the early morning. So did the barking of a dog.

He had to search for his Mercedes. He'd been in such a rush to get into Veronica's knickers he hadn't paid much attention to anything else. He chuckled. Yet another reason he was proud to not be American. Them and their damned paparazzi. If he'd been in the American Congress he'd never have a chance at these dalliances. The first time he'd try he'd be on Facebook and Twitter and Twatter.

There. He spotted his car three rows up.

Dogs began to bark incessantly. As if in answer, a baying came from deep within the fog. The dogs barked madly. He turned in a full circle. What was going on with the dogs? One thing he hated was strays. Not a time to be bit if he could help it.

The baying came again, this time followed by a horn. It didn't sound like a ship's, though. Was there a foxhunt nearby? Why would someone do it in this weather? Never mind that the hunts had been made illegal.

He became aware of figures moving within the fog. He only caught fragmented glimpses of them, but they seemed to be carrying weapons. The fog billowed and covered the cars.

The baying came closer, now with the sound of claws scraping against the pavement as the hidden creatures bore down on him. He had a moment to think, then turned and ran right into the side of a car. The impact drove the air from him. He fell but clawed his way to his feet.

Someone yelled behind him, then sounded a horn.

The baying was now all around him.

He held his hands up in front of him.

"Okay. Okay. Enough of this." An animal brushed his leg. "Do you know who I am?"

The fog parted for a moment and he beheld a man dressed all in green, like a hunter. He wore holly-patterned clothes and an iron crown on his head. But what drew the MP's eyes was the great rack of horns on the white stag the man rode. Even as the MP stared, the man brought a hunting horn to his lips and blew. The stag's eyes blazed red, then the beast lowered his antlers and charged.

The MP screamed and turned. He managed four steps before the tips of the antlers pierced his back. The pain caused him to stagger, but he was unable even to fall. The stag lifted him and picked up speed. Soon they were careening through the fog, baying beasts running all around them. He wanted to scream for them to stop. He wanted to beg them to let him go. But amidst the clatter of hooves and the blowing of the rider's horn, he felt his spirit ripped from his body. By the time the stag shook his great head and dislodged Miller's body many miles later, he could barely remember who or what he'd been. All he knew was that there was a hunt, he was part of it, and it gave him so much joy that he bayed.

CHAPTER 3

TUCSON INTERNATIONAL AIRPORT. DAY.

Timothy Laws watched as Jack Walker reached airport security, then was waved through. Such a fucked-up thing to happen to such a great couple, Laws thought. The universe was a fickle bitch. As was their controller. Holmes had been on the phone for two hours last night trying to get clearance, but Alexis Billings had ordered them to stand down. Where SEAL Team 666 might be able to go into places like Myanmar or Mexico with little political blowback, conducting operations in Mother England was another thing altogether. They were forbidden to lift a finger, England was handling it, and they were not to get involved. End of story.

But no one said that Jack Walker couldn't go on a little Bereavement Leave to England. And no one asked permission either. After all, it was an administrative function, which could be approved by the team leader.

Holmes grabbed Laws's shoulder. "Let's go. We don't want to miss our flight back to San Diego."

Laws turned and confronted him. YaYa and Yank stood nearby and stepped forward. "Listen, why don't you put us all on leave? I'm feeling bereaved."

"I'm fucking bereaved too," Yank said.

"Me too." YaYa placed his right hand on Yank's shoulder. "Bereaved times ten."

Holmes lowered his gaze. "As am I, but we can't all take leave."

"Why not?" Yank asked. The white scars on Yank's African-American face stood out when he was angry and now they looked like a road map of rage. "There isn't a place on the planet we can't be in twenty-four hours. In fact, if the balloon went up, it would make it easier if we were in the same place."

"What he said," YaYa added. Ever since the replacement of his left arm below the elbow by DARPA doctors, Yank had been helping YaYa by using martial arts as therapy and they'd become as close as brothers.

"It's not that easy," Holmes began, but Laws interrupted.

"Sure it is. It's as easy as we make it. We all go on leave and help Jack out. If we happen to get into a firefight then it was one of those wrong-place-wrong-time things."

"That's what I'm talking about. I have the bigger picture to keep in mind. It's what one does when he's the leader. There could be political consequences for our actions. We also don't want to bite the hands that feed us."

Laws knew his boss and best friend was right, but he didn't like it at all. Helpless was not a feeling he appreciated. "So we just do nothing?"

"I never said that. We're going to do something. It's just that I don't know what it is yet."

"Is that a promise?" Laws asked.

Holmes looked up sharply. "Is this kindergarten? Is it recess? Do you want me to fucking pinky swear? This is a goddamn military organization, Laws. I am the commander and I said we're going to do something. Do. You. Get. That?"

Laws grinned. "You look good when you're angry."

Holmes's face remained granite hard.

Yank interjected, "Meanwhile back at the Batcave, Jen's people are working on getting data from the NSA. They should have something by the time we get back."

Holmes sighed. "We've been told to stand down."

"Getting information is not an operation. Using the information is," YaYa pointed out.

Holmes shook his head and walked away. "We're going to miss our plane."

The others caught up.

"I know you have a plan," Laws said, unwilling to let it die. Then he saw it. A twinkle in the corner of Holmes's eye. Laws laughed. "I knew you had a plan."

They walked another twenty feet and Holmes asked, "You're not going to ask me what it is?"

"No. I figure when it's set, you'll let us all know."

"Finally. Someone acting like this is a military unit."

"Hoo-aahh," said YaYa and Yank simultaneously.

They were indeed a military unit. Lieutenant Commander Sam Holmes, the blond-haired, square-jawed paradigm of a SEAL, life dedicated to the cause of freedom; Chief Petty Officer Ali Jabouri, or YaYa, Arab-American, dark skinned, dark hair, built like a runner, trying to prove that he was as apple-pie American as everyone else; Petty Officer Second Class Shonn Yankowski, African-American, shaved head, tattoos, burns along the left side of his face from a house fire back home in Compton; Senior Chief Petty Officer Tim Laws, blond haired, lanky, unable to forget anything he ever read or saw; and Petty Officer First Class Jack Walker, blond haired, dead fiancée, hair-trigger sniper, and supernatural early warning device. Together they were SEAL Team 666 and by god they better have a plan, because they were the last line of supernatural defense for America. And if they didn't have Walker when they needed him, then they didn't have a team.

CHAPTER 4

HEATHROW INTERNATIONAL AIRPORT. AFTERNOON.

Ian clocked Walker the moment he left the plane. He had an un-
mistakable military gait. He was a man on a mission and for the
most part kept his gaze focused on each step in the process. De-
plane. Get baggage. Head through customs. Find rental car counter. Get car. Inspect car. Drive car.

Ian understood. He'd had to act that way enough times in the
past, especially with the recent loss of four Section 9 contractors.
They were down to three members and needed their numbers
increased badly. But with all the budget cuts and the new culture
of austerity circulating England like a fiscal plague the likelihood
that their hidden line on the defense budget would be filled was
slim. But, until then, he'd have to make do. Losing men who were
committed to the defense of a nation in battle was one thing. Losing a wife or fiancée was completely different. He couldn't imagine the emptiness he'd feel, which was why when Holmes had
called him Ian had dropped everything to see what he could do to
assist.

Ian pulled two car lengths behind Walker as he maneuvered
his rental onto the M3 toward Southampton. Unless he'd been

here before, he must be using a GPS, because he was going in the right direction.

What had Holmes said? "Do what you can to help him, Ian. He's impetuous and in his current state, there's no telling what he'll do." Not only had Ian been asked to babysit a U.S. Navy SEAL but also to keep the man from doing something irrational. Ian owed Holmes for pulling his ass out of a tight spot in Somalia. Perhaps this would make them square. Regardless, he rode a wave of compassion as well as a little guilt for the poor man's fiancée dying at what should have been a safe event.

He envied Holmes and his SEAL Team 666. They had resources and military backing. When they identified targets, they went after them. For the most part, there weren't too many organizations who opposed them and their country. The problem with being a much older nation like Britain was that those who opposed her were frequent and many. Opus Dei, the Nine Unknown Men (three of whom they knew), the Priory of Sion, the Followers, Dee's Men, the Golden Dawn, Ordo Templi Orientis, the Rosicrucians, the Hellfire Club, the Fenians, and any number of druidic orders were constantly stirring Her Majesty's pot. The men of Section 9 had been a sad lot. That they'd had success was more a matter of the occult groups getting in one another's way, rather than anything Section 9 had done.

Founded in 1569 by Sir Francis Walsingham, Section 9 had defended Britain for centuries under many different names. Their current nom de guerre had come from the organization's name in World War II. MI9, or Section 9, as it was called, had reported directly to the War Office and was overtly responsible for aiding resistance fighters. While there were those in Section 9 who did this, the majority of personnel and resources were allocated to stopping Hitler's Thule Society, who had been intent on helping the Reich reach her pinnacle through magic and artifice.

No. SEAL Team 666 had it easy.

Walker entered a roundabout. He missed his turn onto A303 and had to go around again. Ian had no choice but to follow him.

If Walker was actively detecting surveillance, then he was as good as made.

They continued for another ten minutes then pulled into the parking lot north of Stonehenge.

Walker got out of his car. As he passed Ian sitting in his own car, Walker turned and gave him a steady look. Ian had no doubt that the double roundabout had been a provocative move and part of the SEAL's surveillance detection. Not that Ian had been trying to hide. Walker approached the policeman at the barricade. Although the crime scene had been released, until the blood was cleared the place was closed for tourism.

Ian watched as Walker tried to talk his way past the guard but got stopped. When Walker began to yell and gesticulate, Ian decided it was time for him to get involved. It would be neither right nor proper for a SEAL to kill one of their bobbies.

Ian made his way up the path to where Walker was about to attack the policeman.

"Walker," he called.

The response was immediate. Walker ceased his engagement with the bobby and strode purposefully toward Ian. Fire blazed in the man's eyes. It would do no good to talk to him now. Instead, Ian sidestepped him, saying, "Wait here a moment."

CHAPTER 5

STONEHENGE. DUSK.

Walker was furious at the world. Not only weren't they going to let him see the place where his fiancée was murdered, but some man, probably a government flunky, had trailed him all the way from London also. By his poor tradecraft, the skinny guy who knew his name must be some low-level worker bee they probably assigned to trail him based on his use of his official passport when he went through customs.

Fuck it. If the man wanted to play a game, then Walker was ready to play. But now he had to wait until the man spoke with the police officer. Walker realized his hands were fists and forced them to relax. After a moment, the man began walking into Stonehenge.

What the fu—

Then he gestured for Walker to follow.

Walker jogged past the policeman and couldn't help but give him a look as he passed. He soon caught up with the man and slowed. They walked the rest of the way in silence. The man stared at the ground, his hands shoved deep into the pockets of his jacket. Walker had a sense of expectation as he approached the monolithic stones. They were at once so real and present as they seemed impossible. Part of him wanted to reach out and touch them, but then this was where Jen died.

Walker paused at the outer stones, but the man continued inside. He stopped, then turned to look at Walker. He pointed at the ground. "They found her here. Her throat was cut; then she was mutilated."

Eyes riveted to the grass, Walker took a reluctant step forward, as if he were being pulled.

"Seventeen civilians were killed in the same way. Some ceremony by some whacked-out neo-pagans or druids. MI5 is still trying to figure it out."

There was so much fuzz in Walker's head he barely heard the other man's words. Walker suddenly felt the need to touch the spot. Three quick steps, he was down on both knees, his hands against the cold ground. He stayed there for a long while. He pressed his cheek against the ground. He didn't know what he'd expected to find. He didn't even know what he'd feel, maybe a piece of her. He had the ability to detect supernatural forces. Maybe if her ghost had been nearby he would have detected her, maybe put himself in position to communicate with her somehow.

But there was nothing here.

The ground was cold.

The place was empty.

He stood. Stonehenge had the feeling of an old battlefield. Like Chickamauga or Gettysburg, whenever he was at a place where a lot of people had died, it felt different. Reverentially empty.

He suddenly felt cold and shivered. "A lot of people died here," he said.

"This used to be a ceremonial place for the druids, some say all the way back to two to three thousand years before Christ."

Walker shook his head and blew into his hands. He hadn't prepared for the cold. Coming from Tucson and San Diego before that, all he had was jeans, a T-shirt, and a light Polo jacket. "Do they have any leads at all?"

The man nodded. "I expect they do. We can ring them up tomorrow morning." He stepped forward and held out a hand. "Ian Waits. Commander Ian Waits. Retired Special Air Service. Your commander called me and asked that I look after you a bit."

Walker should have known. Looking at the man now more carefully, he realized he'd been mistaken when he'd thought of him as skinny. That wasn't the right word. "Lean." "Wiry." Those were better. He stood about five foot six or seven. His head was clean shaven, but in the dying light of the day Walker could make out scars on the man's face and scalp. And his eyes were definitely the eyes of a military officer—someone who'd seen too much and didn't miss a thing. Like Holmes's.

He took Ian's hand. "Jack Walker, but you already knew that."

Ian nodded. "What happened here was egregious. We'll sort this out. It might take a few days, but we'll take care of it." He turned to leave. "For now, however, let's get to someplace warmer. We'll have a pint and discuss our way ahead."

Ian's phone suddenly rang. He pulled it from his pocket and brought it to his ear. Walker couldn't hear the conversation, but by the look on the man's face it wasn't anything good. When it was over, Ian stared at the phone, then slowly replaced it.

"Come on," he said. "Let's get your bag out of your car."

"What? That's my rental!"

Ian shook his head. "No reason to have two cars. I'll have the rental company come pick it up. We have somewhere we need to be, anyway. It might have something to do with the murders. If nothing else, it should shed light on what happened." Ian stepped out of the stone circle with long, quick strides.

Walker struggled to catch up. His head was spinning. "Who are we going to meet?"

"A seer we use from time to time."

"A what?"

"A seer. A witch if you will."

Walker put a hand on Ian's arm to stop him. "Wait a moment. Who do you work for?"

Ian smiled, revealing a gold tooth on the lower left side of his mouth. "Section 9. We do what you do, only we do it here. Who'd you think I was? The welcome wagon?"

The man took off again, leaving Walker to stare at his receding back. *Well, of course England would have its own group.* Walker broke into a run to catch up.

CHAPTER 6

WOKING, ENGLAND. NIGHT.

They drove in silence for forty minutes before they pulled into the town of Woking. Walker noted the interspersed new and ancient architecture. It had begun to mist and Ian had put on the wipers. Through the prism of wet glass, the land seemed surreal. To think that twenty-four hours ago he'd thought that Jen was still alive and that the life they'd planned together was his definitive future. He squeezed his fists together until his knuckles cracked.

Laws had sent him a text with a few kind words and then a link to what was called the Kübler-Ross Model. It's also referred to as the Five Stages of Grief, but Walker believed that Kübler-Ross had little to no idea what she was talking about. Her theory was that a person went through each of these stages in order and it was through these stages that a mourner felt at peace. According to her, they were denial, anger, bargaining, depression, and acceptance. If he was to build a model of stages, it would have at least ten stages, beginning and ending with rage and interspersed with enough anger to fuel movement to the next stage.

He reflected back to his last mission and how dangerous it had been for Jen. Not only could she have been killed by one of the Flayed Ones or the Los Zetas or the Obsidian Butterfly, but Ramon the werewolf could have killed her at any time. To think she survived all of that so she could die on a fucking vacation made him want to explode. What a sad fucking universe this turned out to be.

They passed a sign that read: "Horsell Moor" and Jack immediately thought of the Hound of the Baskervilles. Was the seer's cabin somewhere on the moor? They turned onto Broomhall Road, a narrow way bordered on either side by shrubberies that blocked the views of the nearby homes. They reached the end of the road where a sign read: "Turning Point No Parking." Ian turned the vehicle around, then parked.

Ian switched off the car. "It might say no parking, but no one's going to mess with this car."

"Do they know who it belongs to?"

"No, and that's why they won't mess with it. It only comes back as belonging to Her Majesty's government with no other affiliation. They're afraid they might piss someone off if they so much as give the car a parking ticket."

"So you can drive however you want."

"With impunity if we have to." Ian opened the door. "Come on, let's go."

They exited the car and headed back down the street. The moor stood dark with multiple layers of shadows on their right. On their left stood homes, brightly lit windows warding off the night above the shrubberies. They turned into one of these homes, which surprised Walker. Doubly surprising was the way the yard was decorated with landscaping lights and cat statues. *Seriously?* His gaze panned over a plaque with a kitschy slogan about a house never having too many cats. This was the home of a witch?

He meant to comment to Ian, but he was already at the front door and ringing the bell. An old-fashioned buzzer rang from somewhere inside. The front of the house was painted white and lined with dark beams. Walker thought it was the Tudor style but wasn't exactly sure.

They heard footsteps on a hardwood floor inside coming toward the door.

When it opened, Ian dipped his head. "I appreciate you seeing us, ma'am."

The woman couldn't have been a day over thirty. She wore jeans, impossibly tall high heels, and a blouse that could have been at home inside a dance club. Her black hair was tied into a ponytail. She had blue eyes and wore deep-red lipstick. Skeleton earrings hung from each ear. She looked like someone's sister, not a witch. This was the witch?

"What'd you think I was going to look like?" Her hands were on both hips as she addressed Walker. "A big old warty nose and a broomstick?" She rolled her eyes, then to Ian said, "Where do you get these people?" Then she turned on her heel and clomped back into the house.

Ian gave Walker a look. "I did pretty much the same thing myself." He gestured for Walker to go inside, then followed.

The brightly lit interior smelled of incense and cooked chicken. Down a short hall and into the modernly appointed living room, two men sat. One was perched on the edge of a chair eating a plate of food, while the other sat back on a sea-foam-green sofa, drinking tea from a small china cup.

The witch sat at a card table and regarded Jack and Ian. A deck of Tarot cards was already on a white lace tablecloth.

"Jack Walker, this is Ms. Moore," said Ian. "The git over there shoveling food is Trevor Jones, Royal Marine Sniper, and the effeminate one holding the teacup like a poof is Jerry McMahon. He's our intelligence specialist."

Trev nodded but kept chewing.

Jerry gave a single hand wave, then sipped his tea.

The witch gestured to the couch, then turned to her cards. "Why don't you both have a seat?"

Ian folded his hands in front of him and remained in place. "I thought there was a pressing—"

"Oh, dear lord, why didn't you tell me?" The witch stood and came to Walker. She put her arms around him and hugged him tight. Walker wasn't sure what to do with his hands and eventually returned the hug. When she released him she said, "I'm terribly sorry for your loss. I'm just stunned that you're holding up so well."

Walker smiled weakly.

"And you're angry too. I don't blame you." She leveled a stern gaze at Ian as she went back to her cards. "You really should have told me. It's going to be easier now for me to help."

Ian glanced at Walker. "Easy how?"

"Now we have a personal connection to the event. His spirit was most certainly intertwined with that of his fiancée. That link will serve as a bridge."

Walker spoke up. "I'm not sure I want anyone messing around with any memories I have. They're all that's left."

"It's not your memories we need, Mr. Walker. It's your love."

Walker stared at the hardwood floor as he fought back emotion. He found he was blinking rapidly, his body's autonomic response to keep his tears at bay. "What do I have to do?"

"Not much. Sit down, hold my hand, and keep still."

Walker was having trouble reconciling her youthful appearance with the authority with which she spoke. He hesitated a moment, then sat in the other chair at the card table. She laid her hands across the table and indicated that Walker should place his on top of them, which he did.

"Now, Mr. Walker—"

"Everyone calls me Walker." He closed his eyes for a moment. "Even Jen sometimes."

The witch smiled softly. "Probably when she was mad at you. I can see her doing it. You can call me Sassy." She hesitated a moment when Walker looked at her funny. "It's my name. Seriously."

"Ma'am, there is absolutely no way I can call you Sassy."

Jerry laughed from the couch. "We all told her the same thing."

She shook her head. "You military men are all so formal. Let's just get started."

"What do I do?"

"You be quiet, luv, and let me do all the work."

Walker closed his eyes and tried not to think about anything, but his thoughts automatically strayed to Jen's death. He visualized her lying on the cold, hard earth of Stonehenge, her eyes staring deep into his, asking him why he hadn't been there to help her. His eyes snapped open as he searched for something to look at, some visual input to dampen the accusation in her eyes. He noticed that a few of the Tarot cards had been turned over. In fact, his and the witch's hands were resting on two cards—a card with a tower being struck by lightning and a card with a kingly figure on a throne with a sword. Of the other cards facing up on the table, all had some sort of sword.

Suddenly his body stiffened as if a jolt of electricity had taken control of him. His vision went blank, then was replaced by an image of a green man standing in the snow, then of a red-robed figure, then of the stones of Stonehenge, then of someone racing through a thick wood. He heard the sound of baying and realized it was coming from himself.

His eyes snapped open and he found the witch staring at him, a look of terror on her face.

Jerry, Trev, and Ian were also on their feet.

The witch let Walker go and stood. She paced back and forth for a moment, then went to a bookshelf.

Walker was breathing heavily. He wiped sweat from his forehead using his jacketed forearm. "What is it?"

Jerry said, "You were howling like a wolf, mate."

"And growling too," Trev added.

Walker felt hoarse. He brought a hand to his throat. "For how long?"

"Five minutes at least," Jerry said.

Walker shook his head. "Impossible. It couldn't have been more than a few seconds."

"Try six minutes, Walker," the witch said, coming back to the table with a large book. "We're lucky you were able to come back at all."

Ian stepped forward. "What is it? Earlier you mentioned that you might know who was involved in the ceremony."

"First things first." She spoke a few words in a guttural German, then put her hand on Walker's head. She did the same for the other three men, who stood by like this was a normal every-day occurrence.

When she was finished, she explained, "I needed to hide you from any interested eyes."

"What about you?" Walker asked.

"I'm very well hidden already. I've had people chasing me for more than fifty years. Don't worry about me."

Walker looked at her. She was definitely a lot older than she appeared.

"So . . . ," Ian began.

"So something's returned that the Isles haven't seen in more than a thousand years. Maybe longer." She flipped through the book and came to a double-page picture of a woodcut that showed a hunt. On the left was a cart pulled by a team of great stags. To the sides and in front were dogs and misshapen beasts of all sizes caught mid-action. Some were running; some were fighting each other; one even held the body of a baby in its twisted mouth. Standing in the cart with a whip in one hand and a sword in the other was a figure that looked like a demented Santa.

Walker said as much.

"That's because part of our lovely Yuletide holiday tradition comes from this. Gentlemen, may I present to you the Wild Hunt."

"The wild what?" Jerry asked, his eyes wide.

Trev punched Jerry in the shoulder. "Hunt. She said 'hunt.'"

"Glory be. I thought she was describing a date I had last week."

Ian punched Jerry in his other shoulder.

"The Wild Hunt was first reported in the seventh century, but it could be far older. I've read where they believe it to be the last vestiges of the Sidhe, or Tuatha Dé Dannan. Perhaps those who didn't cross over to the other world with the coming of man. Like the Baen Sidhe, or banshee, they populate much of the mythology of the Isles." She gave the men a gentle but stern look. "Only this isn't mythology. It's real."

"You're talking faeries?" Trev asked.

"I knew you'd be interested if there were faeries," Jerry murmured.

"Like red caps and mermen and boggles?" Ian asked. When Trev and Jerry gave him a funny look he added, "My grandmam used to tell us about them. Wouldn't let us go outside at night because she was afraid the faeries would come and eat us."

Walker shook his head in disbelief. "Those don't sound like the faeries I learned about."

The witch scoffed, "Walker, dear. Don't you get it? America has managed to Disneyfy everything that should be scary. Do you really think Tinker Bell was a sweet little pigtailed pixy? The faeries that were left behind—those still on the Isles—were the dregs, the rejects, those too imperfect or too insane to be with the rest."

"You're serious," Walker said.

"As a heart attack. No one really knows where the faeries went to or for what reason. It's believed that the Sidhe mounds are avenues to small pocket realities where they reside until they feel the need to come out. The Wild Hunt is shared cross-culturally, but primarily in Western Europe and Scandinavia. Many of these areas, now countries, describe the Wild Hunt differently, but there is one universal truth. When it appears, it doesn't go away until its mission is complete."

Walker mused for a moment. Where was Laws when he needed him to simplify things? "What does this Wild Hunt do?"

She smiled patiently. "It's a supernatural hunting party that hunts specific things. What those things are depends on the mission."

"And what's its mission?" Ian asked.

She shrugged. "Think of this like a homicide. If you were a detective, what would you want to know? The motive of the criminal, right? Knowing the motive will help you narrow down who it was who committed the crime. If we can figure out the motive of those who brought it back, we may know its mission."

"Wait a moment," Jerry said, crossing his arms. "Are you saying that there's a supernatural wild hunt out there killing people?"

Ian looked at Walker. "Jerry's new. Only been with us for a month."

Walker nodded. "I can relate. I fought homunculus the first day on the job."

"What's a homunculus?" Jerry asked.

"Little fucking Freddy Krueger–Stretch Armstrong serial-killing mini-golem."

Jerry blinked. "I don't know what that means, but it sounds terrible."

"It is. I've made my share of them too," the witch said. "Making them is even harder than killing them, if you can believe it." She winked at Walker. "Back to the Wild Hunt. The reason Trev called you, Ian, was because I think I might know who it was who held the ceremony."

"The one who apparently called forth the Wild Hunt—that ceremony?" Ian asked.

"The very same. So normally, it's the British Druid Society who puts on the show and performs the ceremony at both solstices. They're a mundane, fairly lame group of non-magicals who do a lot of pretending."

"Like reenactors," Walker noted.

"Exactly. Their shows were—"

"Wait, what are reenactors?" Trev asked.

Jack responded, "Middle-aged men with bad hobbies who dress up in American Civil War or American Revolution uniforms and pretend to do battle. Like the Society for Creative Anachronism except with guns and using real history?"

Trev shook his head. "I only understood half of what you said. Do they ever reenact the American Revolution where we win?"

"Uh, not that I know of," Walker said.

"And back to me." The witch rolled her eyes and pointed both thumbs at herself. When she got full attention, she continued. "So the British Druid Society is really just a bunch of actors. It's why none of us magicals ever worried about them performing ceremonies, because we knew they didn't know what the flaming hell they were doing. As it happens, and we're just now finding this out, except for those of us who felt a shuddering of the veil, a different group arranged to perform the ceremony this year."

"And this group is?" Ian asked, losing a little of his patience.

"The Red Grove. A magical I know contacted the chair of the British Druid Society. The society was given a hundred thousand pounds to silently not show up and my magical friend says that the check was written from an account owned by the Red Grove."

Ian nodded, hand beneath his chin. "So it's a business. We should be able to track financial data through our associates at MI5." He looked up sharply at the witch. "Have you ever heard of this Red Grove?"

"*The* Red Grove, and no, they're new to me."

Ian nodded, deep in thought. "Anything else?"

She shook her head.

"Right then. We'll be leaving you be. Jerry, clean your bloody plate for the lady."

"There's no need. One of my cats will take care of it. Plus, I have my own little homunculus who cleans for me."

"Can I see it?" Jerry asked.

Ian grabbed Jerry by the shoulder and pushed him toward the front entrance. "I apologize for my man, Ms. Moore. He doesn't get out much."

"Quite all right," she said. "And please call me Sassy."

Ian leveled a gaze at her. "Not on your life, ma'am." Then he swept the other three before him and out the door.

CHAPTER 7

RAF CHICKSANDS. NIGHT.

An hour's drive found the three members of Section 9 and the lone SEAL Team 666 member pulling through a guarded gate and onto a military base. Ian explained that RAF Chicksands, which had once been a functioning air force base, closed in 1997 and became the Defence Intelligence and Security Centre and the Headquarters of Britain's Intelligence Corps. Since most of Section 9's personnel came from British intelligence, their collocation made recruitment an important tool for their success. Unlike SEAL Team 666, Section 9 was populated by civilian contractors, and to obtain the specialties they required interaction with military intelligence was important.

Their offices were in the basement of the Chicksands Priory, a former twelfth-century Gilbertine monastery. "The entire monastery actually belongs to Section 9, but we've been relegated to the basement because my predecessor ran afoul of several Members of Parliament. Our funding was cut to the point we could no longer afford its upkeep, so instead of letting it fall apart and needing major construction upgrades, we turned the rest into an officers' club and visiting VIP rooms."

So they passed several drunken service members as they

entered the priory. Had they turned left, they would have entered a large paneled room filled with leather furniture. Had they taken the broad staircase, they could have climbed to some well-appointed rooms. But instead, they turned right and entered a door marked: "Staff Only," which opened on to a staircase that took them down into a basement in need of a face-lift.

"Most of the furniture is left over from World War II. With the exception of the installation of fiber optics and a fresh coat of paint, the basement hasn't seen any improvement," Ian said.

A tight hallway was lined floor-to-ceiling on one side with boxes. As they squeezed past, Walker felt a buzz building in his skin. He hoped it wouldn't get worse. The last thing he needed was to fall down and do the kickin' chicken in front of Section 9. They turned left through the first door and entered a large room with several beat-up couches, a table and chairs, and a small kitchenette. Trev tossed himself down on one of the couches while Jerry helped himself to something that looked like cold, limp French fries in the refrigerator. Ian grabbed a bottle of scotch and two glasses. He poured two fingers into each glass, then held one out for Walker.

Walker accepted it and sat at the table, feeling like he weighed a thousand pounds. He let his elbows support him as he took half of the golden drink, closing his eyes as the liquid left a fire trail down his throat and exploded in his empty stomach. He reminded himself that he couldn't get sentimental. A weepy-eyed widower wouldn't do anyone any good. He needed to keep his wits about him, especially if he was going to track down Jen's killers.

He opened his eyes and finished the scotch. "So, what do we know about the Red Grove?" He gestured for more and Ian obliged.

Ian had called ahead when they were in the car. Even as Walker asked the question, a young Indian girl came into the room. She was beautiful, with black hair framing a narrow face. She wore jeans and an Indian blouse that fell to mid-thigh and tapered at her wrists. She could have been a model had it not been for the twin crutches she needed to propel her crooked legs. Hell, she could still be a model, just not on any runway Walker had ever heard of.

"I have a preliminary report," she said, moving both smoothly and awkwardly at the same time. She smiled at Walker. "The Red Grove is an American 501.3c, meaning it's been classified as a tax-exempt religious organization. Their recorded headquarters is Lake Arrowhead, California, and their employee identification number indicates the Red Grove is headed by Hubert Van Dyke, who also sits on the board of the Bohemian Grove, as well as a company called A Celestial Worry LLC."

Ian poured Walker and himself another two fingers each. "What do we know about Mr. Van Dyke?"

"There are two records in California; both seem to be for the same person. Mr. Van Dyke was a movie star during the 1950s and 1960s. His IMDB credits include *Ironsides, The Andy Griffith Show, Cannon*, and *Bonanza*. Not a top-tier actor, but no slouch either. He has more than a hundred credits to his name." She turned to Walker, balanced on one crutch, and shoved out a hand. "Hi, I'm Preeti Jones." The smile was broad and genuine.

Walker gave her his hand. "I'm Jack Walker. You're not any relation to—" He glanced at Trev Jones slouching on the couch and caught his smile. "It appears that you are." He glanced from her to Trev and back, then shook his head.

Trev got up and gave Preeti a kiss on her cheek. He spent a moment touching her hair and staring into her almond-shaped eyes; then he gave Walker an apologetic look. "It's strange how things are so similar. I understand your fiancée worked with your team."

"It's like a fucking *Twilight Zone* episode," Walker said as he took a drink. Then he looked up sharply. "Sorry about that."

Preeti shook her head. "No worries, Mr. Walker. I'm very sorry for your loss. We're all torn up about it." She pushed Trev away.

Walker looked at her and saw the truth of it. They knew it could have been them. It could have been anyone. The universe is random. Section 9 was much like SEAL Team 666 in that it was a small, close-knit unit that was really a family. Triple Six and Section 9 could have been cousins.

"How long have you two been together?"

"Two years, three months, and fourteen days," she said.

"You say that like it's an incarceration," Trev said, making for the refrigerator.

Preeti grinned playfully. "Sometimes, dear boy, it feels like it."

Trev chuffed but didn't say anything. He opened the fridge and pulled free a pint. "Anyone else?"

Everyone shook their heads, but their eyes remained fixed on him. By the time he got to the couch and sat down, he said, "What? Is this a Benny Hill sketch? If it is, I want the girls with boobs ASAP."

"And what would you do with them, Trev?" Preeti asked.

"I'd—" He struggled for something to say, then just put the beer to his face and began drinking.

Jerry exploded with laughter.

Even Ian cracked a smile.

Walker felt the ghost of one at the corners of his own mouth. He knew what Trev Jones was feeling right now and would give anything to feel that way again. He shook the sadness away.

"So we have an American company that came to England to perform a ceremony designed to bring back the Wild Hunt. Again I ask *what's their motive?*"

Trev added from the couch, "And is the Red Grove the actual group who performed the ceremony or are they a shell corporation?"

Jerry joined them at the table. "What do we know about the Bohemian Grove?"

"Now that's interesting," Preeti said, sitting down. She rested her crutches on the edge of the table, grabbed Ian's glass, and took a small sip of the scotch. She made a face but licked her lips happily. "The Bohemian Grove is quite the place. Imagine a twenty-five-hundred-acre private compound in California's redwood forest where for two weeks every summer the most powerful men in the world, including our own Tony Blair, go to enjoy themselves."

"What sort of things do they do?" Trev Jones asked from the couch.

"All we've found on that is lots of rumor and supposition. The group's been around since the late 1800s and is a men's club.

There's talk of cross-dressing and some odd sexual rituals, but mainly it's some sort of Bilderberg-like group that plans the fate of the world." She raised a finger. "But there is one thing that stood out. The summer festivities start with an arcane ceremony called the Cremation of Care. It's an elaborate performance where everyone wears robes and they burn a papier-mâché man in effigy at the base of a sixty-foot-high stone owl."

"An owl?" Walker asked aloud.

"I looked into that." She took Walker's glass and took a sip of it and made another face.

"Would you like your own glass?" Walker asked.

She shook her head. "Oh no. I can't stand the stuff. Where was I? Oh yeah, the owl. It's believed by many that this is an Aleister Crowley influence and that they're worshiping Moloch, an ancient Ammonite god worshiped by the Canaanites. But the Freemasons disagree and their rituals indicate that the owl really represents Isis, whose modern incarnations include Columbia for America and Britannia for Britain. So by worshiping at the feet of the giant owl, they are sacrificing something to the symbol of their country."

"And what are they sacrificing?" Walker was trying to get things straight, but he realized he hadn't eaten since that morning and he was quickly filling his stomach with scotch.

"Most believe a duality. The Cremation of Care is described as being symbolic of the destruction of each member's worldly concerns so that they can spend the next two weeks in peace."

Jerry laughed. "That's rich. But what does it really mean?"

She cocked her head as she answered, "Oh, it could mean that, Jerry, or it could also mean it's a dark ritual sacrifice to Isis, or Columbia, the female personification of America, right out of the Dark Ages, asking for the goddess to bless them and guide them as they decide the fate of the world."

Trev got up and approached the table. "Is this for real? Why hadn't we heard about it before?"

She smiled and put an arm around his hip. "Maybe because Rupert Murdoch is a member."

"Seriously?" Ian asked.

She nodded vigorously.

Walker felt himself falling. The events of the day combined with his exhaustion and his lack of food and the scotch had all conspired to do him in. He stood wobbly. "Can we get this information to Holmes?"

Ian stood as well and held out a hand to steady Walker. "Definitely. Now let me get you some food, and then show you where you're staying."

"But I have a reservation at the—"

"We canceled that, don't you worry." To Jerry, Ian said, "Can you fetch something to eat from upstairs? I think we all need to eat."

"They're serving fish-and-chips," Preeti said.

Walker lurched to the side as he felt his stomach boil halfway up his throat. "Bath—ulp." He slammed a hand over his mouth.

Trev Jones grabbed him and both hurried out and down the hall to the loo. Walker barely made it inside before he fell to his knees and vomited into the toilet. He was suddenly feeling like eight miles of hell's road.

CHAPTER 8

WOKING, ENGLAND. MIDNIGHT.

The wind howled as it buffeted Sassy's home. She'd sensed something impending in the minutes after the boys from Section 9 had left. She couldn't put her finger on it, but it was like a psychic buildup of magnificent proportions. The pressure inside her head was so high her ears kept popping. At 11:00 PM she'd decided to move downstairs into the basement to her safe room. She cast as many protection spells as she could, with the limited time and resources she had. Luckily, she'd planned for the possibility of this day long ago and had her spells and protections in place. The only question was what was coming and how strong it would be.

She lit her candles and began to read from *Liber Al vel Legus,* the Book of Law. The Fraternitas Saturni had adopted Aleister Crowley's book as their foundation, but upon obtaining higher levels they were provided greater insights. Now as a Thirty-First Degree Magister Templarus, virtually everything was available to her, but at the moment the words of the Egyptian goddess Nuit, Goddess of the Night Sky, comforted her and she allowed herself to be lost in them.

Sassy had more enemies than most successful witches. Never mind that she'd *stolen* her knowledge of the Fraterni Saturni.

What had always been a men's club had unknowingly allowed a woman to infiltrate their temple. Her adopted father, who was one of the early temple masters, had reveled in the idea that a woman might learn the secrets and felt that it was a much-needed balance to the preponderance of male magic. He'd continued her education on his own until his death ten years ago. But in doing so, he'd lost all of his friends, been forced to flee Germany with his step-daughter, and had to cut himself off from the astral plain, lest he be discovered and the Cull Teams come in search of Sassy.

Above her the house began to rattle.

Then the rattle became as loud as a freight train.

She began to scream a spell of protection, invoking Bes. She imagined the protector of mothers and children wearing the Armor of Anhur, fire and damnation pouring from her eyes into the face of Sassy's unseen enemy.

The noise became so great it obliterated all thought and reason until her own words were sucked from her before she could even form them.

CHAPTER 9

WOKING, ENGLAND. PREDAWN.

They'd woken Walker up at 4:00 AM and sped back to Woking. No one said anything because they didn't know anything other than that the witch had been attacked. Thanks to the club kitchen preparing for breakfast, they all had hot coffee and meat pies. They also wore body armor and carried weapons. There'd been some conversation about whether Walker should be able to carry, but thankfully common sense bore out.

Two SA80s with ACOGs and Viper II thermal sights rested in the trunk and each of them carried a Glock 17 in a chest rig under his jacket. Not exactly enough ammo to take over Somalia, but enough for them to respond if they needed to fight whatever threat was still around Sassy Moore's house.

They weren't able to get within two blocks, however. Police and firemen had already cordoned off the area. They were checking people going in and out. Ian parked his car and ordered Trev to go and take a look. The former Royal Marine exited the car and loped across the street. When he got to the cop, he argued for a moment, then was able to get past. It was about ten minutes later when he suddenly appeared at the back of the car and slipped into the backseat.

"It's fucking gone." He sucked in air to control his breathing. He must have been running.

"What's gone?" Jerry asked. "The house?"

"Like Dorothy rode it to Oz."

"You're serious." Ian stared. "Is there anything left?"

"I'm kidding you not. There's a basement open to the world but no house. The houses all around it didn't so much as lose a paint flake. It's crazy."

"Was there any sign of the witch?" Walker asked.

Trev shook his head.

Walker sat back in his seat. "Fuck me."

Ian pointed out the window. "There she is. Everyone act normal."

"Normal? Sure," Trev said straight-faced. "Perfectly normal for four men in a car to pick up a hot woman beside a place where a house went missing."

Ian pulled up about a hundred feet. Jerry hopped out and let Sassy Moore climb inside. She had a birdcage with a cover over it and a bag. These she set on her lap.

Ian put the car in gear, turned a corner, and they were gone.

Everyone wanted to ask the question, but they deferred to Ian. Finally, after he'd maneuvered them out of the neighborhood, he asked, "What happened, Ms. Moore?"

Her voice was ragged and weak. "Can't . . . won't talk here. Get me to your place."

Walker turned and noticed she was gritting her teeth. Her eyes were bloodshot and her face showed great strain. "Better do it, Ian."

The Section 9 leader simply nodded. They took the M25 to the M1 and headed north, reversing their trip. But at Breakspear Way she had Ian turn off and pull into Woodwells Cemetery. She got out, taking the birdcage with her. Trev and Walker got out as well. She asked for a flashlight and Trev gave her one. They followed her until they found the grave of an infant who'd only lived three days. The witch fell to her knees and dug until she had a pile of dirt. Then she pulled a knife from her pocket and sliced open her palm. She let the blood drip onto the dirt until it was glistening. Once she was satisfied, she waved Walker over and did the same to his palm, also dripping his blood on the dirt. Once she was finished, she removed the cover, pulled the bird free from the cage, and held her while she picked up handfuls of dirt and let them fall on the bird. She finally stood, whispered into the bird's ear, then let her go. The bird took to the air and vanished in the dark sky.

"Now that's done," Sassy said, "we can go."

She left the cage, but after following her for a dozen feet Walker returned and took it. He'd spied a trash can on the way in and hustled to get the cage inside it. The last thing he needed on his conscience was for some mother and father to come to the grave of their child only to find that it had been used for some arcane ceremony, even if it was an arcane ceremony for good.

They drove the rest of the way in silence. At RAF Chicksands, the guard seemed not to notice Ms. Moore. Dawn was lighting the early-morning sky as they climbed down the stairs into the basement of the priory.

When they hit the common area, Sassy plopped onto one of the couches and held out a hand. "Scotch."

Ian complied but didn't pour one for anyone else, which was just as well as far as Walker was concerned. He didn't know if he'd be able to handle it. He stared dull eyed at the room's old wooden walls, shined to a burnished gold by multiple hands over several hundred years.

Jerry pulled a first-aid kit from the wall, opened it, and began to treat the cut on Walker's palm. It was fairly deep and about two inches long.

Sassy drank the first one fast. She treated the second one like a long-lost friend and took her time with it. When she was sated, she went to the sink and washed her face and hands. Finally, with everyone watching, she turned, putting her back to the sink.

She glared at Walker. "We're in the shit now."

Walker gave her his best *what the hell do you mean* look.

"That little hand-holding we did to discover what was happening created a connection between the Wild Hunt and us. It knows where I am and it knows where you are."

Jerry, who'd been standing beside Walker, took a step away from him.

Sassy turned to Ian. "But we're good for now. This priory has more prayer and magic than most anything. It's lucky for us that this is your home."

Ian glanced around. "Such as it is."

"No, you don't understand." She held her arms out to encompass the walls. "The priory is shielded. I'm not sure you knew this, but when this was built, it was not only as a place of worship, but also as a place of refuge from entities such as the Sidhe and the Wild Hunt. That's why it has survived for so long. There was a time when the church sought out the help of those such as myself instead of shunning us . . . hunting us."

"So as long as we stay inside, then it can't find us?" Walker asked.

"It might be able to track you here, if you ever leave again, but it can't get inside, nor can it do what it did to my once lovely home." She frowned and shook her head. "You have no idea what I lost to the Hunt. It's going to be difficult to replace."

"Was there something in your house that could help us defeat the Wild Hunt?" Ian asked.

"Possibly." A look came over her as she sized up the men in the room. "Although, with a little ingenuity and firepower, we could get replacements for many of the items. I actually know of a man who has what I need."

It took a moment for Ian to react to the statement, and when he did his face held a disappointed look. "You want us to steal for you?"

She offered a sweet smile. "Is it stealing if the person is a horrible warlock who sacrifices other people's family pets?"

"Yes, it's still stealing. But if he sacrifices family pets then that's what we might call mitigating circumstances."

She clapped her hands together. "Excellent. At least one good thing's going to come out of this."

Jerry went to her to apply a bandage to her cut, but she waved him away, showing him her hand, which had already healed.

"What was it we did back there?" Walker asked, rubbing the bandage covering his wound.

"Poor pigeon. We put our sign on the bird. When the Wild Hunt catches up to her, they won't leave much, but it was a necessary sacrifice that got us to safety unscathed."

Walker didn't like it. The idea of sacrificing anything was anathema. He'd killed enough and been almost killed enough times to appreciate the sanctity of life. He acknowledged that the witch had just condemned a warlock for sacrificing family pets, but she had little trouble, if any, sacrificing a bird herself. He decided not to point the contradiction out.

Still, he felt the need to ask, "Does he really sacrifice family pets?"

She flashed her *trust me* smile but then noticed it wasn't exactly working. Walker was too tired, too pissed, and too miserable to fall victim to it. "I'm sure he does."

"You don't actually have evidence of it then."

"Nothing that would stand up in court, Your Honor."

Ian interrupted the exchange. "You mentioned that there might be something here that could help. You meant the powers here were left over from the old priory days, right?"

She nodded.

Walker turned to Ian. "What's inside the boxes in the hall? My guess is that they're relics and souvenirs from operations going back I don't know how long."

Ian's eyes narrowed. "How did you know?"

Walker turned back to the witch. "You used the words 'a shuddering of the veil' earlier."

"The veil between this reality and any other. If it's breached by something large enough and we're in proximity to whoever or whatever came through, then we can feel it on a spiritual level."

"Sort of like early-warning radar." Walker understood the concept better than most.

She nodded. "Something like that."

"I have this . . . ability." He almost said "curse." "When I get close to something supernatural, I get this feeling in my body, like electricity. Sometimes it makes me have seizures."

"Wait a minute. If that's the case, then why didn't you do that when you met Ms. Moore?" Jerry asked.

Walker caught the witch giving him a look much like he imagined a vet would a polydactyl rabbit. She spoke up before Walker could answer. "It's because I'm not made of magic. I conjure it and cast it. I'm a funnel." To Ian she said, "If you really have relics and pieces of beasties in those boxes, maybe you'll let Walker and me go through them and see if there's anything handy."

Ian shook his head. "Back when defending Her Majesty against the supernatural was a popular occupation, they graced the walls of the priory as mementos of missions past."

She gave him an intent stare. "And now they're in boxes gathering dust. A lot of good they're doing."

Ian returned her stare with equal intensity for a moment, then relented. "Fine. Just don't break anything. We'll eventually get our building back, and when we do I want something to put on the damn walls."

Preeti entered and evinced surprise at seeing the witch. Trev brought her up to speed after a brief introduction; then she spoke. "I ran a scan of the closed-circuit cameras in the area of her home in Woking," she said to Ian. "The cameras ceased working during the event as if there was some sort of interference."

Ian crossed his arms, then brought his right hand up to scratch his jaw. "Do you think something's jamming them? If so there could be a more mundane than arcane solution."

Preeti considered it. "I suppose it could be microwaves, but the interference is localized to any camera that had optics on the street leading to her home. You'd need at least seven microwave dishes to pull it off."

Ian scratched his chin. "Still not an impossibility."

Walker asked, "Was the interference static?"

"Do you mean was it fuzzy?" Preeti looked confused.

Walker shook his head. "No, what I mean is . . . did it merely appear right or did it arrive from another location? Consider the possibility that the interference might be moving."

Preeti's eyes widened. "Oh. I see. No, I didn't consider that. Very smart, Mr. Walker. Very smart indeed."

CHAPTER 10

CHIPPING SODBURY GOLF CLUB, ENGLAND. MORNING.

Jonathan Fitzhugh considered himself a good worker. Not a great worker and not a bad worker, but a good worker. He got to work on time most mornings, at least those when he hadn't gotten too deep in his cups the night before. He was conscientious every evening, ensuring the groundskeeping equipment was clean and put away. And he was polite to the club members, always remembering to call them sir and their lady friends, whether they be an obvious tramp or an overweight wife, ma'am. So the idea that he had to go see the club manager today at noon was infuriating. They hadn't even explained what it was about, but by the tone of the note attached to seat of the riding lawn mower it was clear that they weren't happy.

There was no way they could have known he'd pawned three sets of golf clubs this year. Not only was there no one around when he took them, but the fact that their owners had left them behind demonstrated that they didn't really want or need them in the first place also. Plus, he'd taken each to a different pawnbroker in Bath. No, there was no way they could have known about those.

The morning fog did little to deter the first foursome of the day. He recognized them as they approached the first tee. The tall one in the middle was Nisam Kazmi, a Pakistani businessman who'd been in the papers. The owner of five car dealerships, he was also interested in the fair treatment of immigrants and was a vocal opponent of any law or policy that inhibited his rights. The other three were his usual partners, two Pakistanis and one Afghan.

Fitzhugh kept one eye on them as he checked the oil level of his lawn mower. There were those down at the pub who'd call them disparaging names, such as ragheads, but then that was just stupid. The real ragheads were the Sikhs, who actually wore turbans on their heads. No, Fitzhugh wasn't one to call the Pakis names. As long as they were good upstanding citizens, why shouldn't they be able to come to the club and play a round of golf?

But Fitzhugh couldn't help but think what if . . . what if they were planning something terrible while they played golf? What if they were arranging for an attack on the Queen or parliament or perhaps something worse involving nerve gas or explosives? He smiled grimly and briefly flashed to an image of him in the newspaper with the headline GROUNDSKEEPER FOILS PLOT TO KILL QUEEN.

He held on to that as he started the tractor and headed toward the third hole where ducks had recently been crapping on the green. The last thing he needed this day was for the Pakis to complain to his boss about a crap-filled green.

The fog wasn't burning off like it usually did. If anything, it was getting thicker as he headed toward the small pond near the green for the third hole. He knew there was a scientific reason for it, but he really didn't know what ten-quid words to use, nor would he have understood their meanings. Plus, this time of December and so close to Christmas, the club was lucky the weather was holding as it was. It might as well be spring.

Sure enough, during the night the ducks had crapped all over the green. He grabbed a flat shovel from the back of the tractor and scooped up all but the smallest pieces and dumped them in the water. He searched for one of the ducks to curse, but they'd made themselves absent. Good thing; he might have found a rock and had something for dinner if he'd been able to find one.

He next grabbed a bucket. Then he was on his hands and knees picking up the smaller piece because god fucking forbid one of those little white balls goes off course because it struck a microscopic piece of duck crap. He'd be bottled for sure.

Fitzhugh wasn't positive how long he'd been on his hands and knees when he heard some yelling. He glanced up and saw the Paki foursome halfway down the fairway waving at him. Had he been there that long? A wave of fog passed between them and him obscuring them for a moment.

Where the hell was that fog coming from?

He stood, wincing as his bum left knee reminded him that he was old, drank too much, and could do with losing a bit of weight.

They yelled again. "Fore!"

Of course.

They wanted him to move out of the way.

He glanced down and checked to see if he'd gotten all of the duck crap, then limped back to his tractor. He decided to wait until they finished before he started it up. No use having them complain about the noise when they were trying to hit their bloody damned balls.

He could just make out Mr. Kazmi lining up to hit his ball. It looked like a five-iron shot would do the job, but the damn Paki was using a fairway wood. Fitzhugh moved behind the tractor. If the man was going to overshoot the hole, he'd be damned if he'd be hit.

Kazmi swung, and as his club made it to the apex of his backswing a gigantic creature came from his right and hit him square in the chest, ripping out his throat. Part human, part beast, it was terrible to see. Its front two legs were human arms, but bent in the way of an animal's legs. The back legs were those of a dog or a wolf. It had a gray hairless body like an armadillo's and the face of a long-nosed baboon.

Five more beasts loped out of the fog and took down the three other golfers. They went for the soft places like the jugular, the stomach, and the crotch, ripping and chewing. Their human hands gripping the bodies as they fed and tore flesh free.

Fitzhugh felt warmth flood his own crotch as urine evacuated down his leg. He wanted to run, but he couldn't move. He managed to get down on his trembling knees and then onto the ground, where he watched the men being eaten from his view beneath his tractor.

Then a giant white stag appeared with a man on his back.

The beasts howled and the man laughed.

He looked like a king, regal and broad shouldered. Not at all like that big-eared Prince Charles with the small chin and smaller shoulders. No, this was a true man. Fitzhugh knew without knowing how he knew that if asked he'd follow the figure and do whatever he was told.

The man glanced his way as did the beasts, their heads turning to stare at his hiding place at the exact same time. Fitzhugh felt like puking. They knew he was there. He closed his eyes. If this was the end and they were going to rip out his guts, he didn't want to see it happen.

He counted to fifty.

Then he started over and counted to a hundred.

Then he counted to a hundred again.

He opened one eye but didn't see a thing. He slowly turned his gaze behind him but saw nothing there but the pond. After what seemed like ten minutes, he finally got to his feet. At first he couldn't stop shaking, but the more time passed, the more it seemed that he'd been spared.

He climbed on his tractor well aware that they could be playing with him, but as the fog began to dissipate and he saw more and more of the course he felt increasingly certain that he would make it. He started the tractor and began to head for the clubhouse. He had to tell someone what had happened.

But he paused. He turned in his seat and saw the four sets of golf clubs still on the ground. Of the golfers there was nary a trace.

Then he remembered the note to see the manager. What was he going to tell him? That a king riding a white stag brought some monstrous hounds who ate the golfers? No way. No how. No. He was already in trouble. Four club members being eaten on the third hole would somehow become his fault too. He turned the tractor around and grabbed the golf clubs. Just in case, he'd wait two weeks for his trip to Wales, then he'd find a pawnbroker.

He felt an ache in his back from picking up all of the duck poop. Damn but he was a good worker. When were they going to realize that?

CHAPTER 11

TEN PIN LEIGHTON BUZZARD BOWLPLEX, ENGLAND. AFTERNOON.

The three members of Section 9, Walker, and the witch sat in the rear of a hard-sided van around the corner from the Leighton Buzzard Bowling Club. Evidently Leighton Buzzard was the name of a town. If this had been America, Walker thought, they would have changed it by now. He sort of admired the steadfastness of the Brits. Then again, America still had towns such as Climax, Truth or Consequences, Intercourse, and Lizard Lick. He guessed there were some who reveled in their weirdness.

Walker was surprised that people bowled in England. It had never occurred to him that it was a sport outside of America. Not that he really ever played, but he knew a lot of enlisted friends who used to get together on Saturdays with their family and spend time at the bowling alley. Their salary didn't go far, but bowling was something they could all afford.

Of course the fact that this bowling alley was condemned might indicate that the British didn't bowl. He still found it strange that their target, a warlock named Van McKee, was using this as his home. The witch had said he needed the space because of his experiments and preferred someplace private.

REIGN OF EVIL • 57

Walker inventoried his gear and visually checked the others. They were a sad lot. That Section 9 once had more than two hundred members and had been the paradigm supernatural defense agency in the world was impossible to believe. Even their equipment was out of date. Whatever self-serving politicians had allowed this to happen should be staked to the ground, covered in honey, and fed to a herd of rabid homunculi. One look at those tiny long-armed devils and they'd shit money to fund Section 9.

While the SAS had new Mark 7 Body Armor, Section 9 used the Osprey Mark 2. While both were equally adept at stopping most rounds, the Mark 7 was more ergonomic and could withstand the rigors of combat. They all carried SA80s with ACOGs and Viper II thermal sights. The mainstay of the British military, the SA80 was a bull pup–style combat rifle, meaning the trigger housing was forward of the magazine. Although Walker liked the feel of it, he knew from experience that one of its downfalls was a weak firing pin, which was why Ian had issued them extras. They also carried Glock 17s, which rested in quick-draw chest rigs. Based on the Browning system, the Glock 17 had a counterrecoil system that helped keep the sights on target during trigger pulls. Walker would have preferred his HK416 and Sig Sauer P229, but such top-of-the-line equipment wasn't available to him.

Beneath the body armor, they wore black fatigues with black ballistic gloves and neoprene half-face balaclavas. The witch wore the black fatigues but had demurred when asked if she wanted to wear something on her face. Ian had insisted she wear body armor. They'd actually fought about it, but once she saw that Ian wouldn't even conduct the operation if she wouldn't wear it she capitulated.

What they lacked was an MBITR or its like. With no interteam communications gear there'd be a lot of yelling to get information across, which meant chaos. Hopefully it would be controlled chaos.

"Listen up," Ian said, pulling down his balaclava to be clearly heard. "Jerry and Trev, you're stacking at the rear door. I want you to breach at *GO* plus thirty seconds. Walker and I will be in the front and breach on *GO*. Shoot anything not human. Try not to kill our target. Ms. Moore will be behind us to take care of him."

"There's one thing I might have forgotten to mention," the witch said with absolutely no apology in her eyes.

Ian's head snapped around. "What?"

"He may not be alone. Scratch that. He probably won't be alone."

Ian glared at her, then in a steely voice said, "I'm two seconds away from canceling the op."

She waved her hand. "No reason to do that. Walker's handled these things before. It's probably going to be a piece of cake."

Walker felt worry bitch-slap the nervous butterflies in his stomach. He'd handled a lot of things he'd hoped he'd never see again, number one probably being that absolutely fucking unbelievable obsidian butterfly he'd fought beneath Mexico City.

"What is it?" A frown underscored Ian's words.

"Remember when I mentioned that he needed the space for his experiments? Well, Van McKee specializes in creating simulacrums. In fact, he makes them and sells them. I know he has a contract with several members of the Chinese Mafia."

Walker groaned. *Not those.*

Trev's eyes narrowed. "What is it?"

"Motherfucking homunculi," Walker said. "Little fucking Freddy Krueger–Stretch Armstrong serial-killing fucking mini-golems. Okay, here's the deal. They swarm. As long as we pair up and keep moving, they can't hurt us, but I saw them chew through the neck of an FBI agent who insisted on doing things solo. They die like anything else. Put enough bullets into them and then put some more."

Ian looked to Walker. "How much does this change things?"

Walker shrugged. "It changes a lot, but we can do this if we have fire and position discipline. But it's going to be easy for this warlock to cast a spell or escape while we're trying to survive his minions."

"That's where I come in." Sassy gave a quick, mean smile. "I'm a far better witch than he is a warlock; I just couldn't handle his creations." She pointed at him. "That's where you come in."

Walker hated the feeling of being used. But if it got him one step closer to the killers of Jen, he'd let it happen. "What do you think, boys?"

Ian gave Trev and Jerry looks and in turn they nodded.

Ian turned to the witch. "Okay, mission is still on, but if you do this to us one more time we're going to have a serious conversation."

To give the witch credit, she looked appropriately scolded, but Walker could still detect a smile wrinkling a corner of her lipstick-painted lips. Then she looked at him and he saw the sparkle in her eyes. She'd known exactly what she was doing and how her ploy would turn out. Walker had no doubt that she'd be up to this again and probably soon, regardless of her promise to Ian.

They synced watches and left the van. It was almost midday and there was plenty of traffic on the street, so the chances of them being seen were pretty good. But Ian had coordinated the operation with the Home Office and local police were supposed to ignore any calls about four armed men assaulting an old bowling alley. Plus, unlike America, where any given city could face four men in assault gear ready to attack a bank, the illegality of weapons in Britain made this much less likely. So when people did see heavily armed men dressed uniformly, they tended to assume it was just the government about to do something they didn't want to know about. Or at least so said Jerry.

Ian and Walker stacked toward the front doors, close enough that they were touching. Ian was first and Walker could tell the man knew his business. They covered the distance to the door in a matter of seconds, then flattened themselves on either side. Old fliers were taped to the doors advertising family bowling nights and a missing kitten. Brown paper had been taped to the windows behind the old fliers to keep anyone from seeing into the interior. The double doors were boarded from the inside. Also on the outside of the doors was an official-looking memo purportedly from the health department stating that this *edifice has been con-demned until appropriate biological defense measures can be employed.* It was ambiguous enough to make anyone pause.

Since the doors had been boarded shut, their plan was to go through one of the wide side panel windows to the left or right. They chose the right-hand panel, and when the time came Ian used the butt of his rifle to shatter it.

When the glass was down, they surged into the entry only to find themselves in a vestibule standing before another set of glass doors, these completely covered in plywood.

Ian and Walker looked at each other. If they had some Semtex they could have blown their way in. As it stood, they didn't even have grenades. They both came to the same conclusion and, with a running start, slammed their shoulders into the doors. They gave an inch or two as the glass cracked and the plywood buck-led. The men backed up and tried again; this time the glass shat-tered and the wood cracked. Three more times and they were able to break through. But now any chance of surprise had been destroyed. Plus, the pain in Walker's right shoulder was quickly spinning from an ache to something worse.

The interior of the bowling alley was lit with seven glass chandeliers, which by their placement had to have been in-stalled when the warlock took residence. They cast electric light and hung lower than head height in line across the twenty lanes of the bowling alley. Directly in front of them was the reception desk, complete with bowling shoes still resting in wooden slots. The area to the left had been an arcade, but it had been cleared and was now a sitting area. The area to the right had been a concession but was now a library, books and manuscripts on bookshelves placed where the stoves and fryers had probably once been.

What they didn't see was the warlock or any homunculi. Nothing stirred.

Walker kept his feet moving and his weapon at low ready as he scanned the immense space. "Ian?"

"Yeah, Walker?"

"Where are the bad guys?"

"Not sure."

Suddenly Jerry and Trev burst into the room from the staff access door on the far left. They had their weapons at low ready as well and mimicked Walker's perplexed response. Where the hell was everyone?

Then Walker felt it. It was subtle, but it was there, a minute buzzing just below the surface of his skin.

"Careful," he said. "Something's going on."

"Do you feel something?" Ian asked. "What is it?"

Walker shook his head. "I don't know." He moved left, then right, then forward to the reception desk. The feeling didn't increase or decrease. The magic seemed to be everywhere. Then he had an idea. He raised his weapon to ready carry and aimed at a point below one of the chandeliers. He moved his finger over the fire selector lever and switched from single to automatic. He fired three controlled bursts, raking his weapon from left to right.

"What the hell?" Ian moved next to him. "Did you see something?"

Walker stared at the area he'd fired in. It was as if he could almost see shapes, but it could just as easily have been a trick of the mind.

Sassy Moore swept in behind them. "You had the right idea, Walker, but it'll take more than that to dispel the illusion." She waved her hand and spoke something in harsh, guttural German and the chandeliers sang as they jingled, one reality snapping into place over the fake reality. Where there had been nothing, there was now everything: homunculi lying dead below the spots where Walker had fired, others standing and glaring, others hanging from the chandeliers, others holding bowling balls as if they were giant hand grenades, and of course the warlock, standing about forty-five degrees off to Walker's right in the middle of lane five, a look of pure rage reshaping the doughy features of his middle-aged face into those of a wild animal.

It was like a switch snapped on and everything came to life. Walker opened fire even as the homunculi surged toward him, some swinging from the chandeliers, others running like Chucky Doll–sized linebackers. They were like the ones he'd met before in San Diego, San Fran, and Mexico. Just shy of three feet tall, they had arms long enough that they almost dragged on the ground. Bulging with muscles, their skin was a jolting orange as if their makers were trying to create monstrous versions of Willy Wonka's Oompa Loompas. But what got Walker every time was their sublime expressions that telegraphed such disinterest, it was as if they knew more than him, that they knew when they were eventually going to kill him and that it was already a fait accompli . . . . But even that sublime look disappeared once they opened their piranha-fanged mouths.

Walker took down some of them but missed as many as he hit. He'd forgotten his selector was on automatic and switched it to single shot for more control. Then he leaped on top of the counter in front of him to put some vertical distance between him and the ground.

He gestured for Ian to follow. After a moment's hesitation he did. Good thing too, because the little creatures were already up to the counter and trying to climb. So it was with some well-placed kicks and quick-fired shots that Ian and Walker were holding their own. Enough dead homunculi littered the ground that the others had to walk on them.

Jerry and Trev weren't faring as well. Jerry was down on his knees and trying to get back to his feet. Beside him rolled several bowling balls, which had evidently been thrown at him. By the stunned look on his face, at least one had found its mark. Meanwhile, Trev was firing madly into the crowd of creatures rushing toward him.

Walker did the math. Even if the Section 9 guy hit every target with a kill shot he didn't have the ammo to get them all without switching out magazines. Even if it only took a few seconds, those precious few would be enough for the homunculi to bring them down.

Walker leaped off the counter into a clear area and began running, heading for the wall Trev and Jerry had at their backs. Walker leaped on a mezzanine above the lanes as he began to fire into the herd of homunculi. Firing until his weapon was empty, he dropped the rifle and let the sling catch it, then in one smooth move pulled the Glock from its quick-draw holster and began to fire. He slowed to a walk, keeping his aim steady as he pulled the trigger with metronomic regularity. The words *slow is smooth; smooth is fast* ran through his mind as he found a stair down to lane level and moved into lane seventeen.

Jerry suddenly found his senses and lifted his rifle. He was still on his knees, but he fired from the hip. At last, the combined firepower of Walker, Jerry, and Trev was enough to stop the onslaught. Surviving homunculi turned and fled, flinging themselves into the chandeliers and swinging swiftly across the lanes back to where the warlock was now engaged with Sassy Moore in what appeared to be nothing more than a staring contest.

Ian came up behind Walker and the two of them ran to Trev and Jerry.

"Reload!" Walker shouted. He changed the mag in his Glock, reholstered it, then dropped the mag to his SA80 and replaced it. He chambered a round and brought his weapon around just in time to nail a homunculus square in the head coming down the stairs.

Walker kept his voice steady. "Everyone ready? With me, move steady. Slow is smooth; smooth is fast."

The four moved shoulder to shoulder across the lanes, sweeping everything in front. While Ian and Trev had the flanks, Walker and Jerry had the center. Each of them fired as needed, knowing to preserve his ammunition and aim at only targets that presented danger.

Walker kept his eye to the chandeliers in case any were hiding there, but with their bright orange coloring he doubted they'd be able to disguise themselves.

Meanwhile he kept track of the warlock and witch out of the corner of his eye. They still stood quietly. If there was a battle occurring, it wasn't something Walker was able to see. Just as well.

He was beginning to feel confident when something immense began to crawl out of the far end of lane five. Jerry and Ian began to fire at it, but the rounds had no visible effect.

They'd come to an immediate halt in lane eight.

Walker and Ian fired at other homunculi arrayed across the lanes while the creature emerged and stood to its full height.

Jerry's eyes shot wide. "Bleeding Barney!"

"Crumbs!" exclaimed Trev.

Walker stared at the most terrifying aspect he'd never envisioned. It looked like Krampus but was too huge, its face too void of features to be the same as its namesake. It stood fifteen feet tall with four-foot horns curled like a ram's. With a triangular head, where its eyes, nose, and mouth should be were blank, as if its creator hadn't finished. Mottled-gray skin tightly covered a body with broad shoulders, long arms, and legs with the reversed knees of a goat. Its talon-tipped hands reached toward them.

The remaining homunculi gathered at its feet. Several clambered up its body and rested on its shoulders or clung to its legs.

"What in the holy hells," Walker said, each word coming with shotgun force. "Back," he said. "We gotta get back."

The moment they began backing up, the giant horned being began moving forward. It had no eyes, but it had ears and could discern their location by the noise they made. The smaller creatures arrayed themselves in front of and beside it. No longer were they rushing pell-mell to their deaths. Now they were in a tactical formation meant to keep their god nearby.

The giant creature came to a chandelier and swept it down from the ceiling with one swipe of the arm, pieces shattering and skittering across the lanes.

Walker knew then that he had to stay out of its reach.

Jerry and Trev still fired at it but with absolutely no effect.

"Save your ammo!" Walker shouted. "Kill the small ones first."

They backed away keeping the three-lane distance between them and the oncoming creatures. Their shift of fire had great effect as the smaller, more susceptible creatures fell beneath their well-aimed 5.56mm rounds.

The giant horned Krampus-like creature came to the next chandelier. Instead of sweeping this one aside, it wrenched it from the ceiling, then hurled it at them. It crashed against the lane in front of them as they dove out of the way.

Trev ended up in the pinsetter of lane thirteen.

The others dove the other way.

Walker climbed back to his feet and continued to fire.

Ian was slower to get up.

Jerry didn't even try to untangle his limbs from the pinsetter. He continued to fire from the prone position.

Two homunculi attacked Trev, who was forced to drop his rifle. He pulled his Glock with his right hand and his knife with the other. The knife was long and thin, unlike the K-bar. It was a Fairbairn-Sykes fighting knife, used exclusively by the British Special Air Service, and had more of a stiletto appearance.

Walker watched while Trev shot one of the creatures in the head, then stabbed the other several times and finally, in a rush of screams and adrenaline, sawed off the thing's arm.

That's when Walker had an idea.

Now that all the smaller versions were dead or dying, he had more freedom of movement. He ripped his rifle free and tossed it aside as he ran to a rack of bowling balls. He picked one up but couldn't get his fingers in the holes. He ripped off his balaclava and, using his teeth, pulled his glove free. Then he stuck his fingers in the ball and turned.

The giant Krampus tore yet another chandelier from the ceiling.

Walker windmilled his arm and let the bowling ball fly free. It soared in the air, missing the giant but striking a chandelier, shattering the glass.

"What the bloody hell are you doing?" Ian yelled.

Walker grabbed another ball. "We've got to bring it down." He threw again. This time the ball hit it in the midsection, knocking it back a step.

Ian and Jerry ran up beside him.

"Then what?" Jerry asked.

Walker turned with another ball in his hand. He shouted loud enough for Trev to hear, from where he was crouched in the pin-setter recess, "Then we cut off its fucking head!"

Walker let loose with a ball, catching it in the chest.

Jerry and Ian did the same, both missing.

"Come on." Walker unleashed another missile. This one hit the creature in the head and it reeled.

Both Ian's and Jerry's balls hit the creature too. Bullets couldn't hurt it, but blunt-force trauma was doing something.

It came at them, but they were protected by the giant score screens above the ball racks.

They spread out. Now that it was closer, it was an easier target. That said, Walker was tiring quickly and his shoulder felt wretched from not only breaking through the plywood but also hurling ten- to fifteen-pound balls at a giant monster.

Jerry scored a forehead shot and the thing went to a knee.

That was all it took for Trev to make his move. He leaped to his feet and sprinted the short distance to the homunculus.

Ian and Jerry unleashed two more balls, each one impacting the giant's head.

As the creature put out a hand to steady itself, Trev climbed up its back and wrapped an arm around its neck and began to plunge the knife in and out as rapidly as his arm could piston. Orange goo came from each hole as the monster screamed.

Jerry pulled his own knife and ran forward. Walker shouted for him to stop, but Jerry was so intent to join the fray that he missed his obvious mistake. As soon as Jerry got close enough, the beast lowered its head and thrust one of its horns into the unlucky man. The horn pushed out his back, severing his spine, killing him instantly.

Ian yelled, "No!"

Walker stared numbly.

Trev had begun to saw at the creature's neck but was having trouble holding on as it began to shake its head back and forth. He had no choice but to plunge the knife into the side of the beast's neck and use it to hold on, kicking at the hands that were constantly trying to pluck him free.

The giant monster shook its head, sending Jerry flying across the lanes. Trev lost his grip and fell hard to the ground.

Walker flung his last ball, then pulled free his blade. He ran forward and grabbed the knife Jerry dropped. Sliding between the giant's legs, Walker came up on the backside of the creature and used the knives to climb, plunging each of them into the back, then higher and higher, until he was on the other side of the neck from Trev. Using one knife to hold on, he began to saw. He noticed right away that the creature was constructed. It was like sawing through semi-hard clay. He managed to saw through most of the neck. The weight of it did the rest as it ripped free, falling to the lanes. Walker fell with it and slipped several times trying to get to his feet.

Ian ran over to where Jerry's body lay.

Walker got shaking to his feet. He drew his Glock and crouch-walked along the front of the lanes to where the witch and the warlock were doing battle.

Only they weren't doing battle.

The battle was over and the witch was sitting on the couch flipping through a magazine. A high-heel-clad foot rested on the chest of the dead warlock, whose hair had turned a stark white, a close match to the color of his skin.

"Are you fucking kidding me?" Walker bellowed. "You're just sitting here while we fight and die for you?"

She glanced up and then back down, flipping a page. "Put the gun down, Mr. Walker; we both know you're not going to be using that on me."

Walker's hands were beginning to shake as leftover adrenaline searched for a use. He reloaded the magazine just in case and replaced the weapon in its holster while Ian came up behind him.

"Ms. Moore, Jerry's dead," he said.

She put her magazine down and draped an arm across the back of the couch. "And for that, I'm very sorry." She flicked her gaze at Walker, then back to Ian. "There was nothing I could do to help, sadly."

"Why, because you found an interesting article on the best-dressed witches of New Brunswick?" Walker sneered.

"Not at all, Mr. Walker." She toed the warlock's face with her foot. "He was stronger than I anticipated. He's been learning. The truth is that it was touch and go. He almost bested me."

Trev came up and stood next to them.

"I can't stand at the moment," she said, an embarrassed smile on her face. "I might need some help."

"All that's going to have to wait," Ian said, command returning to his voice. Everyone turned toward him. "A member of Section 9 is dead. There's going to have to be an investigation. This place is on lockdown until MI5 gets here."

"Lockdown as in no one or nothing can leave?" Walker asked.

Ian turned to him and was about to say something when Walker interrupted.

"I get it that we lost Jerry and we'll have long enough to mourn him, but if we let the bureaucrats hold what we need just because it's procedure, then our mission might as well be over." He put an arm on Ian's shoulder. "I've been there. We've lost men mid-mission. We have got to Charlie Mike—continue mission."

Ian chewed on his cheek. "You are a fucking cowboy, aren't you?"

Walker shrugged and removed his hand from Ian's shoulder. "My fiancée's death destroyed the happy future I was meant to have and a fellow soldier has perished. If we don't continue the mission, then they died for nothing."

"He has a point, Commander," Trev said.

Ian sighed. "I bloody well know he has a point, Trev. Walker had me at Charlie Mike." He turned to the witch. "You have twenty minutes to gather whatever you can. You and Walker take the van and head back to Chicksands. I'll have Preeti clear you through the gate." He turned and stared across the bowling alley toward

Jerry's body. "I'll take care of things here. We'll be along when we can."

Walker stared toward Jerry's body as well and fought down a lump in his throat as visions of Jen's body lying on the cold Stonehenge soil presented themselves like a Hollywood horror movie. The shit was starting to get serious.

CHAPTER 12

CORONADO PEST CONTROL. MORNING.

Timothy Laws left his room and entered the base's main salon. One entire wall was covered with relics of missions past. Among these relics were bones, knives, a carved and inlaid fighting stick from the Philippines, fangs, talons, and a large gnarled hand. His eyes briefly scanned these, acknowledging the sacrifices his predecessors had made; then he went to Holmes, who lay sprawled on one of the several couches. He'd just turned forty but still had the body of a much younger man. Laws acknowledged that there weren't too many younger men in the same shape.

"You back from a run?" Laws asked.

"Ten miles. Sucks getting old." Holmes sat up. "What's up?"

Laws held up a tablet. "I got Walker on the line. Want to talk to him?"

"Of course." He took the tablet and rested it against his bottle of water. When he toggled the screen to on, he was greeted by the haggard, drawn face of Walker. He glanced at Laws, who nodded.

Laws had answered the call five minutes ago and they'd spent the time talking about the boy's dead fiancée. Walker was definitely on the edge. What worried Laws was that he might do something irrevocably stupid.

"What's up, kid?" Holmes asked, trying to be light.

"We're in the shit here, Boss."

"Isn't Ian taking care of you?"

"Best that he can." Walker looked down, then back at the screen. "As of two hours ago, Section 9 has two operators left and one analyst."

Holmes's eyes narrowed. "What happened two hours ago?"

Walker gave them a mission report, complete with the information he had about the witch. "The witch and I evacced with several boxes of the warlock's stuff. Books, odds and ends, jewelry, and a bunch of bottles of ingredients."

"Do you trust her?" Laws asked, leaning over the couch behind Holmes so he could fit into the camera's view.

Walker glanced to the side. "I don't know. Not really, I guess. I think she has her own agenda, but frankly, she's all we have." He laughed hollowly. "You know, you don't really appreciate what you have until you've seen it bad. And this is pretty bad."

"I remember doing an op with Section 9 where there were twenty operators, all read on to the mission and fluent in supernatural esoterica. You say there's two left?"

"Three if you count me."

Holmes shook his head. "My, but how the mighty have fallen. What is it we can do for you, son?"

"Bring the team over," Walker said with complete seriousness.

"Billings won't allow it. If you can find some overarching reason why we need to be there, something that involves the safety of American citizens, we can get involved. Otherwise there's no way." Holmes sat forward. "Trust me, Walker. There's nothing I want more than to come over and get the bastards that killed Jen. All of us feel that way, but right now our hands are tied."

Walker was silent for several moments. Finally, "Did Preeti get in contact with Musso?"

Laws answered, "Sure did. We have a line on Van Dyke up at Lake Arrowhead. We're leaving at noon and plan on being on target by fourteen hundred hours."

"Full battle rattle?"

Holmes shook his head. "It's a tourist spot. We're going to infil by helicopter five miles from the target. We have a Suburban standing by courtesy of Alice Munroe, NCIS. Remember her?"

Walker cracked a smile for the first time. "She forgive YaYa yet?"

"When hell freezes over. You should see them in the same room. Poor kid feels terrible about what that creature made him do. He tries so hard to apologize, but she's making him pay for it."

"Thirty hours tied in the trunk of a car, I'd be pissed too," Laws chipped in.

"Which is why I made YaYa our official liaison to NCIS." Holmes crossed his arms. "It gives the kid the opportunity to make it up."

Walker continued smiling for a moment; then it fell like a brick, his face returning to the mournful frown that had become the new normal. "What about the Bohemian Grove? According to Preeti they've been doing some sort of ceremony there."

"That place is politically sensitive. You wouldn't believe the number of politicians on both sides who attend the events. Senator Withers isn't one of them, but he has friends who have attended, who are members. Our official orders are to keep our hands off."

"Some things never change," Walker said. "Did Musso get anything on the Wild Hunt?"

Laws spoke up. "I've been doing research. I agree with everything Preeti sent. There's a lot of open source material, much of it compelling, especially about the Cycle of the Holly King and the Oak King. Not only does this ritual go back almost two thousand years, but there's a solid pagan-Wiccan belief system built around it. Probably the most interesting factoid I came across was a version of the Wild Hunt that has King Arthur as the leader."

This got Walker's attention. "King Arthur as in *the* King Arthur."

"I was surprised as well, when I saw it," Laws said. "Of course, it seems that popular historical figures have been attached to the Hunt through time, so this might not be anything more than wishful thinking on behalf of the people of Britain."

"Even so," Walker said slowly. "If it turns out that it is King Arthur, we'd have to go up against him."

"First things first," Holmes said. "Right now we need to find out about the Red Grove and discover who they are. We might not have to do anything about the Wild Hunt. Frankly, we don't have any evidence that it even exists."

"You should have seen the hole in the ground where the witch used to live. Then you'd have your evidence."

"Did you see it? Did you see who did it?" Holmes shook his head. "We're all acting on the word of people we don't know."

"We've acted on less before, Boss," Laws said.

"But things weren't as politically sensitive as they are now. This is England. This country has had a relationship with them for more than two hundred years. Good or bad, we're like two brothers, a younger and an older. Sure we fight, but at the end of the day we're family."

"Just like SEAL Team 666 is a family," Laws chimed in. "We're on your side, Walker."

Walker nodded. "I know."

"If we have something compelling, I'll find a way for us to come over . . . regardless. And Walker, remember . . ." Holmes pointed a finger at the tablet's screen. "You find a good enough reason for us to come, then send it. I'll fight for it until they either let me go or fire me. Find that reason, Walker."

Walker shrugged. "I'm trying. God knows they need help here. Frankly, I just don't know how they're able to do anything. What I'm afraid of is that MI5 will shut them down based on the loss of Jerry in this last mission."

"Then stick with the witch," Laws said. "Watch your six, but she seems to be the best bet."

"I agree." Walker stared down for a moment, then looked up. "I better go. Tell the guys I said hi, will ya?"

Holmes gave Walker a bright smile. "Sure, son." When they signed off, the smile fell hard. "It's worse than I thought."

Laws plopped down on the couch facing Holmes. "You slow-rolled him on the Wild Hunt."

"I did. I don't want him going off half-cocked. It's tough trying to manage a mission I'm not a part of from five thousand miles away, but it's the best I can do."

"You know, if this Wild Hunt really exists, it could be the reason we need to get over there. On a curious note, I read where there were historical reports of hell hounds chasing down the unbaptized. It's intriguing because this is a pagan tradition, so why does it care about baptizing into a faith?"

"Probably just an appropriation of legend. We've seen it before; just look at the American Bigfoot legends and how we've taken what the Native Americans believed and made it our own, changing it to suit our culture. After all, it was the Algonquin tales of the Windigo which spurred our modern idea of a big-footed forest monster."

"You're probably right, but it just as easily could be something else. 'Baptize' is very similar to 'sanctify.' I can get behind that a lot easier."

"If the Wild Hunt's mission is to sanctify, then what is it supposed to sanctify?" Holmes asked.

Laws spread his hands. "Dunno. Everything? The land?" He stood and retrieved his tablet. "Oh, one more thing."

"What's that?"

"I checked the logs for hell hounds."

"Yes?"

"Battle New Orleans. January 8, 1815, actually. The British Ninety-Third Highlanders used hell hounds against Stonewall Jackson's forces. They were described as *making chupacabra look like lambs.*'"

"How'd we eventually destroy them?"

"Stonewall had a few witches of his own. One of them was none other than Madame Laboy. Remember her?"

"She's still in our employ. The zombie exercise in the New Orleans cemetery. I remember it well." Holmes made a grunt of acknowledgment. "Let's hope we don't have to go up against any hell hounds."

"If we have to fight the Wild Hunt, then those are odds I wouldn't touch."

"We'll cross that bridge when we get there." Holmes stood also. "Get the men ready. I've got something to do."

"What is it?"

"Call Billings one more time. The more information she has, the better our chances. Don't forget, she's on our side. She was close to Jen and wants to get her killers too."

CHAPTER 13

RAF CHICKSANDS. DUSK.

Walker went down the hall into the communications room where he found Preeti crying. She sat at her workstation, four computer screens in front of her and seven thirty-six-inch monitors on the walls, each one showing a different news channel, with the exception of one showing a cricket match. She was slumped in her chair, her head in her hands.

When Walker saw that she was crying, he stopped in the door. "Excuse me," he said, backing into the hall.

Preeti wiped her eyes with her fists and shook her tears away. "No, it's okay." She smiled weakly. "Come in, Walker."

"I can come back later. Really, I—"

"No. I'm just being silly. What is it?"

"I just got off the line with my boss. He said if there was any link we could make to something that might be of interest to the U.S. then they'd be able to come over and help. Do we have anything like that?"

She grinned, the sudden change to her demeanor remarkable. Then she laughed. "It's a sad day for us, isn't it? We used to be so large. Now all we have is Ian and Trev." At the mention of her husband, her voice cracked.

Walker couldn't help himself. He went to her, knelt, and put his arms around her. She accepted and leaned into his shoulder, where she sobbed violently for several minutes. Walker rubbed her back and said soft things to her. After a while, she lifted her head and pushed him away.

"Thank you, Walker. I needed a good cry." She wiped at her eyes. "Bollocks. I bet my makeup is all a mess. My eyes probably look like Rorschach blobs."

Walker smiled and stood. "They're fine."

"That fiancée of yours trained you well, Walker. You know how to say all the right things." Then she realized what she said and added, "I'm so sorry. I didn't mean to— I mean, I was trying too— Oh, hell, but I've bottled it."

Walker felt a rush of *what could have been* flow through him, then shook it off. "You're worried about Trev is all. No worries. I get it."

"Desperately. I couldn't help but think of your situation and how we're so similar. Then with the loss of Jerry . . ." She inhaled to keep from crying. ". . . I don't know if I can handle it."

"It's one thing to be killed crossing the street, or by a lightning bolt, or being at the wrong place at the wrong time." *Like being at the Winter Solstice ceremony at Stonehenge on the exact fucking day when the Red Grove was going to sacrifice everyone there.* "That's random and can't be helped. It can't be planned against. Trust me, I've been thinking about this non-stop for the last seventy-two hours. But it's another thing altogether when someone dies while doing something they absolutely believe in. In the case of Jerry, it was the protection of England, his homeland, and his team members. I've been there. I've been face-to-face with death and ready to give myself up for my team and country. Lucky for me I've never had to do it before, but there will probably come a day when it happens."

Preeti regarded him for a moment. "If this was supposed to cheer me up, it didn't work."

"Preeti, if you want me to make some shit up to salve our emotions then I can do that just like any bullshit Hallmark card.

I'm laying it on straight. If Trev dies in the service of his country, then it's something proud, something honorable. It's what he signed up for."

"But what if I don't want him to die?"

"It might never happen, but to be sure . . . well, then you have to convince him to quit."

"He'd end up hating me."

Walker shrugged. "There you have it. It's what every spouse of a service member has to deal with. What we do is a service. We serve. It's something that's in our DNA. In America less than one percent of the population has this desire to serve the other. It's a sad fact, but there it is."

"It's about the same in England." She wiped at her eyes. "I get what you're saying. I have to accept that this is part of him, right?"

Walker nodded. "It's a hard thing. We had a mission to Mexico where Jen became involved to the point where she was in firefights with me. The shoe was on the other foot then and I felt terrified for her. But like me, she was there to serve."

Preeti was silent for a long time as Walker dove deep into his memories.

When she finally spoke, her voice was full of authority. "You're upset because she died. You're trying to say that because she died in such a random way it's somehow worse. Is it really? I think you'd feel the same way had she died in one of those firefights in Mexico. Don't add to your troubles, Walker. They're bad enough as it is."

He nodded. "You're right, of course. I've always had a tendency to take something bad and make it worse. I guess it's the optimist in me." He smiled weakly. "But enough of this emotion."

She made a mock-serious face. "Right. Enough of that. Time to serve." She flashed him a mock salute, British-style. "What can I do for you?"

"Did you manage to track the video disturbance?"

Her eyes brightened as she leaned forward and began to punch keys. "Not sure if you know it, but your NSA has nothing on our Home Office. There are almost two million closed-circuit television cameras throughout England at a ratio of about one camera for every eleven citizens. It's such a massive network; they must be using supercomputers to keep track of everything. At times during the last few hours I felt I was going blind."

"I doubt they have people monitoring every camera," Walker said.

"You're right, although I sometimes imagine a giant building with monitors and people walking back and forth as they follow the people under surveillance, traveling from monitor to monitor to monitor." She waved a hand. "But that's just my brain being crazy. To answer your question, yes and no. Let me explain."

She typed in a few commands and brought up a map of Woking. Not an ordinary map, this one showed nodes, which Walker immediately deduced represented cameras. As she typed, some of the nodes began to turn red, leaving a trail. More than fifty nodes lit up, then stopped.

"It took some time, but I was able to find the disturbance. You were right. It originated somewhere else. In this case, Horsell Common where there are three barrows."

"Barrows, as in *Lord of the Rings* barrows?"

She nodded. "The same . . . well, not the same, but the same thing. Remember, J. R. R. Tolkien was English. The barrows of Horsell Common have been dated to three to four thousand years old. But now it's basically a public park with thousands of trees and several dozen walking paths."

"And you traced the disturbance back to there?"

"I did."

Walker narrowed his eyes as he leaned down to stare at the last node. "Is the Common big enough to hide a Wild Hunt?"

"Given that we don't know how big the Wild Hunt is I'd have to say yes. But I'm a step ahead of you. I sent in a false complaint of a child being abducted into the woods. Seventeen bobbies were dispatched and searched the woods without finding anything. My guess is if the Wild Hunt was there, they would have found it."

"They wouldn't be inside the mounds, would they?"

She stared at the screen. "I couldn't imagine that."

"So they just appeared there, attacked the witch's house, then went back."

She nodded. "It would appear so."

Walker was used to dealing with magic on a small scale. A chupacabra or a skin-wearing religious fanatic he could parse, but this was on a much larger scale. He wasn't sure what to think.

"Have there been any other disturbances like this?"

"I've been working on an algorithm to find that out."

"We can't just go to the Home Office and ask?"

She was about to answer when she smiled, sat back in her chair, and shook her head. "That would be the obvious answer, wouldn't it?" She put on a headset and began to make a call, acting like Walker wasn't even there.

He paused a moment, then said, "Glad I could help."

She waved a hand but was too deep into her problem set to pay attention to anything else.

Walker left the room thinking about the barrows and the Wild Hunt. There was something the witch had said that he felt was important, but he couldn't remember exactly what it was.

CHAPTER 14

TWIN PEAKS, CALIFORNIA. AFTERNOON.

Director David Lynch made the place famous, but there was really nothing to the town of Twin Peaks other than several hundred homes and a quickie mart. The TV series by the same name started out with a mysterious naked body wrapped in plastic found on the side of the road. Nothing like that really ever happened in this sleepy out-of-the-way hamlet overlooking the Rim of the World Highway and downtown Los Angeles. Which is why many old Hollywood movie stars settled in the greater Lake Arrowhead area. A normal day out near the lake or in one of the nearby towns such as Twin Peaks or Crestline could find a person passing Will Smith or Heather Locklear or Vince Neil from Mötley Crüe. One of the unspoken rules, however, was not to approach them and to give them their space. Although there were tourists who didn't know this, the locals treated it as dogma.

So when SEAL Team 666 landed, loaded into the NCIS-provided SUV, and headed toward Lake Arrowhead it wasn't any surprise when they found themselves at a stoplight next to a Mercedes convertible with a woman behind the wheel who resembled a star from a famous 1970s TV show.

Yank drove. Holmes sat in the passenger seat. Behind him sat

Laws. Behind Yank sat YaYa. They all wore jeans and T-shirts and light jackets to cover their shoulder rigs, which carried Sig Sauer P229s.

Yank thumbed toward the Mercedes. "Isn't that that actress from *The Love Boat*? What's her name, Jane?"

All four SEALs turned to stare at the older woman in the car next to them. Although she couldn't see them through the heavily tinted windows, she turned and looked at the SUV that towered over her car, giving them all a clear look.

"That's Julie," Laws, the man with the eidetic memory, said. "And it's *Love Boat* minus the '*The*.'"

"Julie, right," Yank said, smiling wistfully. "She was the cruise director. Never knew she got so old."

"It's called the passage of time," YaYa said from the backseat. "It's been more than thirty years since that show was on television. Which begs the question, what's a Compton kid like you watching an all-white show like that?" He snapped his fingers. "That's right. The bartender was black. What was his name?"

"Isaac Washington played by actor Ted Lange," Laws said flatly.

Yank spoke into the rearview mirror. "You're always so cliché, Yaya. Why is it a black guy like me only watches black people on television? Do you only watch ragheads?"

"That would mean I'd spend my days watching nothing but Al Jazeera. We're seriously underrepresented on television unless it's some terrorist blowing themselves up. What do they expect me to do, clap and shout, *Hooray, another one for the seventy-two overworked virgins!*?"

A car honked from behind.

Yank looked up and saw that Julie in the Mercedes was already three car lengths ahead.

"We can go anytime," Holmes said.

"Yessir." Yank cursed inwardly. YaYa was always getting him in trouble. He put the SUV in gear. They drove a mile farther before he added, "Anyway, my adopted father watched it as reruns. He made me sit in the living room and do my homework when he watched it. I couldn't help but watch it. It was either that or math."

They drove in silence for several minutes, during which Yank thought fondly of the man who'd adopted him and given him a new life after his mother had perished in a house fire. He wished the man was still around so he could see how his work in progress, as he sometimes called Yank, turned out. Being a Navy man, he'd have been very proud his adopted son had become a SEAL.

"Let's review," Holmes said. "YaYa, give us the rundown."

YaYa glanced into the mirror nervously, catching Yank's attention. Whereas before the mission to Mexico YaYa had been the most outgoing member of the team, the loss of his left arm to the elbow and the installation of the new DARPA mechanical replacement had made him feel less than who he'd been, culminating in a loss of confidence. Yank had told him that he should see it as an addition, rather than a subtraction, but it was hard to dissuade the lithe young Jordanian-American from what he'd already come to believe. Still, both Holmes and Laws had been forcing him to brief and debrief recently in an effort to get his confidence back to the Navy SEAL norm of 1,000 percent.

"So the murder of Jen has been tied to an organization called the Red Grove. It's a 50 . . ."

"501.3c tax-exempt religious organization," Laws supplied.

"Right. What he said. A payoff check was traced to this organization, whose chair is Hubert Van Dyke, a former television actor who had bit parts in pretty much every show that came out in the fifties and sixties."

Holmes nodded. "What do we know about him now?"

"Now, according to *Who's Who,* he is a philanthropist and an environmentalist. His net worth is believed to be around thirty million dollars. He's a member of virtually every conservancy group and also every Wiccan religious group. Interestingly enough, he's on the board of trustees for Loyola Marymount University, which is a Catholic college." YaYa paused and stared at Holmes.

"Continue."

"He also sits on the board of the Bohemian Grove, which we've been asked not to even think about. He's also on the board of A Celestial Worry LLC, which is a young adult organization which promotes *thoughtfulness on the control of Earth by corporate religions*. Its list of religions to watch includes Scientology, Judaism, and Catholicism."

"Which makes his affiliation with Loyola Marymount curious," Laws said. "What's that tell us?"

YaYa narrowed his eyes. "I—uh—am not sure."

Laws looked to the driver. "Yank?"

"That he might care more about money and connections than about his own philosophy."

Laws smiled. "Exactly. It's difficult to make someone cooperate who believes strongly in an ideal. Greed, on the other hand, is something we can work with."

Yank made several turns, then pulled into a cul-de-sac. Two-story houses stood back from the road between towering trees. The grass on the ground was brown, not only from the constant shade but also because of the layers of pine needles that shoaled here and there. The temperature was fifteen degrees cooler in the mountain than it was in the valley. The air was also noticeably cleaner.

"Laws, you ready?"

He put on a pair of glasses that made him look like a fit Berkeley professor, if Berkeley professors wore their hair high and tight and had trained-killer eyes. "Ready."

Yank watched as the second in command left the vehicle and headed down one of the longer driveways. The plan was to determine if Van Dyke was actually there. If they'd been in any other country in the world, they could have used the full intelligence powers of the U.S. government, but Americans, especially in their own country, were provided a privacy barrier that they weren't allowed to cross. Nor should they. Although it would have been easier, Commander Holmes said it best. *We can't trample the rights and freedom we're sworn to protect.*

"YaYa . . . move," Holmes commanded.

The SEAL pulled a Dodger cap low over his eyes, grabbed the bag from the seat beside him, and exited, closing his door softly behind him. He jogged into the woods, then began to angle toward the house. He'd set up in the wood line to monitor Laws's engagement with the persons on the premises.

Holmes toggled on a tablet to magnify the view and waited.

Through the mask of trees, Laws could be seen approaching the front door and knocking. The house was Tudor-style with a pitched roof, dormers, and timbers offset by the white cottage covering. It appeared perfectly suited for its secluded position, deep within the San Gabriel Mountain woods.

They waited.

Laws turned and looked around, but not in the direction of the vehicle.

He knocked again.

The door was opened several seconds later by an older woman, dressed in a housedress, apron, and sensible shoes, right out of a 1960s *Better Homes and Gardens* photo.

Laws smiled, held out his hand to shake, and waited.

The woman ignored it, however, and seemed about to close the door when—

The tablet came to life as YaYa's equipment came online. A zoomed-in side shot of Laws and part of the woman's face appeared along with audio. "But ma'am, I'm just a courier from Loyola Marymount." He spread his hands apologetically. "I have a registered letter that I have to deliver to Mr. Van Dyke regarding an emergency meeting of the Board of Trustees."

"Again, Mr. Van Dyke isn't here at the moment. If you can leave it with me, then I can—"

Laws shook his head and frowned sadly. "That's unfortunate. The board requires an immediate response. It's why they sent me out here." He glanced around and lowered his voice. "It has to do with a windfall they want to distribute among the board members. I don't know any details, but it's supposed to be a considerable sum."

The woman was silent for a long moment, then said, "Wait one moment," and closed the door.

Laws turned to where YaYa was sitting and gave a huge grin.

"Show-off," Holmes said quietly.

Yank noticed that despite the word, his boss had a secret smile on his face. They were lucky to have Laws. Not only did he have a photographic memory, but he could also speak several languages. Yank was just happy to be able to speak a little L.A. Spanish, much less Chinese.

A minute later, the woman returned to the front door. She opened it. "Come in, Mr. Fogbottom. I'm sure you understand we get people wanting Mr. Van Dyke's autograph all the time." She smiled softly and stepped aside. "He asks me to keep them out."

"I'm sure you do an excellent job, ma'am." Laws stepped inside.

With no one outside, the image snapped off, but the audio continued, provided by Laws's wire. "Sure glad he's here. It was a long drive and that road—"

She chuckled. "Rim of the World. It keeps many from coming, thank the gods."

Yank and Holmes glanced at each other.

"It also keeps me from getting down to L.A.," she added. "I can't stand those sheer drop-offs."

"Me neither." The sound of several footsteps on a hardwood floor.

"This is Mr. Van Dyke's sitting room. If you'll wait a moment."

The sound of a single set of footsteps retreating.

Laws whispered, "East-facing window. Walls lined with floor-to-ceiling built-ins, except for one wall with pictures with movie stars and . . . is that Schwarzenegger?"

"Yes," came a raspy voice. One could tell it had once been deep but now was edged with sickness.

"I didn't hear you come in."

"I'm not one to clomp around my own house like Ms. Murphy. Plus, these slippers don't make much noise." After a pause, "Ms. Murphy said you had something for me."

"I do." The sound of paper ruffling. "If I could see an ID, though, Mr. Van Dyke."

Rasping coughs. "Look at the man in the pictures and look at me." More coughs. "What you see is a younger, handsomer version. Plus, that young man doesn't have my particular sickness."

"Very sorry for your—illness, sir."

"It comes and goes. Now the correspondence."

Sounds of papers shuffling. "If you can sign here, please, sir."

"Fine. Give."

More paper shuffling.

Then a sharp intake of breath.

"There you are. And thank you very much for your time."

"Leaving so soon?"

"I have several more of these to deliver." Sound of footsteps on a wooden floor. "I'll let myself out."

"You don't understand," began the raspy voice. "You can only leave when—"

The door opened, then slammed shut. "Start the engines. We need to leave. Now." Laws was walking as fast as he could.

YaYa picked himself up from the ground, then began to run.

They made it to the SUV at the same time, jumped in, then Yank sped away.

Holmes turned around in his seat.

"What was it?"

For one of the first times Yank noticed fear in Laws's eyes. They'd been in plenty of situations and the man had seemed always in control and capable of taking anything thrown at him. Seeing his fear stirred the butterflies in Yank's stomach.

"What was it?" Holmes repeated.

"I think . . . I think it was a vampire."

CHAPTER 15

Laws still wasn't certain what he'd seen, but the uneasiness it had created within him had sent his Spidey senses thrumming. He'd seen Ms. Murphy lock the door from the inside behind him when he'd entered, but what she hadn't seen was the wad of Silly Putty he'd shoved into the space where the lock would go. It was a good thing too, because it had appeared that Mr. Van Dyke hadn't intended for him to leave.

Van Dyke's appearance was that of a two-hundred-year-old version of the man in the pictures. The man standing next to Schwarzenegger and Nicholson and Magic Johnson had a vibrancy the man who'd stood before him lacked to such a degree, he might as well have been the husk of who he'd been. And why?

They sat in a booth in a corner of the bar by windows facing the water. They'd only ordered waters, much to the displeasure of the sixteen-year-old waitress who snapped gum like it was an Olympic event.

"Let's go over it one more time," Holmes said.

His back was to the corner, and he occasionally glanced up to see who was entering and leaving. So far no one had sat by the booth next to them. It was mid-afternoon and there wasn't much traffic.

Laws took a drink of his water as he glanced at his three team-mates. He was normally cool and collected, living by the dictate WWSMD—What Would Steve McQueen Do. Growing up in Holly-wood, Laws had been surrounded by the uncool, the wannabe cool, and the supercool. Although he'd never met McQueen, Laws's father, who'd worked on several of his films, including *Bullitt*, told him that the man was the coolest he'd ever met.

Laws began slowly describing the man's appearance. "I just thought he was sick, but then as he was signing the document, I happened to glance at one of the pictures. I could see my reflec-tion perfectly, but his was smudged. I remember blinking my eyes several times, thinking it was me, but no, it was as if someone had come and wiped their hand across his image."

"I thought vampires didn't have a reflection," Yank said.

"That's fiction written by people following the tradition of Stoker," Laws said, unable to keep from being the Encyclopedia Supernatural.

"Our mission logs reference human smudging in reflective surfaces," Holmes said. "But it could refer not only to a vampire, but to someone possessed, like with a demon."

"Like that makes it better," YaYa said. "Thanks for the clarifi-cation."

Holmes sipped thoughtfully at his water. "No problem."

"Let's talk this out, though. If it is a demon, what kind? Given we're dealing with druids, it could be anything, not necessarily those from Christian ideology. Perhaps like the thing that had you," Laws said, nodding his head at YaYa.

The young man absently rubbed his prosthetic hand. "The *obour*," he said softly.

YaYa had been infected with an ancient forest demon on his first mission while they were operating in Myanmar. The crea-ture's malignant influence had become so bad, YaYa had been co-opted by a shape-changing Los Zetas hit man, which almost led to the death of the entire team. In the end, the only way YaYa could fight the demon was to remove the site of infection, which was his left forearm.

"Although we have the entire pantheon of demons from which to choose," Laws began, "considering we're dealing with druids, one would have to believe it would be a nature spirit of some sort. Remember any readings on those, Boss?"

Holmes shook his head, then held up a hand.

A family of four, mom, pop, son, and daughter, trundled by and took a seat two booths down. Both kids were sulking. The waitress was on top of it and took the orders for two double martinis like it was a military operation and was moving fast toward the bartender before Laws continued.

"Me neither." He leaned back. "Then I guess we follow SOP."

"Wait," Yank said, looking from Laws to Holmes. "There's a Standard Operating Procedure for dealing with demons?"

"Of course there is. Why wouldn't there be?"

"Well, it's just that . . ." He seemed to fight for a way to articulate what he wanted to say. "It's just that we've been flying by the seat of our pants for the last few missions, so the idea that we have manuals and SOPs for these things is . . . well, incredible, I guess."

Laws grinned for a moment, then turned to Holmes. "FNG just said it's incredible. What do you think about that, Boss?"

Holmes shook his head. "Remind me when we get back to the shop that we're going to begin practicing immediate action drills."

"Like how to remove someone's head from their ass?" YaYa said, staring plainly at Yank.

"Or how to remove someone's foot from their mouth?" Laws added.

"More like weapon improvisation against catalogued supernatural enemies." Holmes sighed. "Yank's right in a way. Although I prefer to call it operational flexibility instead of flying by the seat of your pants, we've barely had a breath since our last op. Last time we practiced at all was in New Orleans against the undead."

"Scenario development?" Laws asked.

Holmes nodded. "Think about how we're going to build the training around specific circumstances and environments."

"I can get Musso to begin working on that for us. I hear we're getting a replacement for Jen as well. Someone named Riley Ferguson."

They all stared at nothing for a moment; then Holmes spoke. "Everyone order something. I'm going to call back for our go bags to be delivered. We're not leaving this mountain until we've engaged the demon." He stood up and pulled his phone from his pocket as he headed out the door.

"You heard the man," Laws said. "Let's eat." He kept his smile on and his eyes bright, but inside he felt the darkness in the creature known as Van Dyke. Soon they'd know it was his real name.

CHAPTER 16

BANKS OF THE KENNET RIVER, MARLBOROUGH, ENGLAND. DUSK.

Adam Neville's passion had always been fishing. The major contributing factor for him quitting his job in London ten years ago had been the lack of acceptable trout fishing nearby, not to mention the sheer mass of shuddering humanity. He'd moved to the country, bought a home on the Kennet River, and proceeded to spend his days telecommuting to the brokerage and his mornings and evenings communing with the fish. It was in these moments as he slung a nymph into a ripple of water that he felt the most content.

Of course his mates would be on him for using flies, since the season ended October 1, but being a coarse fisherman wasn't in his veins and he couldn't stand trying to catch anything other than trout or her cousins, salmon and char. Carp and perch and dace and sanders were dumb enough to eat empty hooks. With flies it was a game of strategy, in which sometimes the fish won and sometimes he won. With bait and other techniques it was hardly a challenge. If he'd wanted to fish merely to catch fish he would have learned how to net the fish and spared the cost of a decent rod.

He glanced back at the warmth of his house, his wife, Sarah, staring blithely at him through the patio door, glass of chardonnay in one hand, cigarette in the other. She'd detested the move from the city. He smiled weakly as he shivered from the cold. He couldn't be sure if it was the weather or her stare. She sent him a steely grin, then turned away from the window to the fire. He sighed, realizing it was only a matter of time before she left him.

But of course he'd always have the fish.

He cast a small unweighted nymph in the clear water and let it drift over the ripple. A swirl of silver, then it hit. His rod bent double as his heart soared. The feeling never changed. Not from the first fish up to this most recent one. It was always a luxurious and rewarding feeling.

He reeled the fish in, letting it play long enough that it could have gotten off if it had shaken its head and body the right way, then pulled it onto the bank. It was a brown, probably eighteen inches. He put his left hand gently on the body.

The fish stared at him, its mouth opening and closing in exhausted gasps.

Adam slid the barbless hook free, then released the brown back into the water. He watched as it disappeared. He stayed squatting, watching the poetry of the river for a time before he stood.

Maybe just once more.

He moved fifty feet down the river, leaving the shadow of his own home. He noticed fog coming from the west, hugging the water. He cast toward it, as if it were a geological feature rather than a weather phenomenon. He let his nymph drift a moment, then recast. By the time his fly hit the water, the fog had moved to obscure its position. Then the fog covered him and the river, moving on.

He sighed, reeling in the nymph and hooking it to the place just above the reel on his pole designed to hold it. Although his fishing was done, he didn't want to go home. So instead he stood in the cold, shivering slightly, listening to the land and trying not to remember the words of his wife just an hour ago.

"You're bound and determined to drive me bloody insane. How can you pass the opportunity up? It's double your salary!"

"But it's in Hong Kong," he'd said. "There aren't any trout in Hong Kong."

"Trout. Trout. Your fucking trout. I think if you could find a trout with tits and a slit, you'd get rid of me in a second."

The words had so shocked him that he'd stood there speechless until she'd laughed at him. The laughter broke the spell, sending him outside.

"That's right. Go and find your trout mermaid."

Then the silence of the Kennet River.

It was true. He'd done well for his Chinese trading firm. Because of him, they'd been able to buy two buildings in the heart of the London Financial District, allowing for local representation that gave them leverage when trading on the Heng Seng, Nikkei, and Shanghai Composite Stock Exchanges. He'd even married one of the senior partners' daughters. And now they wanted him to be a vice president, would provide him a car and driver, and would even set him up in an old estate overlooking Kowloon Bay that had once belonged to a sheik and before him an opium king. It was truly what dreams were made of and she had a right to be angry.

But was it his fault if all he wanted to do was fish?

He heard the sound of hounds in the distance, followed by a horn.

Foxhunting? The Marlborough Hunt Club didn't have anything scheduled this close to Christmas. Plus, the hounds didn't sound like any he knew. He listened to them bay again and couldn't place the breed.

The sound of the horn came again, but closer.

He peered into the fog, trying to make out whether it was coming from across the river or on his side. Water and fog always played tricks with sound.

He suddenly felt something brush past him. Then another thing. This one knocked him off balance, forcing him to stumble to his right, where he knew the river was. He fought to keep his balance and would have regained it had he not been pushed one last time.

He hit the water sideways. He lost his grip on his rod but was unable to reach for it. He'd lost his breath, the cold of the water paralyzing him. He tried to suck in air, but his head went beneath the frigid water. He scrambled for footing but couldn't find it against the mossy bottom.

Then he heard her calling from the nearby bank. "If you won't go to Hong Kong, then I'll go without you."

His arms began to move finally as they freed themselves from the sudden shock of the water.

The sound of hounds came much closer. The horn sounded like it was right on top of him.

Sarah screamed and began shouting, "No!" over and over again until it was cut off by what sounded like dogs fighting over a stick.

He finally managed to get his feet under him. By the time he reached the bank, the fog was dissipating. Such a strange weather phenomenon, especially the way it had thrown sound. It was as if the hunt had been right here. He pulled himself up and climbed to his feet, shivering uncontrollably. He ran toward the warm glow of his house. Once he got warm and had a few glasses of scotch, he'd go find his wife and have a word with her. Then when he was finished with that he'd go online and order a new fly rod. He had a spare, but now that he'd lost his best rod he had the chance to order one he'd had his eye on. It was a thousand dollars, but it was a piece of art.

Shivering uncontrollably, he'd almost made it to the steps of his patio when he heard a growl from behind him. He turned, almost falling because his frozen feet refused to cooperate.

It was a hound, but like no hound he'd ever seen. As tall as a Great Dane, it was part human, part beast. It had what looked shockingly like human arms for its front legs and a gray hairless body. But what captured him was the gaze from the dark eyes in the almost simian face. It was recognition. He knew those eyes. And then it leaped, grabbing him by the leg and dragging him east toward Silbury Hill. He tried to scream, but he was dead within the first hundred meters, his head having banged against the ground over and over until it split open. That he could still see did very little to calm him. That is, until he felt himself jerked and pulled and hammered until he was no longer being dragged but was running beside the other hound, a beast he had once called his wife.

CHAPTER 17

CHICKSANDS RAF. NIGHT.

Walker had been helping the witch organize the warlock loot for two hours when Ian and Trev returned. Trev went straight down the hall to Preeti's command center. Ian came to the common room. Behind him were two steely-eyed men in thick-soled shoes who Walker thought had to be cops. The last man was dressed in a Savile Row suit and overcoat and appeared impeccably manicured. From his hair to his hands to the cut of his attire, it all screamed money.

Walker leaped to his feet. "Ian, how are you—"

Ian held up his hand. With his chin high, he went to the sideboard and poured himself three inches of scotch. Without turning around, he slung it back and swallowed.

"So this is what it's come to," the posh man said, glancing around the room in distaste.

The men who Walker had thought were cops stood behind him. *Probably ex-cops. Bodyguards. Muscle.*

"You once had the ear of the Queen," he continued, "and now you're in the basement of an old officers' club. Looks like you bollixed it up good. How pathetic." When he spied the witch, his entire demeanor changed. "Now who's this pretty little dish?"

She'd stood when they'd entered the room. She fell right into the shy schoolgirl act and smiled sweetly. "Sassy Moore, Your Highness. But you can call me Sassy."

The two bodyguards exchanged glances.

A look of pure lechery came upon the posh man's face. "I like your name."

"It's more than just my name," she purred. "It's who I am. Sassy."

Walker felt the power in her words.

The man took a step forward, then halted. His eyes narrowed; then he turned to Ian. "You trying to work me, Ian?"

Ian had watched from the sideboard, a refilled glass in his hand. "Never in a million years, Sir Robert. We're at your service, as always."

"What is she then, a witch?"

"I don't have to be a witch to be hit on by you," answered Sassy. "I'm sure each and every schoolgirl in Sheffield knows your number, Sir Robert."

He glowered at her as he backed up until he was bookended by his bodyguards.

"And look at the right proper benighted Englishman," Sassy continued. "Taking time out of polluting the countryside and de-spoiling young girls just to see us."

"Enough!" Ian shouted. He shook his head and sighed as if the weight of the world were on his shoulders and he could carry it, just in a different position. Addressing the room, Ian said, "Allow me to introduce Sir Robert MacDonald from Sheffield. He's here to shut us down."

Walker jerked his attention back to this MacDonald character. "He can't do that."

"Let me assure you, I *can* bloody well do that and more. I *am* doing that. Your kind was once needed, I agree. But times have changed. We're in the modern era. There's no reason for a unit like yours in this time of instant information and computers." He spread his hands. "And if something were to happen, CCTV would pick it up."

Walker thought about the disturbance they'd tracked. He almost brought it up, but something told him to keep it quiet.

"Plus, we hate to see such an egregious loss of life. What is it, Ian? You've lost three people in three months?" Sir Robert shook his head in a mockery of utter sadness. "Too many lives lost. Just too many. I think you're way past your prime."

Trev and Preeti came in from behind. Sir Robert and his men, who made room for them, then resumed their place.

"Is this everyone?" Sir Robert asked.

"All that's left." Ian's voice was even, his demeanor implacable.

"Pathetic. No one's going to blink an eye with me shutting you down, Ian. To believe that a unit composed of a psychopath, a cripple, a pet American, and a witch servant all led by an old drunk was responsible for the supernatural protection of England is hysterical."

Trev made a move toward Sir Robert, but one of the bodyguards stepped in front of him at the same time as Preeti grabbed his arm with both of hers, letting her crutches fall to the ground.

Everyone stared at them a moment, then back to Sir Robert.

"You have twenty-four hours to pack up your things and put them in official storage. I have orders for you three." He held out his hand and the other bodyguard handed him three slender envelopes. Sir Robert then handed them to each of the remaining members of Section 9. When he was done, he smiled, King of Smug. "You'll be thanking me for this next year. This is best for England." He turned and exited the room. His guards went with him.

Walker broke the intervening silence when Sir Robert was well and gone. "You. Cannot. Be. Serious."

"I'm afraid so, chap." Ian set his glass down carefully. "Sir Robert has been working to shut us down for the last three years. When he began we had thirty people and had strong representation in parliament, fighting for funding lines."

Walker still couldn't believe what was happening. "So what changed?"

"Everything. Nothing. It wasn't a single event. It was a bunch of small things, really. Reassignments. Reallocations. Promises for future personnel if we shifted some current staff to other defense-related operations. Re-elections. Most of those who'd traditionally watched out for us either retired, passed on, or weren't re-elected."

"I hate to ask this," Walker began, "but I came over here to find out who killed my fiancée. Now we know the Wild Hunt is on the loose. Are we just going to stop?"

Trev stepped forward. "Yeah. Can't we complete this last mission and show Sir Asshole how valuable we are?"

Ian shook his head. "He doesn't care. This is a personal vendetta and I've never been able to get to the heart of it. Walker, it's game, set, and match. Sir Robert played us and won. There's just nothing to be done."

"That's not exactly true," Preeti said. She glanced in Walker's direction and smiled secretly. He felt a moment's hope. "There have been some developments." She looked at her crutches on the floor and then to the chairs around the table. "Can we sit?"

Ian stared at her, then went into motion. "Of course, Preeti."

Soon everyone was sitting around the table.

Ian had provided glasses for everyone and had poured an inch of scotch in each. "Before we begin"—he took up his glass and held it—"to Jerry."

Everyone raised theirs as well and they clinked glasses. "To Jerry," they said.

Once everyone had drunk, Ian composed his face. "We'll have services the day after tomorrow. No, that's Christmas. The day after that then, on the twenty-sixth." He turned to Preeti. "You now have the table, madame."

She brought them up to speed about what she and Walker had discussed and done earlier. Then she said, "With the help of my brother, who telecommutes from the Home Office and is so good with computers I might as well be a child by comparison, we were able to track down some additional disturbances. Trev, will you run and get the map on my desk?"

Trev got up and hurried out. He was back in less than thirty seconds with a map he placed in the center of the table. Seven markers were in place at Woking, Chipping Sodbury, Bromley, Shapwick, Marlborough, Penrith, and Notgrove.

"I tracked disturbances from each of these events to nearby mounds."

"Wait a moment." Ian had raised a hand. "Events?"

"Right. We know what happened at Woking. In Penrith, an orphanage for displaced Nigerian children disappeared. It's believed to be a highly localized F5 tornado which only damaged the orphanage, even though it was wedged into a tight little neighborhood."

"What?" Ian shook his head. "An entire orphanage gone? Why aren't we hearing about this?"

"It'll be in tomorrow's news. All of this has occurred only in the past seventy-two hours. There could be more, but these were the only things we were able to discover in the little time we had."

"Continue," Ian said.

"In Chipping Sodbury a local businessman and his associates were found ripped apart on the golf course. Owners of an Indian restaurant in Shapwick went missing. I've been there, by the way, and they have the best vindaloo. In Marlborough a local resident and his wife were found mauled on the bank of the Kennet River. In Penrith there were reports of a man being chased down the street by misshapen hounds, which the police are discrediting because they were called in at three AM by several drunken witnesses. In Notgrove the parish priest reported odd howls and the blowing of horns. There's only three CCTV cameras in Notgrove, so there was no tracking. They all went fuzzy at the same time."

Ian pointed to a spot southeast of London. "What about Bromley?"

"Saving the best for last. The body of MP Gordon Miller was found gored in a parking lot by a hotel. Looks like he'd spent the night with a local girl, then was killed when he went outside."

"Are you telling me that we believe that the Wild Hunt killed a Member of Parliament?" Ian asked.

"I don't think the Wild Hunt gives a shit about an MP," Sassy Moore said. "They don't even know what a parliament is."

"How come we're just hearing about this?" Trev asked.

"The Home Office has it under wraps until they can determine what caused the wounds." Preeti frowned distastefully. "It was reported his insides were torn out."

Ian nodded. "This might change everything. If we have a supernatural event or entity which threatens English sovereignty, then we need to be around to combat it." He stood and grabbed the map. "I need to make a call. Wait here."

After Ian rushed from the room, Sassy leaned back and crossed her arms. "You know what's going on, don't you?"

Everyone looked at her.

"The Wild Hunt is building itself. For some reason it's not large enough."

"Building itself? You mean like recruiting?" Walker asked.

She shook her head. "It's long been held that the Wild Hunt only comes around when changes need to be made. It often comes back a mere shadow of itself, becoming stronger as the souls of its victims come to populate the Hunt. Some become hunters, others become stags, but most become hounds."

"Wait." Walker struggled to parse the information. "All of the victims?"

She nodded. "It was why we saw what we saw, the rush and rumble of a beast hunting. It was the connection to your fiancée."

The knot in his chest turned to iron. "They're using her soul?"

Her expression remained grim. "And those of everyone else they kill."

"Why do they need their hunt to be so large?" Trev asked.

"It depends on what their endgame is. We still don't know their motive."

"We might," Preeti said, interrupting. "It's not something you would notice, most likely, but it's something I hit on right away."

"We're all ears, sweetie," the witch said.

"The businessmen in Chipping Sodbury were Jordanian. The

wife of the man in Marlborough was Chinese and he worked for a Chinese bank. The MP was an outspoken proponent of immigration rights. The orphanage that just vanished was Nigerian run and operated. The owners of the restaurant were Indian. I'm sure once we discover what happened in Penrith and Notgrove, we'll also see a similar trend."

"All immigrants," Walker said.

"We're all immigrants in England," the witch said. "More aptly, the victims were not Anglo or Saxon."

"Or if they were," Trev added, "they were in support of non-Anglo-Saxon activities."

"What are we concluding?" Walker asked. "That the Wild Hunt is a supernatural white supremacist welcoming committee?"

The witch grinned. "You Americans have a way with words, but it's as apt a description as I've heard."

But Walker still didn't get it. "Why would the Wild Hunt care? Do they even know who Indians or Jordanians are?"

"Don't you get it? They're a tool. Someone is using them," Preeti said.

"The Red Grove," Trev said.

"And until we can find one of them and ask, we're going to be guessing at the endgame," the witch said.

Ian entered the room. "We have a stay of execution." He wore a satisfied smile. "I spoke with Lord Robinson—Deputy Minister of the UK Border Agency—and explained the situation." Ian glanced at Walker. "I hope your team is going to be able to help, because the only way he'd accept my proposal was if I included them. Without them, we're only two operators and not enough to make a real difference."

Walker felt something growing inside of him. He recognized it as hope—hope that avenging Jen's death would be much closer with the coming of SEAL Team 666. "Are they invited?"

"Yes."

"Officially."

"If your man in the Senate wants to confirm, he can contact the office of Lord Robinson."

Walker grinned from ear to ear. "Hell yeah! I need to make a call." He made to get up, but Ian had put a hand on his shoulder.

"Call's already been made, son. I spoke to Ms. Alexis Billings. She's aware of everything I just said."

Walker pushed his empty glass forward. "How about another drink?"

Ian grabbed the bottle. "How about drinks for all of us."

CHAPTER 18

TWIN PEAKS, CALIFORNIA. NIGHT.

Navy Senior Chief Genaro "The Genie" Stewart escorted SEAL Team 666's go bags, additional weapons, and the Belgian Malinois, Hoover, in the MH-53J special operations variant Pave Low helicopter. Built like a defensive end, he passed out the gear with a no-nonsense attitude. YaYa knew him from previous missions before he'd joined Triple Six. A SEAL from Team 7, Genie wasn't read on to Triple Six's mission, but at Holmes's request through NAVSPECWAR for sniper support, Genie was coming along. He'd already suited up in black fatigues and body armor and stood by while the others got into theirs.

One by one, the SEALs from Triple Six introduced themselves. Not that they had to. They were from a special brotherhood. But knowing the man next to you enhanced the connection. When it was YaYa's turn, Genie gave him a hug. "Been what . . . since the P.I.?"

YaYa grinned and shook his head. "Three years. Has it been that long?"

Genie pointed. "Heard about the arm."

Although he'd left the rest unsaid, YaYa had experienced it

enough to know how to answer the unanswered questions. "It's strong. The boys and girls at DARPA really know their business."

"With all the casualties from Iraq and Afghanistan, they've had plenty of practice."

The sobering statement cut short any further conversation.

Finally, everyone was up-armored, wore MBITRs, had sound-suppressed 9s strapped to their right thighs, knives strapped to their left thighs, and checked their sound-suppressed HK416s. Outside their armor, they wore black Rhodesian military vests because of the multiple pockets for storing extra ammunition and other useful items. Pro-Tec skate helmets painted black did little to protect their heads but allowed for the mounting of a curiously alien-looking set of night-vision goggles with four lenses. Called QUADEYE, four 16mm lenses reduced the need to pan left and right by re-creating peripheral vision and incorporating the multiple feeds into a Heads-Up Display (HUD) similar to those used by combat helicopter pilots.

The team's only odd uniform concession had been to wear ballistic masks that looked like hockey masks, covering their faces but leaving holes for the eyes and slits for their mouths and noses. Not only did the masks keep their faces from being recorded; they also gave the team the appearance of a Jason Voorhees look-alike contest.

Holmes's mask was black with a white slash across it.

Laws wore a mask with a green camouflage pattern.

YaYa wore a solid white mask in honor of Fratolilio, the SEAL he'd replaced who'd been killed by the chimera in Macau.

And Yank's mask, from the tried-and-true tradition to fuck with the new guy, was so pink that it was fuchsia.

Genie, not being a member of Triple Six, didn't have a mask but was given a plain gray ballistic mask to wear in the event he was needed inside.

Their CQB stack included Hoover, who was in the fifth-man position. She wore tactical body armor that protected her sides and chest. Her eyes were protected by specially designed canine ballistic goggles.

After a short drive, they left the vehicle and traveled the last mile through a stretch of wood.

Genie set up in a tree on the side of the house with the most windows. He carried the SEAL-issue SR-25 Stoner sniper rifle with a Leupold Mark 4 scope. He had a view of the front and back entrances and, after Yank secreted a camera on the far side of the house, also had a view of the area he couldn't physically see.

The choice had been either to walk up and knock on the door, then force their way inside, or to break the door down and clear rooms until they found their quarry.

When Genie notified them that their quarry was in the first-floor drawing room, their decision was made for them. The sniper had a clear shot and was ordered to take it if things went south.

They removed their night-vision devices and cached them at the base of Genie's tree. Yank and Laws were ordered to take the rear entrance, while Holmes, YaYa, and Hoover took the front door.

With their HKs sunk into the meat of their shoulders and the weapons at low ready, Holmes depressed the doorbell.

"Target not moving," came Genie's voice.

They waited about ten seconds and Holmes depressed the doorbell again.

YaYa felt exposed beneath the light on the front stoop. He'd have much rather they'd turned off the power and CQBd inside, instead of this awkward Jehovah's Witness waiting on the front stoop nonsense.

They heard the sound of footsteps on hardwood, then the sound of several locks disengaging.

The door opened and the same woman from earlier stood there. But instead of screaming or showing fear, she looked nonplussed at the three scary men with weapons. "I'm sorry, it's too late to call on Mr. Van Dyke."

"Back door. Move," said Holmes into his MBITR.

He pushed past her into the home. YaYa grabbed her by the arm and pushed her against a wall, knocking a picture to the ground. Quickly and efficiently he frisked her. Seeing Laws and

Yank come in from the kitchen, he pointed upstairs. They hurried up and began to clear rooms.

YaYa put zip ties around the woman's hands, then lowered her to the floor. "Sit here. Don't move." Then he joined Holmes and Hoover in the drawing room.

Van Dyke was sitting in his chair staring straight ahead. He didn't appear to be moving. He didn't even appear to be alive. Whatever his condition, it wasn't anything Hoover appreciated. The dog stood ready to attack, a low growl coming from deep in her throat.

Holmes finished scanning the room, then grabbed a picture from the wall. He held it at an angle, which provided a perfect reflection of the man. Holmes set the picture aside, then checked for a pulse. He waved his hand before the man's eyes, then prodded him in the chest. No response.

"No sign of smudging. Laws, report."

The second in command came loud and clear over the MBITR. "Second floor clear. Nothing out of the ordinary."

"Check the basement. We'll stand by." To YaYa he said, "You and Hoover clear the rest of this level."

YaYa turned and motioned for Hoover to follow. Then, with his rifle at low ready, he pushed into the dining room, then to a library, then back around to the kitchen. He peeked into the sole bathroom on this level and opened the closets. All the while, he was aware of the nature spirit somewhere in the home. He didn't know how he knew it, but it felt like a line of fear tickling his spine. He had to gulp several times as it felt as if it came closer. He wasn't used to the fear. But then again, he also had never been possessed before. What the *obour* had done to him, at least what he could remember, had been so terrible it haunted most of his waking and sleeping moments more than any number of deaths or visions of dead bodies.

As he was moving back to the front of the house, Genie spoke breathlessly. "There's something moving outside."

"Define 'something,'" Holmes said.

"Small tree with legs. Hell. Walking. Fuck me."

"Easy, SEAL. Give us location."

"Right outside your fucking window."

YaYa entered the room in time to see Holmes run to the window to look outside. Then he raised his rifle as if to fire.

"Careful," whispered Genie. "What the hell? It just fell to pieces."

Then YaYa watched as the man in the chair turned to him and smiled. Then he stood and turned to Holmes, who was at the window three feet from him.

"Behind you!" YaYa fired a single round into the man's lower leg.

Holmes spun, in time to catch the man as he fell forward. He held Van Dyke by the collar of his shirt and lowered him to the ground.

Laws and Yank burst into the room.

Holmes pulled Van Dyke into the middle of the room and laid him on his back. He was conscious and evinced both anger and pain.

Holmes pulled his mask free. "Ask the woman if there's a medkit."

"What woman?" Laws said. "She's gone."

"Genie?"

"Nothing here."

"Fuck." Holmes turned to Laws. "Find her. Take Hoover." To YaYa he said, "Watch my six."

Holmes removed the man's shoes, then the blood-soaked sock on the left leg. Then he ripped the pants, exposing the lower leg. He had Van Dyke raise his knee, to allow for the bend to compress the vessels delivering blood to the affected areas. He glanced around, then grabbed the man's shirt and ripped it, revealing a pale and white-haired torso. He balled a doily he found on a nearby table, pressed it into the wound, then wrapped it.

"What were you thinking?" he said to the man.

Van Dyke replied with gritted teeth, "That I wouldn't be shot in my own home."

"You're lucky I didn't shoot you in the head," YaYa said. He could feel the thing inside the man. "It's back in him, Boss. What-ever the fuck it is feels like greasy nightmare shit."

"Be easy, SEAL, and plug him if he moves." Holmes finished tying the field bandage. "What the fuck was that out there?" Then he saw the tattoo over the man's left breast. Holmes pointed to it. "Triple goddess. Tuatha Dé Dannan."

YaYa noticed the surprise in the man's eyes. He leaned in and saw the tattoo. It was three crescent moons, interlocked. And whatever it was lived inside of it. As he watched, the tattoo seemed to pulse and grow larger. He felt its pull and took one uncontrolled step toward it.

"Fu-fuck." He fought the urge to move forward with every part of his being. "Lives in the tattoo. Don't—don't touch."

Van Dyke leaned his head up and met YaYa's gaze. The man spoke in a strange language and YaYa felt himself fall. The last thing he saw was the superimposed image of a man made of sticks and leaves and an unholy glow where his eyes should have been.

Then he heard gunfire.

Then nothing.

CHAPTER 19

VAN DYKE HOUSE. UPSTAIRS. NIGHT.

She came at them from a darkened room. Laws opened fire as he backed away, stitching her in the chest with eleven 5.56mm rounds that should have blown out her back and knocked her off her feet. But she kept coming. He brought the butt of his rifle up and slammed it into her chin. Her head swung back, but it did no damage.

WTF?

The doorway was off the landing to the left. He backed farther left down the hallway, separating himself from Yank and Hoover.

She followed Laws, exposing her back to Yank, who opened fire.

But to no effect.

Hoover growled but waited for a command.

Why wasn't she going down? It didn't make sense. She was a sixty-something June Cleaver hausfrau. She should have died five times by now with the amount of rounds they'd poured into her.

He adjusted aim and fired two more into the center of her forehead. Her skin pulsed with red light and with each pulse revealed an interlocked three crescent moon. Laws recognized the symbol from the mission logs. The glyph of the three goddesses—Maiden, Mother, and Crone. It was the holy trinity of ancient Pict mythology and had been adopted by neo-pagans. A precursor to Triple Six had gone after a group who worshiped them during the Dust Bowl of 1931. The log had recorded nature spirits but nothing like this creature. If he wasn't mistaken, it had all the characteristics of a—

"Golem!"

He dropped the rifle and let it hang from its strap and began to draw his knife. But she was too quick. She fell on him, driving him to the ground, pinning his hand where it was on his left thigh. She was incredibly heavy. Their impact as they hit the floor slammed the air from him and he couldn't move his chest to get a deep enough breath.

Her hands went to his throat. He fought her grip with his left hand, but it was as if he were a child. He didn't have the strength to stop her.

Fuck! Was this how it was going to end?

The glyph began to pulse with regularity now.

His vision began to dim.

Then the pressure reduced.

His vision cleared enough for him to see her right arm moving back. Was she letting him go? But then he saw the arm was being held by Yank, who tossed it down the hall. The other SEAL, with his feet pressed against the baseboard, levered the golem off Laws, who gasped as he breathed, finally able to pull his knife free.

He got to his knees and saw Yank sawing at the woman's other arm. It came bloodlessly free halfway down her triceps. Flesh-colored clay encompassed what looked like a branch, now severed. Yank tossed the arm after the first, glanced up, then paled.

"Oh hell no." He stood and ran down the hall, where he began to kick something.

Laws turned his attention to the golem, whose fierce eyes detailed her desire to kill him. He was about to stand when her legs shot out and caught him in the stomach and chest. He slammed into the wall, all air once again gone. He felt broken as he struggled to stand.

Hoover shot in and put her jaws around an ankle, but the creature kicked the dog free with her other foot. Hoover squealed as she flew to the landing, coming to rest in a painful splay of legs.

Fucking golem, Laws decided then and there. He absolutely hated golems. Hated them even more than those ridiculous homunculi.

Glancing down the hall, he saw where Yank was fighting with the golem's hands, which were still alive and grabbing at him.

Laws fell to the floor beside her and removed her head in five hard strokes of his knife.

It should have killed her, but her legs continued to move. He tossed the head over the rail and heard it strike the stairs several times before it landed on the first floor below. Then he began to saw at one leg, then the other, until they were separated.

He got to his feet, grabbed a leg, opened a bedroom door, then tossed it inside and closed it. He did the same to the other leg but tossed it into a different room.

Then he ran down the hall.

Yank had chopped off the fingers of one hand, but they had moved back to it and were reattaching themselves. He glanced up at Laws and shrugged. "Fucking arm won't die."

Laws brought his knife down and impaled the hand into the floor, like a specimen.

Yank did the same thing.

Then they both stood, staring at the impaled hands, gasping for air, sweat pouring from inside their masks. As one, they removed the masks and wiped their faces.

Yank shook his head. "What the fuck?"

Laws answered in gasps, "Golem. Your first time. Can't be killed."

"Remind me to scratch them off my bucket list."

Growling caused Laws and Yank to turn around. Hoover had returned and was pulling the torso toward the stairs. But the torso was undulating, as if unwilling to leave without its other body parts.

"Dog has the right idea." Laws ran up and cleared Hoover away. Then he kicked the torso down the stairs.

Yank came after.

When Laws got to the first floor, he saw her head lying against the front door. He grabbed it by its hair and carried it into the drawing room. He held the head up by the hair. "Found her."

He saw that YaYa was unconscious on the floor. Holmes knelt next to Van Dyke. The SEAL team leader had his P229 9mm pressed against the man's head.

"What took you so long?" Holmes asked without moving.

"Turns out she was a golem."

"You have to cut her," Van Dyke said. "You can't kill her."

"We found that out."

Then Van Dyke said the unexpected. "Thank you. Thank you, very much. She was holding me prisoner."

CHAPTER 20

CHICKSANDS RAF. NIGHT.

The loot from the warlock's bowling alley HQ was extraordinary. Sassy Moore had spent the night going through the tomes and trinkets, impressed with his ability to collect such a diverse library of the arcane. What the warlock had had before his delightfully untimely but uniquely appropriate demise easily rivaled her collection in its magnitude and scope, but then again she'd concentrated on her own path and hadn't diverged as much as her dear dead enemy. He'd concentrated most of his efforts on fabrication; at least it had appeared so from the immensity of that gargantuan creature. Had Van McKee spent half his time concentrating on astral battle tactics, she wouldn't have been able to disembody him so easily.

But at least now he was dead. He'd been a thorn in her side for years. He was a controller and wanted her tidily working for him, whether it was under the auspices of one of the covens or druid circles he belonged to or as his own personal servant. Now that Section 9, with the help of the remarkable Jack Walker, had helped her to remove him from this plane of existence, her path toward her own supremacy was clear.

Normally, she'd take her new things and slip away. She had to rebuild her life and establish a new magical focal point. But with the Wild Hunt running amok and the mysterious Red Grove controlling its actions, she'd have to pretend to be a team player. Oh, how droll it was to smile and grin at mortal humor. She'd much rather poke her eyes out and so much as promised herself that she would if she ever found herself in a similar position—one in which she'd have to go hat in hand to the nice military men for support.

Walker came into the room, wearing boxers and a T-shirt, wiping his face with his hand and yawning. He'd only been sleeping for a few hours. He reached into the refrigerator, grabbed a water bottle, twisted it open, and drank it half down before he noticed the witch regarding him.

He glanced down at his boxers, then back to Sassy Moore. "I didn't see you sitting there."

"That's okay. I was invisible."

His eyes widened. "Really?"

Dolt. "No. I was just teasing. I can't really make myself invisible."

Still, he looked at her warily. It seemed to wake him and he regarded a box of books on the coffee table in front of her. He came over and lifted the top one free. "Are these helping? Funny-feeling book cover. What's it made from?"

"Anthropodermic bibliopegy."

"What kind of animal is that?"

"Not an animal. It's a term used to define books bound in human skin."

He dropped it like a sheet of acid and wiped his hand on the side of his boxers.

"You could tell a guy."

"You might not just walk up and grab stuff."

He shook his head and gave the entire box a distasteful look. "What's it about?"

"The Red Barn Murder. William Corder murdered the mother of his child near Suffolk in 1827. He was later killed for his crime, and a surgeon stripped and tanned his skin to use it as a binding for the book about his deed, the subsequent trial, and execution."

"Morbidly dreary. What's it used for?"

"Not sure. My guess is it's a focal point for someone to contact the soul of William Corder."

"Why would anyone want to do that?" Walker thought better of it and waved his hand. "Never mind. It would probably be disturbing."

She smiled primly. "People sure love to eat sausage, but they can't stand seeing it made."

He nodded. "I've used that saying before myself. It's absolutely true." He drank the rest of the water, then broke down the plastic bottle, the crinkling sounds filling the silence. "I've been tossing in bed going over the day's events. I've been especially thinking about Sir MacDonald and why he'd be so keen on shutting down a unit almost no one knows exists. It's not like he can take public credit for it."

"That's true. What's his motive?" She eyed Walker speculatively. Perhaps he was more than the sum of his handsomeness and muscle. "I did find it interesting that he was so quickly able to deflect my power. He's either shielded or a warlock. I don't recognize any of the warlock tells I'm familiar with, so my bet is that he's shielded. How and why is what I'd like to know."

"How does one go about being shielded by a warlock? Is there a section in the yellow pages? Craigslist?"

"I don't know what either of those is, but I think your attempt at humor referred to something available to the common man. To answer your question, no. A warlock, or a witch, for that matter, wouldn't advertise. We prefer our privacy. No, whoever is involved with Sir MacDonald was involved from well before this day."

"Could it be someone from the Red Grove?" Walker rubbed an itch in the center of his chest. "Perhaps we should see where he goes. I wonder if Preeti couldn't develop an algorithm which would allow the CCTV cameras to trace his comings and goings."

She raised an eyebrow. U.S. Navy SEALs weren't the knuckle

draggers she'd believed them to be. It seemed the selectors valued intelligence. And to think that there were more coming. *Yum.*

"I'm going to go see if she's still awake." He took a few steps, then paused. "Do you need anything?"

"I'm fine, Mr. SEAL."

He stared at her a moment, then shook his head. Soon he was out of the room and headed down the hall.

She leaned over the box and stared at the book he'd picked up. Beneath it was another book bound in human skin titled *L'Esprits des San Ignacio Mini.* Although she'd never seen the book, she'd heard of it. Who hadn't heard of it? Written in 1613 by a Jesuit priest who was also known to be a practicing warlock, it was the record of life and death and daily events at a small mission run by Spanish conquistadors in the northeastern corner of present-day Argentina. Father Jose Cataldina finished writing the book in 1721, then had the skin from his back removed and used it to bind his work. For years it passed from hand to hand. It wasn't until 1852 that it was found once more when Vicar John Baptist Miège, Vicar Apostate to the American Indian Territories east of the Rocky Mountains, came into contact with the book. As he wrote in his own private ledger, he discovered a simple Elizabethan substitution cipher hidden within the text of the book, which revealed a series of resurrection spells of such complexity that they could never be replicated. Many a coven had rumored that a spell of forgetfulness had been placed over the tome to discourage copying. To Sassy's recollection, no one had ever decoded any of the spells believed to be in the book, much less been able to incant them.

She opened the book with the tenderest hands, letting her finger linger on the pages as she turned them. She felt power here. Substantial and ancient. She'd fiddled with Elizabethan ciphers before. As an apprentice witch she'd passed notes to other witches, their true nature hidden behind replaced letters and numbers. The real genius, of course, of an Elizabethan cipher was that it still had to make sense to better hide what it contained.

With the Wild Hunt once again returned to England and the

Holly King successfully resurrected, it was likely that the spell that made that possible was hidden away in this nasty piece of work she now held in her hands.

Knowing the spell would allow her to unmake it.

The question was, did she really want to unmake it? If King Arthur had indeed returned, did she want him there?

She wasn't sure what she wanted, nor would she be until she determined exactly what the reasoning was for bringing back the Hunt. Until then, she'd work on breaking the code and search the remainder of the warlock's materials for a link to the Red Grove.

CHAPTER 21

C-I7 GLOBEMASTER III. ST. JOHN'S, NEWFOUNDLAND. NIGHT.

SEAL Team 666, Genie, a tied-up Van Dyke, and three crew chiefs stared wearily into the brightening day outside the windows of the giant plane. They'd had to stop for refueling and were ready to get to their destination. When the plane took to the air once more, everyone found a comfortable position to rack out except YaYa. The constant tingling in his body because of the presence of the spirit inside Van Dyke was a constant reminder of the *obour*.

He'd never considered that a forest could be haunted before. He'd always attributed ghosts to places like houses or graveyards. But it made sense. The world was covered with more open space than not. It was just his bad luck to run into one during his first mission in the forests of Myanmar.

It had started with the feeling of being watched. At first it had been an anomalous idea of something tracking him. But when he'd stop, look, and see nothing, instead of the feeling going away it stayed with him. Then it evolved into a certain curiosity. He felt the strange attention, whatever it was, try to understand him; just as he might watch an insect pick a path from one tree to the other along the forest floor, so did this thing do to him as it watched him make his way through the forest.

At one point the idea of *twelve* came to him. It began with just the idea of the number. *Twelve. Twelve. Twelve.* But then it became more, once he exhibited a curiosity about the number. Then he had the idea of *twelve eyes. Twelve eyes* watching him. At the moment of that thought, he remembered vividly halting in the middle of a copse of giant trees of Myanmar. He spun in the silent forest until he spied six birds sitting on a branch of a tree. The birds' bodies faced the same way, their heads were turned the same way, and they watched him from pairs of inscrutable black eyes. He moved away from the birds and felt the weight of their stare. He moved left, then right, but each time the birds moved their heads in unison, tracking him as if they were mere appendages of one larger will.

As he expressed his curiosity about it, it in turn expressed an uncertainty to him. It wanted to know more about him and in turn he wanted to know more about it. He wanted to understand what it was he felt and how he was able to detect something he didn't see.

Then he'd lost time. He next remembered his body aching. The light was different. The entire feel of the forest had changed. He hadn't known it then, but it was because he'd let the creature come into him.

YaYa ran his remaining hand along the mechanism the experts had made for him. Produced by DEKA Research and Development Corporation in cooperation with the Defense Advanced Research Projects Agency, the prosthetic came in two models: one that could pass for a human arm and one that appeared to be half-human and half-cybernetic. He'd chosen the latter, not only because it was stronger but also because its falseness would serve as a reminder of his utter stupidity. Controlled with the help of neurotransmitters implanted into his brain, it was near perfect except for the fact that it wasn't his own.

His thoughts drifted to Walker. Among anyone he knew,

Walker would be the one to best relate since he'd been possessed before as well. YaYa hoped to be able to talk about it but also realized that the SEAL was in mourning. God knew the last thing YaYa wanted to do was to pour on the misery. He'd have to find the right time to bring it up, if at all.

He finally fell asleep staring at Van Dyke. He dreamed of a single crow on a battlefield staring at him with twelve eyes.

CHAPTER 22

CHICKSANDS RAF. MORNING.

Walker stepped into the lounge and thanked God there was coffee. He poured himself a cup, then turned, leaning against the counter, looking at Trevor.

"Sir Robert called you a psychopath."

Trev and Preeti glanced up from eating breakfast at the table. Trev gave him a look. "Good morning to you, Walker."

Preeti frowned. "Can't this wait?"

Walker cursed himself. Ever the bull in the china shop. He began to apologize, but Trev stopped him with a chop of his hand. "You really want to know, then all you have to do is ask."

Walker glanced from man to woman, then shrugged. "Okay, I'm asking."

Trev put down his utensils, took a sip of his coffee, and wiped the side of his mouth. He glanced once at Preeti, who wasn't returning his gaze, then stared openly at Walker. "I beat seven men so bad they were hospitalized for weeks. One of them died. It was very public, it was caught on video, and it almost ended my military career. If it hadn't been for Ian, I'd have been pulling guard duty in some inhospitable place far from everything and everyone I know and love."

Walker blinked. Trev hadn't said how he'd done it, but to imagine putting seven men in the hospital was enough to shock. Physically the man didn't look capable, but then again, Walker had been surprised by what a person who knew how to carry himself could do.

Preeti looked up from her plate. "Trev never likes to talk about it." She glanced at her boyfriend and squeezed his hand. He turned away and stared at the floor. "Do you know what hooligans are, Walker?"

"Soccer fans who get too rowdy."

"Rowdy." Trev laughed. "That's rich."

She patted him on the arm. "Perhaps that's a bit of an understatement, Walker. Hooligans are more than rowdy. It's a way of life to many of them. They want to hurt. They want to break. And in many ways, they want to kill and all in the name of fandom. Long story short, a brother and sister were at a Man U–Arsenal match and ran into a hooligan firm known as the Magogs. Because this brother and sister weren't white, they were separated from the crowd. The brother was curb stomped. Know what that is?"

Walker gulped. He nodded, searching Trev's implacable face. Walker had seen *American History X* and had shuddered when Edward Norton's character had made the black man open his jaw and place it on the curb. When Norton's character had then stomped on the back of the man's head, driving the jawbone into the curb and forcing it to break wide open, Walker had turned away, unable to watch the remainder of the film.

"They broke his jaw in three places and eleven teeth. He still can't talk normally and can't function. Crowds terrify him."

"What happened to the girl?"

"They took baseball bats to her. Broke her legs and her arms. They were getting ready to curb stomp her too when Trev came upon them."

"Everyone was just watching." Trev's voice was low and angry as he took up the story. "If even half of the people watching had jumped in, this wouldn't have happened. I don't get why people watch and don't do anything when shit like this happens." He wiped his eyes with the back of his hands. "Anyway, I just sort of snapped. How these hooligans could do what they were doing was beyond me, but if they wanted to play war, then I was willing to bring it to them."

"He surged into them like a storm, screaming at them the entire time. Then he took one of their bats and used it on them."

"They didn't know how to use it right. I showed them."

Walker's eyes widened as he stared at Preeti's crutches leaning against the side of the table. "You were the girl."

She smiled weakly and hugged Trev's arm. "My hero."

"So the crutches . . ." Walker felt his heart break a little for what had happened to this sweet young Indian girl. "I'm sorry, Preeti, I—"

"Some good came from it." Her smile was incandescent as she stared at Trev. "I met this man."

"Yeah, well, we could have found a better way to meet." He stared at her legs under the table, then looked up. "I rang up Jerry's mum. Ian told her last afternoon. I thought she'd like to know about her boy."

Walker pulled out a chair and sat at the table. "I know how that feels."

Preeti put her hand on Walker's hand that rested on the table, holding the coffee cup. "You must miss her terribly."

"Every waking minute. Thank god for the mission." He looked at Trev. "What did his mom say?"

"It's 'mum,' and she said to find them, break off their legs, and beat them over their heads with them. She went on to describe some further unholy things to do with the human body. Basically, she wants revenge and then she wants me to come back and tell her about it."

"Some lady."

"Ain't no lady there. She hawks beer in Leeds. Probably tougher than any two of us."

"Just the same."

Ian suddenly banged into the room carrying a tablet. "You're not going to believe this." He jerked out a chair and slammed down into it. He put the tablet flat on the table and touched the still image of a female reporter. While the video buffered, he said, "Lord Robinson called and asked me about this." He scoffed. "Like we have any control over this."

The tablet sprang to life as the clip ran. "This is Jonathan Fitzhugh, groundskeeper at Chipping Sodbury Golf Club, who is able to shed some light on the disappearance of Nisam Kazmi and three other men yesterday morning." The screen switched to the figure of a tall, slim-shouldered, bulging-bellied sixty-something with a gin-fueled nose the size of a Christmas bulb, then back to the perky British blonde. "There are growing reports of the strange events occurring throughout England. Chipping Sodbury could be just another in what may be a slew of attacks."

Cut to Fitzhugh. "They was coming out of the fog. I don't bloody well know what they was, but they looked like dogs but with faces. They was all snarling and eating the golfers. . . ."

The four watched with stunned looks as the man described the eating of the Pakistani businessman and his foursome.

". . . then some hooligans came and stole their clubs. I'd run up to the office to report this and when I came back it was as if they'd never even existed. No bodies. No blood. No fucking clubs. Turns out they found the bodies way down on the twelfth hole. Must have been dragged there."

The video cut to a view of a fog-shrouded golf course as the reporter began to give the history of the place.

Trev barked a laugh. "How can anyone be sure he saw anything? He looks like a professional rummy."

"Drunk or not, we know this is accurate. Preeti already tracked suspicious disturbances at Chipping Sodbury, probably due to his call to the police. Now the description combined with the linking of the other events . . ." Ian shook his head. "Lord Robinson is furious."

Trev pointed at the tablet, which once again had the image of the groundskeeper who was making claws with his hands as he described the way the monsters attacked. "I bet he pawned the clubs."

Ian twisted around. "Who the fuck cares what he pawned? We need to get a handle on this." He got up and slammed across the room and through the door.

No one spoke for a moment.

Walker hadn't seen the man this angry, but then again, a lot had gone on in the past several days. This could be the proverbial straw that broke the camel's back.

Walker regarded Trev and Preeti. "What kind of station is this anyway? Does anyone actually watch this sort of shit?"

"It's sensational, yes, but that's England. We don't care about stodgy BBC news, not at least until we're in our forties. We want to know about Beckham. We want to know about musicians. And monsters—hell, if you can give us monsters too, then it's aces ratings."

Trev added, "This is Channel Nine. Everyone watches it, including my *grandmum*. She's probably calling her local MP, then on to her parish priest, wanting to know what they're going to do to keep the monsters out of her kitchen." Trev shook his head. "No. This is serious. Ian's right to be worried. Everyone's going to be worried."

"Perhaps that's what they want," said the witch, coming into the room. "Don't forget, the Hunt isn't only recruiting souls; it's also advertising and marshaling fear."

"Then news coverage is the last thing we need," Walker said.

The witch drank from a bottle of water and shrugged.

Walker stared at the face of the rummy groundskeeper. If this were America, it would be on every station by now. What would something like this do? Alone, probably nothing. But if there were more reports.

Then that would definitely be bad.

CHAPTER 23

BLACKPOOL, ENGLAND. MORNING.

Justin Nguyen rushed back to the tent, eager to show his family the score he'd made. He'd spent the last several weeks volunteering to clean up at Swansea Bakery. He'd helped shut the place down and had swept and mopped, backbreaking work, never asking for anything in return. This was his father's code and to violate it would be to dishonor the memory of the great man. So Justin had suffered on, hoping for some meager reward. And now he had it.

He entered Kingscote Park at a run, weaving past the protestors who carried signs that said things like "Leave Our Land," "Go Back to Vietnam," and less savory things. They were just getting there and hadn't yet rallied their voices into their usual hateful roar. As he passed, they shouted halfheartedly, then returned to their cliques, drinking steaming coffee and tea, grumbling and mean.

Once into the park, he was safe. Police monitored the CCTV cameras and had been making arrests of anyone who attempted to harm the temporary refugee camp put in place after the cargo ship they'd booked passage on crashed on the rocks in the Irish Sea. Half of the passengers had been deported immediately, but those who had relatives who were British citizens were allowed to stay until their status was legally determined.

Thanks to an MP friendly to the Vietnamese community, they were given temporary sanctuary, provided military tents and furniture, and fed three times a day, although the rationing of the food still left many of them hungry.

Which was where Justin came in.

He burst into his family's tent. His two sisters and mother were gathered around the card table on which a heater stood, lava-red filaments radiating heat into the space.

"Mẹ, nhìn kìa!" *Mother, look!* "Tôi có bánh mì và bánh sừng bò!" *I have bread and croissants.*

He placed the paper bag he'd been clutching in front of her and beamed as she opened it. The Army rations they'd been eating were heavy with beef and pork, neither of which his mother's digestive system could tolerate. Not only had Mr. Evans given him a helping of day-old bread, but he'd also provided Justin with fresh croissants. His mother selected one. When she touched it her face lit with a smile, which meant that he'd run fast enough that they were still warm.

"Eat, Mother. Eat, and enjoy. This is just the beginning."

She nibbled at an end and nodded to her daughters to take some as well. Soon the entire Nguyen family was sitting around the table, basking in the heat, eating the warm bread. It was almost as if things were normal.

This new normal lasted exactly forty-seven seconds until someone screamed outside.

Justin shot to his feet and moved so his body was between the tent flap and his mother.

"What is it?"

"I don't know, Mother." He took a tentative step toward the flap but stopped when several more screams sounded. He glanced back at the fearful looks on his family's faces and knew that he wore his own version.

Suddenly a sound like a freight train descended upon them, so loud his sisters clapped their hands over their ears.

Justin felt compelled to investigate. He felt his mother's hand on his arm but shook it off. He stepped to the entrance and opened the tent flap.

Indistinguishable figures hurtled by the entrance at breakneck speeds. Now everyone in the camp was screaming. The tent was ripped from its moorings and flew to the right. A tent pole struck him in his head, sending him to a knee as he fought the starry pain. With his eyes closed because of the dust and wind, he turned and crawled to his mother. He felt around, but she wasn't there.

He opened his eyes to the maelstrom.

Gone was the table.

Gone was the heater.

Gone was the tent.

Gone were his mother and sisters.

He surged to his feet and screamed their names. Looking around, he saw that the land had been cleared of all the tents. Several people lay on the ground. The protestors were fleeing. Where their signs had been dropped, one picket could be seen impaled in an older man Justin only knew as Pham.

Justin searched for his family, but his eyes were drawn toward the dogs who began to turn toward him. Realizing he was the only person left standing in the encampment, he started to back away.

Something growled behind him.

He whirled.

Then the growling grew as the beasts that surrounded him began to stalk toward him.

His mind sought to flee where his body was unable. What was this? Was it a nightmare? If so, he desperately wanted to wake—

They lunged in pairs, grabbing his legs, ripping, tearing, raking teeth along the edges of his femurs. Another beast grabbed his head. He felt a tremendous pressure. His eyes bulged from his face. Somehow, his gaze locked in on a young woman across the street, red hair, white dress, taking picture after picture with an old Polaroid camera.

Then came a pop.

He didn't know how he knew, but he knew that he was dead. For one second he saw everything, knew everything, and understood exactly why he'd been murdered. But then it was sucked away from him and, as if he lived on the end of a whip, he snapped back into an existence he knew all too well.

He ran with the others.

He bayed.

And then came the King.

CHAPTER 24

CHICKSANDS RAF, ENGLAND. MORNING.

Everyone from Section 9 including Sassy Moore stood inside the hangar watching the gargantuan plane pull forward. Although the Royal Air Force had C-17s in their inventory, there weren't many of them. The Globemaster was the sort of plane that looked like it ate smaller ones. Preeti, Trev, and Sassy, on the one hand, stared at it in wonder. Ian, on the other hand, projected the same bored confidence he'd had when fighting the homunculi.

The hangar was a new addition to Section 9 office space. Thanks to a phone call from Lord Robinson, space which hadn't been available to the diminishing equities of England's premier supernatural defense force suddenly appeared. A hangar that had been used for storage was quickly emptied. RAF airmen had then moved Section 9's paltry belongings out of the basement and into the twenty-five-by-twenty-five-meter space. With two offices situated at the rear of the hangar, one was cleared for Sassy and Preeti to stay in for the duration of the emergency and the other was reinforced to hold a prisoner SEAL Team 666 had said they were bringing. The rest of them, SEAL Team 666 included, would sleep on cots in a common area created on the hangar's left side. The right side had been set up with their communications suite, computer systems, a projector that blasted a map on a white screen, and several tables and chairs.

Walker stood at the front of the group waiting outside the hangar. For all the welcome he'd had from Section 9, SEAL Team 666 was his unit and the team members were closer to him than anyone else. Where he'd once set his life against the image of his dead brother, now he had living, breathing replacements against which to measure himself. He remembered the grudge he'd held against Holmes, who'd been in charge of the SEAL team when his brother had died in a roadside bombing. Then after Holmes had relayed the classified details of his brother's death, his feelings had all but evaporated.

Holmes could have no more influenced the way Walker's brother lived and died than he could Walker. Although Walker and his brother were SEALs through and through, their inner cores had been forged long before. Their ideas of right and wrong, their need to be heroic, their desire to make the world a better place, had been engineered within them on a genetic level.

The bottom line was that his brother had died saving children. Some called his actions stupid. Some called his death a waste. But Walker knew that his brother would have done it again given the chance.

Laws had explained it well. "Sometimes the death doesn't mean anything except in context for the living. I think your brother's death can help you understand the man. I didn't know him, but I know people who did and they all say he was a great SEAL and a terrific guy. He was a shepherd without a flock. I think he punished himself for not being able to take care of you and sought out avenues where he could take care of others."

Walker almost laughed. He could absolutely relate. He flashed to Jen, realizing that he'd been feeling his own guilt, wondering if things would have been different had he been there. He struggled to shake the idea free. It was drama. She was gone. The only thing he could do now was stop the thing that killed her and find a way to release her soul, if what the witch said was true. That was his single focus. Blame could wait, if it was ever levied at all.

The Globemaster came to a halt. Aircrew from the RAF ran up and chocked the wheels. Then the rear ramp descended. First out was a pearl-white Cadillac Escalade with smoked-out windows. An unfamiliar man sat behind the wheel. He pulled the car down the ramp.

Behind him came the SEALs, each carrying several go bags.

Holmes, Laws, YaYa, and Yank.

Walker felt elation shoot through him. These were his boys.

When they got closer, he started toward them. He grinned but kept his head down. The closer he got to them, the more full the feeling was in his chest. They dropped their bags and, as one, embraced him. He felt the dam burst and he began to sob. They surrounded him, protecting him, keeping the world at bay, so he could mourn in the comfort of his company of friends.

Ten minutes later, after introductions, Holmes had Genie bring out Van Dyke. The man's wrists and ankles had been zip-tied, but as Van Dyke stood him on the tarmac Genie cut the zip ties on his ankles.

Van Dyke stretched his legs, limping slightly from a bandaged gunshot wound. As disheveled as he was, he carried himself with a certain elegance. With his chin up and his eyes staring straight, he let Genie march him into the hangar. He sat in a chair that had been set up in front of the others. Genie zip-tied his feet to the chair's front legs, then stood and backed away. YaYa handed him an HK416. He took it and held it ready.

Holmes and Ian had the floor. They bade everyone have a seat.

Sassy refused. Instead, she pointed at Van Dyke. "Do you even know what you have here?"

Walker watched as Holmes appraised her. The SEAL team leader knew she was a witch. Walker had relayed every aspect of their interactions. That said, he was curious how Holmes would deal with her.

"We're hoping you can help with that, Ms. Sassy."

Walker grinned, knowing it was an intentional error. Holmes, however, stood straight-faced.

"Sassy is my first name."

"Of course it is. What was your question, ma'am?"

She dropped her arm and gave Holmes a look. Then she turned and approached Van Dyke, her high heels clipping against the concrete floor. She began to circle him, her arms crossed, her face with an air of appraisal. She leaned in and sniffed, then made a face. She backed away and moved her fingers and hands over her face and chest, as if she were casting a spell. When she was done, she looked at Holmes.

"You say he was in America?"

Holmes nodded.

"Was he being kept prisoner by any chance?"

"How'd you know?" Laws stepped forward carrying a box, which he sat on one of the tables at the front of the room.

"Not that I've ever seen one before, but they'd be able to escape given a chance." She concentrated on Van Dyke, who'd been watching her the entire time, his face shifting back and forth between interest and fear. "You have a tattoo?"

Van Dyke nodded and looked pointedly to his left breast.

She waved a hand at the area. "Can someone please remove his shirt?"

Laws came over and ripped the buttons free of the shirt, revealing three interconnected crescent moons.

The witch hissed. She held her hand out toward the tattoo and it glowed gold. Then she spun. "How in the seven bloody hells did someone get a Tuatha Dé Dannan inside this man?"

Laws walked over to Yank, who pulled out a twenty-dollar bill and passed it over.

"I told you she'd know," Laws said.

Yank looked anything but pleased.

Sassy suddenly looked concerned. "You knew what it was and you brought it here?"

"Here's our thinking." Holmes moved to the front of the room and opened the box. He was the only one in position to see inside it. He glanced in, then turned to Sassy Moore. "Hubert Van Dyke is on the board of the Red Grove. A money trail can be traced from the group of druids who usually perform the Winter Solstice ceremony at Stonehenge to the Red Grove. Mr. Van Dyke also sits on the board of the Bohemian Grove, which has long been rumored to be a place where rich men go to get even richer. When we went to see him, we found in his employ a golem, which was not only acting as his housekeeper but was also guarding him."

Holmes tipped the box so the golem's head rolled out.

Preeti screamed as the face of the woman blinked and snarled.

"Hubert, who seems to be possessed by a Tuatha Dé Dannan, and the undead head of the golem seem to be our only clues. We felt it was important to bring them along so that experts might be able to examine them." He turned to look around the room. "You, Ms. Moore, seem to be our only expert."

Her eyes were fixed on the head. "You can call me Sassy."

Holmes raised an eyebrow. "Indeed."

She stepped over to the table and picked up a pen. Then she poked the head. It blinked and looked at her. "You going to tell me who made you?"

"Fuck off," said the head.

Sassy grinned. "This is going to be fun." She pointed at Van Dyke. "That, on the other hand, is going to get us in a load of trouble. I wished you had told me you were bringing one of the Sidhe here. I would have warded the place even more. Everything supernatural, including the Wild Hunt, knows that a Sidhe is out in the open. She will draw them to us." She poked the head in the eye with the pen and sighed. "So now I'm going to have to spend the day warding the entire hangar." She put her hands on her hips and glanced around. "And it's a bloody big hangar."

CHAPTER 25

CHICKSANDS RAF, ENGLAND. AFTERNOON.

As it turned out, she didn't need to ward the entire hangar. Just the room they were using as Van Dyke's cell and a pentacle she placed in a cleared space at the front of the room, beside the worktables that had been set up for her use. The golem head sat in a smaller pentacle surrounded by salt. It looked none too happy but couldn't do anything about it.

The SEALs integrated themselves into Section 9 and were data mining. One set was to determine all the known mounds in England, trying to create an overlay they could use to predict the Wild Hunt's next move. They were also still searching for CCTV disturbances. Finally, Laws was conducting an Internet search for any and all artifacts linked to the Tuatha Dé Dannan.

Walker had just come from the bathroom when YaYa approached him.

"Walk, can I speak with you?"

"You don't have to ask, YaYa."

The Arab-American smiled weakly. "Let's get some air."

Walker glanced at the others who were hard at work, then at

YaYa. Something was bothering the man. Even if they didn't have the time, Walker didn't think they could afford not to have the time. The last thing they needed was for one of them to lose concentration in the middle of the action.

He and YaYa exited the hangar together. They left the flight line and found a path that led through a manicured lawn to a five-story chain-link fence. Like military men the world around, they soon found themselves in step with each other.

Finally it was YaYa who spoke. "Do you ever get used to it?"

Walker smiled easily. "Not sure I know what you mean?"

"That supernatural, early-warning radar you have."

Walker flashed back to when he was a child, locked in a closet and possessed by the Malaysian grave demon. "It comes with a price."

"Don't I know it!"

Walker stopped and turned to YaYa. "Are you kidding?"

"I wish." He related to Walker what happened when they went to get Van Dyke. "It froze me. It was as if the thing inside of Van Dyke reached inside me and turned off a switch."

Walker shook his head. "It's not like that. I know what you think you felt, but that isn't it."

"Are you sure?"

They resumed walking. "Absolutely. This is just new to you, man. For a long time it was new to me because I refused to deal with it. But you have the opportunity to hone it. To refine it and use it as a tool."

"You don't get it, Walker. I don't want any part of it. Every time it happens I remember who I was and how that demon got into me and wouldn't come out." He held up his left arm. "I cut off my own arm just to try and kill it. To have even a shadow of a memory come back is . . . I just don't want it."

"I'm with you. But there's no going back. It happened. You can either deal with it or crawl under your covers, suck your thumb, and never come out." He put a hand on YaYa's shoulder. "But then you knew that, didn't you?"

He sighed. "I guess I just needed to talk about it."

The path ended at the chain-link fence. On the other side was an antenna farm—hundreds of different antennae, all shapes and sizes, as if they'd grown from the loamy earth. The two men stared for a moment; then Walker turned to YaYa.

"I have an idea." He grinned as he took off running back to the hangar. When YaYa caught up with Walker, he added, "If it works, we might be able to get to the Red Grove faster than we thought."

They ran the rest of the way back. When Walker entered the hangar he was ready to tell Laws and Holmes his idea, but he never got the chance. Everyone's eyes were focused on the multiple flatscreens they'd affixed to one wall. Each screen showed a different variation of the same story.

A refugee encampment in Blackpool was overrun by monsters. The CCTV cameras failed to capture any of them, but someone uploaded some camera shots containing some stunning, unforgettable images.

YaYa pointed to an image. "What are those?"

"Hounds from the Wild Hunt. Created from the souls of those who have been culled, molded into something unstoppable, something that makes the bogeyman look like the Easter bunny."

A Frankenstein combination of man and beast, the beasts had human arms for their front legs, and the back legs of a wolf. Their faces were an amalgam, but the eyes that were set in a simian face were unmistakably human.

One screen displayed shots of a man being torn apart, a great hound chewing through his head as it stared into the camera.

On another, a set of hounds were disemboweling a downed man.

Another, a hound was dragging a child away by its neck.

And then yet another showed a side shot of a hound, its neck craning to look at the camera lens, stare right into it. The full shot provided exquisite detail of the mythological beast.

Walker choked back a sob. "Jen."

It was in the eyes. She'd always had a sadness about her. She'd called it her old melancholy. He saw it there in the eyes. The human eyes. The eyes of his dead fiancée.

CHAPTER 26

CHICKSANDS RAF, ENGLAND. AFTERNOON.

Phones began ringing. Not just those belonging to Section 9 but also those carried by Triple Six. Everyone began shouting into a telephone. Pandemonium existed for twenty seconds; then they all hung up at roughly the same time.

Even as Ian addressed the group, the TV screens went blank. "That was the Home Office. They've declared a national emergency. They're pulling all the footage and banning further broadcasts of any nature relating to it."

"They can do that?" Yank asked.

Ian gestured at the screen, which went blank. "Just did."

Preeti hung up another phone. "My brother's been asked to monitor the Internet. He's been given superuser privileges. If anyone tries to post anything, he's authorized to remove it."

"Same thing in the United States." Holmes pocketed his phone. "The networks were set to run this. Senator Withers got the president to sign an emergency declaration. Last thing they need is to scare the average citizen. Better to think such things are sci-fi TV fodder than know that they really exist."

"Even my mother called," Trevor said, holding up his phone. "She was alerting me to the possible dangers of the Wild Hunt."

Sassy Moore shook her head, a grim, knowing smile on her face. "I mentioned this before. It's fear. They need it. The Wild Hunt grows more powerful because of it. Back before television, before cell phones, before the Internet, mothers told their children stories which scared them. It's this sort of fear they're trying to cultivate."

"They're not going to like that we're blocking this, then," Laws said.

"Shit's fucking scary." Yank shook his head. "Television or no television, people are going to be talking about it. That it's no longer available for viewing is going to give it more power. Trust me. I've lived this sort of thing in Los Angeles. Rumor and gossip can be hells more powerful than fact."

"Even if it's not on British or American television, it's going to come out," YaYa said. "Something like this is too big to keep secret."

"Yeah, but when it comes out, it can be discredited," Laws said. "Look at UFOs. It's to the point where national media covers strange-looking lights in the sky and no one gives it a second thought."

Trevor stepped forward. "Wait a minute. Are you admitting that UFOs are real? That America is covering it up?"

Laws laughed. "See what I mean? The idea is already there even if I don't say anything." He turned to Sassy. "What we need is a way to get the Red Grove to come to us. If we could find them, it would go a long way to helping us stop the Hunt."

Walker cleared his throat. "I think I have an idea."

All eyes turned to him. Preeti saw the naked emotion on his face and made to move toward him, but Trevor held on to her and shook his head.

"Listen, the faster we can get this over, the faster I can make those bastards pay." A lone tear rolled down his cheek. "Not just for Jen, but for all these others."

"That's what we want too, son." Holmes stood motionless, but his words had a calming effect. "What's your idea?"

Walker closed his eyes and remembered how he liked to watch her—the tilt of her head, the pursing of the lips. "It came to me when YaYa and I were outside. There's an antenna farm about a kilometer from here."

"It's an old antenna farm," Ian said. "Hasn't been used for years, but no one wants to take it down."

Walker opened his eyes and smiled grimly. "It's not the place; it's the idea. What if we lay a trap? After all, we do have the bait."

Laws stroked his chin. "It would have to be somewhere defensible."

"More than defensible. It would need to be a place where the Hunt couldn't go."

Sassy shook her head. "They can go anywhere."

YaYa looked at her. "Not inside."

She laughed. "They ripped my house down around me."

"Then something a little more permanent," Walker said.

"What about the National History Museum?" Sassy offered.

Laws snapped his fingers. "I love it."

Yank narrowed his eyes. "The Smithsonian?"

"Did your mother drop you as a child? Not the Smithsonian. That's in America. We're in England, McFly." Laws shook his head but kept his ever-present smile plastered on his mug. He turned to Ian. "I saw a special about the basement storage rooms at your National History Museum and how they're discovering things that were right under their nose."

"Spinops," Preeti said. "They discovered a new species of dinosaur they'd had for a hundred years."

"That's it. The museum is perfect. It's a public place, built like a castle, and the logical place for us to store something like a golem head."

Holmes stared at Sassy. "Think they'd go for it?"

"Who they? The Grove or the Hunt?" Walker asked.

Holmes shrugged. "Does it matter?"

The witch nodded slowly. "At the very least, it would get their attention. If I were them, I'd be concerned that their Sidhe has returned to England. It's much more powerful here. If loosed, it might just make it a point to do something to the Red Grove for keeping it away for so long."

"Perhaps we can use the Sidhe, then," Ian said.

Holmes nodded. "Perhaps. But for now, we're going to see if we can't get one of the grove members to pop their heads up so we can play Whac-A-Mole. Everyone get their gear ready. Ian and I are going to plan this."

The teams began to move, but Preeti made them pause. "One thing that's been bothering me." Everyone stopped to stare at her and she blushed. She pressed a few keys to show the pictures from Blackpool. "These aren't digital. They're scans. See these edges?" She pointed to a white border around the images that was larger at the bottom than at the top. "These have to be Polaroids. Who uses Polaroids anymore?"

Laws and Holmes stared at each other. "No one," they said simultaneously.

"So if no one uses them, then how is it that someone was using one at the scene of the last attack?" Preeti shrugged. "An attack that disrupted all the electronic image-capturing devices. Just asking."

Ian put a hand on her shoulder. "Smart girl. You caught what everyone else missed. It could be nothing; then again she could have been put there to get pictures."

Laws nodded slowly. "CCTV broadcasts were disrupted, but not still photography. Then again, no one really uses still photography anymore. It's all digital. From our cell phones to top-of-the-line Nikons. That's something to remember."

"So if she was placed there, then she must be a part of the Red Grove." Yank grinned as he looked at Laws. "Not bad for Marty McFly."

Holmes held out his hand. "Everyone slow your roll. We're piling on supposition and calling it fact because it's so thick. Let's work on the hypothesis that this was just a girl with a Polaroid camera until we can prove it."

"You're right, of course," Ian said. "Preeti, see what you can come up with. She had to have signed a release or something for the pictures to be put online."

CHAPTER 27

CHICKSANDS RAF, ENGLAND. NIGHT.

Preeti knew what she was going to do even before she sat down at her workstation. She'd waited until the team left, assisting them where she could. She provided the SEALs with digital schematics of the museum and basement. Their integrated electronics suites were incredible. It was a testament both to how well-funded the American military machine was and to how impoverished Britain's had become.

They left her alone with only the tall Navy man to keep her company. Of course, he was really there to guard the prisoner, but she'd at least been able to pry a little out of him about his past. The cultural and emotional makeup of military men interested her no end. Before she'd met Trevor, she'd had her own ideas, shared by most of the public, that the people who ended up in the military were those who couldn't do anything else.

Trevor had joined because his family had a tradition of service going back hundreds of years. Walker had joined to be like his brother.

Genaro Stewart, she now learned, had joined because it was the only way he'd be able to afford college. His intention was to stay in long enough to have his loans paid off, then get out, but he'd ended up liking the service more than any possibility higher education could unleash.

They all had reasons for serving. She'd originally joined to help out Trevor, to show her appreciation for what he'd done for her and her brother. But that had quickly changed as she came to learn that she enjoyed doing something that made an impact greater than she could alone. What she was doing had an effect on everyone in her beloved country. And to think she never would have discovered any of this had the hooligans not decided to target her and her brother.

Her brother had provided her a log-in screen behind his firewall. It gave her similar superuser privileges. While he was busy trashing links his algorithms found, she'd do a little detective work. She went straight to the CCTV database. Although the Blackpool cameras had been interrupted during the attack, they wouldn't show any problems prior to the attack. For the woman to have been in place to take pictures at the right time, she would have had to have been there previously.

Preeti spent an hour cycling through Blackpool images before she found her. Wearing a white dress and with blond hair, the woman behaved as if she knew she was being filmed. She kept her face down and away from every camera she came near. Preeti didn't have enough to run face recognition. But she had a better idea.

She walked the woman to the point at which the CCTV cameras were interrupted. She already had her camera out and ready, possible proof of Preeti's theory. When the cameras started working again Preeti was able to find and follow her from camera to camera until she got in a vehicle. The first was a municipal bus, which took the woman to a bus stop on Church Street. The woman got off, waited for ten minutes, walked west for three blocks, then boarded another bus, which backtracked to Devonshire Square. Then she took yet another bus, this one all the way to Blackpool North Railway Station, where she got out and went inside.

Preeti sat back. This next step was a problem. She spent the next twenty minutes hacking into the British Transport Police servers, which got her access to the cameras inside the terminal. She was able to view live feeds but couldn't find any stored feeds. After another twenty minutes she found out where they were supposed to have been.

Someone had gotten there first.

"Bastard."

Preeti could always check the train schedule, but without a clear biometrically capable shot of the woman's face it would mean nothing.

She rattled her fingers on the desk for a moment. Had she missed something?

Of course she had!

She checked the footage from inside the buses. She got access to the cameras and found where the files should have been stored.

Again. "Double bastard!"

Someone was covering their tracks quickly.

She needed to hurry.

Then she had a brainchild!

She went back along the woman's route of travel and marked the location of each ATM and found one at Grosvenor Convenience Store that had the perfect angle. It took her a few moments to hack into it; then she was able to back through the photos taken during transactions.

And there it was.

Or at least, there half of it was. She had the upper half of the woman's face, seen over the shoulder of a haggard-looking man withdrawing money. The rest of the pictures had buses or taxis in them.

Then she zoomed into one of the faces in a bus window in another photo. The route of travel from Devonshire Square to Blackpool North had brought the blonde back by the ATM for the second time. The woman was good, but she wasn't as good as Preeti.

There, in the window of the bus, she could make out a full side shot of the woman's face, even as she kept her head tilted forward so she could hide from the camera in the front of the bus.

Preeti collected the image, cleaned it in Photoshop, then uploaded it to her biometrics program. Then she set it to search. It could take a minute, or a day, or a month, or forever. At the very least, her program would scour the system for matching faces in both real time and storage. Her guess was that the woman—or an associate—had gone in and removed evidence of her in storage, so it would have to be in real time.

She stood and stretched. She went over to the fridge and grabbed a can of Coke. Genie sat at a nearby table watching a TV episode on his laptop.

"Want one?" she asked.

He did. She gave him one, then sat next to him, watching the episode run on the screen. She had no idea what it was, but it looked like nerds sitting in a living room singing songs.

"Want to hear?" He pulled out one of his earbuds.

"No. Just trying to clear my head."

"This shit will do it." He angled his head toward the back room. "Anything to keep from thinking about that back there."

"He just looks like an old man to me."

"Whatever that is inside him was out for a while back at Van Dyke's house. I saw it. It looked like a stick man, walking in the shadows of his house. One minute it was there; the next it was a pile of sticks." He shuddered. "Some things you just can't unsee."

He put his earbud back in and resumed watching the show.

Preeti sat there as long as it took to finish the soda. Then she got up, tossed the can in the garbage, and went to the restroom. By the time she came out, an alert on her screen was blinking.

Stewart stood beside it. When she came up behind, he said, "I wasn't sure if there was anything I should be doing." He pointed to the screen, which showed a live image of a woman in a long coat who was walking down a city street. "Is that her?"

"Absolutely. Where'd she come from?"

He pointed to a car pulling away from the curb. "That one."

Preeti copied down the plate number, then input it into another program, this one assigned to the National Automated Number Plate Recognition Data Center. She set her program to automate, then returned to looking at the woman . . . the woman who had stopped and was staring into the camera at them.

"She's not looking at us," he whispered.

"I think she is."

The woman smiled and began to move her fingers and hands in a complex geometric pattern. The screen began to fuzz and pix-ilate.

Preeti felt fingers of worry dance along her back. She couldn't be sure, but it felt as if the woman was in her head with her. Something. A presence.

She jumped forward and shoved the monitor onto the floor, where it crashed, pieces of plastic and glass shooting out in all directions. Then she ripped the cord free from the wall, removing all power.

Stewart fell heavily into his seat. "What the hell was that?"

"I don't know, but now I'm scared."

"Just now you're scared?" Stewart grinned nervously. "This shit has been scaring me from the very beginning."

"Do you know what I wish?" she asked.

He regarded her.

"I wish that we weren't alone."

They both looked toward the giant closed door of the hangar and the small door set in it.

CHAPTER 28

NATURAL HISTORY MUSEUM, LONDON. AFTER MIDNIGHT.

They'd been in place for three hours and Yank's boredom meter was already pegged. They were on radio silence and no amount of imagination was going to help him pass the time. He hated waiting, which was one of the reasons he'd become a SEAL. Too many nights aboard ship pulling watch, staring at a display or out to sea, had been such a mind-numbingly brutal existence that he seriously had considered quitting the military and returning to Los Angeles.

And now, here he was waiting once more, pulling a sort of watch. The only thing good about it was that at the end of this he'd have a chance to shoot people. Maybe even kick them in the head a few times. He took a deep breath and reminded himself why they were here. It was like Holmes had said: *We don't really give a fuck about someone else's problems. We were formed to protect our country, to deal with her problems. But when someone else's problems become one of our problems, then we're all-in.*

All-in. Yank liked that.

Just as his adopted father, Uncle Joe, had been *all-in* for Yank.

Petty Officer Second Class Shonn Yankowski. That name really told his entire story. He could have chosen the name of his father, who'd ended doing life in Chino. Yank had never met the man but knew he was a thug for the 22nd Street Hustlers and part of the Bloods. His last name had been Johnson, but Yank had refused to take the name of a man he'd never met. He could have kept the name of his mother, who after spending his first six years clean and sober had broken down into the sorry caricature of an L.A. crack whore. Named Rennie Sabathia, his mother had called him Shonny, which went well with her last name. And he'd owned that name, right up until the day she'd died in the fire and he'd earned the burns on the side of his face trying to save her. At thirteen, he'd met Joseph Yankowski, recently transferred from Chicago to Los Angeles as part of the longshoremen's union. Uncle Joe, as Shonn learned to call him, ran a foster home in San Pedro, and Shonn soon found the first stable and safe place he'd ever known. Fostering turned to adoption, and by the time Shonn turned eighteen and made his desire known that he wanted to join the U.S. Navy he also had changed his name to Yankowski, out of respect and love for Uncle Joe—not really an uncle, not even a relative, but more of a father than he'd ever imagined having.

Holmes reminded him of Uncle Joe. They were both hard-ass, no-nonsense types, but you could tell that underneath it all they cared immensely about what they were doing.

Nothing at all like Laws. There were times that he loved working for the brainiac. But others, like when Laws made fun of him back in the hangar, he wanted nothing more than to haul off and slug the guy. Laws seemed to always be yanking his chain about something. While Yank appreciated humor as much as the next sailor, he didn't like it done at his expense.

He sighed.

He'd figure out how to handle Laws. The key was to keep his cool until he did so.

Yank checked the monitors through a toggle on his QUAD-EYE. They'd set up four cameras. Either they'd show when someone was coming or else the image would become distorted. Either way, they'd have some warning.

Holmes had sat him up in an alcove in the main hall. The gargantuan interior was like being in a domed football stadium, that is, if the stadium had marble steps, polished wood rails, wainscoting, and elevated ceilings with tray case paintings and skylights. It was beyond elegant. It was what the British called posh.

The night security lights created pools of luminosity through which a security guard moved along his normal route. He'd been told to ignore the SEALs and Section 9 members. Ian had shown the man a badge and said something about national security and it was all over. The guard had been relieved. He had thought they were there to pick him up because of his wife's overdrafts. That Triple Six didn't care made his day.

Yank shouldered his HK416 and plugged his QUADEYE into the rifle's scope. He zoomed in on the areas of the roof outside the skylights but couldn't detect any movement. If he had to bet, they'd come from that direction. It's where he would come from if he was infiltrating.

His MBITR crackled. "Ghost Four, this is Ghost One. Status? Over."

"Ghost One, this is Ghost Four. Nothing here."

Of course this all could be a crap shoot. The Red Grove might never show. No sooner did he think that then a shadow twisted on his periphery. He turned toward it but saw nothing. Just a wall with a bronze bust in front of it. Then he saw another shadow, this time to his left. But just as before, when he turned it was gone.

They called it ghosting. Seeing things that weren't there. He thought about calling Holmes but didn't want to be the one to sound a false alarm. He was literally just chasing shadows now and would only call if he had anything besides his own tired and inventive imagination.

Shadows twisted twice more in his peripheral vision. Both times nothing was there when he looked. He altered strategy and began staring straight ahead, counting on his peripheral vision to sort itself out. Then he saw them . . . actually saw them . . . shadows, crawling across the walls. Roughly humanoid in shape, they moved fast across the surface, like lizards.

He toggled his mike and was prepared to tell his team, when he felt cold.

Everything went black.

Then he was falling.

Holmes and Sassy Moore were in the sub-basement room called the cauldron. The head sat in the middle of a metal table, upon which a pentacle had been drawn in white chalk. A gag had been placed over the golem's mouth, but the eyes remained fixed on Sassy, as if she'd been chosen as the target of the monster's enmity. Other strange symbols adorned the points of the inverted star. Sassy had her eyes closed and was humming slightly off-key.

Holmes called for another report. All SEALs answered except Ghost Four. Holmes tried again, but still no response. He called the team net. "Ghost Four may be down. Prepare."

"Ghost One, this is Ghost Two," Laws said, keeping radio discipline despite the sudden jolt of concern in his voice. "I'm in the best position to check on Ghost Four."

"Negative, Ghost Two. We'll wait and see if it's not just radio issue."

"And if it's not?" Walker asked, unconcerned with net discipline.

"Then we'll know soon enough, Ghost Three."

Holmes was about to call for Yank again but stared at the head instead, which was now floating five inches above the table.

"Um, Miss Moore? Should the head be doing that?"

Her eyes snapped open. "Oh, hell." She closed her eyes again. This time her hum was louder but equally off-tune as the one before.

The head began to gently lower. But it never did get all the way back to the table. It hovered a mere inch above the surface for a moment, then began to rise again.

"Better try something different."

She opened her eyes, reached out, and grabbed the head. She

pressed it firmly back on the table in the center of the pentacle, then removed her hands. It stayed where it was this time.

"I thought that design meant other witches couldn't touch it."

"I thought so too. But there are so many arrayed against me."

"Will you be able to keep it down?"

"With any luck."

Holmes stared at the head as it stared at him. He called for Yank once more. Nothing.

"Are they close?" he asked the witch.

"Yes and no. I feel someone, somewhere near. But they're also all over the astral plane. I'm having trouble hiding."

"What happens if they find you?"

"If I can't get away or take them down, then I'm stuck there."

"Stuck as in—"

"Forever. Now hush, you big old SEAL, and let me concentrate."

Holmes keyed his mike. "Ghost Two, move out and track down Ghost Four. Report everything, over."

Laws keyed his mike twice, signaling affirmative.

Holmes leaned back against a file cabinet. He fought the feeling of helplessness that crawled on little monster feet into his thoughts. The head stared at him with laughing eyes.

Laws was three rooms over from the central hall. They'd placed him in the Ecology exhibit hall because of its proximity to the only two elevators and two sets of stairs capable of reaching the lower levels where the others were. The idea was not for him to engage any targets but to allow them to descend to where Walker, YaYa, Ian, and Trevor awaited.

But that was before Yank went silent.

Laws moved swiftly through the exhibit, keeping out of the center of the room. He left his QUADEYE off, using the ambient security light, which was enough for him to do pretty much anything but read. When he reached the doorway to the central hall, he took a quick look inside, then brought his head back. He didn't see anything.

He looked again, this time concentrating on the area where Yank was stationed.

Gone.

Where could he have gone?

Then Laws heard scuffling.

He spun around the corner, his sound-suppressed HK416 sunk into his shoulder and ready to fire. There, at the far end of the gallery, was a man being dragged by two immense dogs. Not just any man, but one clad in black with body armor.

Laws sprinted toward them. The immense dogs were the same he'd seen in the still photos the girl had provided to the media. On the screen they had looked strange, but in person they were truly disturbing, especially the reverse bending elbow of the too-human arms each beast had for its front legs.

Of more immediate concern was that Yank wasn't moving.

Laws opened fire, catching each hound with half a dozen rounds. He'd taken down chupacabra bigger than these things with less. For good measure, he unloaded the rest of the magazine into them.

They blinked at him, then dropped Yank and sprang toward him. He did the only thing he could think of—he ran. He took a dozen steps and leaped into the air, grabbing the rear right leg of the Apatosaurus skeleton that dominated the center of this part of the central hall. He pulled himself up frantically and found his perch on the skeleton's back before the creatures were able to follow.

One leaped and failed to find purchase, sliding back to the floor, falling on its back, then twisting to its feet.

The other, however, was able to hang on using the fingers of the human arms. It pulled itself up, where it found its balance on the Apatosaurus's back.

Laws backed away and began to climb the giant dinosaur's neck, using the vertebrae as stepping-stones. The display wasn't meant to hold a man, much less a mythical monster. It creaked and shifted. A low tremble went through the entire skeleton, but it seemed to hold. He climbed as high as the head; then there was nowhere else to climb.

The hound climbed unsteadily after him, using its fingers to pull and hold itself. It snapped twice at him, almost ripping through the fabric of his pants.

Laws let go of the neck and hung from the jawbone of the extinct herbivore. He glanced beneath him and saw the other hound pacing there, occasionally glancing up. Less than six feet away from him stood the other hound on the neck of the dinosaur. It appeared to be getting ready to leap. Or was it just balancing? Laws wasn't sure, but he was sure he'd ended up in the worst possible position.

Check that.

The creaking increased. Suddenly there was a great crack. One of the backbones fell to the floor.

Both Laws and the hound stared at it.

"Fetch the bone," he whispered. "Come on, doggy. Fetch."

Instead of complying, the hound growled.

"Ghost One, this is Ghost Two." Laws's words came between grunts of effort as he adjusted his slipping grip on the jaw. "We have two of the hounds here."

"What's the status of Ghost Four?"

Laws twisted his head to see where Yank was still lying in a heap. "Unclear."

"Why is it unclear?" Holmes paused. "What are you doing?"

Laws thought of saying something like *just hanging out,* but he wasn't feeling his inner Bruce Willis. Before Laws could respond a series of cracks shot through the great space. The neck of the dinosaur collapsed under his and the hound's combined weight, sending them crashing to the floor. He fell hard on the other hound.

He lay stunned for a moment, trying to get the Earth, moon, and stars from revolving around his head.

The hound he'd landed on stirred.

The other jumped toward him, snapping.

Laws grabbed his rifle, which had been dangling by its sling, and brought the butt around to intersect with the head of the leaping hound.

It made a strangling noise and tumbled past.

Laws didn't even look to see how it was doing. He scrambled off the other hound and broken skeleton, found his footing, then took off for Yank. He was more than halfway there before a hound behind him let out a howl. He approached Yank at a dead run, then made a controlled skid as he reached down and grabbed the downed man's collar. Laws hauled the deadweight down a hall and through a side door. He was just able to pull it closed when a weight slammed against it, slamming it shut.

Finally, out of breath, but safe behind the door, he was able to answer Holmes and check on Yank.

Walker and YaYa exchanged glances through the darkness. Both of them wished they were upstairs. They were close enough to hear the sound of battle and the cataclysmic crash of the Apatosaurus skeleton in real time. Then came the telltale howl of the hound.

So many questions ran through Walker's mind, especially ones regarding the fate of his fellow SEALs, but his mission was to secure the stairwell.

The two SEALs were in charge of securing one of the two sets of stairs that could be used to enter the basement. Ian and Trevor held the other.

When Walker heard Laws's hurried report to Holmes, he was pleased that the lanky second in command had made it, but was concerned for Yank. It took a moment for Laws to ascertain his status, but it appeared as if the newest member of the team was unconscious and there was nothing Laws could do to change that.

Walker was so engrossed listening to the play-by-play that he almost missed the attack, foreshadowed only by the sound of metal on granite. One glance at the grenade bouncing down the stairs made him switch his QUADEYE off.

"Flash bang!"

He closed his eyes and a moment later the universe exploded into white. As it faded, he switched his night vision back on. He could see YaYa shaking his head, clearly having missed or been unable to heed the warning. But that was the least of his concerns.

Boots rattled against marble as five men charged down the stairs.

Walker pegged three of them in the chest and one in the leg before he had to swing back around the corner. Return fire exploded wood and stone from the doorway he'd left. Unable to fire back, he tossed his own flash-bang grenade. When it went off, he slung himself back around the corner and to the floor, changing levels. He fired. Two men went down, but two others were pulling a wounded man back up the stairs.

YaYa jerked his QUADEYE free. He'd felt blind with it. At least now, he could operate in the gloom.

"Ghost One, this is Ghost Three. Five *beegees* tried to infil west staircase. One down. Four retreated."

Walker was about to check on the downed man when he heard gunfire from the east staircase.

Ian and Trevor weren't fucking around. They'd dangled a grenade from the upper stairwell, tied it off to the railing, and trailed a filament-thin line so they could quickly pull the greased pin . . . which they did as three men stormed down the stairs. Ian and Trevor twisted around the wall, putting several feet of marble between them and the blast.

One thousand one.

One thousand two.

One thousand three.

Kaboom!

One of the attackers was about to breach the doorway but was flung to the wall like a broken-backed toy by the explosion. When it came, it was like a dragon's roar. Flame, pieces of meat and muscle, and thousands of granite and marble chips shot through the doorway. Whoever they were, they didn't have time to scream or react, and the grenade had been too high to notice.

When the pieces stopped falling, both men stood and surveyed the stairs.

Trevor wiped soot from his face. "Bloody fucking hell."

"Takes care of that." Ian turned to the one who'd been slung free of the blast, intent on a quick interrogation. But one look at the exposed spine and the head spun halfway around told Ian there'd be no words coming from this gent.

"Demon One, this is Ghost One; report."

Ian tapped Trevor on the shoulder and gestured toward the stairs. "Moving to flank."

They stacked up the stairs, slipping a little on the pieces of the would-be attackers. When they hit the top, they got down and turned toward the Fossil Marine Reptile exhibit. Ian peered around the corner and spied five men in black, night-vision goggles, body armor, and black skullcaps preparing to descend. He raised his rifle, sighted in through the fixed optics, and put two rounds into the side of the nearest man's head.

The reaction was instantaneous as the remaining four knelt and returned fire.

Ian ducked around the corner as rounds slammed into the concrete and granite. He pointed behind them where the restaurant was, indicating Trevor should move in that direction. Once he was moving, Ian pulled another grenade, made a silent apology to the Queen for blowing up even more of her museum, pulled the pin, then tossed it around the corner.

He barreled after Trevor, only to come up short as he watched what could only be one of those hounds making its way across the tops of the tables directly toward them.

"Back down!" Ian commanded.

They turned and crashed down the stairs, taking them three at a time. Halfway down they slipped on gore, falling hard to the marble-edged stairs. Their body armor took the brunt of the damage, but the air left them. Still, they were all that was left of

Section 9 and by god Ian wasn't going to allow them to go out as supernatural dog food.

He got to his feet first, then reached down for Trevor. He pushed the kid in front of him just as an immense weight plowed into his back, throwing him face-first to the ground.

Walker had made the stairs and was firing upwards, sending ricochets into the hall above. Ian and Trevor had countered the attack. He had no doubt they were going to stack down and take advantage of the second flash bang. That the Section 9 guys had drawn their fire had been a godsend. Now it was time to repay their effort.

He'd grabbed YaYa and they were about to move up the stairs when they heard Trevor's scream over the net.

"It followed us down the stairs!"

One glance said Walker and YaYa were in tune. As one, they left the stairs and ran back into the basement. They peeled left and after several turns came upon the scene of the beast-like hound trying to chew through the back of Ian's body armor.

Both Walker and YaYa opened fire. The momentum from the bullets punched the creature from Ian's back but had no other effect.

"Fucking kidding me." YaYa fired full auto until his HK was empty. He'd knocked the beast down, but even as he watched, it climbed to its feet and let free an arcane howl.

Another beast climbed down the stairs. The sight of its human arms as forelegs and hands gripping the marble sent chills down Walker's back. He shook his head and backed away.

"One, this is Three; we have two hounds down here. The other staircase is open. Time to bug out, over."

He heard two clicks and reached down slowly to haul Ian to his feet.

"Back away, gents. Let these critters do what they need to."

While the new hound snarled at them, it made no move to attack.

The other hound turned and padded toward the other set of stairs. If they'd planned this right, it would turn left and head down to the lower level where they had the golem head. Walker's and the rest of their jobs were over. They found a utility closet they'd prepared earlier, and backed inside.

Once the door was secure, he called the net. "All Ghosts, this is Ghost Three and Five and Demon One and Two. All secure."

"All Ghosts, this is Ghost Two with Four. All secure."

Walker was gratified to hear that Laws and Yank were okay. He waited for what seemed like a full minute before Holmes called in.

"All Ghosts, this is Ghost One and the Crone. All secure. Wait until you get the all clear, then rendezvous to site one."

Walker let out a sigh of relief. They might be a little beat up, but their mission was a success. Now to see if they could track the head.

CHAPTER 29

CHICKSANDS RAF. MORNING.

Yank was the worst off. He'd sustained a concussion and had trouble coming to. There were no bruises or contusions, but he couldn't explain what happened.

Sassy Moore's migraine was so bad, she could barely open her eyes, brought on by the vicissitudes of astral combat. She claimed that she had fought and defended herself against no fewer than five warlocks. She held a long package to her chest that Laws was pretty certain she hadn't had at the start of the mission.

Ian had two black eyes from where he face-planted on the ground.

With the exception of exhaustion and a few contusions from flying granite, the others were fine.

After conducting a three-hour surveillance detection route, including three changes of vehicles, they made it back to Chicksands. Ian got them through the gate, and they were soon pulling into the hangar and unloading their gear. The SEALs and men of Section 9 had already broken down their weapons and cleaned them. All they needed to do was add a light coat of oil and wipe the weapons down once more.

But that would have to wait.

They had company.

Hoover stood, head low, growling at a well-dressed hulk of a man standing between two bodyguards and with three more arrayed behind them. They each had enough goon genes in their DNA that they could have been related. The central man's demeanor was anything but calm. His hands strangled invisible children while his face threatened to transition from red to purple.

"Do you realize the damage you did? You broke a dinosaur skeleton!"

Ian and Holmes exchanged glances. Ian turned to the man and sighed. "I don't know what you're talking about!"

"You don't—" He seemed to get some control. "Hundreds of thousands of euros in damage and the loss of priceless artifacts. Do you realize that those bones were given to Queen Victoria by the Crown Prince of Prussia?"

"Must have been someone else, Sir Robert." Ian turned to head toward the back of the hangar.

"Don't turn your back on me."

Two of his men drew Glock pistols from shoulder holsters.

They shouldn't have.

The SEALs brought their rifles up at once and began to create separation between themselves and their targets. Trevor paused a moment, then joined them.

Soon all five goons had pistols trained on the SEALs and stepped in front of the man Ian had called Sir Robert. The SEALs had realized he must have been the Member of Parliament Ian had told them about.

It might have remained a standoff, but they forgot to account for Genie during the fracas. Laws watched stone-faced as he came up behind the MP and placed a pistol barrel to the side of his head.

"Drop your weapons or the white guy gets it!"

The goons stepped aside and stared at the African-American squid with a gun to their boss's head.

"We're all white, asshole," said Sir Robert. "Now let me go."

"Maybe that's your problem. You had a brother with you, he'd have watched your back."

Trevor and Walker collected the guards' weapons and tossed them into the back of their SUV.

Holmes came up and placed a hand on Genie's shoulder. "You can let the man go, now."

Genaro Stewart snapped his wrist back and stepped away until he was standing by Laws.

Laws grinned. "The white guy gets it? Did you really say that?"

Genie shrugged. "I couldn't think of anything else to say. Got their attention, didn't it?"

Laws laughed. Moments like this were why he loved being a SEAL. "It sure did, man. It sure as hell did."

Sir Robert snarled at his men and whirled on Holmes. "So this is SEAL Team 666."

Holmes remained silent.

"Are you going to deny it?"

Holmes smiled grimly. "You don't have the need to know."

"Need to know? Do you know who you're talking to?"

Holmes merely stared at the angry MP, letting the moment draw out until it was Sir Robert who broke it.

He spit on the floor. "You Americans think you can throw your weight around anywhere you want. You wouldn't be anywhere if it weren't for—"

Laws couldn't help himself. "—an Italian discovering North America, a German monk creating the Protestant Reformation, and a handful of dissidents you didn't want along with a bunch of profiteers who wanted to rape the land? Is that what you were going to say?"

But he knew the response he'd get. So when Sir Robert spun in Laws's direction, he beamed his very best smile.

Before the British MP could faint from apoplexy, Ian interrupted. "Sir Robert, was there a reason for this visit?"

The MP was sweating from anger. "Just keeping my eye on you. And If I find out you were involved at all in that cock and bull at the museum, I'm going to have your ass."

Trevor stepped forward, lowering the point of his rifle as he did. "Did you see anything on the cameras?"

"I'm told there was some sort of disturbance."

"A lot of that going around lately," Laws said.

Sir Robert pointed a shaking finger at all of them. "Watch yourselves."

Ian simply nodded. "Yes, Sir Robert."

The MP glanced around. When his eyes lit on Laws, he shook his head. "Bloody walking talking Wikipedia entry." Then he turned with his men close on his heels. As they passed, one looked imploringly at Yank, who stood by the rear of the SUV where their guns were held.

He shook his head once, firm. "I don't think so."

The goon frowned and hurried to catch up to the rest of the retinue.

The SEALs and Section 9 watched them until they entered the parking lot and climbed into two sedans.

Trevor plopped down on one of the couches. "Big coincidence he showed up right after the operation."

"Wasn't a coincidence." Ian turned to Preeti, who'd remained sitting and out of the way the entire time. "Did he see our prisoner?"

She nodded. "They tried to get into the room, but Genie here wouldn't let them."

All eyes turned to the big Navy chief, who, apparently unused to the attention, lowered his eyes and blushed.

Laws patted him on the shoulder. "Way to go, big guy. Ever thought of being a SEAL?"

Genie smiled sideways. "Too broken. Bad knees. I'm support. It's what I do best."

"That's okay," said Holmes, in a rare moment of open appreciation. "You're a great asset to the mission."

Laws chuckled. He just couldn't forget the words *or the white man gets it.*

Holmes turned to Ian. "You know what this means, right?"

Ian nodded. "I thought we'd have a little longer, but you're right; we need to move." To the room he said, "Pack up your gear and break down the electronics. We'll take whatever we can. We need to be out of here in an hour. We're moving to Point Bravo." Then, realizing he'd just ordered the Americans, he glanced at Holmes.

But Holmes was ahead of him. "You heard him, SEALs. Get your ass in gear." When he saw YaYa and Walker exchange looks, Holmes added, "You want to sleep, you can do it when you're dead."

Everyone sprang into motion, using muscle memories from countless deployments, exercises, and inspections. The need to pack and unpack and prepare one's gear had been imprinted on their DNA.

Preeti hobbled over to Ian, who was packing sheets into a kit bag. "There's something I need to tell you."

"Can this wait?"

She glanced around. "I suppose it can."

Seeing the conflict in her eyes, Laws interrupted. "Let's hear what she has to say."

Ian stopped folding and regarded her. "What is it, dear?"

"The woman in white . . . the woman who took the pictures in Blackpool . . . I found out where she lives."

Ian stared blankly, his jaw dropping slightly. "You what?"

Laws laughed; then he called over to Trevor, "You got a winner here, kid. The girl's a keeper."

Trevor looked up from stuffing the kit into his bag. "What'd she do?"

"She made Ian lose his composure."

Ian turned, his face once again composed. "She did not. I might have been a little surprised, but then I only hire the very best."

Laws nodded slowly. "Right. Just surprised. Right." He dramatically looked at the floor by Ian's feet. "Oh look, there's your jaw. . . ." Then Laws glanced up at Ian's face. "Nope. You're good. You got it."

CHAPTER 30

The air inside Saffron Gold smelled of curry, turmeric, and a dozen other spices, which made Walker's mouth run with anticipation. Indian food was Walker's culinary kryptonite and Preeti's cousin had once worked at Saffron Gold. Although all the way out in the Midlands, it frequently made England's "Best Indian Restaurants" list and was a go-to destination for culinary enthusiasts. It was also a go-to restaurant for special operations teams trying to hide under the radar.

A sweet Indian girl, who could easily be the next target of the Wild Hunt, packed four bags into a box and stuffed napkins in between them.

Walker thanked her, pulled his skullcap over his head, and turned up his collar. He headed out the door, then turned down Friars Street. About a half block down on the right was a sign that read: "St. Paul's Church." Built in 1824, it was a small stone chapel with yellow construction tape across the front and a sign that said: "Grand Reopening Next Easter." He followed a path along the right-hand side of the church. A construction tent stood around back that hid the SUV.

Genie met him at the back door and relieved him of the food.

Walker secured the door, then followed the Navy chief down the stairs into a long and wide basement which had become their new operational HQ. Pews had been dragged down from the chapel and were being used as couches, chairs, and cots. A table scrounged from the sacristy held Preeti's computers and monitors. Van Dyke occupied a pew in the very back of the space.

They'd been lucky to find T1 lines already installed, due entirely to the previous friar's love of soccer. He'd been known to disappear for hours, only to be found downstairs on the couch watching Premier League soccer, or passed out from too much alcohol—which was where they found him one morning when he didn't show up for mass. Whether it was West Brom beating Manchester by four goals or too much wine, his heart gave out, which left the archdiocese with the decision to either close the church or remodel, since no significant work had been done to it since 1932.

Ian had already arranged for this or an abandoned home in Brighton to be available if they needed a temporary HQ. Preeti had her brother wipe away any record of the location.

Walker wasn't sure if it was the smell of the food or the sound of the box hitting the pew, but everyone suddenly took notice.

"About time you got back. Getting hungry in here." Yank rubbed his hands together, clearly no worse for wear from being dragged away by a Wild Hunt hound other than a concussion.

"We could have done a cover stop at any number of fast-food joints." YaYa elbowed his way past Yank. "I still want to try those ketchup-flavored crisps to see what they taste like."

"Probably like ketchup and potato chips." Laws pulled the smaller enlisted man back and stepped forward.

Soon everyone was pushing and prodding. Unsure if it was a game or survival of the fittest, Walker found himself in the middle, scrabbling for a samosa.

"Stop!"

Everyone turned to see Holmes standing with hands on his hips. "Let the young lady get in there before you men start grazing."

Everyone glanced at one another, then backed away.

Preeti smiled, then began to load a plate. Walker could have sworn she was taking her time. Probably hadn't had this sort of deference and positive attention from so many in a long time. He sighed. His stomach could wait if it meant something good happening to her. Not only was he empathetic for her injuries, but he saw a mirror image in the relationship she had with Trevor with the one that he'd had with Jen.

Plus, Preeti and her brother had arguably done more to move the mission forward than SEAL Team 666, Section 9, and a certified witch.

During their four-hour surveillance detection route, she'd explained her sleuth work and how she'd figured out how to track the mystery woman. With brains and guile, she'd found a location whose address matched a name from a list of Bohemian Grove donors. If he wasn't involved, he'd have to know someone who was.

And her brother had been largely responsible for their escape. They now had no doubt that Sir Robert Montgomery was involved with the Red Grove and possibly the Wild Hunt. There was also no doubt that once these entities learned of the demise of their golem guard, they'd be searching for the Tuatha, having determined that it had returned to the Isles during the brief period before the witch shielded it. So as they knew that the SEALs had been at the museum, it would be a simple task to track them back to Chicksands RAF, that is, if the MP hadn't outed them already. It would additionally be simple to track them once they evacuated and headed to Point Bravo. All the surveillance detection routes in the world couldn't evade a network of CCTV cameras. So, just as they'd planned it, Preeti's brother launched an immense DNS attack on the British Transport Police Servers, using underground networks in Romania and Uganda. The denial of service attacks successfully blocked all incoming traffic feeds, replacing them with live streams from various sex cams from around the globe for two orgasmic hours, allowing Section 9 and SEAL Team 666 to fall off the map. With the additional change of vehicle, their vehicular biometrics was now also different. The only way to find them now would be through witchcraft, which Sassy was spending all of her time thwarting.

Once Preeti finally filled her plate, then Sassy, the men approached the food in a less aggressive manner. They found space on the pews and ate in silence. This was the first nourishment they'd had since before the mission at the museum and Walker had to force himself to eat slowly. He'd almost finished when the witch, who'd been in the rear of the room, writing runes on the floor around Van Dyke with chalk and dust, approached them.

"He's dying," she said flatly as she took the plate that Holmes had prepared for her. "It's only a matter of days." She shrugged. "Might be hours."

Laws spoke first. "He said he had cancer."

Sassy shook her head so her hair almost covered her face as she chewed. She spoke around a bite of vindaloo. "The cancer should have killed him two years ago. It's the Tuatha Dé Dannan that's keeping him alive." She laughed huskily as she wiped her mouth and set her plate aside. "It's clear what the Bohemian Grove is all about now. I don't know if this is the only one, but they have at least one Tuatha Dé Dannan that they let someone host in order to prolong their lives. They might even give it to healthy people, because what this thing does is share its life force, giving the host strength and, in the case of Van Dyke, enough strength to live a few more years."

Walker suddenly understood. "And the golem was there to protect their property."

"They're going to want it back," Holmes concluded.

"You saw how interested Sir Robert was, as if he knew Van Dyke was there. Had they gone to the hangar instead of the museum, they would already have it."

"But I had it well shielded. Going to Chicksands would be a crapshoot, while the museum was a sure thing."

Walker gestured at the Navy chief. "Thanks to Genaro for holding him and his thugs off long enough for us to come."

YaYa, who'd been looking sideways at Van Dyke in the back of the room, joined the conversation. "It still doesn't answer the question of why they want it."

Sassy's eyes widened. "Alas. The million-pound question. I think I have the answer to that." When she was certain she had everyone's attention, she told them, "It's the mounds. Legend states that the Tuatha lived in them. I believe the mounds are a sort of parallel universe. It's clear that they are connected somehow, which would explain how the Wild Hunt can move around so swiftly."

Holmes nodded, got up, and stuffed his plate and plasticware into a garbage bag. "Van Dyke is the key."

"Not Van Dyke, the Tuatha," she corrected.

"He—*it* can get us access to the mounds. Will *it* cooperate?"

"Not as long as it's in Van Dyke's body. It wants a new host."

Holmes stared for a long moment, then shook his head. "No way. It could be a parasite. Maybe it lets the host live longer because it needs something from the host to live? Did you think of that?"

"Perhaps, but—"

Laws joined in as he was throwing away his plate. "Legend has it that after their defeat by the Milesians, the Tuatha descended into the mounds. Hence their other name, Aos Sí, or Sidhe, 'people of the mounds.' Now this is where Tolkien stole his ideas for elves, from legends resident in the British Isles. Although the term 'Tuatha Dé Dannan' is of Irish origin, there are cognates–different names for the same entities–throughout the peoples who populated Dark Age Briton. Realize that when the texts came out, they were referring to a race of people who existed more than nineteen hundred years before Christ."

Sassy laughed tiredly. "He really is a walking talking Wikipedia entry."

"He has an eidetic memory. Remembers everything he sees." Holmes gestured for Laws to continue.

"It's a curse." Laws found a runaway samosa and snapped it into his mouth. "Tolkien's elves leaving Middle Earth for Valorian mimics the Tuatha leaving England for Tir Na Nog. Both left because of the coming age of humans. Both left some of their kind behind. This thing inside Van Dyke is probably one of those left-behinds."

Genie shook his head violently, his hand going to something hanging on a necklace beneath his shirt. "You're saying this as if it's true." Genie seemed as surprised as the rest of them that he'd spoken. "Sorry, it's just that . . ."

YaYa smiled grimly. "This is just the beginning. Everything you thought you knew will change. It happened to all of us."

Laws shrugged apologetically, as if he was sorry for spoiling Genaro's idea of the truth. "We're talking about pre-history. It could be right or wrong; that's sort of beside the point. The fact that we have a Tuatha right here with us and the Wild Hunt killing people around this country by transporting themselves through the mounds is what we have to deal with. The rest is just background, and something to maybe help us put it in context."

In the intervening silence a tune began to form at the back of the room. The sound was high-pitched, almost too high to be made by a human. Van Dyke had been too weak to stand, so they'd pulled two pews together to form a sort of crib to contain him. Around and on this, Sassy had drawn arcane magical symbols. He was sitting up now, singing in a language Walker had never heard before. It was at once lyrical and harsh, words beginning with vowels and ending with brittle consonants.

Everyone stared at Van Dyke for what seemed like five minutes until he finally spoke. *"Tir Na Nog, the place where time is but a memory, 'tis neither hot nor cold, windy nor still, wet nor dry. Tir Na Nog."*

It was clear at once that this wasn't Van Dyke speaking but rather the Tuatha.

Sassy moved forward, but Holmes held up his hand. She hesitated, unsure if she wanted to follow his command, but relented, a curious look coming to life in her eyes.

Holmes stepped forward and held his hands out in front of him, palms up and empty. "I'm Commander Sam Holmes, U.S. Navy SEALs. To whom do I have the pleasure to speak?"

" *'Twas you who brought me back.*" The voice broke from high to low at odd times, as if it wasn't used to the language.

"It was. We thought you might be able to help."

"*I'm trapped here. Weak. Sick. Need to touch the land. Need to feel the spirit of the trees.*"

"We can probably help. You're keeping the man Van Dyke alive, yes?"

"*He sucks at me like a baby to a nipple. It irritates, but it is a pleasure to feel his life.*" Then Van Dyke made a face. "*But his is such an oily soul. The things he's seen . . . done.*"

"Your people left you." Holmes glanced at Laws, who nodded. "Why did they leave you?"

"*Tir Na Nog. Once gone you can never return.*" Van Dyke regarded the humans in the room with a fondness one might show to his pets. "*I love this land. I love the strange race of being known as human. I didn't want to leave.*"

Laws shook his head in amazement, eyes wide. "Do you realize that this being has seen more than four thousand years of our history? What is your name?"

"*When we speak our names, it is with our minds and you are unable to hear it. Dyfed is a good name. He was a poet I once inspired.*"

The name sounded remarkably like "David," but with a residual "f" replacing the "v."

Laws smiled. "You're a muse."

"*I inspire. Yes.*" Then Van Dyke looked startled. His eyes searched the room, appearing neither to fall on an object or person or to recognize them. He let out a cry, then collapsed, falling roughly back into his pew-made cradle.

CHAPTER 31

POINT BRAVO, WARWICK, ENGLAND. LATER.

Holmes was the first to the man. He reached over the pew and checked for a pulse. Nothing. He shoved the pews apart and laid the man gently on the floor. He made sure the man's clothing was loose, then began to give him CPR.

Walker and Laws came over to assist, moving the pews farther apart. Laws loosened Van Dyke's belt and removed his shoes. Walker took over compressing the man's chest while Holmes supplied air.

Everyone was silent as the three men tried to save the life. After thirty seconds, Holmes checked for a pulse. He found one. As thready and weak as it was, it was at least there.

"I don't know how much longer he'll last." Holmes glanced at Sassy Moore. He didn't want that thing in her. He didn't know what it would do to her and, frankly, he was still concerned about her loyalties.

"You have to let me do it," she said matter-of-factly.

He wanted to weigh his options, he wanted to build a virtual decision matrix, but he just didn't have enough data. "Fine. But if you turn into a raving monster I'm going to put you down."

She grinned savagely. "Sounds harsh."

"This is a harsh world. Do you understand?"

"Sure. I'd rather you do that anyway. No way will a raving monster be able to work these pumps like I can." She raised her left foot to show off a red three-inch-heeled shoe.

Holmes stood. "How do we do it?"

"It's not 'we,' big man. It's just old Sassy." She waved her hands at the three men. "Step away, now. Let Sassy get at it."

Walker and Laws gave Holmes a look. He nodded to them and they stood and backed away.

Sassy immediately went into action. She stripped off her blouse, revealing a white bra. Her back was covered with some tattooed symbology Holmes didn't recognize. Inverted stars, circles with lines, runes, and all sort of patterns created an almost dizzying array of the arcane. A fresh tattoo had been inked just above her navel. It was so new that the flesh was still raised and puckered. Seeing everyone's eyes on it, she said, "I thought I might need it."

She straddled the body and let her head hang back, her arms dangling beside her. Her pupils rolled so only the whites could be seen. She began to hum, the sound coming from somewhere miles deep within her. After a few moments, Van Dyke's body began to jerk beneath her. Her knees tightened so she wouldn't lose her balance. She rode him for a few moments, then snapped forward until her face hovered over Van Dyke's. She spoke too fast to discern, the words falling over each other one after the other. Van Dyke's eyes snapped open. She placed her mouth above his, her hum once again returning. They stayed in this embrace for a full moment, until Sassy raised her torso up and inhaled greatly. A look of joy suffused her face. Beneath her Van Dyke lay, eyes open, pallor gray, not breathing.

She stared at the ceiling a moment as she gathered herself; then she carefully stood, as if she weren't used to the motion. She wobbled slightly, reaching out. Holmes ran to her and took her hand, feeling the coldness radiating from it.

"You okay?" He stared into her face and searched her eyes. "Did it work?"

Her hand became warm, then hot, so hot he had to let go. She began to shake. Smoke came from her skin. Her face turned bright red. Power shone from her eyes. Then came the sound of something cracking.

Everyone looked around, but the sound had come from Sassy.

She slowly returned to normal, finally wiping sweat from her face with the fabric of the blouse covering her left arm.

"That should do it." She shook her head and closed her eyes as if to dislodge a headache. "Dyfed is amazingly powerful. I could barely subdue it." She laughed a little crazily. "Almost had me."

"What'd you do with it?" Walker asked.

"Stuffed it in a corner and made it stay."

Laws's brows came together. "Can it see and hear us?"

"I get that impression."

"How are we going to be able to talk to it?" Laws gave Holmes a look. "We were doing just fine until Van Dyke suddenly kicked it."

"Coincidence, I'm sure," Sassy said.

Holmes didn't like it. They had a mantra—*one man's coincidence is a Triple Six mission.* "Can we speak to Dyfed?"

"You can speak through me. Now give me a second. I need something to drink and to catch my breath."

She walked over to the table and grabbed a bottle of water, then went over to the pew that had become her private area. She sat heavily and stared at the floor.

Holmes glanced at his men, who all seemed to be expecting answers from him. He definitely didn't like the situation now. How was he to know if Sassy was telling him exactly what the Tuatha said? She was a filter and the only one able to speak directly to the creature. He couldn't help but sigh heavily.

"Laws, where are we with mission planning?"

Holmes's tall second in command sighed as well. Laws understood. Like the rest, he didn't like it, but he understood. They'd deal with Sassy when they could. Until then, they had a rendezvous with the woman in white.

CHAPTER 32

GLASTONBURY TOR, GLASTONBURY, ENGLAND. NIGHT.

The trip from Warwick to Somerset would normally take two and a half hours, but because of their constant concern for surveillance they took five. It was decided that Walker, YaYa, and Trevor would go while the others remained with Sassy and the Tuatha to see how they could best leverage the creature.

Preeti was busy trying to find the radio beacon they'd placed in the golem's head, but with no luck at all. She also pointed out to them something they'd completely forgotten. Tomorrow was Christmas. Not only was it one of the pinnacle Christian holidays, but it was also a well-known pagan holiday, predating the determination that the twenty-fifth of December was the birthday of Jesus Christ.

Holmes made it clear that this was not a time to celebrate. They were neck deep in pagan mythology and needed to be aware of its dangers.

Laws, ever the encyclopedic mind, shared that more than four hundred years before the birth of Christ early Romans celebrated the birth date of the deity Saturnus. It originally began as a simple banquet on December 17 but then grew to a five-day affair, highlighted by gambling, gift giving, and a general bacchanal celebration. It eventually became something different as Saturnus's darker aspects were celebrated. In addition to everything they'd done previously, Romans introduced the Lord of Misrule as part of the holiday. Every Roman community selected a man or woman to become the Lord of Misrule, who would represent the enemy of their people. Beginning on the seventeenth of December, they'd feed and treat this person as if he or she were an actual lord, denying him or her nothing. But then on December 25 they'd come together and kill the Lord of Misrule. Ancient Greek poet, Lucian, mentioned in his texts that revelers would also travel from home to home naked, singing the songs of the day; performing deviant sexual public acts, including rape; and eating human-shaped biscuits to symbolize the eating of your enemy.

Walker found the information creepy, especially when he thought of the similarities to the Christmas he and every other American kid normally celebrated. To think that the gingerbread man had a violent and terrible past was stunning.

Holly, ivy, the giving of gifts, the use of an evergreen tree, and many more symbols of modern Christmas were derived from ancient Roman pagan customs. Laws and Preeti weren't sure how December 25 would affect the power of the Red Grove or other neo-pagan groups but had to be aware that it might have an incongruous effect on the success or failure of any mission they might be conducting. Just as the Winter Solstice was a special day for the Red Grove, Triple Six had to consider that Christmas might be as well.

The house they needed to surveil was a two-story Tudor with four chimneys and seven dormers. Records showed it to belong to Jason Belair, who ran an import-export business specializing in North European antiques and collectibles. He'd been referred to in a *Financial Times of London* article as being the *kitschy king of secondhand Ikea*. Although the description was unflattering, his net worth was upwards of 100 million pounds.

The home was less than two hundred meters from Glastonbury Tor, which held an interesting place in British history and mythology. No one exactly knew how it was formed, but because the hill rises 150 meters above the surrounding plain it had been used since at least 400 BC as a place to defend from.

"Tor" was an English word referring to a high rock or hill. But the name used by the Celts for the hill was Yns yr Afalon, which translated meant "The Isle of Avalon," linking it directly to King Arthur.

When this piece of information had been discovered, it had set off a murmur of excitement among them in the chapel basement. But what they found next was even more intriguing. According to the twelfth-century poet Gerald of Wales, monks from the nearby Glastonbury Abbey discovered a coffin buried in the side of the Tor. It bore an inscription identifying it as Queen Guinevere's. Although this presented an exciting prospect, experts now believe that the monks, who'd recently lost their abbey to a fire, might have had a more commercial reason for finding and selling the artifact. Gerald of Wales also indicates that Glastonbury Tor was one of the possible locations of the Holy Grail, especially because of the discovery of the Nanteos Cup at the same abbey. The cup was allegedly brought to Briton by Joseph of Arimathea, who was believed to have founded the Christian settlement at Glastonbury Tor.

Finally, what was arguably most interesting was the connection of the Tor in Celtic mythology to Gwyn ap Nudd, also known as Annwn, and later called King of the Faeries. The hill became known as the entrance to Avalon, the land of the faeries. Yet even with all that history, the Tor usually wasn't considered a mound but rather a fortification. Those gathered in the basement were coming to believe something a little bit different.

"I always wanted the legend of King Arthur to be real," Walker said when they were still twenty minutes out. "The whole Knights of the Round Table and the quest for the Holy Grail seemed so spiritual."

Trevor, who was driving, scoffed and couldn't help but reply, "Your romanticism is amazing. Kings are just like anyone else. They are fallible, sometimes mean, most often greedy, and rarely considerate of the common man."

YaYa was sitting in the backseat and leaned forward. "Is that the way you feel about your queen?"

Trevor kept his gaze straight ahead, but he replied quickly. "Not at all. Queen Elizabeth, God bless her soul, is completely different."

Walker laughed. "Now who's being a romantic? I heard she's a billionaire many times over. I've also heard the theories about her and Princess Diana."

"Rubbish. Pure bloody rubbish. It's in no way the same as your Americans' reverence for a king you know nothing about."

Walker couldn't help himself. He crossed his arms. "Explain?"

"It's because of your movies and books. No, it goes back further. It goes back to Washington. Sure, you had a general for a president, but you lost your king. Americans have always had a love affair with the idea of a monarchy. It's why you put so many of your cultural icons on pedestals."

"Like LeBron James and Brad Pitt," YaYa said.

Trevor pressed harder. "What do you know about King Arthur? Have you as Americans read any of the actual historic texts or the academic dissertations or are you a victim of American pop culture? Your movies have become encyclopedias to your young. Look at Arthur. You have one movie where he wears chrome armor and another in which he is a Roman wearing leather armor. In one movie Camelot is a ten-story gleaming castle with pinnacles and in another it's an old fort made from stone and mortar. Your love affair with the myth makes reality unreachable."

Walker sat back for a few moments, then said, "Wow. Where'd that come from?"

YaYa nodded. "Probably some pent-up anti-American sentiment."

Walker's brow creased. "So what you're telling me is that Arthur doesn't look like Richard Gere and doesn't wear chrome armor? I drop the bullshit flag on that."

YaYa shook his head. "Lancelot. Richard Gere played Sir Lancelot. It was Sean Connery who played King Arthur."

"Sean Connery. Yeah. That fits with me. He even talks like he's from around here."

Trevor turned to Walker and gave him a deadpan look, then shook his head and turned forward. "All I'm saying is that when we meet King Arthur I think he's going to scare the shit out of us."

Walker uncrossed his arms. "That I believe."

They parked a mile away from their target. They were dressed for recon, not for battle, although they did wear body armor. Instead of helmets they wore baseball caps. Their night-vision goggles were in pouches hidden under their jackets. They carried Sig Sauer P229s with silencers and knives. They had their intersquad radio system but wanted to keep it silent until they knew what they were up against.

There were no CCTV cameras in this area near Glastonbury Tor, so they didn't have to concern themselves with their actions being seen by police. Three men dressed in black approaching a home on Christmas Eve would have been odd.

They made their way down the lane with Trevor on one side and the SEALs on the other. They'd traveled halfway to their objective when they passed a house that was under construction. They checked for security, but there wasn't any. In fact, the front door was unlocked. The serendipitous find would serve as their forward observation post.

Walker and YaYa each carried a small plastic case containing a PD-100 Black Hornet Personal Reconnaissance System. Comprised of two micro-unmanned aerial vehicles called Hornets, a base station, a recharging station, a remote-control unit, and a seven-inch screen by which to watch the footage.

The Black Hornet was little more than a camera molded into a tiny helicopter, weighing less than sixteen grams. It was invisible at ten meters, almost completely soundless, but lacked the ability to film in night vision. The smallest FLIR camera weighed twice as much as the entire Hornet. Even without night vision, what the three-inch UAV would do was allow them to get up close to the house and surrounding compound and see what was going on without being seen.

At least that was the plan.

Trevor placed infrared trip wires at both the front and back doors downstairs and on the stairwell. If one was tripped, a signal would travel to the receiver in his pocket, which would then vibrate in series, with the number of repetitions corresponding to whether it was from number one, two, or three.

It was about ten at night and snow just had begun to fall when YaYa and Walker were ready. They'd chosen a second-floor bedroom to use as their launch bay. The glass in the window had yet to be put into place, so the space was open to the elements. Walker could already feel the cold seeping into his fingers as he prepared the tiny UAVs.

He launched his first Black Hornet by sitting it on the ground and remotely controlling the minute helicopter blades, enabling it to rise. It was hard not to control the UAV while looking at it. Instead, he forced himself to use the small monitor, forcing himself to become the Black Hornet and shrinking his universe to what could be viewed by the nose-cone camera.

Tunnel-visioning in, he found himself rising, then moving forward. White snowflakes fell like down feathers. He could feel a slight crosswind and had to adjust by turning into it. The result of this was that in order to travel in a straight line, he'd have to aim the camera slightly left of his target. He found it tremendously difficult to do that and stay online. Thankfully, the wind subsided and he was able to point his nose at his goal. The downside of having a MUAV was that wind was its kryptonite.

He negotiated the Black Hornet through tree branches, which were already beginning to be covered in the Christmas Eve snow. He passed over a backyard occupied by a dog staring woefully into a warm-lit living room where a family was huddled around a cozy television. Then an empty lot. Then the compound.

He rose to an elevation of fifty meters so he could see the whole area. The backyard was enclosed by a wall. People were outside around several bonfires. Judging by the people, the wall was ten or twelve feet high—high enough to hide activity from outside view, especially since there were empty lots on either side. It seemed as if every light was on inside the home, creating a nimbus of warm orange light. In addition to the bonfires, four floodlights mounted on poles in the four corners of the wall shone inward.

He counted twenty-seven persons in the backyard. Walker moved the Black Hornet closer to resolve the images of the people. The wind began to pick up and he found his ability to focus severely constrained. He fought to keep the MUAV still for several minutes, but to no avail. He cursed and heard YaYa swearing beside him too as he tried to control his own MUAV.

"I'm going to find a place to put it down," Walker said.

"What about the corners?" YaYa asked. "We can put them in the protective lee of the poles supporting the floodlights."

"Good call."

Walker manipulated the MUAV until it settled on the northwest corner post on the side of the light pole opposite the wind. He adjusted the aim of the camera, then turned off the blades. To anyone looking, the MUAV would just look like a black blob the size of a dragonfly sitting on top of a pole.

"Take the northeast corner."

YaYa rogered and soon after landing the other MUAV they were looking at a complete feed of the entire backyard. The area was so well lit, their lack of night vision wasn't going to be an issue.

Now that they were close enough to see the images of the people, what they saw made their eyes go wide.

Trevor leaned in to look. "Are they—"

"Naked. Absolutely."

"And what the hell is wrong with their faces?"

"I have no . . . idea." Walker couldn't help but bring his hand to his own face and touch his lips with his cold fingers. Where his lips were warm and smooth, the lips of the seven naked women they counted in the backyard were scarred and sewn shut by an inexpert and vicious hand. Other than their lips, their faces were free from any mark and would have been beautiful, had they not been so gaunt. The women's hollowed-out faces, prominent cheekbones, and bulging eyes made them look like victims of a famine. But once Walker was able to take in the totality of their appearance, he understood what was going on; he just didn't know why.

"See their rib cages? I bet they don't weigh even a hundred pounds."

Trevor's voice was low and reverential. "They're being starved."

Each woman stood beside an outdoor heating element that rose half again as tall as they were. On occasion, a man dressed in a suit would walk by and place his hand on a woman's crotch or lean down to kiss her breast. The women remained unfazed, their faces blank as if they were in another place.

"They're stoned. Someone drugged them . . . thankfully." YaYa made a fist with his prosthetic hand. "I suddenly want to kill every one of the fuckers who did this."

"Something tells me we'll get the chance." Walker tore his gaze away from the women and regarded the yard. He counted twelve men dressed in expensive suits and cloaks. Servants circulated among them with trays. Three figures were clothed completely in red robes, their faces hidden behind masks, and a conical matching red hat that rose several feet. They looked like scarlet KKK robes. These three were treated with clear deference.

"Wish I could get close enough to hear what they're saying." YaYa stared at the scene for a moment, then shook his head. "I still can't get over the women. I get they're starving, but how can they survive without water? They have to drink."

Walker shrugged. "I'm sure they've figured it out. They've been starving for a while. Let's get back on mission. Trev, you still watching our six?"

Trev replied from his sentry position in the hall, "And seven and eight. Roger."

"I don't see the woman who took the photos." Walker prepared a second Black Hornet. "I'm going to check out the windows on the second floor."

It took him a few moments, but he was soon controlling a second MUAV, flying it well above the trees and bringing it in over the top of the Tudor house. He could see the party in full swing down below. He decided to check the front of the house first.

If he thought he'd seen it all in the backyard, he was terribly mistaken. The view into each room was a different study in debauchery. Men on men. Men on women. Some were tied. Some were being taken violently. In all cases, their faces were covered by brightly colored carnival masks.

He moved around the eastern side of the home and found a room where several men and women were putting their clothes on. Walker figured this for a dressing room and was rewarded with the sight of two men dressed in masks and nothing else entering into the room. They removed their masks and could have been the most normal people one would encounter. They glanced at each other, their gazes lingering for a moment, then went about putting on their clothes.

That's when Walker noticed that one of the women was staring directly into the camera.

She couldn't possibly have seen the Black Hornet, but just in case, Walker backed it away from the window. But she came closer and began to point.

He swung the camera north just in time to catch a flash of light from high up on Glastonbury Tor, as if there'd been an explosion. He glanced out the window, to where he could see it in real time, but the light was gone.

The feeds on all the cameras began to static.

It dawned on him what was happening about the time the camera on the northwest pole winked out.

He directed the Black Hornet to pull up and head south of the area, hopefully getting far enough away to be out of the disturbance zone.

YaYa took a knee and stared out the window, now that the feed on his screen had gone blank as well. "Do you think it's the Hunt?"

"What else could it be?" He let the craft hover and put in a call to Holmes, using his MBITR Bluetoothed to his cell.

Holmes answered on the first ring. "We've been watching."

Walker peered into the night but couldn't see anything. He focused on the view from his remaining Black Hornet, but the Tor was too far away for him to see much of anything except blobs. "Then you can tell us what the hell is going on."

"Sassy says it's the Carnival of Fools. They're using sex magic to pool power."

"You can get magic like that?" YaYa asked.

Sassy got online. "Jack, it's the collocation and derivation of energy. Magic is all about gathering and transmitting energy. By the looks of it, they're creating enough energy that were I on the astral plane, I'd be able to see it from here. Think beacon."

"Well, I think the beacon is working. Looks like the Wild Hunt is coming." Walker strained to see, but the images were too grainy.

Laws joined in. "They've been busy. We have seven more reports of missing persons, including an entire population of Basques who'd established a sheep farm in Wales. MI5 is keeping everything quiet, but the Prime Minister is raging."

Holmes returned, "Stay put. Looks like we may have found their headquarters."

Walker rogered out. If they were going to stay put, he could at least see how close he could get. He began to ease the Black Hornet forward. He was at about two hundred feet and the wind was buffeting him pretty badly. As soon as the camera found the yard below, it would turn away. The view was akin to looking through a porthole on a small boat on high seas.

YaYa wondered aloud, "I wonder which one of them it is."

"Which one of who is what?" Walker realized his sentence was an egregious violation of the rules of grammar, but in context it made sense.

"Which one of them is the Lord of Misrule," YaYa said. "If this is the Carnival of Fools and they're celebrating Saturnus, then someone has to be the Lord of Misrule."

Walker was finally able to get low enough on his bucking MUAV to get a glimpse of the backyard. Several hounds from the Wild Hunt were climbing over the wall. No one seemed disturbed by them. He saw one of the hounds approach a naked woman, leap at her, only to disappear inside of her. The woman arched her back—

Then the feed blacked out.

Walker felt a moment of panic. The last thing he wanted was for the MUAV to fall into the yard where it could be found. So he turned the MUAV south, or at least he was hoping he had, and he powered it out of the area. Only the feed never came back on. He continued powering it away, praying every second that he'd get it back. He really had no way of knowing if he was powering anything.

Finally, he gave up and slapped the remote control into his lap.

"We have entry from the front door." Trevor moved to the doorway of the room. Then he whispered, "We have entry on the stairs. Prepare yourselves."

CHAPTER 33

GLASTONBURY TOR, GLASTONBURY, ENGLAND. SECONDS LATER.

YaYa stayed by the window while Walker stacked behind Trevor, who'd assumed a kneeling position, his pistol locked in front of him. They slid their NVDs in place and dialed up their familiar green universe.

Walker reminded himself to be careful. It could be anything from a cat or a dog to maybe a couple of teenagers looking for a private place to do something frisky. He'd be mortified if they gunned down some kids by accident. But they didn't have to worry about that.

The first sign was the sight of a rifle barrel. Walker immediately recognized it as belonging to a submachine gun, which meant the barrel was very short.

"Let me." Walker's voice was a hint of a whisper over the MBITR.

A balaclava-covered head appeared. Walker gave twin trigger pulls and sent a pair of suppressed 9mm rounds ripping into it. The man fell flat, his face planting on the top step.

"Watch for grenades," Trevor whispered.

Walker didn't like not knowing their situation. "Anything outside?"

YaYa responded, "Negative," and Walker ordered him to prepare the fourth Black Hornet and to deploy it around the front. While Walker wasn't sure if they'd have time, they might, if the man was either a singleton or paired. There was only one way to find out. He ordered Trevor forward to retrieve the body, an effort that would put the Section 9 man's hand and arm at risk for as long as it took for him to grab and jerk.

Trevor held his pistol in his right hand at high ready as he squat-walked to the head of the stairs. He peeked around the corner fast, then turned and held up his fingers showing two.

Walker held out a fist, which meant to halt operations.

Trevor flatted himself against the wall.

Walker moved forward, his P229 at low ready, repeating his mantra, "Slow is smooth; smooth is fast." He counted to three with his trigger hand, then put his finger back on the trigger and smoothly twisted his barrel round the corner. He put eight rounds into the two men, but only one fell.

When he pulled back, Trevor had grabbed the dead man and was pulling him into the room.

Walker backed to the door of the bedroom and took up position.

"YaYa, give me something."

"Launched. Moving over the top of the house and—shit."

"What is it?"

"One of those girls is standing out there along with two of the red-cloaked things. Uh, Walker?"

Walker cursed. Things were going from bad to worse. "What?"

"I feel something."

"I feel it too, bud. Just relax."

"It's them, isn't it? It's their magic. Feels . . . greasy."

Walker couldn't agree more. "Trev, what do you have?"

Trevor had searched the prisoner. He found an amulet with a silver tree inside a circle, which he took a cell phone picture of, then pocketed. He also found a tattoo on the prisoner's chest of three interlocked crescent moons. The man had nothing else besides equipment, which was top-of-the-line. He took pictures of the man's face and the tattoo, then sent all three shots to Preeti.

"The feeling's getting worse," YaYa said.

Walker's teeth were on edge. There'd been a time when magic or proximity to the supernatural would have made him fall on the ground and do the kicking chicken, like his first mission in the hidden snakehead sweatshop in San Francisco. He could only imagine how YaYa felt. It was so new to him.

YaYa cursed, "Fuck me."

"What is it?"

"The naked girl with the sewn-shut lips pointed at the Black Hornet and it fell from the sky."

Walker thought through his options. "Is the back clear?"

"For the moment."

"Okay. We're going to *un-ass the AO*. Trevor, you watch our six. Once we're down, we'll cover you."

Trevor nodded and took up position at the door.

Walker gestured for YaYa to go first. The roof had a ledge outside the window large enough for a man to stand on. YaYa climbed out, then swept the area with his pistol.

"Clear."

"Then move."

YaYa reached out and grabbed the lip of the roof. He hesitated a moment, then pulled himself over the edge. Walker saw his fingers; then he was gone.

A moment later, "Clear."

Now it was Walker's turn to exit. He glanced back at Trevor, who gave him a thumbs-up. Walker nodded, then climbed out into the cold Christmas Eve night. Somewhere people were warm and celebrating. Somewhere people had already exchanged gifts or were preparing to do so the next morning. Christmas Eve had always been a time of joy, even at the orphanage. But he felt anything but joy at this moment, fear raging through his spine from the proximity of this strange Red Grove magic.

He lowered himself, then dropped the remaining five feet.

YaYa had already taken up position beside the trunk of a tree, his weapon sweeping both corners of the walled-in backyard.

"Clear," Walker said into his mike, then moved beside YaYa. With the trunk to his left, he aimed toward the window. "Sectors of fire." YaYa left the right corner of the house alone and concentrated on his 180 degrees.

"Come on, Trev. Move." Walker glanced behind him. Wall with concrete blocks and lots of dead grass. He turned back to the window.

YaYa gave Walker a quick look. "What's taking him?"

Walker was beginning to get a sinking feeling. "Trev. Radio check. Come in, Trev." It had only been a moment. Not ten seconds.

Walker felt it before he saw it. "Something's coming."

YaYa was sobbing beside him as his whole body began to tremble.

Walker put a hand on him. "Control. Fight it."

YaYa nodded, wiping unbidden tears from his face with the back of his hands.

When Walker looked again to the window he saw her, sewn lips, blue piercing eyes seeing through him, her long blond hair moved delicately by an unfelt breeze. He felt her power. His teeth began to chatter. He raised his pistol but couldn't control his aim. He fired over and over and over, but the rounds never came close. He kept firing until the pistol clicked back at him.

A moment of panic took him, but he fought it.

He grabbed YaYa.

"Where is he?" YaYa asked through sobs.

Walker glanced once more at the window. She was gone. As was Trevor.

"They have him."

CHAPTER 34

POINT BRAVO, WARWICK, ENGLAND. CHRISTMAS DAY, ZERO DARK THIRTY.

He expected Preeti to scream and shout, *How could you?* and *You of all people?*, but all he got was silence. He caught her glancing at him with red swollen eyes, but she wouldn't say a word. This uncharacteristic response to the capture of her boyfriend worried Walker enough that he wished she were screaming at him.

It had taken them four hours to make it back. Once they'd cleared the wall behind the home, they'd headed for the car. But even before they reached it, they'd realized that Trevor had the keys, and neither Walker nor YaYa knew how to wire a car. So they'd been forced to continue running. Near Glastonbury Train Station they'd found a car with keys inside. Then, they'd taken extra care not to drag surveillance back to the chapel. Preeti's brother had tried to do what he'd previously done to the CCTV servers, but cybersecurity had found and closed his back door.

Just as they thought the universe was against them, they had help from an unsuspected arena. Lord Robinson had provided a platoon of Royal Marines to Ian for assistance. The chief of Section 9, for all Walker knew the last member of Section 9, had finally managed to convince the senior MP that the only way they were going to stop the Wild Hunt was to dedicate more assets to the effort. The Marines weren't pleased to be pulled away from their families at Christmas, but in the end they were Marines and acted the part. So it was a taxi that picked them up outside of a Sainsbury's superstore in Gloucester. They'd switched to foot, then boarded a bus, then went back to foot once more. Scrubbing any last vestige of surveillance by transiting an all-night grocer, they got into the taxi in an area identified by Preeti's brother as having no active CCTV cameras. The taxi driver introduced himself as Corporal Alex Cope and took them straight to Warwick.

Hoover was the first to greet them. Walker spared the dog a small pet, then strode straight to Preeti.

"We'll get him back."

Dark circles under her bloodshot eyes along with a red and running nose detailed a bucket of shed tears. "I know you will." Her voice was flat.

"No, really. I'll do everything I can." Then his voice got husky. "I'm so sorry."

She nodded, then turned back to her work. "I know."

Then he'd briefed Ian, Holmes, and Lieutenant Rory Magerts, platoon leader of the Marines, who'd been read onto Section 9's mission, but by the increasing level of incredulity present on his face it was not something he wholeheartedly believed. The witch, Laws, Genaro, and Yank listened in, but from a distance. Everyone occasionally glanced in Preeti's direction, especially when Trevor's name was mentioned.

After the second run-through, Holmes asked Sassy to join them.

"Can it hear us?" Holmes asked.

"It hears everything."

"What were those women Walker described?"

"Vessels. Fonts. They are empty and have no soul."

That explained their emotionless appearance. But Walker wanted to know where their souls had gone, so he asked.

Sassy frowned and shook her head, looking almost like the regular woman she'd been pretending to be all this time. Looking at her now, no one would know that she was a powerful witch who'd forced the mythological creature to possess her. "There's a type of magic that uses people, uses their souls for power. It's distasteful."

"What are they used for? I thought I saw a hound leap into her, then disappear."

Sassy regarded Walker. "I know what you're thinking, but stop that right now." Walker was about to respond, but she shushed him with a wave of her hand. "You're thinking of your girl, aren't you? If her soul can survive in the body of one of these ghouls, then you can be together again." She shook her head again, this time looking 1,000 percent witch. "She is not at all like she was. What's left of her soul has done terrible things, things from which she can't come back. Ever."

Walker stared at Sassy, understanding and not caring. He repeated his question. "What are they used for?"

She sighed and glanced at Holmes.

"Answer his question," he said.

"The hounds are formed from the strength of a person's soul. They manifest as real when attacking, but spend most of their existence as a wisp of wind or a billow of fog. They are sustained by Tuatha magic and belong to the Hunt. But on occasion, if an empty vessel is available, a witch or warlock can summon a hound to do their bidding. The soul of the person who was harvested for the hound is pleased to be once again in a human form and shows their gratitude through sharing of the magic that made them."

"Have you ever done that?" Holmes asked.

"I told you. I'm not that kind of witch."

"Why do they sew their lips shut?" YaYa asked, joining the conversation.

"The Tuatha have their secrets and don't want them told."

YaYa couldn't help himself. "So they take some poor waif, rip out her soul, sew her lips shut so she can be a vessel?"

She stared at him flatly. "Being judgmental isn't going to get us anywhere."

Holmes jumped in. "She's right. Let's figure this thing out."

Just as they were about to start, the lieutenant's cell rang. He stepped away from the table and carried out a brisk conversation. He glanced at Holmes and Ian twice. When he finished, he rejoined them.

"Don't know what to make of it. I sent two men to Glastonbury to keep tabs as requested. They're sure that the people in the house know they're there, but they don't seem to be concerned. In fact, they're still having their party."

Holmes uncharacteristically cursed.

"What is it?" Ian asked.

"They're not worried about freedom of movement."

Walker figured it out the same time everyone else did. "It's happening today, isn't it?"

Holmes nodded and checked his watch. "We have less than twenty hours and they could do it anytime. We've got to get out there."

"And do what?" Ian smacked his hand down on the table. "We don't even know what they're trying to do."

"No, but at least we know where they are. There's got to be something we can do . . . whatever it is." To Laws, Holmes said, "Have everyone ready to go in twenty."

"What are you going to do?"

"Sassy and I are going to speak with the Tuatha. If something's going down then it knows. It's time for the Tuatha to come clean."

CHAPTER 35

POINT BRAVO, WARWICK, ENGLAND. LATER.

While everyone else checked weapons and loaded kit, Holmes and Sassy had a private conversation in the back of the room. He decided to begin, letting her know as close to what he felt as he could afford.

"First of all, I appreciate everything you've done for us. We're more used to things we can shoot and kill. A lot of folks might think that to do our job we'd need a lot of special equipment. But they'd be amazed at what a simple round from a rifle can do if delivered on target." He checked to see if she was listening and she nodded. "But the hounds are another matter. We can't affect them. Our bullets do no damage. That is, unless you or the Tuatha have something to help us."

She started to say something, then stopped, as if she was listening to something. When she looked up, she said, "There's little mortal hands can do to deter the hounds of the Wild Hunt."

"What about magic? Is there something, I don't know. . . ." He felt silly saying the words aloud, but there was no other way he knew to describe what he wanted. "Can you make magic bullets?"

Sassy smiled, but it wasn't her smile. It was too wide and too strained. There was a flash of fear in her eyes before it was replaced with a competent calm. *"The residual of our magic is what mortals like my host tap into for power. These are nothing but slick shadows of what we once were. The hounds were created from original magic. It is pure."*

"So you're saying there's nothing we can do?" He had a hard time believing that. He frowned. Was this some sort of test? He knew he was speaking to the Tuatha now. However it was happening, he wouldn't have much longer if it was against Sassy's will. "Then how were you defeated before? Who was it, the Milesians?"

Again with the alien smile. *"You've studied my people. What is it you want to know about them?"*

"They defeated you. What did they use?"

Gone was the smile, to be replaced by a look of such intense hate that had it been one degree worse her face would have cracked and broken. *"They were given the gift of iron before they were ready."*

Swords. Metallurgy. Arrowheads. Holmes could see it. He tried to remember the eras. Where was Laws when he needed him? No, there wasn't time, plus this was a commander issue. Hadn't it been the Bronze Age? With everyone using weapons made from tin and copper, the appearance of iron would have been as a super-weapon.

"What's the other thing?" Holmes asked.

"Faith."

"What? Like Catholic or Baptist?"

"Those are words, not faith." Then Sassy's face slipped into something more akin to a coma patient's. Her eyes went glassy; her mouth dropped, lengthening her face. The only thing that told him that she was still alive was a tic jerking the corner of her right eye.

He waited about thirty seconds, wondering what he should do. Just as he reached out to give her a gentle shake, she shook her head, blinked several times, then curled her lips into a knot of anger.

"How long?" she asked in a voice that would make a snake shed its skin.

"A minute. Maybe two."

"What'd it tell you?"

Holmes thought about it but decided to tell her. So he did. He still wasn't entirely convinced she was on their side. He was certain that as long as he and the team were doing the same thing she was doing she'd help. But if his mission went cross-purposes to her desire, he had no doubt she'd do whatever it took to get her wish, even if it meant stepping all over SEAL Team 666.

She listened, her brow knotted. When he was done she said, "It has the feel of truth. Listen, I know you don't entirely trust me, but you have to trust me on this. The Tuatha does not care about us. We are humans, mortals. We are nothing to it, no matter how easily it's able to manipulate us through its charismatic magic."

"But you said it was telling me the truth?"

She smiled for the first time, her own smile so unlike that of the Tuatha. It was as if the Tuatha didn't know the limitations of a human face. "You should know, Sam, sometimes it's what they don't tell you."

Holmes hated this part of it. Why couldn't he just plan a straightforward mission to take down a terrorist in Waziristan or pirates in Somalia? Why'd they choose him to lead Triple Six? He frowned inwardly and smacked down the little devil who was distracting him. He knew exactly why they'd chosen him. The same reason he couldn't go into any casino in Vegas or Atlantic City. He had luck. No, it was more than that. He had the ability to miraculously pull victory from the jaws of defeat. This could be part of it. What had she said . . . *it's what they don't tell you*? In order to know what they don't tell you, you have to know what questions to ask.

"What'd it leave out and why?"

"The why is the most important. Once you realize this, once you get it through your head, make it your mantra." When she saw he was ready she said, "It will do anything to keep you from killing another Tuatha. Anything."

Holmes thought about this for a moment. "How strong are you? Will it take over during the battle?"

"I'm strong, Sam. I'm stronger than most any you'll see. And after all that, I'm also a fairly good person too. At least I have my moments."

"I've known plenty of strong women who found themselves in the wrong place at the wrong time and lived to regret it. What happened to you back there?"

"Think of containing the Tuatha as holding down a thousand-tentacled octopus. I thought I had all of them pinned down, but I must have missed one. . . . I triggered it when I tried to communicate with it. Well, it won't be able to pull that one again."

He'd take that one at face value. "What is it that it didn't tell me?"

"While I was in there I saw flashes of things yet to be . . . alternates. Things that could happen. The Tuatha are vulnerable inside the mounds. How can I explain it?" She closed her eyes. "The insides of the mounds are like our outsides. It's their normal universe. Inside they are as mortal as we are."

"And their magic? The hounds?"

"The same."

"Then we need to figure out a way to get into the mound of Glastonbury Tor."

"I've been working on that and I have an unconventional idea."

"What is it?"

"We go through a back door."

"How are we going to manage that?"

"I'll need to exert some control over the Tuatha. It might even hurt a little."

"Are you sure that's good?"

"After today, I'm positive."

CHAPTER 36

POINT BRAVO, WARWICK, ENGLAND. 0400 HOURS.

They left Preeti and Genaro in the basement. It was obvious why Preeti wasn't invited to the party, plus she'd be in a better position to support them where she was. In addition, although he was a U.S. Navy chief petty officer, Holmes was unwilling to send Genaro Stewart into combat untested, so he was asked to remain with Preeti, if for no other reason than to protect her, especially once she briefed the team on what she'd found.

While Walker and YaYa had been making their way back, she'd cleaned the footage, combined the two feeds, and run it through MI5's biometric processor, which had just been upgraded with new software, thanks to a partnership with the Israeli Defense Forces—the pre-eminent biometric-capable organization on the planet. It wasn't long before she discovered the identities of nine of the persons at the party. Five were Members of Parliament, three were high-ranking military officials, and one was the Deputy Minister for Education.

That this group reached the highest levels was both unsettling and expected. All along Ian and Holmes had found it difficult to believe that the Hunt was something a previously unknown organization could pull off. Ian and Holmes argued whether or not to contact Lord Robinson, but in the end Holmes relented. After all, this was Ian's country and ultimately Ian's battle. Triple Six had been sent in for support, even if Ian was the sole surviving member of the organization they'd been sent in to support.

Lord Robinson doubted Ian's contention at first but came around when Ian offered to show him pictures, including the image of a naked Minster of Education, returning from a romp with some anonymous masked partygoer. Lord Robinson promised to send them additional help, as well as pulling together a group of trusted MPs and Ministers whom he knew to be honest and uninvolved. Ian tried to dissuade Lord Robinson from doing this, since he couldn't be sure who was who, but the Lord would hear nothing of it. He'd insisted that he could judge character well enough to determine who was a *devil-worshiping sot and who wasn't.*

When the conversation ended, Yank was the one who pointed out the danger. "As much effort as we've spent to find them, I can't help but think they're expending exponentially more trying to find us." He'd pointed at Ian's phone as he put it into his pocket. "Once Lord Robinson outs himself, it won't take long for them to trace his phone calls and find you. The phone's Global Positioning System will give you away like that," he said, snapping his finger for emphasis.

Laws held out his hand. "He's right. Let me have it."

But Ian hesitated.

Holmes stepped in. "Got to give up the phone, Ian, or we're not going through with the mission."

Ian nodded. "I know. I just can't believe it's come to this." He pulled the phone out and handed it to Laws. "To think I can't trust my own people."

Laws began taking the phone apart. "These aren't your people. These are folks who want an all-white England. You have no more in common with them than I have with Jeffery Dahmer."

"Well said, I suppose."

Lieutenant Magerts offered Ian the use of his phone, but he had the same problem. His could be tied to Lord Robinson as well. So Laws eviscerated that phone of its sim card too. Preeti offered the men the use of her phone, so it was with a pink, rhinestone-encrusted phone that the mission began.

They were literally heading out the door when Preeti screamed and began to sob. Her brother had sent her a URL, which had recently propagated. When she'd clicked the link, it took her to a picture of Trevor. His face was beaten. His eyes were swollen. Blood was crusted in his nostrils. If there'd been any doubt before regarding the Red Grove's desire for Trevor, it was now obvious that he was designated as Lord of Misrule. The sign around his neck said so. The conical party hat on his head was so out of place to make the image even sadder.

Walker placed his hand on her shoulder. "This means he's alive. We'll get him."

"Do you promise?" Her gaze lingered on the image on the screen.

"I do. I promise." As he said it, he caught the gaze of Laws, who shook his head slowly. Walker knew good and well that he shouldn't have made that promise. But he was serious about it. He'd lost his girlfriend to the same people who now had Trevor, the same people who were the architects of the largest coordinated serial killings in England. Walker was going to be a success if it killed him. And if he died, at least he'd ensure that he'd take some of the bastards from the Red Grove with him.

CHAPTER 37

WARWICK CASTLE, WARWICK, ENGLAND. 0430 HOURS.

Ian didn't plan to survive the day. But that didn't matter. He'd lost everything he'd cared about and he wasn't about to lose England. A corporal drove them to the marshaling area, which was the parking lot of Warwick Castle. Magerts had thirty men and they'd need every one of them. They were in full kit and each carried an SA80 and a knife. But Holmes had different ideas about what weapons might work, based on a conversation he'd had with the Tuatha. So Ian woke the director of the Warwick Castle museum and forced him to open the museum to them. At first the man was squeamish about what he'd been asked to do, but after Ian pulled out a letter signed by the Queen authorizing them to do anything he so desired in the defense of England the man had no choice but to comply.

Ian had used the letter–what they affectionately call the Queen Letter—on less than a dozen occasions. She'd signed it back in 1973, long before he was part of the organization, but it was designed to provide them agility of movement, despite the ponderous reaction of British bureaucracy.

He first went to the display case and pulled out every sword he could find, noticing that many of them were irreplaceable national treasures. Lot of good they were doing gathering dust. He then ordered the curator to lead them into the storage rooms, where they found two dozen swords used by a local reenactor group who came together once a month to use the ballistae and pretended to attack the castle while others dressed up to protect it. The swords were cheap and had dull blades, but they had points on them. At least there was that.

Then, with thirty-three swords, he had all the Marines don the scabbards as best they could. Magerts passed around a roll of 550 cord, which they used to form sword belts. Soon they had the blades slung over their backs.

"Give yourselves a few minutes to familiarize yourselves with them," Ian bellowed. "Just don't cut yourself or a fellow Marine."

He turned to Magerts, who wore an immense smile.

Ian had chosen Guy of Warwick's sword for himself. Although several of the other swords, including the one carried by Magerts, had enough gems and gilt on the scabbard that he could probably trade one in for a London flat, Guy's sword was old, flat iron. The grip had long ago lost any padding and was only black metal, as was the pommel and guard. The blade was of the same material but still held an edge. All told, the sword was fifty inches of black metal. It didn't look like much, but Ian had a special place in his heart for the mythological hero of the twelfth century who was purported to have killed the giant named Colbrand, the Dun Cow, and even a dragon. If even a sliver of the legends was true, then this was the only sword Ian could see using this day.

"What are you so happy about?" Ian struggled to make his own sword belt. "I never thought I'd see the day when my Marines went to war wearing swords."

"We'll be lucky if they don't kill themselves with them."

"You'll be surprised at how fast they pick it up." He nodded toward them.

Ian turned and his mouth fell open. The Marines were moving the blades through the air in complex patterns. Although not at all similar to any way Ian had seen swords function, it seemed no less deadly.

"We've been doing Filipino Kali Arnis training for the last nine months. They learned some stick-fighting sequences. Looks like they're applying the principles to their swords."

Ian regained his composure and shook his head. "Isn't it ironic that after four thousand years of weapons evolution it's the simple sword that's going to make the greatest difference?"

Magerts winced as one of his men dropped a sword. "Let's hope they don't have to use them too much."

"They'll use them as necessary. Using them might just be the only thing that will win the day. Have them form up. I want to speak to them."

Magerts brought his men to attention.

Ian finished making his sword belt. He took his time putting it on, well aware that the men were watching him. When he was ready, he marched to the front of the formation, where Magerts stood waiting. They saluted; then Magerts stepped aside. Ian put the men at parade rest.

He took a moment to regard them, acutely aware that he might be leading them to their deaths, just as he had the men of Section 9. That he was the sole surviving member of his unit made him feel small and unequipped to lead, but there was no one else. He fought against an avalanche of self-doubt—after all, how effective could he be if he'd lost his whole team? Still, one incongruous part of him demanded he stay on the path. Whether it was the spirits of his men or his own damned desire to continue the mission, he needed to finish it. He believed with every molecule of his unworthy body that to quit was to lose England. Somehow, he had to convince these men that their lives might actually be forfeit, and a necessary loss for the preservation of England. It was a hard thing, but such was the lot of a soldier.

So it was with a heavy but proud heart that he addressed them. "You should be with your family. You should be getting baked ham, drinking too much, and making bets about who falls asleep first. You shouldn't be here. Let me say it again, you shouldn't be here." He paused. "But you are here and you're here because you are professionals. I thank you for that. The reason I thank you is that when you die, no one will thank you. They'll never know that you tried to stand in the way of a supernatural force created for selfish ends.

"The things you are going to see this night, should you survive, will haunt you for the rest of your lives. But know, Marines, that without you, England is surely lost. With you, we have a chance to win her back. Now get ready to fight hard."

Thirty curious faces were now stunned. Several of them glanced at their partners, but no one was laughing. He wasn't sure if his speech did the trick, but it was something he'd felt compelled to do. He'd have wanted someone to tell him if he'd been in their place.

He brought them to attention.

Magerts stepped in front of him.

"Not exactly a Saint Crispin's Day speech, was it?" Ian asked.

Magerts's face was stone cold. "They need to understand the seriousness. I think you provided that."

Ian turned the platoon back over to the lieutenant.

After a weapon and ammo check, they boarded into three vans and a car. The vans were white with dark smoked-out windows. The insides had been stripped and allowed room for ten Marines to sit. Each van had a driver. The car was a white BMW sedan also with smoked-out windows. The vehicles all had military license plates. Magerts would drive the BMW with Ian in the passenger seat.

Ten minutes later they were heading for Glastonbury Tor.

CHAPTER 38

SOUTH FROM WARWICK, ENGLAND. 0530 HOURS.

Walker drove with Laws in the seat beside him. Holmes, Sassy, and Yank were in the middle row. The last row held YaYa and Hoover. Walker kept glancing in the mirror at Sassy. Her plan was simple, but Walker doubted they'd be able to execute. It was based on too much theory. He'd rather charge through the front door, but the hounds had already proven to be unaffected by their rounds. Now they were on their way to meet a fellow witch who lived in Godalming. She was going to provide some items that would assist them. Then it was off to Sassy's Boondoggle, as he was privately referring to it.

Her idea, once posed, was co-opted and coordinated into the larger effort. While Ian took the platoon of Marines to secure the home south of Glastonbury Tor, arresting as many of the party-goers as they could, Triple Six and their pet witch were heading for Bratton Castle in Wiltshire. The castle had been built in the Iron Age, but the hill fort it had been built upon was constructed during the Bronze Age, which according to Laws, meant about two thousand years before Christ.

What very few people knew was that the hill fort was erected on an even older Tuatha mound. Sassy had drawn a map of all the mounds she knew of and this one had been the nearest to Glastonbury Tor. The idea was to use the Tuatha inside Sassy to enter the mound, then use the Bratton Mound as a transit point to Glastonbury Tor.

That is, if the Tuatha had the power to get into the mound.

And if the Tuatha could bring them with it.

And if the Tuatha cooperated.

And if they could figure out how to travel through the mounds.

There were just too many ifs.

"You know, if you squeeze it hard enough I'm sure it will bleed."

Walker glanced at Laws. "Huh?"

"The steering wheel. If you were planning on strangling it, then you're done."

Walker loosened his hands. He glanced in the mirror, then whispered, "I just don't think this will work."

"It might not, but I think what really bothers you is the whole going-through-the-mounds thing."

"That's doesn't bother me."

"Then you need your head examined." Laws glanced behind them, then leaned close to Walker. "We've never done anything like this before. Sure, we've run, walked, crawled, and jumped into the mouth of danger before, but we've never traveled through an interdimensional portal. You realize that that's what they are, right?"

Laws had put his hand on Walker's right arm. Walker shook it off. "Now who's the excited one?" But Laws was right. That was what was bothering him. He'd dealt with magic and seen it done, but he'd never really been in a position to use magic for his own ends. "We'll be lucky if we don't find ourselves stuck inside a hill."

"You're a complaining lot of military men, aren't you?" Sassy said from the backseat. Her words dripped with condescension.

Walker felt his grip tighten on the steering wheel once again. He was about to say something when Laws jumped in.

"It's been like this since Christ was a corporal, Miss Moore.

We talk about it now and get it out of our system; then we're clearheaded when the fighting starts."

"I just never thought this was how you acted."

"You've been influenced by the movies, I can tell. You expect us to be stoic, silent, strong, rugged. That sort?"

She nodded. "That's closer to what I expected."

"We do that sometimes. But that's also why we have Commander Holmes around. He's our official stoic, silent, strong, and rugged SEAL team leader."

"Enough already," Holmes growled.

Walker pulled off the A3 into Godalming and followed Sassy's directions until they came to a quaint house on a side street. One-story, made from stone, and with what looked like a thatched roof, it was right out of a storybook. He watched Sassy walk up the sidewalk in her dress and high heels. This whole experience seemed like it was out of a storybook. Witches . . . the commonplace, almost casual references to magic and all things magical . . . supernatural creatures . . . and faeries. Not the faeries that populated the stories he'd read when he was a child, but the faeries from which those stories originated. And much like the stories from the Brothers Grimm were watered down over the ages, so had the complexity and terribleness of these faeries.

She was gone for ten minutes, during which time the only sound inside the SUV was the occasional sweep of the wiper blade and the panting of the dog. When she returned, she wore black jeans and black high-tops with sparkles. A black blouse peeked out from her black down jacket. She wore a baseball cap with a picture of a witch on a broomstick inside a circle with a line through it. Holmes got out and let her in. She carried a heavy canvas bag, which she deposited on Yank's lap. She slid into the seat, keeping a smaller bag on her lap.

"What's this for?" Yank unzipped it and his eyes shot wide. "Sweet." He pulled free a short sword made from a black metal.

YaYa leaned over the seat to peer into the bag. "What's that?"

"Gladius," Sassy said.

YaYa reached out to touch it, but Yank moved it out of reach. "As in what a Roman gladiator used?"

"As in what the common Roman soldier used. But this is no antique." Yank tested the heft and weft. "My guess is carbon steel." He counted. "There are six in here."

"A gift. They're gladius machetes. The young lady who helped me out has a boyfriend who works at a knife store. She talked him into letting us borrow them." She smiled flatly. "You're supposed to return them as good as new."

Yank snorted, then turned the metal over in his hands. He stared at it the same way some men stare at a beautiful woman.

YaYa managed to reach in the bag and pull one for himself. He sat back in the seat beside Hoover, who could care less about the dull-colored piece of metal. "You're giving this to us in order to . . ."

"Kill the hounds," she said.

"And whatever other *beegees* there are that don't like bullets," Laws added.

Walker felt himself flinch when she said *kill the hounds*. He was acutely aware that Jen's soul had somehow been co-opted and used to form one of the creatures. The idea of killing her all over again, killing her soul, made his breath shallow, his chest tighten. He fought back the emotion that threatened to take over his face and swallowed hard as he stared into the dawn of Christmas Day.

"What's in the other bag?" Yank asked. "More goodies for us?"

"In a way. I need each of your body armor and those mask things you wear." She unzipped this bag and pulled out a few small bottles of what looked like paint and a tiny brush. "I'm going to put protection runes on you. These runes will be from the Elder Futhark runic language, which is about two millennia old. Elhaz was used by the Norsemen when they invaded, ironically, to protect them from Christianity. Because of its rich history in the Isles, I've found it works considerably well against nature spirits, which you could call Tuatha."

Yank turned to her. "I'm not giving you my armor or my ballistic mask."

Holmes sighed. "Give it to her."

Yank tried to draw in the other SEALs with pleading looks, but no one was biting. "But we can't be sure if she's—"

"Enough of that." Holmes shrugged out of his body armor. "Do mine first and make it pretty. Walker, we going to sit here at the curb for the rest of the day?"

Walker shook out of it and put the SUV in gear. Soon they were heading toward Farnborough. When he hit the M3, he turned left. They'd traveled about ten kilometers when Holmes got a call from Preeti. A few moments into the conversation, he told Walker to pull over. There were no turnoffs, so he had to pull far to the edge. Luckily, there was hardly any traffic.

After a few moments, Holmes hung up and let them in on the conversation.

"Looks like the Red Grove is marshaling its forces. Preeti's been monitoring the CCTV cameras and discovered that there are seven roadblocks, all at major intersections that would bring us to Glastonbury Tor."

"But we're not going there," Laws said.

"As it turns out, their roadblocks have put the whole area out of reach."

Ever in need of a fight, Yank shrugged. "Why not run them? We have the firepower."

"This part of our mission requires a little subtlety and surprise." Holmes shook his head. "Suggestions?"

Walker continued staring out the window. "We could jump in."

YaYa laughed. "Like we're going to find a plane and chutes on Christmas Day. Nice try."

But Laws wasn't so dismissive. "That would work if we had a place to go."

"What about that?" Walker pointed out the front windshield to a billboard that read: "SKYDIVE COTSWALD—Five Locations," with a picture of two grinning civilians making a tandem jump.

"But it's Christmas," YaYa persisted.

Walker turned to Laws. "My guess is that they have the chutes and the plane. All we have to do is jerk someone out of bed and have them fly us to altitude."

"Let's do it." Holmes got on the phone to Preeti. She checked the locations. The closest was in Salisbury, but it was on the other side of a roadblock. So the next nearest location was Redlands Airfield in Swindon. Holmes ordered Walker to take them there. He told Laws to plot them a drop azimuth because they'd be using commercial chutes, which would force them to remain in the air longer.

Laws called Genie and ordered some weather data.

"So we're really going to jump in?" YaYa grinned. "That's the best thing I've heard all day." He scruffled Hoover's neck. "Hear that, girl? You're gonna jump. I'll need to work up a Palmer rig, but it'll be good."

Sassy looked up from where she'd been concentrating on Holmes's body armor and ballistic mask. She'd painted what looked a lot like an upright pitchfork on the forehead of his mask and several dozen symbols on the front and back of his body armor.

"Did someone say 'parachute'?"

Holmes nodded.

Her eyes narrowed. She pointed at her hat. "This witch doesn't fly."

"You will today," Holmes said. Then he gave her his stoic, strong look. "Suck it up. It's the only way in."

She had no response other than to stare at him in stunned silence.

For the first time that day Walker found something to laugh at. So he did.

CHAPTER 39

WARWICK CASTLE, WARWICK, ENGLAND. 0730 HOURS.

It had stopped snowing. Cold fog hugged the sides of the road. Dawn had just come. Ian had wanted to get on-site before light, to take advantage of the night, but it looked like he wasn't going to make it. The drive from Warwick had been too long.

They were headed southwest on the A361 and less than three kilometers away from their objective when Ian saw the roadblock. He knew in the pit of his stomach it was there for him. Each driver had been issued a radio. He ordered the last van to pull up and continued to the roadblock with the rest of the vehicles. Two police sedans were pulled across the road. Three men in jackets stood to one side. They had pistols in holsters on their hips, which meant they weren't just police. They all wore military uniforms, although their name tags had been removed. One was a large Irishman with the flattened nose of a professional fighter. Another was a young kid, his eyes wide and nervous. The last one was a mousy man with a weasel's face.

Magerts pulled the BMW to a stop so its nose was a few feet from those of the police cars.

Both Ian and Magerts got out.

Ian decided to take the offensive. "Can you move these out of the way? I need to get through."

The big Irishman stepped forward. "Easy there, mate. You're not going nowhere."

Ian allowed a look of surprise to cross his face. "What do you mean? We're on a mission from the Queen. You stop us at your own peril."

A slim mousy-haired man with glasses frowned. "What's he talking about, Bill?" His ill-fitting uniform showed he was a lance corporal.

"Take it easy, Geoff. Man's all bluff." To Ian, Bill said, "Now run along. No one's getting through this way for quite a while."

"What's going on?" Magerts asked.

"I wouldn't know," sniffed the man named Bill.

Ian addressed the mousy man and the young kid who hadn't yet spoken. "You men are participating in an illegal action. Stopping men of the Queen in a time of war is treason."

That had the intended effect. The other two men were suddenly very nervous. "Listen, we're just here because Bill says—"

"Shut it, Tim. I told you, the man is all bluff."

Ian shook his head. "No bluff here." He pulled the Queen Letter out and proffered it for them to read but held on to it. As Tim and the mousy one read it, their eyes widened. "You'll notice the official seal and Her Majesty's signature."

Tim backed away. "I don't want to be part of this."

"Like you have a choice, Tim Thompson." Bill squared his shoulders and addressed Ian. "How do I know this is real?"

"Seriously? When's the last time someone tried to get through a roadblock with a fake letter signed by the Queen?" Ian flicked a hand at the cars. "Now get out of the way."

Even Bill seemed worried now. He'd begun to step forward when the sound of a vehicle approaching from behind him caused everyone to pause. It was a pickup with four men in the back and two in the cab. They got out when it came to a stop. The four in back were dressed all in black with body armor and balaclavas. One of the men in front was a civilian. The other was dressed in fatigues. An SAS patch and colonel's rank stood out against the camouflage.

"What's going on, Bill? These men refusing to turn around?" The colonel stared imperiously at Ian.

The four men in black brought up MP5s with silencers,

"They have a letter from the Queen which says they should be allowed to pass."

The man held out his hand.

Ian merely stared at it.

The man snapped his fingers.

"To whom am I speaking?" Ian asked.

"Colonel Wilson Picket. Now give me the goddamned letter."

Ian handed it over. "You're a little out of your jurisdiction, Colonel."

Colonel Picket glanced at the letter, then unceremoniously ripped it in two and dropped it to the ground. "It's a fake."

"So you've seen one of these before?" Ian struggled to keep the anger from his face.

This stopped Colonel Picket for a moment. But he recovered and said, "It's obvious. Why does the Queen need someone like you to—"

Ian stuck out his hand, "Colonel Ian Waits. Section 9, Special Services." He'd watched Colonel Picket's eyes and it was obvious he'd heard the name before. Even the twitch of a smile at the corner of his mouth gave him away. "But you knew that already. Let's cut the bullshit."

"Yes. Let's."

"Someone convinced you to come out here and stop me. I'd like to know who!"

The colonel paused a moment, then shrugged. "You'll know soon enough. Sir MacDonald swore out a warrant for your arrest."

"Oh, he did, did he? On what grounds?"

"I'm not privy. All I know is he asked a few trusted men of Sheffield to assist him and he decided to call on me."

"Us," Bill added.

The colonel frowned at Bill's addition but nonetheless concurred. "Us."

Ian couldn't help himself. He started to chuckle.

The colonel didn't like being laughed at. "What's so damned funny?"

"You've been played." Ian pointed to the four men in black. "Those four are part of a group planning the overthrow of the British government. Sir MacDonald is part of it. A man of Sheffield or not, he's hitched his tail to a kite being flown by men from an organization called the Red Grove who have brought back King Arthur and the Wild Hunt."

Everyone was silent for a moment as the words sunk in.

Then they started laughing.

Ian waited for the laughter to die down. "As funny as it sounds, it's true. I'd like to offer you and your men a chance to surrender to me now."

Everyone began to laugh once more. Ian and Magerts joined in.

"You ever play poker?" Ian asked when they were done. The colonel responded, "Yeah. Sometimes."

"Good, then I'll see your squad and raise a platoon."

"What's that supposed to mean?"

A squad of Royal Marines appeared out of the darkness behind the four men. A corporal called out, "Put down your weapons and lay flat on the ground. You so much as twitch I'll have my men go full auto on your asses."

The look on the big Irishman's face was priceless.

But not as priceless as Ian wanted. He took one step forward and delivered a right hook to Colonel Picket's jaw, delivered with all the outrage of a man trying to save his country only to be delayed by the grossly incompetent. The man fell hard to the ground and landed on his ass. "It means you lose and I win, you pompous ass."

CHAPTER 40

POINT BRAVO, WARWICK, ENGLAND. 0700 HOURS.

Preeti was beyond exhausted. But there was no way she could sleep. Now that she'd assisted SEAL Team 666 and Section 9, it could be argued that she deserved some rest. But she just couldn't bring herself to stop. The feeling of helplessness only served to accentuate her fear for Trevor. She'd loved him from the dizzying moment when he'd waded into the group of hooligans and saved her and her brother. Perhaps she loved Trevor too much. She was constantly pulling back, trying to mete out her love, fearful that if he ever knew the true breadth of it he'd run away. Was that a missed opportunity? Had she denied herself and him some true joy because of her fear? She made a promise that when this was all over and he was returned to her she'd confess to him, profess to him, trusting that their love was strong enough.

She'd been organizing files on her server for half an hour before she ran into an audio file she'd recorded. She listened for a moment; then it came to her. She'd heard the Tuatha Dé Dannan speaking once when Van Dyke was asleep. It had sounded like a song. She'd only gotten thirty seconds of it, but she'd wanted to capture it in the event it was something they might need.

First she ran it through a filter to remove the graininess of it.

The question was what language was it. Was it Welsh? It had the tonal structure. Or was it Middle or Old English? In her mind the words lacked some of the hard notes of those languages, so she searched for translation engines. She found several, three of which were commercially available and two from universities. The university engines required a log-in, so she pushed them to the side and concentrated on the commercial engines. Two of them were text-to-text translations and would do her no good, but the third looked promising.

She dropped the file into the search engine and watched the hourglass spin. After thirty seconds, the screen flashed and text spit out beneath the drop box. Sheer gibberish. Or almost gibberish. She recognized a few words like "men" and "sword" and "head." Farther down she saw the word "Arthur." Was it the same as King Arthur?

She felt a rush of excitement. If this was about King Arthur, perhaps it could help the teams. Maybe this was more than an effort to keep awake after all. She copied the text into a Word document and saved it.

She checked out the two university links. One was for Wales and the other for Oxford. It would take some time to hack into the membership directories and find a suitable name and password to use. So which one? Although Oxford held prestige, it seemed obvious that any serious study into the Welsh language would be occurring at the University of Wales.

She spent the next hour hacking into the system. Genie came over and asked what she was doing. She told him and he went away uninterested. But then he returned sometime later with some hot tea and an orange scone. She devoured the pastry and sipped the tea. Then half an hour later she was in. It wasn't long before she found the internal links to the language engines. To her surprise, there were four of them: Primitive Welsh, Old Welsh, Early Welsh, and Modern Welsh. A quick check online told her that "Primitive Welsh" referred to the language spoken from roughly AD 300 to 800. "Old Welsh" referred to the language spoken from roughly AD 800 to 1200. "Early Welsh" referred to the language spoken from AD 1200 to 1800. Modern Welsh was the current incarnation of the lyrical language.

All this was good, but it did nothing to help her, especially since these were text-based search engines. She searched the directory trees but could find no place to drop an audio file. Which only made sense, especially since there was probably no one except for a few eccentric literature professors who could speak Primitive or Old Welsh.

What to do?

She opened the Word document and stared once more at the gibberish. What if it wasn't all gibberish? What if it was some version of Welsh the engine couldn't translate, but it still recognized it as Welsh and rendered it in the language?

She selected the oldest engine first—Primitive Welsh—thinking that if there was a King Arthur link then it would be here. She copied the text, then dropped it into the translation engine drop box, then clicked on the TRANSLATE button.

After a few moments, it spit out the text, revealing a more succinct translation, but still with words she didn't understand. There were several whole phrases that appeared:

> *In Llongborth I saw the rage of slaughter*
>   *and*
> *In Llongborth, I saw the clash of swords*
>   *and*
> *In Llongborth I saw spurs*
>   *and*
> *In Llongborth I saw the weapons*
>   *and*
> *In Llongborth I saw Arthur's*
> *Heroes who cut with steel.*
> *The Emperor, ruler of our labour.*

She sat back, pleased with herself. She knew she was close. The remaining question was what was Llongborth. Since it didn't translate, it was definitely a place. She decided to Google "Llongborth."

She had immediate hits. She selected the first one from Brittania .com, which explained that "Llongborth" was present in an Old Welsh epic poem and is believed to be the modern location for Portsmouth. She read the passage again.

> In Llongborth I saw Arthur's
> Heroes who cut with steel.
> The Emperor, ruler of our labour.

This poem referred specifically to Arthur and identified him as Emperor. Conducting an additional search for the Battle of Llongborth, she learned it was believed to have occurred circa AD 510 and was reputed to have involved King Gerren of Dumnonia, who was killed in the battle, and Prince Rivod of Brittany, who murdered his brother King Maelew and usurped the Briton throne. She could find no mention of Arthur.

She returned to the Britannia site and scrolled through and discovered the poem in full, which began:

> Before Geraint, the enemy's scourge,
> I saw white horses, tensed, red,
> After the war cry, bitter the grave

Then she ran through to the last lines:

> When Geraint was born, Heaven's gate stood open;
> Christ granted all our prayer;
> Lovely to behold, the glory of Prydain.

She soon found that "Prydian" was the Primitive Welsh word for Britain. She decided to search other sources and soon found that the location of Portsmouth as the site of the battle was in academic dispute, as was the year in which it took place. A scholarly text from a King Arthur site, citing earlier documents, believed that Llongborth was actually Langport in Somerset and that the year the battle occurred was actually AD 710. It also went on to say that King Arthur probably wasn't present at the battle but that his men were, hence the sentence *In Llongborth I saw Arthur's Heroes / Who cut with steel.* The poem never once mentions that the narrator saw King Arthur.

Which made sense later when she saw that the birth of Arthur was believed to have been circa AD 465. She continued searching and learned that Arthur was believed to have ruled the region known at present as Somerset, Devon, and Cornwall. His castle was located in Cadbury and was presently known as Cadbury Castle. Bones and artifacts from the area date back to 3300 BC, but it is argued that the fortification on the giant mound was created circa 70 BC.

An interesting excerpt tied Arthur into the poem: *If Arthur was conceived at Tintagel, then as a prince of Dumnonia, Cadbury Castle would have been within his dominion.* Dumnonia had been mentioned before as being the seat of King Gerren, the Geraint referred to in the poem.

Another detail caught her eye. Several sources said that Merlyn was purported to have written the poem but then explained that as he was a right-hand man to Arthur it would have been impossible for this to be true because of the time difference.

Unless Merlyn happened to be a Tuatha, she thought.

She blinked hard. What had she stumbled on?

She remembered that Cadbury Castle had been built upon a mound. What kind of mound? And what sort of artifacts had been found there?

Half an hour later she'd discovered enough to make her worry. She checked the time. It was 0912 hours. She put in a call to Ian. She got no response. She put in a call to Holmes, then Walker, and received no response from either. If she was right, then everything they were about to do might be wrong. In fact, it might be the very worst thing they could do.

CHAPTER 41

Paul Legerski lay in bed with the sweet smell of sex still welling from his body. He'd seen Megan at the pub three times before and had always wanted to talk to her, but she was just too bloody beautiful to approach. But last night was Christmas Eve and he told himself this was the night. Completely lubricated with courage juice, he'd gone over, only to find her crying.

This he was good at.

Her aunt had passed away that morning and Megan was at the pub drowning her sorrows. He spent time asking about her aunt, what was it she loved about her, what had she learned from her. In the back of his mind, he knew this was unfair, but he really wanted her to work as quickly through the stages of grief as possible.

And it had paid off. An hour before closing, they went out for some crisps, then found themselves back at his place. He had the best closing lines around.

What is it you do? they'd ask.

I'm a pilot.

As in a plane?

Then he'd shrug and add, *I teach people to parachute too.* Then he'd look at the girl and say, *Do you want to learn how to jump out of airplanes? Do you want to fly?*

Once he got his courage up, those were the magic words and rarely did they miss. Just as they hadn't last night.

He pulled the covers up to his neck and imagined the mole she wore just below her left breast. He was reliving the moment when a pounding came at the door.

Bollocks! Don't they know it's Christmas? He closed his eyes and was determined to ignore it.

But the banging came again along with someone yelling, "Open the damn door!"

First of all, he'd never open the door if someone yelled that. Second of all, the voice sounded American.

He slid out of bed and wrapped a sheet around his midsection.

The man hammered at the door again.

Paul was getting brassed off. He didn't know who it was. It could be someone on drugs or—he thought quickly. Did Megan have a husband? He hadn't seen a wedding band and she sure didn't mention it.

The door suddenly exploded inward. Splinters from the door-jamb flew past him as the door landed on the floor. An immense black man in black fatigues was putting his foot back on the ground.

"Knock knock, Avon calling." The man strode into the room. "Are you the pilot?"

All Paul could do was nod dumbly. Although he never took his eyes off the man's face, Paul knew he wore some sort of body armor, had a pistol, a knife and a machete, and a rifle slung across his back. If Megan had an African-American soldier husband and she never told him about it, then he was as good as dead.

The man poked him in the chest. It was a simple move, but it hurt tremendously and woke him from his stupor. "Chop-chop. Get some clothes on. We need to get the plane in the air."

Paul stood there, waiting for the man to leave, but the man merely crossed his arms. His eyes narrowed and it looked like he might have been getting ready for a growl. Paul sprang into motion. He grabbed pants and a shirt and ran into the bathroom. After doing what he needed, he exited and grabbed some socks and boots and a jacket.

"You have the whitest skin of any white guy I have ever seen," the man said. "Do you get out much?"

Paul didn't dare answer. He grabbed a set of keys and headed for the door. The man fell in behind Paul. They marched across the tarmac from his trailer to his own private hangar on the south end of Redfield Airport. He was fumbling with his keys when he noticed that the lock on the door had been wrenched away. He entered the hangar to find utter chaos. His cabinets had all been broken open and their contents removed. Odds and ends were in one pile while another pile held nothing but packed parachutes and a group of people dressed in black were sifting through them.

"Are . . . are you robbing me?"

Four other men and a woman stopped what they were doing to regard him. One man looked like he was cut from a solid block of stone. Another was tall and blond with a wide smile. Another was a short Arab with a robotic arm. Then there was a regular-looking blond guy. The woman was older, but beautiful in an intimidating sort of way.

The man with the chiseled face approached Paul. "You're not being robbed. And we're sorry for all of this, but we need your plane and your parachutes ASAP. We also need you to fly us."

"I—I can't just fly. I have to file a flight plan and—"

"You don't get it. You're going to do this and when it's all over you can come back and get shit faced at the pub. Now, where are your other parachutes? There's only four here and we need two tandems."

"Why—are we—"

A dog with body armor padded by, giving him a look.

"For god's sake." The angry black man grabbed him by a shoulder. "This is a matter of national security. We're trying to help England."

"But you're American?"

"Well, look at Captain Obvious. Haven't you heard of our

exchange program? We get Anthony Hopkins and Michael Caine and you get us?"

The tall one spoke in a husky voice. "I ate his liver with some fava beans and a nice Chianti."

Paul felt himself begin to tremble.

Then the woman approached him. She put her hand on his arm. "It's going to be fine. You're going to be fine. Everything is going to be fine." She stared into his eyes. "Say it."

"Everything's going to be fine."

"Say it again."

"Everything's going to be fine."

"Good boy. Now tell us where the other parachutes are."

He pointed toward the back of the room, where a large industrial-sized box sat. "In there. But they haven't been recovered yet."

Four of the men, minus the angry black man, headed toward the container.

"Now that wasn't so hard, was it?" Then to the black man she added, "Brutes. Think he'll be able to fly the plane if he's too busy peeing his pants?"

Paul thought it was odd that she would say that. Because he knew that if he could possibly produce any urine at this moment then he'd be well into peeing his pants.

CHAPTER 42

IN DARKNESS SOMEWHERE NEAR GLASTONBURY TOR. 0750 HOURS.

Darkness and pain. He knew he was outside because of the cold that had long ago seeped into his bones. At first his body had rebelled, whatever nerve endings that hadn't been broken by the beating screaming for him to get them warm. But the longer he'd remained outside, the softer their cries became, until now they were silent, relegated to the reality that the numbness masked the pain that had taken permanent residence in his body.

His legs trembled as they struggled to hold him upright. Although he couldn't see through the blindfold, he'd known the instant the spike had touched his palm what they'd intended to do. And it was the merging of their laughter with his screams as they nailed first one hand onto a length of wood, then the other. He'd been crucified *in honor of his Christian upbringing. Let Christ come down and save you,* they'd howled, then added, *But then he couldn't save himself.*

Of course he'd had his chance to escape. He'd thought he'd had the time. Walker and YaYa had exfilled the window and he'd heard a scratching in the hallway. Part of him had screamed for him to flee, but he'd paused, raised his weapon, and readied to fire. He hadn't wanted to leave anyone behind him who would shoot him in the back when it was his turn to exfil the window.

When it came around the corner, he'd tried to pull the trigger but found himself frozen, incapable of even calling out. It stood there. She wore only a stitched smile, her naked body blossoming with pendulous breasts. Her pubic hair had been shaved, revealing a pierced vulva. Her arm came up and pointed to him and he felt himself pulled in her direction. He fought against it, resulting in a hobbled walk like a two-year-old, crossing the floor of the room until he was in her arms. She closed them, giving him a cold embrace; then she kissed him through the stitches.

He'd vomited then and lost consciousness.

When he next came to, he was standing in the middle of a pentacle being struck in the face over and over by men in suits, men dressed as women, women wearing strap-ons, and women dressed like animals. He remembered seeing an impressive figure sitting in a throne-like chair, laughing at him. The figure was regal and wore an iron crown. He was completely cloaked in green, the cloth patterned with holly leaves.

But that's all he remembered. He'd been hit so frequently and violently that his memory of that period was like an old 8mm movie, skipping ahead, with black spots between images. Then his vision had stopped, but the beating had continued.

Sometime afterward, he'd awoken to find them cutting him. Thin lines of pain along each arm and each leg, one by one by one. He was beyond screaming and whined like a broken dog with each pull of the knife, trying desperately to ignore the bombastic hilarity of his cutters as they laughed uproariously at their deeds.

Then they began to touch him. He'd cried as his body ignored his complaints. A part of him had a will of its own and ignored his protests. He imagined himself trussed somewhere on the ground so he could be cut, then a man, or a woman, or both, wrapping themselves around him and making his body tremble.

And now, as he hung crucified in the middle of the vile celebration, he pushed all those images aside, forgot about the abuse

and the pain and the cold, and instead focused on a single image—
Preeti standing, her head cocked, her long hair falling down to
one side, a self-conscious look on her face, not for a second realizing how beautiful and how wonderful a person she was and
how lucky he'd been to know her for a time.

CHAPTER 43

REDLANDS AIRFIELD, SWINDON. 0755 HOURS.

Yank sat behind the pilot, making sure he wasn't going to do anything stupid. At this point, Yank doubted the pilot would do anything that would make him mad. He'd intentionally tried to terrify the poor kid, both because he needed the man to be afraid of something immediate and because Yank was pretty sick and tired of this whole idea of creating a white-only England. Each time they'd discovered a group had gone missing or someone was killed who had been involved with helping immigrants and refugees, it had served to fuel his anger. Add to that the ineffectiveness of the government and he wanted to punch something or someone. Not only had they emasculated Section 9—which should have been ten times the size of SEAL Team 666 because of all the supernatural shit going down in England—but it was clear that there was compliance at the highest levels, making him wonder how long they'd been planning this. That it took Jen's death for anyone to notice was a terrible thing, but at least they had the chance to stop what had been inevitable before.

He tried to imagine how England would look without Queen Elizabeth and parliament and instead having King Arthur sitting on the throne. Would there be a round table? How would this sixth-century ruler be able to survive in the modern era? Or would it be kept a secret, King Arthur working from behind the scenes, ordering the complicit MPs to do his bidding? It was all too much.

The plane rumbled down the runway and took to the sky. Holmes and the witch were set up for a tandem, just as YaYa and Hoover were. They'd had to work on the straps for the team dog, but they'd managed finally. The rest of them wore regular commercial chutes, which would get them to the ground, albeit more slowly than their military counterparts.

Yank glanced out the window. They were in a Super Twin Otter de Havilland. He'd jumped out of this model before, so knew how to exit, but it didn't mean he liked it. He remembered his first mission with Triple Six when they'd HALOed into the Sea of Cortez. Laws and Walker had given him no end of shit for supposedly being afraid of heights. Not that he'd let on, but someone must have let the secret slip.

Truth be told, he was terrified of heights and spent most of the time while he was in the air with his eyes closed in some form or fashion, even if it was only to pretend to sleep.

They were heading to Bratton Castle. He'd had the pilot program the coordinates into the navigation system. He glanced at them to make sure they hadn't been changed. 51° 15' 49.32" N, 2° 8' 36.6" W. *Check.*

Laws had checked the wind and weather and had plotted for them to jump from an altitude of 4,000 feet north and west of their target. It would be a cold jump, but they wouldn't be in the air for long. The two tandem jumper pairs were going out first, separated by ten seconds. Then the rest of them would pile out together. What the pilot did after that didn't really matter. Either there'd be an entirely different England within a few hours or Triple Six would have accomplished their mission.

And what was that mission?

To kill the mythical King Arthur or at least stop him from becoming king once more, all while trying to not get killed by supernatural hounds and whatever else might be thrown at them.

A hard-core terrorist looked easy by comparison. He fought the urge to rub at the bruises the hounds had caused when they'd taken him.

He glanced out the window, then averted his gaze back to the controls. He heard Laws laugh behind him but wouldn't give him the chance to bring the phobia up again.

It wasn't long before the pilot announced they were ten minutes out.

The SEALs set their watches.

They'd expected to hear from Ian and his Marines, but there had been radio silence. Several times during the short flight, Holmes had tried to establish contact but with zero luck. Everyone tried to keep their thoughts positive, but the mind could very easily spin lemonade into citric acid.

Laws posted by the open door hatch and got everyone in line.

Yank kept his eye on the pilot.

At five minutes, the pilot slowed the airspeed.

The SEALs did a radio check on their MBITR.

Laws counted down the last thirty seconds and sent YaYa and Hoover out first. After a ten-second gap, Holmes and the witch went next. Then it was Walker and Laws.

Yank patted the pilot on the back of his head, then slid out the door into the air. He let three seconds pass, then pulled his ripcord. He saw the line before him, with YaYa far to the front and lower in altitude. He searched for his landmarks. Keevil Airfield was northeast. He found the town of Bratton, then spied the white horse drawn on the side of the mound. He didn't know where it came from, but it was made from something white and seemed as large as a football field. The plan was to land west of this landmark, then climb the mound together.

He watched as YaYa landed and rolled.

Holmes did better, standing up, using the witch's weight as ballast.

Then Walker, then Laws, then it was his turn.

Just as he was about to hit the ground fear surged through him as he realized he'd just leaped from an airplane. He'd been so focused on the mission that he'd forgotten to be scared. He closed his eyes and winced as he landed. Still, with the extralarge commercial parachute, he was able to stand and walk it down.

They recovered their parachutes and placed them in a pile.

The witch looked like a freshly bathed cat.

"If there ever comes a time when you want me to jump out of another plane, don't bother coming around. I won't do it. England or no."

"Wasn't so bad," Laws said. "Yank here is terrified of heights and he jumps all the time."

"Of course we sometimes have to kick him out the door," Walker added, "but he's getting better."

Yank rolled his eyes. He'd known the jibe was coming. Laws couldn't help himself. *Always the fucking merry prankster. Mr. Joker boy.*

Laws patted Yank on the back. "What? No comment?"

"I'll reserve my comment for the next time we're sparring."

Laws shut up at this, probably because he knew that Yank had forgotten more about fighting than Laws had ever learned.

Holmes checked his HK416. "Let's remember this is a military mission."

Yank watched as Laws almost came back with a smart-assed reply, then thought better of it when Holmes gave him a firm glare.

They all wore body armor over black sterile uniforms. Their Pro-Tec helmets had mounts for night vision, but their QUAD-EYES were in their cargo pockets, as were their ballistic masks. They wore Rhodesian military vests over their body armor, which had numerous pockets allowing them to carry ten spare magazines, as well as white phosphorous and fragmentation grenades. They wore their usual MBITR and Holmes did another radio check.

YaYa and Hoover took point, the dog ranging a dozen feet forward. Walker and Laws followed. The witch and Holmes came next. Yank brought up the rear.

He checked his watch. 0840 local time.

They reached the top of the mound without event. The pinnacle was mostly flat, running lengthwise for more than seventy meters, with a width of nearly twenty meters. Several piles of wood and sticks had been placed in the center, making Yank wonder if they might not be planning a bonfire later.

The witch found a location on the northeast side. It looked like any other place, but she'd stopped and said, "This is it."

The rest of the SEALs faced outward around her while Holmes stood beside her as the witch unwrapped the item she'd brought.

Yank glanced back and saw a length of metal a little more than a yard long with a hooked end like a shepherd's crook or a giant fishing hook.

She pulled the last of the canvas from it. "I found this laying around the museum. Belonged to a ninth-century Norse witch."

Holmes's eyes narrowed. "You stole it?"

"They didn't know what they had. There's more power in this than anything I've ever seen. It drew me to it." She shrugged. "What do you want to do? Look at it behind a case or use it to help us save England?"

Holmes didn't answer. Instead, he asked, "How exactly are we going to get in?"

"That's where the Tuatha comes in. It knows the secret knock."

She began to hum. Her pupils rolled back, revealing nothing but white.

Yank shuddered. He hated when that happened.

She spoke something guttural in a language he didn't understand, then struck the ground three times with the end of the metal staff.

Yank didn't see what happened, but he heard her say, "Oh hell no," then heard her fall.

He turned to see her splayed facedown. No opening. No doorway. Nothing except cold, wet grass.

"What happened?"

Holmes knelt and checked for a pulse. "She's alive. Pulse is strong." He glanced at Yank. "She acted surprised."

Yank made a face. "Can't be a good thing if a witch gets surprised."

Holmes nodded.

Walker pointed toward one of the woodpiles. "Look. There."

They watched as several pieces of wood fell from the pile to the ground as if there was something inside the pile pushing it free.

Yank and the others raised their silenced HKs but refrained from firing.

Then more wood fell until the entire pile had flattened across the ground. Yank saw both Walker and YaYa grit their teeth. When Yank looked back at the wood, he watched as the pieces began to come together. Small and large pieces, thick and thin pieces, they were moving together on their own for a common purpose. He couldn't be sure how long it had taken, but it was suddenly a being. He could see legs, bent the wrong way, like an animal's. A tall, slender upper body with long arms, a triangular head with what looked like horns jutting free. Only it wasn't a body or a being, just wood somehow hewn together to make this . . . this creature.

When it turned its head to regard them he couldn't help but let out a gasp.

Then it took off running.

"Hoover, YaYa, Walker, get that thing," Holmes ordered.

All three looked at one another, including the dog. Then they were off. YaYa and Walker slid their rifles on their backs, barrels down for better ease of running.

He turned to Yank and Laws. "You two, help me and Ms. Moore." He bent down to pick up the staff but snatched his hand back when it sizzled on the metal. "I think we've been tricked."

"But who would do it?"

"My guess is that Tuatha was playing possum."

Laws grabbed the witch under her arms. "Where to now?"

"Wherever that thing is going."

"Do you have any ideas?" Laws motioned for Yank to grab her feet.

"Glastonbury Tor."

Yank did the math. It was about forty miles away. They couldn't possibly run it. They'd have to steal a car to get there in time.

Then they heard Walker give a shout over their MBITR.

"Oh hell! A truck just creamed it."

CHAPTER 44

SOUTH OF GLASTONBURY TOR, ENGLAND. A FEW MINUTES LATER.

The party was still in full swing. Revelers could be heard inside and outside the home. Here and there a naked torso or butt could be seen pressed against one of the upstairs windows. Ian had never seen anything like it. What they were doing didn't seem fitting on Christmas and certainly was not a tradition his family cultivated.

After a brief conferral, he and Magerts placed the men where they had planned, based on reconnaissance using Google Maps. The lots to the right and left of the home were empty, but across the road was seven-foot shrubbery capable of hiding men from view of the house. There was also a rather dense blackberry thicket in the empty lot to the right, which seemed to present an impenetrable view both to and from the home. Neither would provide cover enough to stop any rounds, but they'd provide excellent concealment.

Fifteen men were placed behind the shrubbery. They all carried SA80s, a suite of white phosphorous, smoke, and fragmentation grenades, Fairbairn-Sykes commando knives, and of course their swords. Eight men with the same armament were placed behind the thicket and were under the command of Magerts. The remaining seven Marines were stationed at the house where they'd previously conducted surveillance. Two of these men carried L7 General Purpose 7.62mm machine guns, which were placed so they could fire from the front and rear of the structure. The remaining five were armed as the others and were to be the Quick Reaction Force, moving where designated if needed. They were under the command of Sergeant Ronald Scott, who was eager to engage and disappointed he wouldn't be part of the initial fight.

Ian and Magerts had decided to try to lure whatever forces were waiting for them outside. Attempting to break into the place would be suicidal. Ian stared up toward the height of Glastonbury Tor, which rose five hundred feet above the plain. The Tor was topped by St. Michael's Tower, which was still standing even after much of it had been destroyed by a twelfth-century earthquake. The far side of the Tor was terraced, but the near side had a gentle slope, only slightly disturbed by terracing. A thin path ran from the summit down to the rear of the Tudor home. A wider, more formal path bisected the hill from southwest to northeast.

They observed their target for forty-five minutes to ascertain whether there were any roving guard forces or security elements, but there were none.

Ian checked his watch. 0830 hours. It was time to knock on the front door. He wore a black turtleneck under a black leather jacket. He wore black 5.11 pants with black boots. A black beret covered his head. He felt the heaviness of the amulet he wore beneath his shirt. He'd never used it before, but since they were going against magic, he thought he'd try. Taken from the body of a dead seventeenth-century witch hunter by one of his predecessors, the logs from the 1800s professed its ability to provide protection to the wearer against magic. Whatever the truth of it, he was about to find out.

He pulled free an M34 model United States white phosphorous grenade. The UK had ceased to use them in 1997, but for Ian they were so much more useful than his other options. On the one hand, a smoke grenade would merely conceal the door. A fragmentation grenade would destroy it and possibly innocents behind it. The white phosphorous grenade, on the other hand, could burn at 5,000 degrees Fahrenheit for up to sixty seconds. He liked it because of its duration and its disruption.

He pulled the safety, then the pin from the cylindrical grenade, then stepped free from the shrubbery and walked across the street. When he was ten feet away from the door, he tossed it. The spoon flew free and it rolled until gently bumping into the door. Then he turned and walked into the street, continuing east down the road.

He heard the pop and the hiss, then the roar of white phosphorous burning violently. Walking away as he did would put eyes on him instead of the two hide sites. He felt an itch in the center of his back like someone was training a rifle on him. Would he even feel the bullet? Not if it hit his spine or the back of his head.

Then he heard Magerts through the radio coms. "Front door is on fire. They're breaking it down from the inside. They've tossed a body on top of the grenade. Jesus. It burned right through."

Ian prayed that it wasn't Trevor but suspected that it probably had been. *Bastards.*

He kept walking until he knew he was out of sight, then peeled off to the right and made his way back using the shrubbery as cover.

A howl went up from somewhere behind the house. As it died in the overcast morning, it was followed by another.

A minute had gone by, but the grenade was still spouting flame. The doorframe was on fire. He could see shadows through the flames but couldn't make out anything inside.

And the party still went on.

The howls came again . . . closer.

A hound tore around the left side of the house. It skidded to a stop and regarded the burning canister in front of it. As it circled it was joined by another. They both regarded the grenade as it died, their heads turning at odd angles, as if they were trying to decide what it was.

Their presence made him uneasy, especially when he observed their eerily human fronts. Their simian faces held human eyes and bore odd expressions. Sometimes it seemed like they were in pain, sometimes it seemed as if they were trying to laugh, neither of which they could accomplish with their animal facial structure.

"Get ready." He backed away from the men standing in front of him and drew his sword. When he was ready and when his men had their swords drawn, their Fairbarn-Sykes commando knives in their other hands, he made the call. "Here, doggie, doggie. Come to Poppa."

The machine gunner up the road with the front of the house vantage spoke through the coms. "You got their attention. Call again."

Ian whistled. "Here, doggy, doggy."

"Here they come."

The men heard it as well.

He gripped Guy of Warwick's sword tightly.

Instead of coming through the shrubbery, the hounds leaped over the seven-foot hedge. They came down on the other side of the line of men, facing Ian all alone.

This was not exactly how the plan was supposed to have gone. One of the hounds rushed at him and he brought his sword down on its shoulder, the black blade slicing through meat until it struck bone. He jerked the blade free and brought it down for another attack, but this time the beast backed away.

Meanwhile three Marines had caught the second hound by surprise and were busy hacking it to death. Even as it tried to spin, pieces of it fell away. Once separated, they turned to smoke and drifted away.

Ian feinted.

The hound jerked back, then leaped forward.

Ian was forced to backpedal. He barely kept his balance.

The hound leaped.

Ian brought his sword up in a blind defense and ended up skewering the creature, the tip of the blade entering through the mouth. It fell hard, ripping the sword free from his hand. For a moment, he was worried that he was now weaponless. But the hound was dead and he watched it first fall to pieces and then those pieces turn to smoke. His sword was left lying in the grass. He snatched it from the ground and looked for something else to attack.

But the hounds were gone.

Not that they'd won the day or anything, but succeeding in killing what they'd previously been unable to kill elated him.

He could see the Marines smiling at their accomplishment, but he had to force himself to remain unaffected.

"They weren't prepared. They will be now."

The Marine at the back of the vacant house with his machine gun reported, "They're massing a platoon of men with weapons—looks like SA80s—up on the Tor. Looks like there are some robed figures with them and several dozen hounds."

Ian wished he could see their formation. "Are they coming down, or are they performing a blocking maneuver?"

"They're not moving, if that's what you mean."

Ian had worked his way back to the shrubbery and the party at the house was still going in full force. He ordered four of his men to the door.

They ran the length of the shrubbery, then exited onto the road, east of the house. If they were being observed, now was the moment for an observer to fire at them. But no shots came. They were able to stack themselves on either side of the smoldering doorframe.

"The body is Asian," one of the men said.

Ian let out a sigh of relief. At least it wasn't Trevor.

One of the Marines peered inside, then jerked his head back.

"Report?"

"Uh . . ."

"Come on, Marine, what do you see?"

"A lot of bloody fucking."

Ian had no response.

"Everywhere. Everyone. It's one big orgy. What do you want us to do?"

Ian had been prepared for pretty much anything. But not this. He'd been ready to defend or to attack, but what could he do to rooms filled with people in coitus?

"We have more hounds coming your way," a Marine said hurriedly.

Another Marine added, "Oh shit. Here comes one of the—"

The four Marines at the door stood as stock-still as mannequins.

A figure was coming through the darkness from inside. It was a woman. A tall, naked woman with her lips sewn shut. Tresses of long black hair fell down her back. She made the doorway and put a hand on each of the men in turn. When she touched them, they fell, immediately falling into a seizure, their entire bodies shaking and jerking.

Then she pointed toward the shrubbery. Ian watched as all eleven remaining men jerked straight as if invisible strings attached to their limbs had been pulled tight. Then she pointed toward the thicket.

"Magerts, report," ordered Ian.

Nothing.

His amulet felt warm beneath his shirt, but he was still able to move. He sheathed his sword, snatched up a rifle, and took aim. He locked on her face and fired six times. She fell backwards and then went down.

His men immediately relaxed their poses and began to whisper among one another.

"Quiet," he reassured them.

The four men at the door had stopped seizing and began to get up.

First two hounds, then one naked possessed girl. They were being underestimated. It was only a matter of time before they'd realize it and attack.

But for now, he had to prepare for more hounds.

Even as he thought it, they attacked.

Four hounds came for him and his men. Two of them burst through the shrubbery, creating gaping holes. The other three leaped over the top of it like the previous pair. Although their bodies were the same diseased-looking hairless gray, they were different sizes by degrees.

One set of blue eyes flashed at him; then the beast came for him, low, mouth open with protruding fangs.

Out of the corner of his eye, he saw three of his men go down. *Damn.*

"Do you need help?" Magerts shot through the coms.

Ian brought his sword back into *First Point*, which presented the tip of the blade toward the target, his sword hand beside his right ear. "Got this." The tip of the sword quivered from his barely controlled fear.

The hound clawed for his leg.

Ian jerked his foot back.

The hound immediately clawed at his other leg, before Ian could put his foot down.

He was forced to hop backwards and in doing so lost his balance.

The hound leaped forward, grabbing his boot with a claw. He felt talons bite into his leg directly above his ankle. He fought back a scream and jammed his sword at the hound's face. It jerked back, but not before he sliced off an ear. But even as he looked, the ear grew back.

He pushed himself back and stood.

The hound moved on again.

This time Ian feinted, stepped back just as the hound lunged, and spun to his right, finishing a 270-degree arc by slicing the black blade through the creature's neck.

It fell soundlessly and began to melt into the air.

Ian turned to his men. Eight of them were down. A single hound held the rest at bay. Try as the Marines might, they couldn't get past the hound's defenses, and vice versa.

The hound was facing away from Ian so it was an easy five long strides before he hacked off this one's head as well.

With no current opponents, he began to check the men.

Five were dead, one of whom had his chest ripped open and

another with his spine ripped out. Ian saw it lying a few feet away but didn't have the stomach to return it to the dead. Three others were wounded, one of whom didn't have long to live.

"Observation Post, report," Ian said.

"They're arguing on the hill. They must know what you've done. The hounds *are* dead, right?"

"Affirmative."

"They seem to be trying to decide. One's pointing this way."

The observer in the front of the home joined the conversation. "I bet he's pointing at the troop trucks."

Ian could hear trucks coming up the road. Sounded like several of them. A sinking feeling replaced his sense of impending victory. "Did you say 'troop trucks'?"

"The trucks stopped. Men are disembarking. They're wearing black and carrying SA80s. They're forming into two groups and look ready to come down each side of the road."

"How many?"

"Thirty. Fifteen and Fifteen."

"Stand by." Ian sheathed his sword and grabbed the nearest Marine. He spoke in a harsh whisper. "Listen up. We're crossing the road and going into the house. We leave in five seconds. Magerts, stand by. QRF, stand by. Two, one, move!"

He jerked free his pistol and pulled the Marine through the shrubbery and let the others follow. He rushed across the narrow two-lane road, through the charred doorframe, and into the house. Parlors stood off either side of the entry. He posted the men in each one as they came through. The last two in line were the wounded as they came under fire from the new threat. One took a bullet in the back. The other made it in.

"Magerts, when they get in front of the house, open fire with everything you have. QRF, establish positions to their rear. Machine-gun fire on my command. You lot in here. I want you to clear the first floor. Kill anyone who is a threat and zip-tie everyone else. And for the love of god, look out for Trevor." Ian faced ten sets of wide-eyed stares. "Move!" And they jumped into motion.

He remained by the front window. He didn't like being forced to bring his men inside without knowing what they faced, but the alternative would get them killed. And they weren't even close to completing their mission. He tried to call Holmes but got only static. He tried Preeti with the same results. Could someone be blocking cellular coms? If so, he was thankful their short-range radios were working.

Several shots rang out behind him. He didn't dare turn. He just had to trust that the Marines were doing their jobs.

The radio crackled as the machine gunner spoke. "One group is moving behind the shrubbery you just vacated."

"And the other?"

"Moving slower toward the near corner of the house."

Ian pulled a fragmentation grenade from his belt, slid free the pin, and held the spoon in place. He put his back to the wall just left of the window. It gave him the angle to see the first man of the group of black-clad soldiers closest to him. He was dressed like the others, and his and the faces of the men behind him were painted with black and green camo.

"Magerts, fire on my signal." He let the spoon slip free and cooked the hand grenade for two seconds before tossing it through the window. He had just enough time to see the surprised expression on the lead man's face before Ian was forced to dive to the ground.

The grenade went off, peppering the outside of the home with shrapnel. Screams were cut off by a surge of SA80s firing from Magerts's hide site. Then a few seconds later, the rattling of the machine gun began to eat the rear of the line of men.

He pulled his last two fragmentation grenades, removed the pins, then tossed each of them across the road until they rolled beneath the shrubbery. He jerked his head back. Both went off simultaneously, throwing superheated shrapnel in all directions. When next he looked, a pair of truck-sized holes had been blown in the shrubbery. Men were picking themselves off the smoke-hugged ground. Many had hands over their ears. They never heard the machine-gun shots that took them down.

Then as suddenly as the violent confluence started, it stopped. The machine gunner said it simply. "They're all dead."

"Rule number one." Magerts laughed. "Never walk into an L-shaped ambush."

But Ian didn't find any of this funny. Thirty men with families had just died much like Jerry and probably Trevor. And for what? For a mythical king to come back to life? *Fuck!*

One of the Marines approached from behind. "First floor cleared, sir. No sign of Trevor."

"Clear the second floor. Magerts, clear the front, and bring your men inside."

Ian turned and walked into the main salon where his men had already zip-tied several dozen revelers. It had been an orgy of epic proportions. Many of the men were still erect, trying to edge their way closer to the nearest zip-tied woman. There wasn't a single piece of furniture or square meter of carpet that wasn't occupied by someone.

Some of the men still wore masks. Long beaks of birds. The mane of a lion. The whiskered snout of a rat. He pulled the rat's mask off and recognized the man immediately.

"You looked different on television."

The flab of the man's midsection almost covered his semi-erect cock. The mad, lust-filled look in his eyes showed no signs of diminishing. It was either drugs or magic or both. Whatever was in these people, it wasn't anything Ian wanted to be part of. He glanced over at the naked women and noted that they did nothing for him. In fact, he felt sadness for them. Whatever they'd had that was good had been spent. He wasn't sure how he knew it, but he just did. Something evil had come to harvest and laid them bare.

A few shots echoed in the street out front; then Magerts and his men fanned inside.

Magerts whistled. "Now this is what I call a party." He waggled a finger at one of his Marines. "Treat this like a museum, boys. Look, but don't touch."

"Pretty fucked-up museum," one of them said.

Magerts's face held the afterglow of battle. "We'll follow you anytime, Lieutenant Colonel Waits. Those bastards never knew what hit them."

Ian shook his head at the pure sadness of it. "No, they didn't."

It had been a little while since he'd heard from the other Marines he'd sent upstairs. He found the staircase and looked up at the landing. His heart chilled as one of the lip-sewn women stood there, her eyes glowing with power.

He felt the amulet grow hot against his chest.

Magerts began to approach, but Ian waved him back. He didn't know what the woman had done to his men upstairs to overcome them and didn't want it to happen to Magerts and his men. Ian alone seemed to be impervious to her powers. At least for now.

"Where are my men?" Somehow he managed to keep the terror from his voice.

She pointed at him and he felt his amulet grow warmer. He was so thankful he'd worn it.

"I'll ask again, where are my men?" Then he laughed softly. Here he was asking a question of a woman whose lips were sewn shut. Correction. Not a woman but something that looked like a woman.

He put a foot on the first step just to see what would happen.

He was rewarded, so to speak. One of his men stepped woodenly beside her. Ian had talked to him. His name was Todd something. He had a kid who was in some Christmas pageant somewhere.

And now he stood, staring dumbly at Ian, holding a rifle, but not yet pointing it at him.

Please don't point the weapon at me.

Ian had his hand on his pistol and was ready to draw it but hoped he wouldn't have to exacerbate the situation.

"You don't have to do this," he said as much to her as he did to the Marine.

Then the Marine raised his rifle.

Ian had no choice. He drew quick and fired three times, catching the young man named Todd in the chest, head and throat. As his first target fell, he shifted his aim to the woman and fired three more, catching her in a similar pattern. But whatever success he'd found outside with the other lip-sewn girl, this one was different. She remained standing, and as he watched the bullet holes in her skin closed. He heard in his mind the voice of a famous actor known for his deep voice who said simply, "Oh, shit."

Then two Marines stepped forward to replace the one he'd just been forced to shoot.

Instead of participating in this insane assassination of his own men, Ian turned and walked away. He saw a tabletop covered with liquor bottles. He grabbed a bottle of twenty-year-old Highland Park, flipped off the top with a finger, and brought it to his face. He gulped deeply, holding the bottle there, knowing full well that he was a babe suckling at his mother alcohol. Images of all the men who'd been under his command and not survived slid past in a parody of a mortician's photo gallery until the final face caused him to jam shut his eyes. Trevor. Good kid to have helped Preeti like he'd done. Even better to have loved her after. He blinked away his tears, heaved back, and threw the bottle against the wall. He breathed deeply, then drew his sword. He knew what he had to do.

CHAPTER 45

BRATTON, WILTSHIRE. 0900 HOURS.

Walker slid into a ditch along with YaYa and Hoover. He breathed heavily through his mouth, trying his best to ignore the cold, wet mud. YaYa held the dog down as they all peered over the edge. At street level, they could see the sticks strewn across the road that were once the Tuatha. The cargo truck had hit it going fifty at least, exploding it into tinder.

But what of the Tuatha? Did the impact of a truck carrying a heavy cargo on a long flatbed kill it? Or even injure it?

Walker had his answer right away.

The driver climbed out of the cab and walked to the front of his truck. He was tall and broad shouldered with a gut that told of a lifetime of off-duty beers and taking up space in pubs from here to London. He held a hand on his head as he stared at the sticks, then looked at the front of his truck. From Walker's vantage it didn't seem to have done any damage. But he doubted the trucker cared. At this point, he probably thought he had been seeing things, such as a human-shaped stick man running across the road.

What the man couldn't see was what was happening beneath

the truck—a single stick began to drag itself into the brush on the other side of the road.

Hoover saw it and began to growl, but YaYa hushed him. But the man had heard. He turned to the sound, but the SEALs ducked as low beneath the lip of the ditch as they could.

They heard the man begin to walk in their direction, the heels of his boots clomping on the pavement. Walker reached toward the 9mm pistol under his left arm, wondering what he was going to do once the man saw them. It wasn't like they were chartered to kill random civilians, nor did he want to.

Holmes spoke over the MBITR. "Walker, what's your status?"

He didn't dare speak. The man was almost upon them.

Then a horn honked. Then another. It looked like the local Bratton townsfolk didn't appreciate a truck stopping in the middle of the road.

The footsteps stopped as the honking increased.

"All right, all right," he hollered. Then in a softer voice he added, "Bloody eyes are seeing things."

The restless locals stopped honking. His footsteps receded, then were stopped by the sound of the truck door closing. Soon the truck had pulled away, followed by the seven cars that had stacked up behind it.

Holmes's voice was filled with stress. "Walker, report!"

"Think it's on the move again. Stand by."

YaYa pointed and Hoover took off across the road. The SEALs waited for a car to pass, then followed. Soon they were running across a field. Hoover was sprinting straight for a stick figure. It looked different from the other. Probably because of the shape of the sticks and wood that was available. But Walker had no doubt that it was the same creature.

"Got it. Heading west northwest."

YaYa pulled ahead as Walker slowed, his legs becoming leaden. Gone were his stress fractures that had plagued him in BUD/S, but the sprinting was tiring him out. But not YaYa, who was an ultramarathoner. He could run for days.

Holmes spoke. "We think it's heading toward Ian."

"That far?" Walker figured it would take them hours to run that far. Correction. It would take YaYa hours. It would take Walker days.

"Break off and meet us in Westbury."

"Dressed like this?"

"Make it happen."

Walker slowed to a walk. YaYa did as well and called Hoover through his own MBITR connection. The dog slowed but kept going. YaYa called in a stern voice and the dog stopped. She turned and loped back with a disappointed look on her face. Not that she was disappointed she couldn't keep going, but that her human team members were so damn slow. If the dog could shake her head in exasperation she would have.

YaYa found a minivan parked on the side of the road in front of a nineteenth-century stone house. He checked the driver's side door. It was unlocked. Although it would have been nice if the keys had been inside, they weren't that lucky. But it was an older model and it wasn't long before he'd hot-wired the ignition and they were backtracking to where the others waited with the witch in a copse. It was the farthest they had dared go. After those trees were open fields with homes and travel trailers. None of them thought that they'd go unnoticed.

The three other SEALs got in after the witch was loaded into the back.

Walker wondered if Holmes had spoken to Ian on his private command channel. "Any word from Section 9?"

"Not a one."

"We going there?"

"Only place to go." Holmes glanced at Laws. "He thinks that's where it's heading."

Laws shrugged slightly. "Only reasonable place to go."

Preeti called and Holmes automatically put it on the squad frequency. The first thing she said was, "The Tuatha. Don't trust it."

"Too late," Holmes said. "Tell us what you know."

"The Tuatha wasn't just any faerie. It was perhaps the most powerful of them all."

Holmes's eyes narrowed. "What do you mean?"

Preeti began to recount her research, but Holmes soon cut her off. "Get to the point, Preeti."

"I think the Tuatha that the Bohemian Grove had taken and used is none other than Merlyn the Magician."

"Seriously?"

"Absolutely. Let me explain. In the body of English literature Merlyn appears more than six hundred times spanning fifteen hundred years."

Yank interrupted, "But it's fiction."

"Very true. But there's a tradition in England, as there is in most countries, to use folklore as the basis for literature. The continued incarnations of this historical figure set a pattern."

"Couldn't they all be referencing the original source?" Walker asked.

"They could, but that wouldn't explain some of the divergence. Especially his disappearance from English literature and his appearance in German literature in the early 1800s."

Laws shook his head. "Wasn't he just the creation of Geoffrey of Monmouth, though? Merlyn is and has always been a literary figure."

"Nope. Geoffrey just associated him with Uther Pendragon and gave him credit for moving the stones that make up Stonehenge. And it was Sir Thomas Malory who first paired Merlyn with King Arthur. What I'm talking about is a series of Middle Welsh poems which were later retold in the Black Book of Carmarthen and which refer to Merlyn and his relationship with Arthur centuries before Malory or Geoffrey.

"His original name was Myrddin and first came to light while he was living in Caer-fyrddin, or Carmarthen, which stakes its claim as the oldest established town in Wales. *Caer* means 'Fort' and *fryddin* is believed to be a version of 'Myrddin,' meaning 'Fort of Merlyn.' Modern scholars agree that the name is eponymous to the town—that the town derived its name from 'Myrddin'—but doubt that Myrddin existed prior to the town, despite what medieval scholarly texts assert the same."

"So modern scholars doubt what scholars closer to the era believed?" Laws asked.

"Exactly. These same modern scholars associate Myrddin with Lailoken, who was a sixth-century prophetic wild man mystic."

"But you disagree."

"There are Roman texts identifying Myrddin as a guide in the area circa AD 27."

Walker could tell by his expression that Holmes was getting impatient. "And this is significant how?"

"Camarthen wasn't founded until it became a defensive fortress in AD 75. Forty-eight years later."

Holmes's eyes lit up. "Now you have my attention."

"The rest is supposition, with me asking myself how a being could exist over the span of at least two thousand years. And that was as—"

"A Tuatha Dé Dannan jumping from host to host," Holmes finished.

"But let me tell you the best part."

"Go ahead."

"Section 9 has a record from 1909 of killing a man known as Isaac Manuel Francisco Albéniz y Pascual, who was a Spanish pianist and composer working and living in London. He was identified as being part of a plot to kill Edward the Seventh, son of Queen Victoria. He'd created an opera during which assassins associated with the Golden Dawn were going to kill the King by flooding his private box with acid vapors."

"The Golden Dawn are of German origin," Laws interjected. "They're organizationally descended from Rosicrucians."

"Isn't the Bohemian Lodge tied to the Golden Dawn?" YaYa asked.

Holmes waved them silent. "I don't get it."

"The opera to be performed that night was called *Merlyn*."

The inside of the van was silent for a few moments. "You have a lot more, don't you?" Holmes asked.

"Oh yeah."

"So tell me again why we need to know this."

"It's simple. If Merlyn, or Myrddin, is a Tuatha, and he had a close relationship with King Arthur in the past, where do you think he'd most like to be?"

"By Arthur's side, especially if there's to be the dawn of an Arthurian hegemony."

Laws snapped his fingers. "And we helped him get here. My guess is that the Golden Dawn sold, traded, or gave the Tuatha to the Bohemian Grove, probably shortly after their failed attempt on the King's life. The people of the Bohemian Grove have been protecting their investment with golems since then, knowing how valuable the Tuatha's life force is. Even if the Tuatha had wanted to return to its home, it couldn't have, not with the protective measures in place, such as the tattoos and magic."

Walker nodded. "Then came SEAL Team 666. Do you think it was that well planned? Was Jen invited to Stonehenge on the Winter Solstice to set this chain of events in motion?"

Yank whispered, "Feels like Mexico City all over again."

Laws put a hand on Walker's shoulder. "We'll never know, Walker. I doubt their information is that good, but we can't rule it out. Remember, our information and existence is special-access code word."

Sassy Moore moaned as she sat up. "So what you're saying is that we're all a bunch of chumps? And look at me. When the Red Grove couldn't get him from us, the Tuatha killed its host so I'd be forced to take it inside me, in order for me to *personally* escort it to the mound." She closed her eyes and held her head. "I felt the surge of power when it touched the mound. Like a charging system. It went from weak to full charge in a second. I didn't stand a chance."

Preeti interrupted, "I heard what she said. Listen, there's one last thing. Cadbury Castle was the home of King Arthur and is largely believed to be Camelot. If King Arthur is going to rule England, then—"

"It's going to be from Camelot." Holmes glanced at the others inside the van. "Any news on Ian?"

"We're monitoring reports of gunfire and explosions in the area. Locals are calling the police, but their calls are going ignored."

"Are they just not answering?" Walker asked.

"Yep. Ringing off the hook."

Laws turned thoughtful. "So the calls could have been hijacked, the police might not be in their office, or they might be intentionally not answering."

"Could be any one of those. We have no way of knowing."

"The roadblocks have also been removed," Preeti added.

"Maybe that means they needed the men to fight against Ian and his Marines." Holmes chewed on his lip for a moment. "Keep monitoring local traffic referencing Glastonbury Tor and surrounds." Holmes paused, then added, "You might want to send a warning through Ian's contacts with MI5 and the Home Office. If this thing gets out of hand, the Queen might need to be evacuated."

Silence hugged the line for a few moments. "It's come to that?"

"Yeah," Holmes said. "I'm afraid so."

"Okay. Roger. And, boys?"

They all answered, "Yes?"

"Be careful, please."

No one said a word. They didn't have to. Preeti's voice warmed them. Not only was it hers, but it was also that of their mothers, dead or alive, their wives and lovers, dead or alive, and every other woman who'd ever showed concern for them.

Be careful, please.

CHAPTER 46

SOUTH OF GLASTONBURY TOR, ENGLAND. 0905 HOURS.

Ian ordered Magerts and his men to hold at the bottom of the stairs. The other man had argued to let him be part of the attack, but Ian wouldn't have it. This was something he had to do alone and was his cross to bear. One thing he vowed was not to kill any more of his men. He was well aware that the lip-sewn woman had them under her control and would use them against him. But that didn't matter. He would not participate in her farce. If he could get to her first, then maybe he had a chance; otherwise, he'd wade through an avalanche of bullets until they brought him down.

He drew the blackened-iron sword of Guy of Warwick with one hand and pulled a Fairbarn-Sykes commando knife with the other. Then he marched to the bottom of the stairs. She hadn't moved. Neither had his two men beside her. One's name was Jim. He didn't know the other's, but Jim was saving his money for a trip to Australia, where he knew some blokes who would teach him to surf and introduce him to a platoon of sheilas. If everything worked out, he wouldn't be coming back. At least that had been his plan.

Ian felt his amulet warm as she tried to work arcane magic on him. He met her gaze and he saw something there that gave him hope. Frustration. He'd seen it enough in his life. His ex-wife had owned the look. He'd been known to kindle it in the last few years of their horrid ten-year marriage. Now to see it in this vessel for a rogue Tuatha spirit gave him hope.

And he took advantage of the hesitation by storming up the stairs. He took them two at a time, his sword in *First Point* position, his knife held low. Although he was focused on the woman, he saw when his men raised their rifles. He heard two shots and flinched, but no bullets took him. Instead, his men went down.

He shouted, *"NO!"* as he took the last two steps and plunged his blades into her. Her body went rigid, but she didn't go down. She clawed at his face with her hands. He pulled the sword free, stepped back, and swung it through her neck.

Her head rolled free as her body fell, blood gushing with the last pump of her heart.

He stepped aside, remembering that she'd been a victim as well. Then he went to his men. Instead of dead, they were merely wounded. Magerts had shot them in the legs.

Ian felt a hand on his back and turned to it.

"Couldn't let you be the Light Brigade, sir." Magerts smiled apologetically. "I thought there might have been another way."

Ian stared at him.

"They're my men too," Magerts added.

Finally Ian nodded. "Have someone bind their wounds. Let's see what happened to the rest of our men."

Five rooms ran off the landing. They checked the two on the right and found men and women zip-tied, much like downstairs. The Marines had made it this far. On the other side of the landing were three rooms. One was a bathroom and was empty. They opened the door next to this one carefully and also found it empty. So where were they?

He exchanged a glance with Magerts, who appeared equally vexed.

When they opened the final door they found what they'd been

looking for. It was an immense bedroom with a second sitting room off of it. Seven of his men stood like statues around another seated in a chair. His face was contorted around the stitches that had been applied to his lips, pulling them shut at odd angles. Blood had seeped from the inexpertly made seam of his mouth but was now dried. He wore so many wounds his skin had taken on a reddish hue. He had holes in his hands and feet like he'd been crucified.

"Oh, Trev." He pushed aside the men, who appeared to be waking from a trance, and fell to his knees beside his man.

He pulled away the sign they'd hung around his neck. Trevor was no *Lord of Misrule*. He was a hero and would always be a hero.

Ian turned and saw the bathroom. He rushed into it and grabbed a washcloth and wet it with water. He turned to leave but felt a presence. He paused a moment, then jerked aside the shower curtain. A fat man stood trembling.

"Let me explain," he said.

Ian grabbed him by his hair and jerked him from the shower and threw him into the room.

Several Marines recognized him and made exclamations.

"Take care of Sir MacDonald. Do not let him up until I am done with my man." Ian flashed his rage at the men. "Do you understand?"

They all nodded hastily, then stared fearfully at the Member of Parliament. They'd been placed in a precarious position, but for now they were more afraid of Ian, so they followed his order.

He knelt again in front of Trevor. Wiping gently at the blood on the man's beaten and sewn face, he spoke to him in a low voice, promising him that he'd take care of his mother and Preeti and that his death would not be in vain. He cried as he said these things, eventually bringing forth a knife that he used to cut the threads that had been used to sew Trevor's mouth shut. Then he untied his hands and legs and brought him from the chair. Cradling him like he was his own child, Ian carried Trevor to the bed and laid him in state, crossing his hands over his chest and closing his eyes. He said a simple prayer over the body, then turned.

Ian gazed upon Sir Robert MacDonald, unabashed at the tears that had flowed and were now drying upon his face.

"You were part of this."

Sir Robert held up his hands. "It wasn't me; I swear."

Magerts came from the sitting room. "Found these two trying to hide." He presented two women in their thirties, fit, naked, and tattooed. Their eyes were dull and dilated. "I asked them what happened, but they're too stoned to even talk."

Ian returned to the task at hand. "Then who was it?" He pointed to where the women were being zip-tied. "You going to blame them?"

"I—I—"

"Speak up!" Ian slapped the MP in the face. "Had you any honor at all you'd be ashamed. This man was defending your country."

"Found this in the other room beside his pants." Magerts held out a leather pouch. Inside were long curved needles used to re-upholster leather. Also present was a half-used roll of string-like thread.

Ian took it. He glanced from the MP to the pouch and back.

Sir Robert turned away.

Ian's eyes shot wide as rage fired through him. "You."

"It wasn't . . . you don't understand. They have power . . . power like you've never seen before."

"What does that have to do with my man?"

"Listen. It's not too late." Sir Robert glanced at the Marines who stood watching. "There's going to be a return to greatness. Remember when England ruled the world? Remember when we had colonies? Remember when we meant something?"

The Marines began to look at one another.

"There was a time when being English meant something to the world. There was a time when we carried ourselves proud. If it weren't for David Beckham and the fucking Beatles no one would even care about us now."

Ian had only one question. "What does that have to do with my man?"

"His death can mean something. It has meant something. His soul went to power the new king." Fat and pallid and naked, with his penis lying flaccid against his leg, Sir Robert suddenly smiled beatifically. "You should see our new king. King Arthur. He's wondrous."

Ian delivered a blow that sent Sir Robert across himself. His head bounced off the floor. Ian pounced on him, flipped him over, and straddled him. He stared into the man's eyes. "What does that have to do with my man?"

"We needed a Lord of Misrule. We needed someone."

"It was supposed to be him," came a slurred feminine voice.

Ian held Sir Robert by the neck but turned to the speaker.

It was one of the women. She could barely hold her head up, but she managed to say, "Sir Robert was to be the Lord of Misrule."

Ian stared at the MP as he processed the information.

"You chickened out." How this man had been elected, Ian couldn't fathom. There wasn't a single redeemable molecule in Sir Robert's body.

"Once King Arthur rules we will take care of you," Sir Robert said. "I can make you an earl or a duke. I can give you anything because I'll be his trusted man."

Ian stood and kicked the MP in the stomach. He reached for the pouch, which Magerts handed over. "I don't have a king. I have a queen and I've devoted my life's work to her and the people of England." He nodded toward the door. "Magerts, please leave us for a moment. Take your men with you."

Magerts appeared to be ready to say something, but one glance at the bed silenced him. He ushered his men out the door along with the two women. Then he closed the door behind him.

Sir Robert MacDonald began to cry. His sobs turned to screams by increments as Ian did what he felt he had to. When he was done, the former MP no longer bled from his crotch, nor could he speak. His lips were sewn shut and were forever full.

Ian washed his hands in the sink but never once looked at

himself in the mirror. When he was done he walked to the window and stared up at Glastonbury Tor just in time to see a tall figure wearing a crown pause beneath the arch to St. Michael's Tower. Ian wondered if he'd turn. He wondered if the King would regard him. But then the King continued, disappearing into the tower.

CHAPTER 47

SOUTH OF GLASTONBURY TOR, ENGLAND. 1030 HOURS.

The place was a war zone. Dead bodies lay in the street, some having sat down as if they were resting instead of lifeless. Walker had
seen this before. They'd died so quickly their bodies didn't even
have time to display properly. A Marine leaned out the window of
the top floor of the building and waved. Walker waved back.

Several Marine sergeants were talking to a concerned group
of locals.

"Shit got real serious," Yank said from the back of the van.

They pulled up to the front of the Tudor house and got out.
Magerts and his men were moving bodies into piles on the other
side of the shrubbery. Yank and YaYa went to help. Hoover jumped
out and began inspecting the bodies. Walker joined Laws, Holmes,
and the witch, who went inside.

They found Ian sitting at a table. He sat staring at a glass half-
filled with scotch but made no move to drink it.

No one said anything.

Laws went upstairs.

The witch inspected the head of a lip-sewn girl.

Holmes pulled out a chair and sat in it. "We didn't have any
coms."

It took a moment for Ian to answer. "They put a cell jammer on the roof."

"You didn't take it down?"

"Didn't know if they left behind any cellular-detonated bombs." Ian hadn't moved at all.

"I understand." Holmes regarded Ian for a moment, then glanced at Walker. He flicked his eyes toward the open sliding glass doors that led to the backyard.

Walker stepped silently away and into the backyard. It was clear that there'd been a party here, but with everyone gone it had an empty, almost barren feeling. He saw several marks drawn on the grass in what looked like blood. He couldn't figure out what they were but didn't want anything to do with them. He gave them a wide berth. A man-sized cross had been crudely erected in a corner. Bloody nails marked where someone's hands and feet had been affixed to the wood.

Hoover padded up to him and nuzzled his hand. YaYa and Yank were right behind.

Yank jerked his thumb back toward the house. "What's up with Ian? Man's comatose."

"Magerts said they killed Trevor. Said it was bad."

Walker felt an emptiness well up inside him. A mere echo of what he felt for Jen, but it was still painful. He knew exactly how Preeti was going to feel and mourned for her. "What about the rest?"

YaYa put his hand on Walker's back. "They have the survivors upstairs in the bedrooms. Everyone else is dead. You should see what was done to that British Lord."

"The fat guy with the goons?"

"Yeah. That guy. Someone ripped out his manhood and sewed it in his mouth."

Now it made sense. Walker was able to imagine the rage that had consumed Ian. Had he been alone with the man, especially knowing that he was an integral human part of the conspiracy to bring down England and replace it with something older, nastier, Walker might have done the same. Images ticked through his mind, like CSI photos of what he would have done. His mouth dried and his breathing became rapid. He caught himself and in a voice more husky than he'd planned asked, "What about the red-robed witches and the King?"

"They went into St. Michael's, then disappeared."

"All of them?" asked the witch, coming up behind them.

"That's what Magerts said. His man with a machine gun watched them go and said there was a flash of light."

She frowned. "The only way that could happen is if all the other witches have Tuatha in them. So many in one place at one time. It's as if they came together for this one great event." She harrumphed. "The left-behinds getting their just due."

She turned and strode inside. "Can we get to Cadbury Castle now?" She raised her voice. "We need to get to Cadbury Castle."

Holmes stood up. "Let's go, Ian. This isn't over."

Ian stood woodenly. Then, as if he'd just awoken, he looked at the SEALs. He focused on Walker. "Young Jack. Bring Sir Mac-Donald, can you?"

Magerts made a worried face. "Maybe we should just leave the body here. Let it sort itself out when this is all over."

But Ian shook his head. "This is my abomination. I need to answer for it."

"But he was guilty of helping the enemy." Walker stared at his hands, which had become fists, strangling invisible murderers. "Accessory to the murders of our loved ones. Don't you get it? He knew."

Ian put his hand on Walker's shoulder. "I know he knew. He was a terrible human being. But don't you get it? If we do the same things to them as they do to us, we become them."

Walker tried to find a weakness in the man's logic.

"Get the body and bring it with us. I'll let the Queen decide my fate. I can't go without being judged. I just can't."

Walker tried to think of something to say, but his mind was everywhere and nowhere at once.

Holmes saved him. "Go ahead, Walker. YaYa, go with him." To Magerts he said, "Let's figure out our transportation situation."

YaYa grabbed Walker and pushed him toward the stairs. "Come on, man. Let's get this done."

They trudged up the stairs. Walker followed YaYa, who'd already been upstairs. They went into a bathroom and found Sir MacDonald in the bathtub, eyes staring sightlessly toward the paneled ceiling. Beneath these orbs his face was a bloody mess and looked as if an inexpert hand had frantically sewed and seamed his mouth shut. You could tell where someone stopped, then started. Several of the threads had broken and had been resewn.

Walker saw the dark red stain of blood that had seeped through the terry-cloth robe where the crotch should have been. Yeah. It was fucking terrible, but a growing part of him wished it had been him who'd done this instead of Ian. And if anyone wanted to judge him for this deserved desire, then let it be Saint Peter at the Pearly Gates.

"Let's get this done," he said roughly.

Walker grabbed the arms and YaYa took the legs. They took the body into the master bedroom, laid it on the bed, then bound it in the bedspread, using ripped lengths of sheet to tie it. About halfway through, Walker noticed YaYa had stopped moving. He glanced at the kid and saw his teeth were rattling. His face had paled and sweat beaded on his brow.

"What is it?"

"I feel . . . there's . . . something."

Walker felt something too, but he'd been feeling a low-key supernatural buzz almost the entire time he'd been in England. But now that YaYa was feeling something, he tried to hone in on the feeling. Strange. It was as if it was centered right in front of them, but all that was there was the dead MP and the bed.

Walker suddenly stepped back.

"Did you check under the bed?"

"Of course . . ." YaYa stepped back too. "I don't know."

"You don't know?" All he saw was the dark edge of a solid shadow.

"Once we saw the body, it was all about that."

"Did Hoover come in here?"

"No, she was in the other rooms."

Walker pulled his pistol and dropped to his knees. A set of eyes met his own. "Get out of there."

The eyes blinked at him.

He waved the barrel of his pistol. "Get the hell out."

A hand came out. He grabbed it and pulled a woman free. She wore jeans and a blouse but had no shoes on, nor did she have any jewelry. Her blond hair was mussed, but her face was thankfully free of stitches. She looked for all the world like a regular girl, but Walker knew better. The moment he touched her he could feel the power coursing through her. He let her go and kicked her away.

"Get the witch."

YaYa stared a moment, then broke into motion. He went to the top of the stairs and called down. Soon Laws and the witch were pounding up the stairs and into the room.

"I don't know what she is, but she's something."

The witch took one look and laughed. "Sarah Pinney, what have you done? Did you look under the bed for a robe?"

YaYa reached under the bed and pulled out a scarlet robe, the same ones worn by the Red Grove. He held it in his mechanical hand like it was rotten.

Walker stood and backed away. He crossed his arms low and in front of him but still held his pistol.

The woman named Sarah was older than he'd originally thought. Her mousy blond hair held slivers of gray and crow's-feet lived at the corners of her eyes and mouth. "Sassy, we thought it was you."

"In all of my glory." She took the robe from YaYa and inspected it. "I thought there were a few familiar touches in the Red Grove's magic."

The girl went to stand, but Walker shook his head and lifted the tip of the pistol slightly. She gave him a smile which said *a girl had to try,* then settled onto her butt. "You might as well know, since it's almost over."

"You'd be surprised how much we already know."

Sarah giggled. "We know. Merlyn told us."

Laws stepped forward. "Who is this, Ms. Moore?"

"She and I once trained together. She was going to be a part of the Fraternitas Saturni as well, but she didn't have what it took."

"Except she has a Tuatha inside her, now," YaYa said.

Sassy nodded. "Except that. How'd you know?"

YaYa made a face. "It's like a familiar smell, except it's a feeling instead. Not at all pleasant."

"Even with a Tuatha, this one is no match for me." Sassy knelt next to the woman. "And it's a nasty little beastie inside you, isn't it? What is it?"

"A Baen Sidhe."

"What's her name?"

"I'm not going to tell you that."

Sassy gave her a matronly smile. "Come now, Sarah. You've never been one to like a lot of pain. Do you really want to deny me?"

The other witch looked defiant for a moment, then sighed. She shrugged. "Fine. Have her. It's not like you'll be able to do anything with it. There's nothing you'll be able to do to stop it."

"We'll see about that. Now let me get to that Baen Sidhe. I could use a recharge." She brought her Viking wand up and pointed it at the other witch. "You boys might want to turn away. This is going to get ugly."

CHAPTER 48

POINT BRAVO, WARWICK, ENGLAND. LATER.

Preeti was anxious to get through. The total blackout was killing her. Not only did she need to find out about Trevor, but she'd also been trying to coordinate some backup for Ian and the men of SEAL Team 666. Her brother was helping her as well and both of them were butting up against a wholesale effort to keep information from flowing within the country and to turn the communication networks into a cat's cradle of confusion. She couldn't contact anyone meaningful, and when she could get through they were requiring her to authenticate a phrase for which she had no password. Lord Robinson was completely incommunicado. Even his private cell number was out of service. She was becoming increasingly concerned that they might be winning the battles but losing the war. She said as much to Genaro, who could feel her frustration.

"Have you tried to have someone external contact an internal number? Maybe it's something they've done with the switches."

She thought it was a great idea and contacted Pete Musso at SPG. She explained what she needed. Gave him several numbers, then waited. He came back in fifteen minutes and the news wasn't good. He couldn't get through either, and with a query to a colleague in America's NSA it became apparent that Britain's Government Communications Headquarters had locked down the communications systems and was only allowing connectivity through their master server in The Doughnut, their headquarters in Cheltenham.

Preeti slammed her crutches against the floor. "Damn it. What if they need help? There's no way to get it to them."

"This had to have been part of the greater plan. It makes you wonder how many people in high places are involved."

"It could only be a few if they have the right access. After all, it's Christmas Day. No one's paying attention to anything except their families."

Genaro had another idea. "What about friends from outside England? Help from America is too far, but what about France or Germany?"

Preeti felt a well of hope. "Or Ireland. Trevor and Ian worked with a couple blokes from the Irish Seventeenth Army Ranger Wing. On paper it doesn't exist, but much like Section 9, they've been around for quite a while."

She tried to call out but wasn't able to connect. Which made sense, since GCHQ controlled all of Great Britain. She called back Musso and asked him to contact Conor McGinty and to give him a time to connect, which was thirty minutes from then. Musso said he would, and in the meantime she logged onto Facebook and pulled up a popular application used to play word games.

While she waited, Genaro made them another pot of coffee. She was on the third pot. Her stomach was torn up from the stress and the acid. He urged her to eat and she finally chose a slice of bread with some butter on it. She couldn't bring herself to try anything else.

Two of her Facebook friends saw her online and tried to initiate a game, but she ignored them. Finally, thirty-seven minutes after she began waiting, she saw the word *Laith* pop into her box.

She replied with *Luachra*. Laith Luachra was the mother of Finn mac Cumhaill, better known as Finn McCool. Not only was he a great Irish mythological warrior, but it was also the nickname of the Irish Seventeenth Army Ranger Wing—the Finn McCools.

Then they opened a chat window.

Conor: *Merry Christmas. What's up?*

Preeti: *Nothing merry about it.*

Conor: *Uh-oh. Tell me.*

Preeti: *Jerry's dead. Trevor may be too. Lost three others last week. Might lose the Queen. Need help.*

There was a long pause.

Conor: *Sorry about loss. Terrible. What news with Queen?*

Preeti: *All other coms are hijacked. Highest-level bad guys. Want to overthrow Queen.*

Conor: *We've been tracking something. Bad day to get help.*

Preeti: *Can't help it. Do you have anything?*

Another long pause.

Conor: *Have two choppers at Culdros. Two men. Not going to be happy, but looks like you need it.*

Preeti: *You have no idea.*

Conor: *It must really be bad. How's Ian?*

Preeti: *You can guess.*

Conor: *Yeah. I can. Listen, Patrick Kelly and Keith O'Reilly will be in contact. Keep lines open.*

Preeti: *Will do. And thank you, Conor.*

Conor: *As always, payment in beer.*

Then he signed off.

Genaro, who had been following the conversation over her shoulder, straightened. "Ingenious. I read a book once about spies communicating during MMORPGs. What was your plan B if this didn't work?"

She frowned and hugged her sweater around her. "Carrier pigeon."

"I think they're extinct."

"That says it all." She sat back in her chair. England had a long history of kings and queens and not everyone found the throne through peaceful means. What was that mnemonic they'd made her learn in order to recall the long line of English monarchs?

First William the Norman
Then William his son
Henry, Stephen, Henry
Then Richard and John
Next Henry the Third
Edwards One, Two, and Three
And again after Richard
Three Henrys we see
Two Edwards, Third Richard
If rightly I guess
Two Henrys, Sixth Edward
Queen Mary, Queen Bess
Then Jamie the Scotsman
And Charles whom they slew
Yet received after Cromwell
Another Charles too
Next James the Second
Acceded the Throne
Then good William and Mary
Together came on
Not till Anne, Georges Four,
And Fourth William all passed
Came the reign of Victoria,
Whose longest did last
Then Edward the Peacemaker
(He was her son)
The fifth of the Georges
Was next in the run
Edward the Eighth
Gave the Crown to his brother
Now God's sent Elizabeth
All of us love her.

Then Preeti added two lines:

But now Arthur is here
And if you're not white . . . .

She struggled to find the right word, but all she could think of was:

Then your life is shite.

And to think two Irish helicopters, five Americans, a Belgian dog, and Ian were all who could possibly alter this path. She began to cry, big, choking sobs. She cried for herself, she cried for Jerry, she cried for Trevor, and she cried for England . . . an England who'd embraced her family and every other family, regardless from whence they came.

CHAPTER 49

CULDROS ROYAL NAVAL AIR STATION, ENGLAND. 1115 HOURS.

Lieutenant Patrick Kelly cursed loudly in the cockpit of his Superhawk helicopter. "Seriously? Christmas Day we have to pull some English nit's balls out of the fire?" He'd planned on a nice afternoon with a gal he'd met off base. She was single. He was single. He imagined getting some ribbon and wrapping himself up as a present so he could gift himself to her.

But then Conor had contacted him through flight control. It was strange at first that Conor hadn't called him on his cell phone, but he'd explained that there were *issues* with communications at the current time, which was why Patrick had stood in flight control wearing a headset with an on-duty noncom staring at him while Conor gave him the rundown.

"Get Keith. You two have to meet some friends at Cadbury Castle. You'll take your orders from Ian Waits. Do what he says until this is all over."

Keith stumbled out of the hangar, zipping up his flight suit. He gave Patrick a quizzical look as he made his way to his own helicopter.

Patrick shrugged with his hands. He watched Keith's walk. The kid had been in his pints last night and it was possible he could still have alcohol in his system. He waited until Keith put on his flight helmet and jacked in. Then he called over.

"You okay, brother?"

"Always."

Patrick paused for a second, then asked, "You sure had a good time last night?"

"Fuck you very much."

"Keith, I—"

"Forget it. I'm good. Let's get spun up and over there to see what the hell is going on."

Patrick had done everything he could. Keith was probably okay. He had the metabolism of a twenty-year-old and could fly circles around most pilots. Actually, he was lucky to have Keith with him. They were to fly Nap-of-the-Earth to avoid detection. Although NOE was unusual outside a combat zone, Patrick had gotten the impression from Conor that England had suddenly become a combat zone. Patrick was eager to find out why.

He'd already prepared the flight plans for their return home to Casement Aerodrome in Dublin. So he'd filed those, which meant they'd have to head north over the Celtic Sea, before heading east to Cadbury Castle.

He glanced over at Keith again and watched him go through preflight. They were more alike than different. They'd both lost family in Northern Ireland and had grown up with war all around them. So when they had the chance to spend time in the south of England, even during the cold, blustery month of December, it was a luxury they didn't take for granted.

Both Keith and he had been enlisted soldiers prior to becoming officers. They hadn't known each other when they'd transferred to helicopters, but they'd formed a fast and lifelong friendship in flight school, even if it felt sometimes that he was the older brother in their relationship.

Then they met the Finn McCools. Something in Keith's and Conor's files had made the McCools interested in them and they soon found their missions filled with odd creatures and cryptids they'd previously only seen on badly made movies on the cable

TV channels. Part of him believed it was just this sort of mission that he was about to embark upon, which went a long way to ameliorate the disappointment he felt at missing his much-anticipated assignation.

The sky was overcast with a ceiling of five hundred meters. Visibility was at five kilometers. It had snowed lightly early in the morning, but the day was now crisp and clear, so flying shouldn't be an issue.

With preflight done for both helicopters, he called flight control. The engines whined and the blades spun clumsily. But as they gathered speed they took on a slick appearance and the sound rose in pitch.

"FM One, this is Control. All flights are grounded. Repeat. All flights are grounded."

"Control, this is FM One requesting clearance."

"Negative, FM One. All flights are grounded." The voice had been friendly but firm.

Interesting. "Control, we are en route for Baldonnel. Please grant clearance, over."

"Negative. Stand down."

He toggled to craft-to-craft mode. "Keith, looks like we're going to have to make a run for it."

"What are they going to do, shoot us down?"

Patrick laughed but hoped that it wouldn't come to that. It couldn't. Or could it? "Ready?"

"You lead, I'll follow."

"Control, this is FM One. Request permission return to home base."

"Negative. Stand down." This time the voice was anything but friendly.

"Affirmative, Control. Thanks and Merry Christmas."

He punched the throttle, lifted the collective, and pushed the stick forward. He roared across the tarmac, his ears suddenly filled with commands to stand down and return to base, but he ignored them like he did most things English.

"Patrick?"

"On your six."

He reveled in the power of the new Sikorsky H-92s. The military variant of the S-92 and an upgrade over the S-70, the Superhawk boasted more than 3,000 shaft horsepower. Nominally assigned to the Irish Coast Guard, as was his cover status, they were meant for search and rescue. Of course the Ministry of Defence had ordered two extras for the Finn McCools to use. The delivery last year of these aircraft eliminated the need to keep the older ones aloft with spit, bailing wire, and prayers to all denominational deities. Patrick loved the feel of the craft.

The pair of green and white Superhawks flew at an elevation of thirty meters over the windswept empty grounds of Flambard's Themepark. The Skyraker thrill ride towered over them for a moment; then they were moving on. Patrick switched off his Identification Friend or Foe transponder and had Keith do the same.

They soon passed Helston and turned northeast past Treswithian in order to stay away from the radar present at Nancekuk. When they hit the coast they kept going, then made a slow turn to the northeast. They crossed back over land at Bideford and reduced their elevation to twenty meters. At Tiverton they were forced to head south to avoid yet another radar.

Then they were at Chard.

Then Crewkerne.

Then Yeovil.

Cadbury Castle lay five kilometers to the north and they were on it in a matter of seconds. Rising 140 meters, the hill was surrounded on all sides. A road ran up one corner. Opposite this was a stair-stepping of land leading to the valley floor. It was a beautiful place, but that's not what made both helicopters pull up.

Patrick wasn't exactly sure what he was seeing. It looked as if a line of men had their backs against a drop-off and were defending against grayish hound-like creatures while red-robed figures stood in a line behind the beasts.

"What the hell? Is this some *Lord of the Rings* shite?" Keith asked. "Which side are we on?"

Patrick thought that was a good question. Then he saw one of the men in line waving for them and pointing to a flat of land just below them on the stair steps. The LZ was only large enough for a single chopper, but another stair several steps down was large enough for another. He ordered Keith to take the lower one and he took the upper. He was wary of his blades. Although they were five meters away from the edge of the hill, a person would have to be careful when descending to them.

CHAPTER 50

CADBURY CASTLE, ENGLAND. A FEW MINUTES EARLIER.

Laws scrambled up the second to the last step before the plateau of Cadbury Hill. Holmes was to his left with Yank. Walker and YaYa were to his right with Hoover. The witch was behind them carrying her thousand-year-old Viking wand and was madder than a wet cat inside a hornet's nest.

Magerts and Ian and their men were posted at the road. They were to arrive on command, based on the lay of the land on top of the plateau. There could be nothing. Or there could be a whole mess of *beegees* just waiting for them to arrive.

When the men were in line, Laws pulled a peeper cable from his pocket and slid it over the edge of the hill. Nothing but grass. He moved it around but couldn't see anything. Whether it was the lay of the ground or that nothing was there, he couldn't see anything, which could be good news or bad.

A moment from when he was a child flashed into his mind. He'd been waiting for his father to come home, but it had gotten so late his mother had made him go to bed. She'd left the door cracked, so light came in from down the hall where she sat watching Johnny Carson. Little Timmy Laws could barely make out the words, but whenever Carson said something funny the audience would roar. He'd sat on the edge of his bed for an hour, eager to tell his father about the story they'd read in school that day—one about butterflies and dinosaurs and time travel and how the strangest things can affect the universe. Then the Carson show had ended and his mother had turned off the television and she'd put on a Burt Bacharach record. He must have fallen asleep, because he next heard yelling, his mother hurling epithets toward someone. The sound of a shriek was followed by footsteps thundering down the hall. Was it his father come home? Then a creature with the face of a mad ape sprang into his room and beat its chest and howled. Little Timmy Laws had screamed. Pee soaked his Spider-Man pajamas. He held trembling fists out, wishing so hard that his father had been there to protect him. Then suddenly the ape became his father as he removed a prop mask from one of the sets. His father came in close, smelling of whiskey and perfume. He whispered to his son that he was sorry, hugged him, then staggered out of the room. A week later his mother made his father move out, and Laws saw him less and less until it was only major holidays when he'd make an appearance, even though he just lived across town.

Laws wiped tears from his eyes. He sat down heavily. He didn't want to fight. He didn't want to be here. He wanted nothing more than to be nine again, before his father had an affair with the costumer, before his mother kicked his father out, before he realized that a scary plastic ape mask could change the life of a small child as efficiently as a butterfly crushed under the foot of a time traveler.

He glanced over and saw that Walker and YaYa were sitting like him, sobbing violently into their hands. On the other side Holmes stared into space, tears streaming down his face. Yank punched the dirt, crying, saying, "Can't stop the burning, Momma, can't stop the burning."

The only one not in tears was Sassy, who stood transfixed, gripping her rod until it quivered, her eyes as far away and glassy as Holmes's.

Then the feeling was gone, sadness replaced by a hollow, empty nothing. Laws sighed, realizing that he could never fill the hole that memory made in his soul. A single tear fell; then he wiped it.

"What happened?" Holmes asked roughly.

"Empathetic magic," said Sassy. "They were all working together. I had a hard time stopping them."

"Fucking asshole witches." YaYa glanced around, clearly still in the clutches of whatever memory had captured him. "My father had me in a madrassa for two weeks before my mother found out. Ever been to a madrassa? It's like being a Catholic monk, only I was ten. They took everything away from me, even my name. I was . . ." He wiped his face with the sleeve of his uniform. "Shit."

Walker touched YaYa's real arm. "It's okay, brother. We all have memories we'd rather never remember."

Holmes helped Yank to his feet. "Is that the last of it?"

"Takes a lot to put a spell like that together," said Sassy. "I'd be surprised if they were able to repeat it. They might have something else up their sleeves though."

Laws realized he'd been clutching the snooper cable tight enough to make his hand ache. He rolled it and shoved it into a cargo pocket. "At least it means we're on the right track." He'd hated Halloween masks for years after that episode. Ironic that he'd ended up in an occupation that put him into contact with real monsters. If he were a psychiatrist, he'd probably tell himself that each time he took down a monster he was taking down that version of his father in the mask who'd ruined his life. But then again, what did they know?

Holmes nodded toward the lip of grass. "Let's do this."

All five SEALs and their dog surged over the top. They never got above a squat before falling into a prone position. Even Hoover hugged the ground, ears alert, eyes searching.

Cold seeped from the earth into their uniforms and body armor. Laws checked through his sights and without them and didn't see anything except for some low ground fog near the center of the plateau, where he knew the archeological excavation to be. Laws gauged the distance to be about 150 meters.

On command, the SEALs formed a wedge and moved in a tactical walk toward the center of the plateau, weapons seated in their shoulders, eyes gazing along the barrels. Hoover ranged in front of them. Sassy Moore followed behind, moving with her wand held up as if she were a disheveled shepherd, herding them across a high pasture.

They got fifty meters before a hound betrayed itself by baying.

The SEALs each dropped to a knee. Each one knew their quadrant of a 270-degree arc.

Sassy spoke from behind them. "I can feel them summoning power. They're there; we just can't see them."

"Can you tell me where they are?" Holmes asked.

"What do I look like? A dowsing rod?"

Holmes sighed.

Laws had the same feeling. They just loved it when they had a smart-ass helping them. It made life so pleasant and so worth surviving for.

"What are we doing here?" Yank asked.

YaYa responded, "What do you think we're doing here?"

"No, I mean, aren't SEALs supposed to be near water, hence all of our water training? Kneeling on a plateau in the middle of BFE seems so out of place."

"You're out of place," Walker said.

Laws gritted his teeth as the tension built. The air around him felt like the skin of a balloon filled past capacity. It was only a matter of time. "We're a different type of SEAL. We're pasture SEALs."

YaYa laughed. "BFE. Usually stands for 'Bum Fuck Egypt,' but I guess we're in England, so it fits."

"Do you boys always talk so much?" Sassy sounded exasperated.

Laws knew it was any second now. "Only when there's imminent danger."

Two hounds rushed toward them. One from the right and one from the left.

Hoover squared with the one on the left, running full out for it. They met in midair. The heavier hell hound took Hoover down, its massive jaws clamped around the dog's back right leg. Hoover twisted around and clamped her smaller jaw on an ear, ripping it off. Then she managed to bite down on the hound's neck.

Yank and Holmes let their rifles fall, catching and hanging on their slings as they drew the gladius machetes.

Laws wavered between joining and watching his sector of fire. Holmes stood a few feet from him, and by the way he stood, it looked as if he could take on a pack of hell hounds single-handedly. And Laws hated that. Why was it that the rest of them had to work so hard, yet everything came so easy to Holmes? It was infuriating the way he could be so lucky. Hell, his own ire was shared by half the casinos in Vegas, Holmes's hometown. Even they thought he was too lucky.

The other hound thundered toward them from the right. Yank held his gladius in his rear hand. The creature leaped. Yank sidestepped and brought the weapon down on its spine. The hound cried out as it fell to the earth. Holmes sliced off its head. Then the two pieces of hound evaporated.

Fucking Holmes. Like he wasn't even trying.

Laws was aware his barrel had drifted toward the other two SEALs but didn't care. After all, it was Holmes and Yank. Boy weren't they a pair. Different sides of the same coin. On one hand you had the impeccable Holmes, King of Cool-Ass Luck, and on the other you had Shonn Yankowski, black on the outside and white on the inside. "Hell, he might as well be a—" Laws caught himself at the last moment. He'd pressed the trigger but rode the firing into the sky.

Holmes turned on him, eyes blazing.

Yank turned to Holmes, gladius raised for a killing stroke. Laws could hear YaYa and Walker shouting at each other behind him.

Once more Sassy saved the day.

The feeling of unreasonable anger passed, but it couldn't stop Yank's sword.

"Holmes!"

The SEAL team leader spun, catching most of the descending

blade on his own gladius. The rest of it sliced into his arm, which immediately began welling blood.

Yank dropped his blade. "Oh shit. Sorry, Boss."

"Let me guess." Laws glanced at Sassy Moore. "Empathetic magic?"

She nodded abruptly, then continued her thousand-yard stare. Suddenly she went down as two dozen darts pierced her body.

Laws spun and spied what looked for all the world like a Gatling gun that had appeared forty yards in front of them . . . except this one fired flechettes instead of rounds.

Son of a bitch.

Simultaneously, more hounds bounded onto the plateau from where they'd been hiding in the archaeological dig. A line of seven Red Grove druids also appeared. All the while, flechettes ate through the air. Laws threw himself to the deck as three flechettes bounced off his armor, one dug itself into his face near his left eye, and five of the three-inch steel slivers lodged in his unprotected legs.

"Fucking hell!" he screamed with pain.

What was going on? The witch was down. Holmes was wounded. No telling what the other men were doing. And where was Hoover?

Laws's hand had gone to the wound in his face and was now coated with blood. Still, he found his grip on his rifle, raised up a foot, and began to fire at the guy manning the flechette cannon. This was beginning to feel like a trap. Laws wondered where King Arthur was. Was he at the dig site? Was he even here?

The entire place felt wrong.

Then came the sound of helicopters.

CHAPTER 51

CADBURY CASTLE, ENGLAND. NOW.

Walker shot up from his prone position and fired at the druids and the guy manning the flechette cannon. He saw one druid go down. The cannon began to swing Walker's way again and he dove to the ground. Three slivers of pain caught him in the back of his right thigh. The ground drove the breath from him, but he didn't have a moment. He'd seen Hoover getting her canine ass handed to her by the hell hound. Without help, they might lose her. Hoover was as much a part of the team as any of them. It just couldn't happen.

He lurched to his feet again and began running. The flechette cannon was no longer firing. He didn't know if it was because the cannoneer was down or out of ammo, but he couldn't spare the moment it would take to turn and look. His entire focus was on the interlocked canines—one supernatural, one SEAL.

He stumbled once but soon closed the distance. The last ten meters he ripped free his rifle and tossed it aside. He pulled his gladius. It felt like a fire poker in his hand and he had no idea how to use it. Still, he had to do something. Hoover was howling as the hell hound savaged her leg. Walker raised the gladius, intent to strike, but something in the eyes of the creature before him stilled his hand. As it looked his way with a large blue eye, he could swear it paused and regarded him. Somehow within its brutish baboon face there was something remarkable. The way the eye looked at him, the shape of the orb, the slight sadness surrounding it, sent a shock wave through his memories. A great well of sadness exploded, filling him past bursting. The feeling of loss . . . of nearness . . . of need . . . shot through him like a lightning bolt.

He staggered backwards. Could it be?

He uttered a single word. "Jen?"

The eye blinked at him.

He inhaled emptiness.

He'd known all along that the hounds were fueled by the souls of those they killed, but it had always seemed like an academic idea, something so unfathomable that he just took it for granted. Never once did he imagine that he'd be put in a position to not only face her but also possibly kill her.

She stared at him. My god, how he loved her. A thought struck him. He remembered what the witch had said about the souls of the hounds possessing the fonts. Was there a chance? Could he at least get that part of Jen back that was her essence? She wouldn't look the same, but then that wasn't what made her . . . her. All he had to do was find someone to possess.

He shook his head. What was he thinking? He couldn't do that to someone else!

Not even to have his girl back?

Not even to have the love of his life back in his arms?

He'd give the world to kiss her one more time, the feel of her soft lips, the warmth of her hands as she held him, knowing that he could close his eyes and she'd be there forever.

She blinked at him as if she was reading his mind. He could see recognition in her eyes.

The gladius felt heavy. He knew he needed to use it to save Hoover, but he couldn't kill her. Not again.

Then she did something at once beautiful and terrible. She opened her great monstrous jaws and released Hoover's leg. The hound's human hand that had been holding Hoover let go as well. It reached out to him, slow, tentative.

He choked back a sob. This was not her. This was a hellish creature of the Tuatha. This was . . .

Fuck.

It was her.

He reached out to her.

Hoover had had a grip on the hound's neck before, but it had been inadequate. Now the SEAL dog reared back and sunk her teeth into the hell hound's jugular. Growling and snarling, favoring her wounded rear leg, Hoover whipped her head back and forth.

The expression in the hound's eye changed from wonder to pain. It blinked rapidly. Its hand stalled in its arc to meet Walker's.

Then it screamed.

Hoover ripped the jugular free. Victory shone in her eyes.

Walker let out a barely audible, "No!"

He glared at Hoover, ready now to use the gladius.

But then the hound evaporated, leaving nothing of it behind.

Hoover limped over and licked Walker's outstretched hand.

Walker sunk to his knees. He dropped the gladius and threw his arms around Hoover. Great tides of anguish flowed through him, rocking his shoulders.

"Hoover did it right.

"Hoover did it right."

If he said it enough it might make it all okay.

"Hoover did it right."

Walker spent a lifetime in a single second, living and dying with the woman of his dreams. When it was over, he felt different. Was it a sense of closure? He couldn't be sure. All he knew was that the pain had receded to a dull ache. Seeing her in the hound, knowing that she loved him and had longed to be with him in that gesture of its hand, ameliorated some of his pain. Even so, he knew it wasn't the end of it. He'd need more time. But that was a luxury he didn't have at the moment.

Walker stood, shakily at first. "Come on, girl." He closed his eyes tightly for a second, then collected his weapons from where he'd dropped them.

Hoover licked his back leg and gave him a sorrowful look. "Don't be a sissy. We'll fix you up later. We got *beegees* who need killing."

His words went unheard because Hoover was already limping at a half run toward the line of red-robed druids. It was strange that they hadn't done anything yet. What were they waiting for?

Walker ran after Hoover. The other SEALs were fighting a pitched battle with the remainder of the hounds and the cannoneer was down. So it was him, Hoover, and the druids. *Fuck their magic.*

He raised his rifle and fired several three-round bursts at the druids nearest him. He saw the rounds pass through the material of their robes but have no effect on the wearers. Still, he fired again. He wondered what the hell he was going to encounter when he reached them. After all, who or what could withstand 5.56mm rounds traveling at 788 meters per second? Certainly not anything natural.

He screamed and pulled out his gladius with his left hand as he ran. Firing one-handed with his rifle, he swung the machete above his head in circles until he reached the first statue-like druid. He swept his blade through it and felt no resistance. The material fell to the ground along with the bundles of sticks inside that had filled out its dimensions.

But these things had appeared. They hadn't been staged.

Which meant they'd been populated—were populated—by Tuatha, but to what end?

Then it hit him.

Stalling tactic.

There was nothing here.

He'd felt it in the beginning.

Cadbury Castle, or Camelot, had been part of a wild-goose chase. So where was King Arthur and the rest of the Wild Hunt? If Arthur was intent on becoming the ruler of England, the only way to do it successfully was to depose the present ruler. So, wherever Elizabeth was, Arthur could be found.

Walker ripped apart the remaining stick-figure druids in a brutish rage. Hacking and slashing, kicking and punching, he finished off these ragged druid scarecrows, ripping them to pieces. He paused, panting from the effort, sweat-slick face regarding his work. Then he turned to his team and watched them locked in a desperate battle with the remaining hounds.

His men needed his help. It was fucking time to end this mission. He started to move toward them but felt a malaise take him over.

Hoover whined beside him and gave him a worried look.

Walker's hand came up and he found himself looking at it. Was this his hand? He became aware that he wasn't alone. The hairs on the back of his neck engaged. He felt an itch between his shoulder blades. He spun around, but no one was there. Still, he felt a presence. He looked up, then to the ground, but nothing was there. What was it?

Hoover stood stock-still, her body rigid and locked. Not even her tail moved. Odd that she'd stand that way.

Then Walker felt the same thing. His body was locked as well. And something continued to watch him, as if its face were mere inches from . . . then he knew. *No no no no no no no no no no!* he wailed within his mind. He remembered the Malaysian grave demon that had possessed him all those years as a child. He'd been spectator to what it had made him do, unable to stop it, unable to close his eyes because even his eyes were no longer his own.

Why hadn't Sassy saved him?

Why did he have to be the one to be possessed?

What did it want with him?

And then the images flashed through his mind.

All of his team dead.

Three-story piles of bodies all throughout the country. Anyone without Briton lineage, rotting food for a trillion flies.

There was a change coming and he was to be a part of it whether he liked it or not.

CHAPTER 52

CADBURY CASTLE, ENGLAND. 1355 HOURS.

Ian and his men helped end the battle when they swept up the road and over the hill. Other than the flechette cannon and the shredded empty robes, nothing remained to show the fierceness of the Tuatha's attack. Even the archaeological dig was deserted.

Ian was plainly worried. "Where are they? Was there no sign?"

But as Holmes took care of Laws he ignored Ian. The second in command was bleeding profusely from the wound near his eye. The flechette had come so close to the orb, Holmes was afraid to remove it. The wound had swelled, making the flechette impossible to get to. So Holmes took care of Laws's other wounds and cursed the Red Grove for taking a page out of the Vietcong's book. Knowing they couldn't defeat American forces during the Vietnam War head-to-head, the VC had waged a war of damage, wounding as many American soldiers as possible, delaying them, sapping their will. The flechette cannon was as good as a pungi stick. Not only had it put Laws out of the fight but also the rest of them until they could bandage their wounds and figure out a way to move on.

Yank worked on Sassy. Whatever she'd expected to find on Cadbury Hill, it wasn't a body full of metal. She'd lost a piece of an ear and would have a lasting reminder on her right cheek, not to mention those that had pierced her triceps, quadriceps, and stomach. She fumed silently as Yank and one of the Marines worked on her, first removing the flechettes and then cleaning and bandaging her wounds.

No one had gone unscathed.

YaYa had a leg wound.

Walker had wounds on the back of his upper leg.

And Holmes had one in his arm in addition to the cut from Yank.

Still, they were lucky. Their body armor had caught most of it. Had the enemy really wanted to kill them, though, it could have set up a far more considerable ambush. Claymores, IEDs, machine guns with interlocking fields of fire, bouncing Betty mines, trip wires . . . Holmes could think of dozens of more efficient ways to kill them than the flechette cannon.

Was it a statement?

"Stop looking all motherly, Boss."

Holmes finished affixing the bandage over and around the flechette next to Laws's eye. "Not sure if you lost the eye or not, Tim."

Laws dropped his smile at the use of his first name. Holmes knew it would get Laws's attention. He wanted to make certain that his second understood his predicament. But then the smile returned.

"Can't worry about what's already done. How are the others?"

"You were hit the worst. The witch is next, but her pain is more intramuscular."

"She'd going to be one large bruise."

"She already is." Holmes held up one of the flechettes. "Why?"

Laws took it from him. "I was laying here thinking the same thing. If they'd really wanted to kill us, I can think of better ways."

"Exactly. So why this?"

"You think it's a statement, don't you?"

Holmes nodded.

"Let's look at it from the Arthurian perspective. The Romans used *plumbatas*—small handheld darts with lead weights. The Picts of Scotland also used darts, some tribes exclusively. They were also used by the Celts and the Gaels. One could look at it as symbolic of a return to the past."

Holmes knew that to be true but had a hard time believing that this was the reason now that he heard it out loud.

"But I'm with you," Laws continued. "It doesn't sound as good out loud as it does in our heads. Let's look at it another way. We've done considerable damage to their operation."

"Not enough, it seems. Arthur is still out there. Even though we've removed several high-ranking officials and killed some of his hunt, we don't know how many are left."

Laws grimaced as he brought himself to a sitting position. "You're right. It doesn't make sense."

"Back to the question at hand. Where is Arthur? We'd believed all along that he'd come here to crown himself."

"You're forgetting something." Laws made to stand and Holmes helped him. "There's already a ruling monarch. The people aren't going to follow Arthur as long as Elizabeth lives."

Holmes beckoned Ian over, who'd been speaking to the pilots who'd just arrived. Ian came and brought along one of the pilots, who introduced himself as Patrick.

"Ian? Where is the Queen right at this moment?"

The sole surviving member of Section 9 blinked several times. "Buckingham Palace."

"So she's spending Christmas in London," Holmes said.

Ian snapped his fingers. "No. She's at Sandringham Estate. It's in Norfolk."

"How fast can we get there?"

"By truck about six hours."

Holmes pointed at the helicopters. "And in one of those?"

"Ninety minutes. Maybe a little more," said Patrick. "We can get about one hundred and ninety-five miles per hour out of them."

"Then let's get everyone loaded. We can continue triage on board."

The helicopters were in the air within five minutes. The SEALs, Ian, and the witch flew with Patrick. Magerts and his men flew with Keith in the other helicopter.

Holmes sat in one of the co-pilots' seats and wore a helmet. He stared at the top of Cadbury Hill wondering what it was he had missed. There had to have been a reason for the flechette cannon. He knew he was going to regret not knowing.

CHAPTER 53

NAP-OF-THE-EARTH. ENGLAND. 1419 HOURS.

About fifteen minutes into the flight he turned to the pilot. "How'd you know we needed help?"

"My boss contacted me."

"That would be Conor?"

Patrick glanced at Holmes, an impressed look on his face. "So you know Conor?"

"Just as he knows me. We've worked with the Finn McCools a few times. Were you in on the Isle of Man disaster?"

Patrick shook his head. "That was before my time, but I read the record. Unbelievable."

Holmes smiled wryly. "Not so unbelievable if you'd been there to see it." Then his face went stone again. "It must have been Preeti then. My guess is Section 9 had some sort of back-door communications plan."

"They had to. We can't call or e-mail out. Everything's shut down. Hell, I shouldn't even be flying. We'll be lucky if we don't get some Tornadoes want to tussle."

"Your IFF?"

Patrick pointed to his console. "It's off. And as you can see, we're flying NOE, so we might go unseen."

"I guess it depends on how much effort they're putting into finding you . . . or finding us. They must know we'd be working together. What's your cover?"

"Coast Guard Search and Rescue. And yours?"

"Pest control."

Patrick laughed. "Classic."

Holmes turned to Ian and got his attention. He had the man put on a crew chief helmet so they could communicate.

"Since I seriously doubt the Queen has been left in the dark on this, we can't exactly land and not expect to be shot at. Her security detail will have zero idea who we are until we can explain the situation."

"I can't be sure if Lord Robinson did or not. This is bottled."

"How'd Preeti get in touch with the Finn McCools?" Holmes asked.

"Could be any number of ways. We've been using Facebook Apps lately. Using their in-game chat functions. We found after the Chinese government tried to shut down Facebook that all they could do was inhibit the ability to communicate through the site. The game applications are add-ons and subject to a completely different code set. In order to knock them out, the Chinese would have to either completely shut down the Internet or back into each game application, and there's well over ten thousand."

"Can you see if you can get word to the Queen through Preeti and her brother?" Holmes asked. "As long as they're leaving the Internet on, the least we can do is take advantage of it."

"Meanwhile, we have to find out where the nearest mound is to Sandringham. If by some chance we're able to get to the Queen before Arthur and the Wild Hunt, then we'll be able to plan a defense."

"What do you think those odds are?"

"Slim to none. But I have to try." Holmes went to remove his helmet. "Listen, I'm heading back. If you have any issues, please let me know."

Holmes slid free the helmet, then climbed in back. He wanted to check on Laws and the others. Both Laws and Sassy were sucking on fentanyl lollipops. More than fifty times stronger than morphine, fentanyl was short lasting and would provide them the comfort they needed until the next mission. He'd have to watch them, though. He needed to make sure they weren't completely stoned when they touched down.

YaYa was wrapping QuikClot gauze on Hoover's mauled rear leg, staring at the dog in a funny way.

Holmes found a seat near Sassy. She held her wand in her hand as if she were gathering strength from it.

"How are you feeling?"

"Like a London dart league used me as target practice."

"Fentanyl working?"

"I'd love to have a cupboard filled with these babies." She took it out of her mouth for a moment. "Tastes like doctor ass, though."

Holmes chuckled. "I wouldn't know." He paused to look at Walker and Hoover. There was something off about them. Probably the dog was picking up on Walker's emotion. Back to Sassy, Holmes said, "Don't suppose you know the nearest mound to Sandringham Estate, do you?"

She thought for a moment. "Probably would be Bloodgate Hill. About twenty miles east, I think."

"Anything special about that one?"

She shrugged and pulled the lollipop from her mouth. "It's Iron Age, which makes it old. It's the largest in Norfolk. And like most of them it's built on a faerie mound."

"Sounds like where they'd be coming from. Got anything up your sleeve that could help us combat them? Looks like they hit us with some pretty good magic back there. Laws almost shot me." He glanced at the bandage on his arm. "Yank nearly beheaded me."

"They were able to prepare the area. Those are from spell traps they'd put in place. Only reason I didn't notice them was because of this." She held up the wand. "It's both a help and a hindrance. There's enough power in here to help me defeat, along with the Baen Sidhe, most anything. But if detecting residual magic is what I need to do, then this gets in the way because all I can feel is this."

"But they've never been to Sandringham Estate?"

"Not that I know of, plus the Royal Warlock would have taken care of it had he seen anything."

"The what?"

"You heard me."

"There's a Royal Warlock? And why have I never heard of it?"

"It's not necessarily for the English monarch. That's just the way it worked out. The Warlock is assigned to protect the House of Wettin. This dates back to Theodoric the First in AD 900. He protected a coven of warlocks from persecution and so did his line all the way until the 1600s. In return, we vowed to protect the line."

"When you say 'we' you mean . . ."

"The modern incarnation is the Fraterni Saturni, to which I belong."

"But you're not a warlock."

"Glad you noticed. Let's say I'm ex-official."

He nodded. "Got it. What happened in the 1600s?"

"Praying Ernest, or better known as Ernest the First, Duke of Saxe-Gotha, was the first to allow witch trials and burnings. We lost many because of that ass." She splayed two fingers apart and spit through them onto the aircraft floor, then said a few guttural German epithets.

"Elizabeth the Second is related to the Wettins?"

"Through patrilineal descent courtesy of Prince Albert, she is."

"And your service to the family?"

"Returned when Queen Victoria invited our founder, Gregor A. Gregorius, to continue the tradition in 1900. He founded our order upon her command, revived the tradition, then made it public in 1928." She spread her hands. "Thus is our boring history."

"Anything but boring. This Warlock, are you on speaking terms with him?"

"I know Garland quite well. He doesn't particularly like me, but he does respect me." She frowned. "Unlike most of my fraternity."

"Can you contact him and tell him we're coming?"

She gave Holmes a shocked look. "I already have. He'll be meeting us at the LZ."

Holmes felt exasperated. "Why didn't you tell me?"

"You looked busy running the show." She smiled knowingly. "I didn't want to get in the way."

Holmes thought about that and would have called her on it if he felt it would do any good. "And have you brought him up to date on what we know thus far?"

She nodded. "I have."

"And how are you able to communicate with him? Magic, I suppose?"

"Not magic. Astral projection."

Now it was his turn to smile. "Of course. Astral projection. Makes perfect sense."

She beamed back. "I thought so."

CHAPTER 54

NAP-OF-THE-EARTH. ENGLAND. 1440 HOURS.

Walker felt it inside him. It called itself Myrddin and felt like a giant fucking snail was laying a vile trail through his brain, only to spin into a millipede, scratching the sides with a million spiked feet, then to change into a neon-green dragonfly with razor blades for wings. It hurt so bad he wanted to cry, but the Tuatha wouldn't let him do anything but sit dumbly, laugh at the occasional crack by Yank or YaYa, and act appropriately concerned for Laws's awful face wound.

Was this what Van Dyke had felt? And to think he brought it into his body on purpose. Had it been worth it? If this was the Tuatha's soul then Walker would rather bathe in a cesspool.

He felt it look inward at him, condescending, treating him less like a man, more like a child. It showed him a memory, except in this version he was out of his body watching. Walker knew the scene well. It was Subic Bay, 1985. His father was dead. His brother was gone. And he was possessed by a demon.

And there he was hiding in a pile of trash—Little Jackie Walker. The liquid from banana skins, coffee grounds, and rain-soaked rags seeped through his clothes, making him shiver. His teeth chattered. Beneath the soft skin of his bare chest he felt what could have been gravel. A rubber thrown away by a hooker on Llo-Llo Street in Barrio Barretto rested like a deflated sausage two inches from his nose. A wasp crawled inside, caus-ing the skin of it to wriggle and jump. He felt rats crossing the backs of his legs. When they sniffed at him, he fought the urge to jerk as their whis-kers tickled the soft underskin of his knees.

Feral.

Like a pig.

Or a dog.

He was wild and eager to gnaw on something that screamed.

Twice old men shuffled by, coming home from a day spent at the dump.

Each time he screamed like a dying cat. "Hoy! Hoy! Tanda! Halika. Sayaw tayo." Hey! Hey! Old man. Come and dance with me.

Whenever the men would look over, he could barely contain himself with glee. Although they looked right at him, he knew they didn't see him. He was invisible. He was like the air.

But then came the old cripple, pulling himself along with one with-ered arm, a hand gnarled like the fingers of a twisted branch. His skin was the color of old chocolate. He had a few hairs on his face and even fewer on his head. His eyes were the color of olive pits and were sunken into craters of wrinkles.

Jackie could barely contain his laughter as he leaped free of the trash and high into the air. Pieces of debris sprayed the cripple. Jackie screamed like a beast. He picked up an old hubcap and swung it as hard as he could. He caught the cripple in the side of the head. The cripple screamed. The slick metal slid off without doing much damage, so Jackie brought it around again, this time coming straight down with the hubcap on the crown of the cripple's head. Blood exploded outward, the sight of it fuel for another swing of the arm. This time it came around in a flat arc, catching the old man beneath the eye.

"Hoy! Hoy!" he cried. "Dance with me, you fool!"

The cripple fell to his side, his mouth twisted into a curl of fear as he whined miserably.

Jackie growled and peed on the man's withered arm. Then he turned and ran, giggling, his bare feet slapping at the ground, all the way down La Union Street.

And the memory dimpled his soul.

What was the Tuatha trying to tell him? That it wasn't as bad as the grave demon? That it wasn't making him do these things? Or was it trying to show Walker that he could be evil all by himself, because every time that memory rose to the surface, a part of Walker asked the question: *Did I do it because I wanted to or because the demon made me do it?*

Walker jerked. He realized Holmes was talking to him.

"Sure, Boss. I'm fine," he found himself saying. "Just saving my energy."

Holmes gave him a worried look, then returned his attention to Laws, who was just finishing a fentanyl lollipop.

Laws flashed Walker a smile and a wink, then touched the back of his hand to his patched facial wound. Worry found a home in Laws's eye for a moment, then was gone as he began to work the slide on his pistol.

Walker turned to Hoover. As they stared at each other, Walker wondered how Hoover was dealing with the possession. Was the dog crying on the inside like Walker?

Then the helicopter began to descend.

CHAPTER 55

SANDRINGHAM ESTATE, NORFOLK, ENGLAND. 1520 HOURS.

YaYa felt the change in the pair. At first he'd written it off as nothing, but his new senses told him otherwise. Hoover wasn't responding to him like she normally did. Sure, she was responding like a typical dog should, but then whatever was controlling her didn't know the nuances of the SEAL team dog's personality or the way she sometimes looked at you as if you were a lower life form when you made an off-color joke.

It must have happened when Hoover and Walker charged the scarecrow druids. In fact, YaYa could believe that this was the entire reason they'd been drawn to the location. The whole attack had seemed so halfhearted and not well-thought-out. But then maybe it had been. Maybe the purpose was to possess as many of the SEAL team members as possible, knowing that they'd gain access to the Queen at Sandringham. If his supposition was true, then it meant their foes were more devious than any of them had suspected.

He surveyed the inside of the helicopter. He knew for sure that Hoover was possessed and he'd stake a month's pay that Walker was also possessed. But what about the others?

YaYa stared at Holmes. His leader was who he should be telling, but was it safe? Was he possessed as well? As he stared at Holmes, the SEAL team commander turned to stare at him in return, as stone-faced as if he could see right through him.

YaYa forced himself to adjust his gaze elsewhere, well aware that Holmes was still staring at him. If Holmes was possessed, then he might be wondering if YaYa had realized. If he wasn't possessed, then he'd be wondering why YaYa was staring at him, probably trying to deduce if something was wrong or if YaYa wanted to say something.

Once he thought about it, his brain began to hurt. Possession logic was quantum theory.

And what about Laws?

Or Yank?

Or the witch?

As YaYa thought of each one, they turned to look at him.

How could he tell? Maybe if he touched them. Petting Hoover had felt like he was moving his fingers through static electricity. He'd have to touch Walker first to establish if that was the way it felt with humans as well as canines. If he could establish a recognizable feeling, then it was only a matter of figuring out a way to touch everyone.

He could almost laugh at the irony. It was less than a year ago when he'd been the one possessed, trying to hide it, to keep others from knowing. Now look at him.

The helicopter began to lower. He glanced out the window as they crossed from pasture to manicured estate. Only it wasn't any estate. These sprawling gardens and lawns surrounded a four-story mansion the size of a small college. He spied the landing pad about fifty meters behind the house, screened by a copse of trees. They had a welcoming committee of a squad of Royal Marines dressed in full battle rattle as well as several civilians. He found himself looking for the well-known figure of the Queen but then realized that there'd be no reason for her to meet them. After all, she probably didn't know, nor would she care, who they were.

What bothered him about the scene was the apparent tranquility. King Arthur and his Wild Hunt had had a considerable head start on them and could have easily gotten here first. Had they gone to the wrong place? Was King Arthur traveling somewhere else? He found himself looking at Walker. No. If the Tuatha were here, then there had to be a reason.

"You're doing a lot of thinking over there," Laws said, poking him in the knee. "That wrinkle between your eyes is making my head hurt."

YaYa had felt the hand touch him and it came with no telltale sensation. He still had to find a way to touch Walker, though.

"I thought it was the flechette in your face that made your head hurt."

Laws grinned, then winced with the effort. "That too."

YaYa offered him a sympathetic smile. "Just trying to get ahead of the enemy."

"Aren't we all."

When they were about fifteen meters off the deck, Holmes brought them back to the mission.

"Be ready, SEALs."

Everyone who hadn't already chambered a round and prepared their weapons did so.

Yank adjusted his body armor.

Walker replaced his pistol mag.

Laws removed his fentanyl lollipop.

The witch kept sucking on hers. She hefted her Viking wand and stared fixedly ahead, as if she were not there.

YaYa stood and posted himself at the door. When the wheels touched down, he slid the door open and leaped out. He held his rifle at low ready and stood by the door.

Hoover leaped out next, followed by Walker.

YaYa reached out to guide the other SEAL and felt the same static charge he'd felt when petting Hoover. Static and sticky. Not a combination that felt anything but supernaturally nasty.

Laws was next. Nothing.

Yank. Nothing.

Ian. Nothing.

The witch came next, but as YaYa went to help her she skipped aside, eschewing his touch.

Holmes came last, and like the witch, when YaYa reached out, he zipped ahead of the touch.

YaYa fell in behind them. He was now certain about Yank and Laws, but of the witch and his boss YaYa still couldn't be certain. If he could find a way to speak with Laws in private, he'd let him know what he'd discovered. Maybe the second in command could assist.

The other helicopter landed behind them and expelled twelve Royal Marines, led by Lieutenant Magerts.

Holmes approached the head of the Royal Marine commando squad assigned to Sandringham.

Holmes was all business. "Commander Sam Holmes, SEAL Team 666."

"Lieutenant MacMasters," the young man said with just a trace of brogue. "Mr. Garland is waiting for you in the second study. If you'll come with me." He was stocky with closely cut blond hair and sideburns. His pure blue eyes showed a thoughtfulness in addition to a professional intensity.

Ian touched Holmes on the shoulder. "I'm going to stay out here with Magerts and the men. I need to inspect the grounds." To MacMasters he said, "I'm Lieutenant Colonel Waits. Is this all your men?"

"I have seven standing by as QRF."

Hoover had been inspecting the boots of the new group of Marines. He came up to Holmes, who automatically reached down and placed his hand on the dog's head.

Ian looked at the battle rattle on the new Marines. He smiled grimly. "Sorry to spoil your Christmas, Lieutenant, but get them out here. We're going to need them."

MacMasters glanced from Holmes to Ian. "What's this all about?"

"Shit's about to hit the fan," Holmes said. "Better do as the man said."

MacMasters stared for a moment, then nodded to one of his

men who took off running toward the main house. Then the lieutenant nodded. "If you'll follow me, Commander."

He started to move back toward the house and the SEALs fell in behind him.

They'd gone perhaps twenty steps when the sound of a hunting horn could be heard in the distance.

MacMasters turned toward it, his eyes narrowed.

The SEALs halted.

YaYa took advantage of the moment and intentionally bumped into Holmes. He was shocked as he felt the familiar nastiness of clammy static. Their eyes met.

Hoover began to bark. She went for Walker, trying to bite him.

Walker jumped out of the way and leveled his rifle at the dog.

Yank grabbed the gun right as the SEAL opened fire. Dirt kicked up near Hoover, who was able to leap sideways and out of the way.

The Marines escorting them leveled their weapons on the fighting SEALs.

Yank struggled, one hand on the barrel of the rifle, the other on Walker's arm. "What the fuck, man?"

"Let go of my fucking weapon. The dog . . . she's possessed."

YaYa knew if he said anything that all hell would break loose. He'd lose any advantage that he had.

Yank struggled with Walker, who was still trying to level his rifle at the dog.

YaYa realized that the Tuatha must have passed from the dog to Holmes and now Hoover was trying her best to save the situation. He couldn't leave her hanging.

The witch was struggling to figure out what was going on, glancing from one SEAL to the other. When she rested her eyes on YaYa, he mouthed the words, *Tuatha. Holmes. Walker. Tuatha.*

She got it right away.

She began to mouth indecipherable words as she reached out to touch Commander Holmes with her wand.

But he was prepared.

He pulled his pistol and shot her in the stomach.

She went down hard.

"Sam?" Laws screamed. "What are you doing?"

"It's not him!" YaYa yelled above the chaos. "It's Tuatha. They're possessed. Walker and Holmes."

Holmes spun toward YaYa, but the lithe young SEAL was ready. He grabbed the pistol with his prosthetic hand, stronger than any human hand and reinforced with titanium alloys; he twisted the weapon out of his commander's hand as if it were a toy.

Holmes staggered and fell against MacMasters.

Meanwhile Yank had Walker down on the ground and disarmed him. Magerts came up and helped, bringing zip ties from his cargo pocket. He bound Walker's hands in front of him, then his feet.

Laws had his rifle pointed at Holmes.

"Sam. What are you doing?"

Holmes blinked his eyes. "Tim, it's me."

A horn came again. This time it was closer.

YaYa noticed a bank of fog rolling toward them.

"How do I know it's you?" Laws asked.

"Whatever it was is gone." Holmes glanced around and saw the witch on the ground. "Sassy. Fuck." He ran to her and pulled a QuikClot bandage out of his cargo pocket. He applied it to her wound and pressed to stanch the flow.

"If it's gone, then where is it?"

Everyone began to look at everyone else.

YaYa stepped forward. "I can tell you. I just need to—"

"Marines, disarm these men," ordered MacMasters. "I don't know what kind of bloody shitstorm you're trying to bring to the royal family, but I won't have it."

YaYa's eyes narrowed as everyone turned their weapons on one another. SEALs against Marines. Magerts's Marines against MacMasters's Marines. Then Ian put a hand on Magerts's shoulder.

"Marines," Magerts called. "Follow MacMasters."

The Tuatha had hopped from one person to the other and were now in command of the largest military forces in the area. YaYa finally saw them for what they were. This had been the plan all along. The SEALs were now outnumbered thirty to six. The chances were grim. With all the modern technology at their disposal and the latest gear, the SEALs had been outmaneuvered by the Tuatha Dé Dannan, a race of beings who'd slipped into the shadowy crags of mythology more than three thousand years ago.

In his mind's eye he pulled up and out. His group of SEALs stood in the center of a circle, Holmes on the ground trying to save their witch. They were surrounded on all sides by Royal Marines, all pointing the working ends of their SA80s at them. In the distance came the fog and with it the Wild Hunt. And somewhere inside Sandringham Estate was the Queen. Myrddin and Arthur didn't even have to kill her. All they had to do was possess her and have her abdicate her throne on national television. It would be a relatively peaceful coup d'état with no one the wiser that they'd entered an Era of the Tuatha, when Arthur would once again be king.

What the fuck was SEAL Team 666 going to do?

CHAPTER 56

SANDRINGHAM ESTATE, NORFOLK, ENGLAND. 1540 HOURS.

She was in a deep pool of pain, falling deeper and deeper. As terrible as the flechettes had felt, the bullet in her abdomen was far more awful, introducing her to an ache so profound, she found it hard to think of anything but fleeing from the pain. So she swam away from it, pushing and pulling her soul into a tight little ball where she could rock herself, much like she had when she was a little girl and Hitler's buzz bombs roared across the London sky like nightmares made real.

She was only remotely aware of hands around her wound. She heard chaos, she heard angry voices, but she was too far away to understand them. But then a single voice came to her.

Sassy.

If she ignored it, maybe it would go away.

Sassy Moore.

She pulled herself tighter until she was cloaked in darkness, just like she'd been in the underground shelter, huddled with the rest of the children, each of them trying to be strong, trying not to cry.

Sassy Moore. You have the power. The wand. The Baen Sidhe. Use it.

How many times with the buzz bombs roaring overhead, their

hiccupping journeys heard from even far beneath the surface, had she prayed she could stop them, keep them from doing any more damage? If only she'd had the same power back then as she had now. Fat lot of good that did her against the SEAL commander and his pistol. She saw him draw and heard it bark. Her soul flinched and she pulled in tighter still.

Sassy Moore.

Leave me alone, Garland.

Sassy. The wand. Use it.

Was she still holding on to it? In order to find out she'd have to unlimber herself and feel the pain once again. It seemed hardly worth it.

She felt warmth suffuse her.

I'm too far away to do more. Help us, Sassy. Help yourself. I'll save the Queen.

She cursed and shot free from her body. Looking down from her great height, she saw the trouble for what it was. She saw the predicament and how she and the SEALs were about to die. She cursed again. This had better be worth it.

She shot back into her body and gasped as the pain she'd been striving to avoid hit her like a dozen buzz bombs, exploding into her stomach over and over. Her back arched. She felt a hand on her and heard the words, "Easy, Sassy. Keep still."

Bloody fucking pain. She felt along the ground with her right hand until it found the cold iron of the old wand. She gripped it and pulled from it. The wand went from cold to warm as she sucked hundreds of years of built-up power into her body. She sent it swirling toward her wound and felt immediate relief as it began to bind and repair. She pulled harder, her will sucking at the essence of the Baen Sidhe. She worked yet another magic, empathetic magic, sending her pain to those around her, interrogating each of the men's memories and forcing them to relive the worst pain they'd ever felt. For some it was birth, darkness, light, the transition to breathing air and the panic they'd felt as they left the sanctity of the birth canal. For others it was a gunshot, or a knife wound, or a broken bone, the ends of it pressing through flesh, the very air like acid to the nerve endings. Still for others it was a different kind of pain, a pain of the soul, like when a daughter dies or a wife leaves you.

Sassy hurled pain around her like water flung from a bucket, catching anyone not her. She snarled. She cursed. She gave every one a taste of what she'd felt and more. She sent them to a place where they too huddled beneath the London streets, mothers dead, fathers off to war, homes destroyed, and their entire universe the sputtering, doddering V1 bombs sent by Adolf Fucking Hitler to terrify and destroy.

The more pain she gave the less pain she felt until she was surging to her feet, whole once more, woundless, skin alive, hair moving to unseen winds. Her arms flung out. Everyone around her was on their knees or their backs or curled into fetal positions, heads down, mouths pulled into rictus masks as they relived their own worst moments as well as her own.

Then the wand was empty. She flung it to the ground and screamed.

From nearby came the sound of a hunting horn.

Her mission returned to her.

Garland, she said across her astral channels. *I am back.*

Good, Sassy. Very good. Now do what needs to be done.

She nodded. She was alive. She was free of pain. She had her powers. But what was it that needed to be done?

Then she knew. Without the wand to mask their presence with its own power, she saw the Tuatha and knew them at once. One was Merlyn and the other was Arthur. They moved from one man to the other, trying to confuse her, but she could see them perfectly, glowing from within, illuminated and pulsating.

She snatched the metal wand from the ground. It no longer held power, but it was still a weapon. She strode toward them and managed to separate Arthur from the others. Still recovering from her spell, the man he inhabited found it hard to keep his balance. He fell twice. Enough so that she was upon him, thrusting the wand through his heart.

As the light went from his eyes, so did the Tuatha. She knew the truth and somehow understood the rules. It could only enter another through touch. She watched it travel near the ground like a miniature dust devil, collecting sticks and leaves and twigs, until it was able to form the figure of a man made from debris and detritus. Then it ran, not toward her, but toward the bank of fog now roiling across the lawn several hundred meters from them.

She turned and found the other.

This one didn't run.

It turned to face her.

It wanted to fight.

She smiled grimly, knowing that her entire existence was meant for this very moment. Her, Sassy Moore, once a child afraid of her own shadow, now a Thirty-First-Degree Magister Templarus witch of the Fraterni Saturni against the greatest magician of the Western canon–Merlyn.

She began to battle.

CHAPTER 57

SANDRINGHAM ESTATE, NORFOLK, ENGLAND. NOW.

Walker climbed to his feet, the vile taste of possession still in his mouth. He wanted to lash out, to hit, to beat something until its insides splattered all over his uniform. In fact, he'd been searching for the location of the Tuatha when he'd been struck by such a wave of pain, he couldn't remember when last he'd felt so awful. He wasn't sure how, but he knew it had originated with the witch. Perhaps it was the sheer outrage he felt in the force of her power or maybe it was the residual image of a little girl hiding in a bomb shelter, but she'd somehow saved herself and them all by sharing her pain.

He saw her now, squaring off against a Royal Marine. Although the young man had a knife at his belt, he made no move to use it; instead his hands were moving in a complex series of manipulations. Walker had no doubt who it was. Walker made to move toward him, when Holmes grabbed his arm. The commander was on his knees and trying to stand. Walker helped him to his feet, then looked around to see if he could help the rest of the SEALs, but they were all standing, if not a little unsteadily.

The sound of a hunting horn made him turn.

Through a bank of fog appeared King Arthur riding an imperial white stag with a menacing rack of horns. Beside and behind him were men dressed in all manner of clothes. Some carried swords and knives. Some carried spears. Still others carried long-bows. Intermingled with these were hounds, each one slightly different, their eyes the link to who they'd been before their souls were stolen and reforged into these unholy beasts.

Ian began screaming for the Marines to form a defense. With Magerts on one end and MacMasters on the other, a ragged line began to take shape as the confused Marines picked themselves off the deck and formed to confront the enemy.

Holmes called the SEALs to him as he ran back toward the he-licopters. Walker glanced back to see if Hoover was coming, then, once assured, hurried after his team. Patrick was spooling up the rotors as they arrived. Walker was the last on the helicopter. Hoover had leaped in before him.

"What's the plan?" Laws asked.

Holmes pointed out the front window as he spoke to the pilot. "Can you take us up and behind that bank of fog?"

"Yes, but that's not your only problem. We just got word that a battalion is coming up the road from RAF Markam."

"Whose side are they on?"

"Can't be sure."

"How long until they get here?"

"Ten minutes. Maybe sooner."

"Then we need to hurry."

"Hold on!" The helicopter jumped off the landing pad and over the copse of trees. Beneath them they could see the approaching Hunt a mere fifty meters in front of the line of Marines. Even as Walker watched, the Marines opened fire. Their combined fire should have knocked down the first rank of hounds and hunters, but they had no effect. Magerts's men and Ian had swords. They drew the swords now, explaining to the other Marines what had to be done. With only their combat knives, they had a lot of close combat to look forward to.

King Arthur leaned back in his saddle, staring up at them as they flew over. Fire glowed in his eyes.

The fog wrapped the helicopter in a claustrophobic embrace. Gone was the world of man. Gone was everything they knew. For a moment, there was nothing except the feeling of displacement. Then they were on the other side and the crisp, clean wintery light embraced them. Patrick lowered the helicopter, keeping the wheels six inches from the manicured lawn.

"I knew it." Holmes pointed opposite the fog to where a line of seven red-robed figures stood. "Take us there."

Walker remembered the last time he'd encountered one of the robed figures. "Don't let them touch you."

"They're never going to get near us." He clapped the pilot on the back. "Mow them down."

The helicopter gathered speed as it roared across the lawn.

The figures not only wore red robes, but their heads were covered by conical red hats also, with holes cut out for their eyes.

Walker felt so much magic coming out of them he felt nauseous. His head rang with pain. His skin began to vibrate.

The pilot lowered the nose until the blades were almost clipping the ground. "Hang on." He slowed almost to a stop, then surged forward, the propellers eating through the line of druids, transforming them into red mist. The druids had probably counted on the Wild Hunt being the target rather than themselves. Holmes had demonstrated his tactical genius by realizing that the Hunt had to have been manipulated from elsewhere and had guessed the location correctly.

Walker turned back toward the fog and noticed that it was quickly burning off, revealing Marines and the Hunt fully engaged in battle.

Holmes didn't have to say anything. The pilot was already turning the helicopter toward the action. The windscreen was covered with blood and gore. An ear slid free of the glass. The SEALs dropped their rifles in the cabin and drew swords and knives. Ten seconds later as the helicopter lowered to the ground they leaped out the open door, each of them finding targets.

Walker hit a huntsman, knocking him to the ground. His bow,

which had been pulled back, flew from his hands, the arrow breaking as it struck the earth at an awkward angle. Walker picked himself up and swung his gladius, catching the huntsman down the length of his back. Then Walker stepped to the side and swung, severing the huntsman's head. Instead of disappearing like the hounds had, he remained in place. He'd probably been human once.

Walker moved to his next target, another huntsman who'd just shoved a spear through a Marine's stomach. Walker brought his gladius around again and hacked it halfway through his target's neck. Blood spurted into the air, drenching the Marine, whom the huntsman fell against.

Laws, Holmes, and YaYa were similarly engaged, using the advantage of coming from behind to their benefit.

Beyond them Yank stood toe-to-toe with King Arthur. While the King swung a great two-handed blade, Yank swung his two blades in a dizzying Filipino weave, catching the other's blade, deflecting it, then slicing the Tuatha with his blade.

A hound leaped at Walker and he shoved the gladius in its chest. He tried to pull it free, but the hound pulled back, jerking the weapon from his grip.

Walker had no choice but to dive to the ground and pick up a spear that had fallen. He had no idea how to use it other than to hold it out in front of him, so he did.

The hound leaped again, spearing itself just below where his gladius was stuck. Walker pushed hard against the spear, shoving the length through the beast until he could grip the end of his gladius once more. Then he jerked it free and hacked at the creature's neck until it was no more.

Walker sought out Yank again and saw that the tables had turned. Instead of fighting King Arthur, he was now trying to defend himself from three hounds. Walker began to run to his aid, but Hoover bounded past him, as did YaYa. Walker slowed. He found himself in the middle of a quiet space as everyone fought around him.

"Walker, look out."

He was shoved to the ground by Laws, who took the blow meant for his head. But Laws was taller, so the great sword sunk deep into his shoulder. His face immediately paled as he fell to the ground.

The stocky king pulled the sword free and swung at Walker. But he rolled to his right, managing to come up in a standing position. Somehow he still had his gladius.

"Fucking hell." He leaped backwards, barely able to keep from getting skewered. He studied his opponent. Arthur's crown was made of old beaten metal. His beard was cut rather than ragged. His gaze was fixed and steady. He looked just like what King Arthur should have looked like, just as if he'd walked right out of Central Casting. His armor was made from beaten plates attached to a leather background. He wore a ring on one hand and a watch on the other wrist . . . a watch?

Then Walker understood.

Of course. It might be the Tuathan spirit of King Arthur, but they needed a body to use in order to make him the King. This was never really about the need to have King Arthur from the days of old return. That was just the vehicle the Red Grove was going to use. Arthur was to be their tool so that they could prosecute their program of national segregation. With him would come magic and a promise of a return to proud times and in turn they'd remove all non-Britons from the country and have a beautiful white oasis of peace and prosperity.

So they had to have a human who looked like the popular ideal of Arthur.

Which meant that Walker finally had a target for his rage.

He waited until King Arthur swung, sidestepped the sweeping blade, and hacked at the right arm holding it. His blade missed taking off the arm, but it tore the skin open from wrist to elbow.

The man howled, but even as he did, the Tuatha inside of him worked its magic and the wound began to heal.

"Oh no you fucking don't."

Walker feinted in, then ducked back.

King Arthur switched his grip and shoved the blade at Walker. It hit his chest plate and slid to the left.

Walker trapped it with his left arm and shoved the gladius toward the King's chest.

Instead of taking the blow, King Arthur released his grip on his sword and backed away, searching the ground for a weapon.

Walker took two steps and hacked at his opponent, missing with the first swing but catching the King on the upswing. Then he swung again and again and again, his rage and pain fueling his increasingly expert slashes.

King Arthur staggered backwards.

Walker caught his target on the shoulder.

The man who would be King Arthur reached out.

Walker sidestepped. "I don't think so." He knew what it was trying to do. If he let it touch him, the Tuatha could transfer, then it would probably make him kill himself.

King Arthur turned and ran.

Walker spied a spear on the ground. He snatched it up, brought it back behind his head, ran forward a few steps, and threw it. The spear went true, piercing the back of the man, sending him careening to the ground. His crown fell free and rolled several feet before it came to rest at a pair of high-heeled feet.

Sassy Moore reached down and picked it up. She looked at it, wrinkled her nose, and tossed it over her shoulder.

"Don't touch him," Walker warned.

She pulled a bag from her cargo pocket, opened it, and dribbled it along the ground until King Arthur was surrounded with a circle of what appeared to be white dust. "The other Tuatha ran. I'll not let this one get away. This is bone dust from the Giant of Castlenau and it has trapped you in this place." Her voice was ragged from use but contained a power that compelled. "Hold my hand, Walker. I need your anger."

He gave her his right hand and she took it with her left. Her right hand began to manipulate the air. She began to speak in guttural German.

He stood watching, noticing when the figure on the ground began to writhe, legs and arms beating against the ground. Walker focused his entire being on his anger for the murders of Jen and Trevor and everyone else who'd lost their lives in this attempt at a white hegemony. He focused on Preeti and knew how terrible she'd felt at Trevor's death, knowing it because he'd owned the very same feeling. He thought of Jen and their last night together, how he'd swept a stray hair from her forehead right before he kissed her. He focused on it all, letting memory after memory after memory shoot through him and into Sassy Moore to fuel her spell, until he was once again face-to-face with Jen's soul-forged hound of the Wild Hunt. His hand now felt like it was holding on to an electrical current. He couldn't let go of the witch even if he wanted to. Sobs ripped from him as he screamed at the creature in the circle. Soon he couldn't hear anything except for his own shouts of outrage.

Then there was silence.

He realized that his eyes had slammed shut.

He opened them and saw that only black ash remained in the circle of white.

Sassy pulled at her hand. "You can let go of me now."

He opened his hand and stared at it.

She put her other hand on his shoulder. "You loved her terribly, didn't you, son?"

He nodded dumbly.

"She's in a good place now, thanks to you."

He felt the truth of her words. He closed his eyes once more. An image of Jen flashed and held in his mind. She was smiling. He smiled back at her. She waved and turned and was enveloped by light.

Hands gripped him.

He turned to find YaYa and Yank.

"Come on, bro." Yank pointed toward the helicopter. "We've got to get Laws to a hospital."

Walker realized the battle was over.

He let himself be pulled until he was running with them.

"Anyone else get hurt?" he asked.

"Nah." YaYa flashed a grin. "Just all of us."

"You'll be okay," Walker said to Laws as he climbed into the Sikorsky and it took to the air.

Ever the goofball, Laws grinned. "I know. It's merely a flesh wound."

EPILOGUE

RAF CHICKSANDS. THREE DAYS LATER.

SEAL Team 666 sat in the main salon of the priory, sipping from mugs of dark local ale. They wore civilian clothes and could have been a group of footballers, if they all weren't sporting bandages on their arms, faces, heads, and hands.

Sassy Moore had just left after paying her respects to Preeti. Ian and the team had held a private ceremony for Jerry and Trevor, one that had begun with solemn ritual, then ended up a circle of tearful laughter as each of them began to tell story after story of how the two men affected their lives. When Preeti had told her and Trevor's origin story, Yank and Laws, who hadn't heard it before, had both cried.

Preeti returned from the ladies' room at the same time as Ian arrived with a platter of fresh pints.

"What's the plan now that you've been given the building back?" Holmes asked.

"Magerts is coming on as my second. Of the fourteen Marines who survived the battle, eleven have agreed to join us." Ian passed out the beers, then sat down, bringing his own two-cubed glass of scotch to his lips. He closed his eyes and made a relishing sound. Then he continued. "We still have a long way to go, but it's a start. The thing about disaster is that it tends to remind people what's important."

"And the roundup?"

"Sir MacDonald's chief of staff rolled and gave MI5 a list of everyone involved. It goes all the way up, including several high-ranking military officials."

"Was it really that bad?" Walker asked. "Why go to all that effort?"

"There are some who look at America and places England once called their own and remember how great we were." Ian took another sip. "They forget that America lives today because of our greatness. Had we not set the colonies in motion you might never have existed."

"It's hard not to look back," YaYa said, "knowing the rich history you've had. My own culture has its own share of problems trying to merge past greatness with the realities of today."

Preeti joined in. "Add to that the rising sentiment that immigration is destroying our great nation." She shook her head. "They don't realize that I don't think of myself as Indian first. I think of myself as English first."

"Whenever things start going bad fingers start pointing." Laws adjusted his sling and rubbed his shoulder where he'd had surgery. An eye patch covered one eye. "We have the same issues at home. People forget that America was created through immigration. What is it etched on the Statue of Liberty? *Give me your tired, your poor, your huddled masses, yearning to breathe free. The wretched refuse of your teeming shore. Send these, the homeless, tempest-tossed to me, I lift my lamp beside the golden door.*" Laws grinned broadly. "And look at us. We are the sum, rather than the parts."

Everyone drank at the same time, giving them a long quiet moment.

"Hey," Yank asked. "Anyone hear from Genie?"

He'd been gone when they'd returned. Even Preeti didn't know what had become of him. He hadn't said good-bye.

Holmes set his glass down. "Get this. I got a report from NAVSPECWARCOM. He left his enlistment over a year ago."

Everyone's eyes shot wide.

Walker was the first to ask what everyone wanted to know. "What the hell was he doing, then?"

Holmes shrugged. "By all accounts, he helped us."

Laws regarded his ale with narrow eyes. "But there had to be something in it for him?"

"If there was, I don't know what it could be." Holmes spread his hands. "I'll see what I can find out when we get back."

WEST OF SANTA ROSA, CALIFORNIA.

The rental car turned off Bohemian Highway before it crossed the Russian River into Monte Rio. The driver found himself on Bohemian Avenue. He drove past twenty people holding signs railing against the Cremation of Care and continued down the road until he reached a security shack beside a gate. The guard looked out and recognized the driver. He pressed a button and the gate rose. The car rolled forward, passing several groups of houses until the road ended at a large building. The driver got out and went to the front door of the building. He was met at the front door by an elderly Caucasian man who'd be recognized for his three terms in the U.S. Senate.

"Did you get it?"

"It took a while."

"But you got it, right?"

"A witch almost destroyed it. It's weak, but it's here." He unbuttoned his shirt and revealed a three-crescent tattoo etched into his black skin. It glowed faintly. "Just in time for the next ceremony."

The senator smiled. "You done good."

"Can we get it out, now? It feels a little itchy in here."

"All in good time. All in good time. The board's about to

convene. Come in and have a drink with us. Tell us what happened."

Genaro Stewart thought about it for a moment, then nodded.
"I could use a drink." Then he followed the man inside and closed
the door behind him.